HAMMER FALL

HAMMER FALL

LEGENDS OF LYORION

THE HOPEBRINGER TRILOGY

BOOK ONE

DAVID DUNFEE

TABLE OF CONTENTS

FOR THOSE WE LOST FAR TOO SOON.

YOUR LIGHT ENDURES IN THE *HOPE* WE CARRY FORWARD

ACKNOWLEDGEMENT: A SPOON'S TALE

"Every story begins in shrouded darkness. Lucky for us, I brought a spoon to dig it out," I say, letting the edge of my grin catch the flickering firelight.

Welcome, friends, wanderers, and seekers of the extraordinary, to the Spoon Inn. Tonight, as you gather near this hearth, I offer you more than just warmth and good company. I offer you a tale, one worth your time, your curiosity, and perhaps even your faith.

You see, stories are not merely words strung together for entertainment. They are keys to truths hidden in the shadows, treasures buried beneath the weight of time and silence. This tale is not about distant myths, but about our world, Lyorion, its people, its lands, and its secrets. Here at the Spoon Inn, we have a penchant for finding those truths, dusting them off, and setting them before you like a feast. The world, after all, does not give up its secrets easily, but a spoon is a fine tool for digging deep.

Allow me to introduce myself properly.

I am Spoony Spoons McSpoonerson, collector of lore, teller of candor, and proprietor of this fine establishment. Over the years, my pursuits have taken me to the edges of forgotten ruins, into the depths of perilous dungeons, and even through the shadowed dealings of illegal markets, all to unearth the fragments of history that our world tried to forget. Some would call this work, Madness... But I call it, Passion.

Now, I imagine you might be wondering why I've gone to such lengths to set this scene. After all, isn't this the part where an author usually thanks their mentors and inspirations? Well, my friends, this tale is far from ordinary, just as we are. What you are about to hear is not just a story, it is a glimpse into the veins of Lyorion itself, a reflection of its heartbeat within the continent of Shularix, and together we unlock truths too dangerous to remain buried. The lands we will walk, the voices we will hear. They are not just echoes of the past, but a fabric of a world shaped by choices.

But why this story, you might ask? Why now? You see, history has a funny way of repeating itself. The lessons buried in the shadows often hold the answers to questions we've yet to ask. And those answers, dear friends, may prove vital in days yet to come. As you sit here tonight, I can see the spark of curiosity in your eyes, the readiness to step into the unknown. It's no accident that you've found yourself here. Perhaps it's fate. Perhaps it's something more. Perhaps it is your search for adventure that brings you to learn of another tale, just to ignite that spark of *Hope* within yourself.

Lean in close, for the fire burns low and the shadows are listening. Let us peel back the layers of history, one story at a time, and uncover the truths the Coalition would rather leave hidden.

As we begin this tale, I would first like to share a fragment of written history I unearthed. A recollection penned by one whom we will soon get to know within this tale. It takes us to the night that altered the courses of many lives, ignited the embers of war, and called forth *Hope, Justice, Fury, and Courage* to stand against the encroaching darkness. A single moment, woven from choices and consequences, whose ripples have aged the world we now know.

EXCERPT:
IGNITING HOPE

The flickering light danced across the worn tables and mismatched chairs of the Spoon Inn. The air was heavy with the scent of old wood and damp stone, a comfort to me after so many years on the road. I ran my hand over the leather cover of the journal before me, its edges frayed and corners curling with age. It was a relic of a time long past, its pages heavy with stories too important to be forgotten, and yet, nearly lost to the weight of history and a country's choice to erase it.

I turned the journal carefully, as if the slightest pressure might cause it to crumble into dust. The binding groaned faintly in protest, and a stray page, browned and brittle with age, came loose. My fingers caught it before it could drift to the floor. A smile tugged at my lips. This old thing has seen better days, but it still held its secrets, waiting for someone brave, or foolish, enough to uncover it.

Tracing the faded ink on the page, the words reached out to me, alive with the echoes of the one who had written them. His heart and his soul, engraved in parchment and ink. I glanced around the room, noting the quiet figures lingering in the shadows, the soft clinking of glassware as someone cleared the table behind me. They always left me to my rituals, although their presence was a steady reminder that I was never truly alone, and I thanked them for it every day.

"This," I said aloud, more to myself than anyone else, "is where it begins." My voice trailed softly throughout, the tone meant for intimate gatherings around a hearth. I opened the journal, damp from years of neglect, but its presence hummed in my hand as I opened it to the first marked page.

Taking a deep breath, I began to read.

Running blind, it's all I could do at that moment. Right before being thrown into the air, I heard the commotion of people attempting to leave in a foreign caravan. Tossed like a courtesan's bed dressings in a Cyrillian brothel. I continued to move through the chaotic crowd of what had once been the Lunamani Festival. Echoed screams resonated in my ears from the mangled bodies within the city. One misplaced step was all it would have taken, just one simple moment of hesitation, and my brief life would have ended in the streets of Fall Lake like the countless others.

As I hurried past a group of mages, a mix of races from Shularix, I saw them giving their all, casting spells at the imminent danger. A ball of fire soared through the air and lit up the dark streets just before smashing into the side of a tailor's workshop. I had been responsible for the construction of Mr. Dowling's shop, and it tugged on my heartstrings to see the damage done to that man's life work. I then turned my glance to a man standing just a few feet away from the blast's impact. The debris was about to topple over onto him. He stood in fear, watching and waiting for his approaching doom. I rushed to him, shouting and waving my hands to get his attention before it was too late.

Or so I thought. He noticed me and ran just in time for the chimney to collapse behind him.

I continued forward on my path towards a blackened void of the unknown. A mother sheltering over her two young children caught my attention and pulled me back into this blood-borne reality. I recognized her. With her husband's recent passing, they would soon relocate to Riversend to live with her mother just north.

Overlapped shouting brought a potential escape at the docks for civilians and visitors alike. Further commands were given to the castle or even to the docks. Others were shouting to take arms, but with a monstrosity this size, nothing appeared to even dent the scales of the colossal abomination or delay its inevitable path of destruction.

"Damn the Draconis. This Draconic horror is almost otherworldly. Is this the moment I am forgotten about in this land? Never found my genuine passion or purpose. Is this truly the life I have desired to live for myself?" I kept asking myself over and over in my unsettled mind.

Cries of desperation were enough to pull my focus back into the danger around me and the occupants of Fall Lake. The same children, pleading for their lives, begged their mother to keep them safe. The children barely had an opportunity to find passion or purpose in their lives. That could not be the end of their young lives. With a quick yet careful push through the crowd, I made my way to the woman and her children. The quaking stomps of the beast as it quickly approached told me there was not much time before its path would fall upon this street. So, I could not let those young lives fall victim to that.

"Come with me. I will find you refuge." The tear-stricken woman ushered her children along behind me as her little boy named Jaxon gripped my finger as tightly as he could to ensure I would never let him go. Her gaze seemed never to want to be pried from the beast, so I held out my free hand to scoop hers into mine. "Have hope, Milady. Stay strong for the young ones here and have hope. All is not lost. Sir Seig is with you.

His protection will keep you all safe." I continued to lead them down a different path, a passage between the walls of the city's second gate.

It seemed I would not make it to my hut at the top of the hill at this point. But I knew of a bunker, a safe place she and her young could hide until, hopefully, the danger had passed. I helped build it. Hell, I helped build much of this city's newest locations over recent years. I knew its workings, and if there was one place to call safe, this may be one of the few locations. So I took them there.

What seemed like an eternity was just mere moments. The sound of the monster's roar rang through my ears, deafening me. At least I believed it was from the beast. There was a sudden pause in sounds as I was leaving the mother and children, with some others taking refuge in the bunker. A flash of a blue light appeared in my eyes. I shook it off. It must have been from the mana usage of the mages I passed before. Or was my mind losing itself?

"You shall be safe here. Have hope, everyone, this is a burden we all share." That was all I remembered saying to everyone as they looked at me just before I shut the bunker door. Leaving the bunker, I made my way back towards my original destination. The mother and her children thanking me profusely and begging me to come with them was a scene that forever made its mark in my memory. It was not fair to these children that they should fall victim to a war they held no action in. Perhaps not following them will be my downfall, the end of my story. I told them to stay safe and live their lives to the fullest before departing the bunker. I stood near a nearby statue and looked up towards the Draconis. The beast showed no sign of slowing down. Its rampage, if anything, had hastened as if every bit of flesh, stone, and dirt it ate was fueling the fires within itself. Like an unstoppable, bloodthirsty machine.

I noticed others making their way up the hill towards the top of the city, where my modest home is situated. The beast had made its way further into the city. Echoes of the insufficient weapons clanging against the creature's impenetrable hide, the smell of the metal and blood in the air. Nothing appeared to penetrate or slow it...

By the time I made it up the hill, I saw worrisome eyes meeting mine as they tried to hide. Hoping their stealth would hide them from the monster's path, my eyes caught one man whom I will never forget. Emptiness and despair filled his eyes while his words spoke of a simple prayer to his deity. His tunic held a holy symbol centered on his chest. A false hope, clinging to their faith that something greater awaits them in the next life. I am not the one to judge them, but I couldn't watch them waiting to be slaughtered. I yelled out to them, encouraging words to give them the courage to get further away. There was another exit that I knew of. Pointing and ushering them to the quickest route out of the city. To this day, I do not know if they took the route or lived, but I showed them a hopeful escape. It was better than listening to their cries and prayers and watching them suffer upon its arrival.

I made my way to my home, continuing to aid and guide others in a last-ditch effort to save their lives. I still don't know why I went there, or what I was going to do, but I allowed my gut to take me home one last time. An enormous sigh escaped me once the creaking door was shut. While resting my back on it, I saw what appeared to be a small fox. No, it was another flash of blue, or was that red? At the time, I was not certain, but a silent ring filled my ears, drowning out the dreadful sounds outside. Picking up the smell of thick blood in the air brought everything back into focus. So much was spilled this day that I could almost taste the metallic flavor on my tongue.

Another massive roar gave me the indication that it was much closer to me now. I shook my head to gather my senses, frantically looking around the plain and mostly empty space I called my home for anything that may help others. "Why have we been damned by the Draconis? There must be something that can be done to calm its rampage, to bring an end to this." Just then, another flash of blue filled my eyes, passing sight of that foxlike creature as my eyes lost vision once again.

Despite the sound of the deafening roar, my ears filled with voices, chants, melodies, songs, and gospels. Languages, both foreign and familiar, overlapped one another like an orchestra playing towards a conjoined connotation. All those people were using their last moments for prayer, in a simple hope that their god answers their call. The sounds pounded through my head over and over like a carpenter's nail. "Does this make them happy? Did it give their last moments purpose? No... I think I get it..." I said to myself before shaking a blue light from my eyes. When I closed them, a glimpse of the people that I had helped on my path here became a beckoning light during moments of despair. It was not just purpose. It was.

Hope.

The idea came to me through the struggles we face today. We fight to bring a better and brighter tomorrow. That we can find a light even in the darkest of days. Strength, passion, unity, faith, and love all start with hope... the vision of those people turned back into a blue light. For once in my life, I think I had found a purpose. With faster movements than I could ever recall in my life, I swung the door wide open. Death, destruction, and a million other descriptions of the massacre await me outside. Returning cries, screams, and pleas for hope returned to my lightly ringing ears. Those people needed something or someone to show them a sign of hope.

I thought I had lost my mind during that moment, to have any inclination that I could do something against that massive beast. Once again, that foxlike creature came into view, its movements leaving a trail of blue light along the ground as it sprinted off. I didn't understand what it was trying to do. Whatever it was, I think it wanted me to follow it. I decided to take my chances on the lost mind I now carry. A tower stood at a close distance and along the fox's path, a favored spot of mine, that overlooked the city and water's edge of Fall Lake. After climbing to the top, I looked at the surrounding people. I did not know the words that I was saying... I almost did not even feel like myself. I felt different. I do not even know how to explain it. It is like my body knows what it needs to do on its own. Telling me to go to this tower, I feel drawn to it. I gave a quick shout out to them just before a shock hit my hand, causing another flash of blue essence in my eyes. I felt a sense of energy shooting towards me. Of course, the Draconis monster, but I believed it to be something else...

The people moved as I shouted protective commands at them. Again, the words just flowed from my lips. They tried to find shelter and a way out of the beast's path, but for me, that light was the path of hope I followed. I had hope. An ideal, at least in whatever I did next. I moved with greater strides and a purpose to find whatever awaited me at the top of the tower. My feet moved faster than I believed to be humanly possible. The quakes of the stairs beneath my feet told me the creature was almost there. Drawing closer to my end, I climbed that tower faster. But something about me was different...

I stood at the top of that tower with pride, even if it was to look out onto the beautiful city one last time to watch the glistening sunset across the clear blue waters of the lake. Again, another light, the foxlike creature was absent from my view, nowhere to be seen around me. I saw a flash of blue and red pulse outward. My eyes deceived me as I saw the city in its highest glory. Beautiful architecture going on for miles, blue tinted walls surrounding it in its entirety. A large and exquisite castle sitting atop a neighboring hill. I glanced around to see myself standing on a balcony, no larger than the tower I stood on at that moment. I appeared to be looking out to the lake once again, but the location seemed foreign. The blood, death, torment, and the unholy living weapon that just moments prior was laying waste to the land was all gone. That... was hope, a grand view of the brightest light of tomorrow that could be born from the darkness of despair today. I felt something brush against my leg. The foxlike creature had returned. Its touch was comforting and familiar to me, but within a moment, it disappeared along with the vision.

It all made sense to me at that moment. I did not know how, but I felt the need to want to do something, so I told myself that I would. I needed to deal with this threat, but I was just Arlo Devine. What could I have done? I felt something in my hands, a blue spark coursing through them, encircled by a white mist of energy. Was that Mana? What was happening to me? I heard something, a voice. It was soothing, and echoed through my core, somehow filling a part of the void I felt deprived of in my life. It sounded as if it came from the sky. My eyes flashed with blue light and instantly storm clouds appeared, hiding the eclipsed twin moons within the evening sky. I instinctively turned to the path the beast carved on its way directly up the hill and straight towards me. I held no fear in my heart and mind. A quick glance at my hands once again I appeared to be encompassed in this blue and white light. Sparks continued to form and branch up my arms until I became a living conduit of lightning. I heard voices, visions flashed once again before my eyes of people and their last hopes as they began to fade away from this world. No, they were not fading away. They were the surrounding energy that encompassed me. The beast finally approached, trampling and stomping upon anything and anyone it could. We were all mere ants in comparison to its gargantuan size. I put pressure onto my bent legs, leaning into it and readying myself. Ready to pounce as the hunter, awaiting the opportune moments to strike its prey. The voice spoke to me again. I spoke the same words aloud to let the two voices overlap.

"I have Hope."

My eyes saw everything more clearly in that moment. The buildings, the bodies, the crops, the animals, all left in a wake of despair behind it. I was only Arlo Devine, a man who until that day had lacked a purpose in life, no real thing to truly be passionate about, just a man who worked day and night, giving everything he could for others and taking little in regards for himself. I found hope in those moments, a hope that even if I could not stop the beast. My efforts would delay it so that others would not suffer the same end. Pressing from the stone tower I found myself launched into the air, the tower's stone foundation was crumbling from the leap that propelled me forward. Time seemed to slow, a monstrous abomination of Draconis descent scaled, strong, and invulnerable. Flashes of my life clouded my vision and my slowed ascent into the sky above. My scream echoed throughout the entire city like howling thunder that rivaled the roar of the beast itself. Cracks of lightning struck around the city. My hand reared back high above my head, outstretched completely. I held the weapon of Hope, and I was ready to smite this damned creature that brought darkness upon all these lives. If that is what it takes, then my life for yours. Cobalt energy filled my hands. Closing my hand around it into a fist ready to strike the beast. My eyes covered and lost again behind the blue and white. The last thing I witnessed was the muzzle of this monstrosity, the swirling void of chaos and destruction within its reptilian eyes. Then silence. Blue light. Emptiness. This must be the serenity of death. To wade in the void of nothingness, lost in maddening thought for the rest of eternity. I felt like I was lying in a shallow pool of water, hopeful that my actions were not in vain, and that I could find acceptance in my fate. I had hoped that all would be well, even if my life was only able to save those who remained in the city. More visions flashed over my eyes, things that had been, that were, and what could be. But these were not dreams of my life.

They were the lives of others.

Finally, sound had returned to my ears, or perhaps they were noises in my mind to break the madness that I had fallen to. The sounds were too hard for me to comprehend exactly what they were. At times they came as voices, of strange dialect I have never heard in my life. Some were yelling, others crying, and a few laughing. I then felt a jerk as metal clanged in my head and echoed into an ear-splitting headache. The sound was familiar, hammer hitting metal within a forge, or two warriors engaged in combat, parrying the blows of their iron swords. Swirling sounds of speed, flame and chaotic energy of magic whisked through the air once again. My nostrils filled with a metallic smell, the flavor of blood on my tongue. Echoing voices of the Hopeful, reverberated in my ear.

Then all went silent once again.

The silence was lonesome. The voices I had been hearing at least gave comfort, giving me an illusion that I was not alone in this abyss. But I soon came to the realization that they were gone. I tried to open my eyes as I heard shouting again, the blue in my vision moving in unidentifiable shapes. All I could see was the black emptiness, as the blue light moved towards where my hands should have been. Mixing with the white and formed into the long shape of a road, I heard a tingling in my hand, what sounded like my voice speaking to me, while the energy of blue and white pulsed with every syllable.

If you have hope for a brighter tomorrow. Stand tall and take hope into your own hands. Accept their pain as your own and share hope's light with the world.

I did the only thing I knew how to do. Find hope within despair, and I tightened my hands, gripping upon what appeared to be within my reach. And as I grasped the light, feeling its energy course through my body, and then outward from my body as if I was the conduit for the lightning. Ringing filled my ears from a massive thunderous crack and the weight of something massive falling from the strength of hope in my hands. My eyes fell victim to the deep blue light, and all plunged into absolute silence.

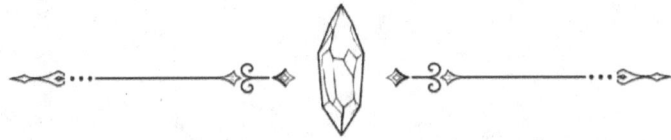

The room stayed quiet as I closed the journal, clasping the worn latch onto the leather binding. I leaned back in my chair, letting the weight of Arlo's words settle over the room like the embers of a dying fire. For a moment, there was nothing but the sound of the wind rattling the windows and the faint clinking of glass from the kitchen.

I placed the journal gently on the table, my hand lingering on the cover. "You see," I said low and steady, "this is more than just a recounting of one man's night. It is a spark, a light born in despair and carried forward through courage. Hope is not a grand thing, my friends. It is the smallest ember, nurtured into a flame. And that flame… Well, it's what lights the way, even in the deepest darkness."

The fire crackled again, a bright burst of light and heat as if in agreement. I glanced toward the shadows where the journal's pages had disappeared, a faint smirk curling my lips as shadows of red hair moved to lock it away until it was needed again. "This is where our story begins. Picking up with the aftermath of what we have just learned. Remember his words as we step forward together, for in them, we find not just the story of Fall Lake, but the heart of what it means to fight for a brighter tomorrow."

I took a sip from my tankard, letting the cool liquid clear my throat as I leaned forward, and began the tale. Hammer Fall.

CHAPTER I

Thump. Thump. Thump.

Heavy boots slammed against the scorched earth, echoing through the hollow silence of Fall Lake. Each step felt heavier than the last, as if the weight of the dead clung to him. The crater before him breathed of chaos and destruction, veiled by a shroud of ash and debris and a distortion of heat radiating upward. He paused at the edge, his breath catching as he stared into the heart of the destruction of the newly built city, one he believed he could have led wearing the mantle of Paladin one day.

In the center, the source of the city's destruction. The young knight took in the sight of the monstrous creature lying dormant at the crater's center. Its body rose many stories high, its hide thicker than a rhinoceros, and hardened, pristine scales formed a protective layer over its massive frame. Its teeth were sharper than any blade he had ever wielded, and its claws were jagged with blood, viscera, and rubble.

None of it belonged to the beast.

Even in its still and quelled state, no wound had seemed to puncture the gargantuan monstrosity... Save for the massive indentation upon its neck where someone, or something, had struck it down.

Fused veins of crystalline glass and stone traced the crater's rim, glowing faintly blue as if lightning had burned belief itself into the rubble.

For a sergeant of the Porters, he was familiar with warfare, battles, and monsters. But the devastation before his eyes spoke of something otherworldly. His mind raced with questions as he considered the source of the powerful blow that had caused its downfall, half-expecting to discover that it was the Paladin, the hero of his youth, or even a miraculous act performed by his own deity, Heir. If this was Heir's judgement, why had Heir not spared the faithful?

A hand grasped his shoulder, but it was not enough to bring his focus back to his duty for his church and the King. "Brother Sorren, may Heir be with us all on this day." A grim voice spoke out from behind him, the owner of the voice shifted his eyes to gauge the taller, younger man's reaction. Despite knowing Sorren could handle himself, he still routinely measured Sorren's reactions.

Sorren knew who the hand and voice belonged to, a trusted companion and mentor within their ranks. Even though he knew his duty, this was still hard for the man to gaze upon. How could someone, or something, cause this sort of destruction and mayhem? And what if there were more of these? Would all of this continent fall victim to its violence? He glanced around to see a single man within the craterous foundation, lost and taken by the moment. He found it strange that anyone survived this creature's path, let alone only this one man.

"You ever see anything like this?" Sorren asked in bewilderment. He placed a hand over his holy symbol in a silent prayer.

"I have seen many strange things in my day, but nothing of this extent. You go in and find any other survivors. I will retrieve the King for escort," Jason directed.

A nod gave the confirmation of the command of his superior. It was the duty of the Porters to escort high-ranking officials through the lands. Having just arrived at the docks of Fall Lake, their squad had missed much of the onslaught that took place. But they did take notice when the lightning struck and watched a man foolishly leap towards the beast. With his focus brought back into view, Sorren quickly assessed the area, taking notice of a crowd growing around the peak of the crater to see what lay within.

"See to the throne, brother. I will seek other survivors." Without hesitation or further conversation, Sorren shifted his way through the rubble, taking notice of no signs of life other than the one man. The man held a strained and grimacing face of agony, his clothing tattered with little intact. Debris floated in the air as if being held by some magnetic force, electrical static protruding off them. Kneeling to help, he took in the sight: raw wounds, old scars split open again, bruises blooming like ink beneath torn skin. The man's body was a testament to agony.

An audience grew, marveling at the beast, some crying from the destruction of their home, and others wanting to see what they believed to be their savior.

A sudden scream tore from the man's throat, his eyes snapping open wide and wild. Sorren's gaze dropped to the weapon clutched tight in the man's hand, a warhammer, gleaming even through the dust and grime. The man's ragged muttering twisted into a hoarse battle cry as he lurched forward, swinging the hammer in a blind arc through the air, not at Sorren, but at some unseen terror only he could see.

The warhammer pulsed with a low, resonant thrum as his arms dropped back to the ground, the swing spent. Through pained, flickering eyes, the man met Sorren's stare, blue light flaring behind his pupils, before his body collapsed, limp among the settling debris that had hovered moments before.

"Aye, watch it now, big fella," Sorren muttered before showing signs of his massive stature and strength by lifting the man with practiced strength. Strength without purpose, he thought, is only weight.

The man needed tending to, and soon. People approached in awe but kept their distance until Sorren's eyes caught with that of a few soldiers amongst the crowd, Kingsguard, clearly a private by the design of their armor.

"You lot! Stop gawking and give me a hand. Or are you waiting for orders from that beast?" he commanded the soldiers with a glare. One scrambled forward, his hesitation melting under Sorren's imposing presence.

Mumbling under the man's breath were signs showing he was still alive. A powerful stench of metal and blood was heavy in the surrounding air. The man occasionally came to and spoke in that same language again, a few words of the common tongue scattered through in ambiguous sentences. With enough thrashing from the man, he soon fell limp again. Sorren was unsure if this was the man that had claimed the title of this beast slayer, but he was the only living person within the area, so it had to have been him.

Upon crossing the peak of the crater, they lay the man next to a building, still intact from the devastation. Sorren thanked the private before dismissing him back to where he needed to be. As a Porter and knight of The Monastery of Heir's Reign, blessed by his deity with some abilities to tend to wounds, though most of Heir's work was done quickly on the battlefield to keep a man going. He hoped his capabilities were enough to ease his burdens. "Heir, help me bind these wounds and relieve this man's pain."

White light blossomed between his palms, sealing cuts but leaving bruises untouched. The flow faltered where it met the sparking scars as if his own powers recoiled.

18

"Hildegarde has fallen! Tell Lieuten..." the mysterious man shouted through his unstable state. For Sorren, he had seen others become hysterical and lose their grip on reality in times of great stress. But what this man appeared to be going through, Sorren was not even sure if the man would survive the night with the pain he appeared to be in. Another prayer to the deity of warfare led him to send another pulse of mana through the man's wounds, but with little effect from the radiant essence.

Mumbling to himself, Sorren took a mental note to spend some time with the clerics in Davenport. He would have time to dwell on that later. For now, he must finish the mission bestowed upon him. It helped that Sorren was of immense size, at over six and a half feet tall, and muscles that rivaled the size of an anvil he was a remarkable sight and a force to be reckoned with. Carrying this man was of little trouble even with his immense sword strapped across his back. Embarking through the city, it took little time for Sorren to notice the signs of six figures in a flanking formation around two individuals. He was familiar with these individuals. Radiant white cloaks pinned together by the lion head insignia of the Lionhart royals covered the royal blue tabards. These were the King's hand selected personal guard. Sorren approached the formation as Jason acknowledged him and gave ease to the guards as he pushed past the two men at a point.

"Is this the man from the crater?" Jason asked, eyeing the half-conscious body draped across Sorren's broad back.

"Aye, it is. Feisty one he is, been in and out of consciousness. Tried treating his wounds and dammit if I didn't have any luck," Sorren answered with a slight grin of seeing Jason's quick find of the King.

Their attention turned to the approaching figure. A seasoned man with short cut gray hair and a thick beard to match. Wearing apatite plate armor, an elegant blue phosphate material with gold trimming and a black wool shirt and leggings underneath. King Frederick Lionhart now stood before Sorren, who gave his best attempt at a bow given the circumstances of carrying another man. His voice was regal and spoke with a commanding elegance. "Sorren, what is the status within the crater?"

"M'Lord, that thing appears to be dealt with. It was not moving, and no other survivors remained. Save for this fella. But I must ask, what happened? What was that thing? More pressingly, is there anything I can do now to help?" Sorren answered and quickly questioned back, keeping pace with the men as they moved quickly towards a destination.

"In Heir's name, I do not know what that thing is. But we are already working in search of an answer. One moment we are enjoying the last of the Lunamani festivities, the next all kinds of chaos consumed us. We were fortunate to hold the creature off, that it was unable to destroy the entire city. It was strange, watching upon the hilltop as a man leaped from a tower. Something appeared to be falling from heavens of Zenith itself before the lightning struck and the crater remained." King Frederick explained hastily, looking upon the mentioned location the beast had fallen. His gaze glancing over at the man in Sorren's arms.

"You said there was only one survivor, and it was this man? Surely, he must be the one who leaped from the tower or have knowledge of what happened if he survived such an attack," Jason added.

"In all honesty, if this is the man who quelled that beast, then we all owe him our highest gratitude. Sorren, the only thing I need you to do is keep an eye on this man, make sure he does not leave and inform me when he awakes. For now, he is your highest priority," the king requested of Sorren.

As Sorren turned away, rage and pity twisted together in his chest. Each injured face he passed was another spark to the fire beneath his ribs. He forced himself to breathe until the heat dulled, lessons of faith that whispered control was its own devotion.

He carried the stranger aboard the vessel, laying him gently in a swaying hammock. Above, the crew readied the sails. The man barely stirred. Sorren checked for a pulse.

Blue eyes flickered open, a glint of light chasing shadows across Sorren's hands, then closed again.

Sorren stared at the fading glow. He did not yet know he was watching the first breath of Hope return to the world.

CHAPTER 2

Echoes of despair clung to Sorren's thoughts, haunting whispers of a land consumed by chaos. Every plea, every cry replayed in his mind, woven into the explosive roar that had shattered Fall Lake and rippled across Shularix like a thunderclap. Taking a swig from his flask, he let the bitter burn silence the ghosts.

Still, the memory hummed beneath his ribs, a faint pulse of light he could not drink away.

"Shouldn't be much longer, mate. Heir be with you," Sorren muttered to the unconscious white haired man beside him while leaning back in the oak chair.

A groan escaped Sorren's muscled frame, causing the man to jerk awake. Blue eyes rolled to the back of his head, speaking some type of foreign chant aloud. Was he some kind of witch or other magical being? Sorren could have sworn the language was not of this world, which only helped aid in his confusion and unsettling concern for being stationed to watch the man. Unable to place the words, and watching as the man began to still and go back to his pain-filled slumber. He knew he must get rest while he still could.

"How is he?" Brother Jason's familiar voice broke through the silence.

"Not much has changed, brother." The raven-haired warrior stated with a hint of frustration. He leaned forward in his chair to greet his superior. Compared to his build, the chair looked like it was meant for a child, a sight that always gave him a chuckle. "Every sign says he should've been dead already, but whatever is keeping him alive is nothing I recognize."

Jason's hands gripped the wool blanket draped across the unconscious brave soul, or foolish, as he had heard some crew members say. The lacerations, burns, and bruises told a story of unimaginable pain that Heir's available disciples were unable to cure. He took note of the swollen mark on his forehead, scattered burns and bruises across his body, and the hammer clutched tightly in his grasp. He gave one more attempt at using Heir's mana to mend him and watched as the mana appeared to absorb into the wounds, but it was as if he had done nothing at all. The wounds remained the same.

"You can keep tryin' but I have given it my best shot at least a dozen times already," Sorren claimed, giving a shake of his head as he moved to stand beside Jason.

"The plan is to take him to see one of the clerics now that we arrived in Davenport. A new priestess arrived from Cyril, seeking to perfect her craft. If she can aid this man of his wounds more than we can, she will certainly have gained recognition amongst the Porters."

On deck, he heard the crew signaling their arrival to the Davenport docks.

"We should get him ready to transport."

Sorren nodded, wrapping the man in a woven blanket embroidered with a lion's head, the sigil of the Lionhart family.

"Things could have gone really south back there. We are fortunate the king is still safe, a tragic blow to Zenaria had we lost His Majesty during the attack," Sorren said through the clambering steps of his weighted boots.

"Let us not weigh the losses of those who have passed from tragedy. I shall lead you to Alysia, then I must go back to His Majesty after. As much as it pains me to admit, I foresee another battle in our near future."

The thought of spilling the blood of those responsible for the destruction at Fall Lake pressed a vengeful smirk over Sorren's handsome features. A hunger had been forming within him since he had seen the destruction that consumed the festival. And justice needed to be served. He whispered Heir's name, not in prayer this time but promise. The silence that answered still felt wrong.

"Aye, and may the bastard to blame be struck by Heir's righteous judgement. Now let's hurry, you shouldn't keep the King waiting."

An eerie calm blanketed the city of Davenport. News had yet to spread this far south, but that would not last long. As they moved through the docks and towards the church, various citizens were muttering to themselves about the King's premature return. Jason led them into the elaborate white and gold church. Twin warrior angels flanked the entrance. A spark hit the eyes of the young warrior, followed by a confident grin as he let his eyes take in the slender beauty before him. Sorren could tell she was around his age, somewhere in her early twenties. Silken raven hair draped down plainly just past her shoulders and comforting olive eyes.

"Brother Jason, it is good to see you again." The woman's soft voice greeted before noticing the load Sorren carried in.

"Alysia, the pleasure is truly mine. This is Brother Sorren, a fellow Porter. A tragedy befell Fall Lake during the festival, and this unknown hero was severely injured. Sorren, if you do not mind informing her of the events that transpired, I must return for orders from the King." Alysia took in Sorren's enormous figure, then glanced at the lifeless body in his arms. She gave a nod, pointing in the direction of the infirmary.

"Do not worry, Brother Jason, I will tend to this man. Do not keep the King waiting. Gracemother bless you." Alysia responded.

Jason parted from the two with a pat on Sorren's shoulder as they passed and disappeared through the church doors. "Heir guides your path, brother." Sorren gave a quick prayer, then followed the woman.

"I am Alysia Erudite, a disciple of the Grace Mother." The woman laid a plain cloth blanket on the bed, dashing through the room to gather instruments and herbs she may need. "Please, lay him on the bed so I may examine his wounds."

"Well met, M'lady Alysia. I attempted to care for him the best I could in my limited capabilities, but since I have seen him..."

Sorren gave a brief pause as the sight of the aftermath fell back into his vision.

"Since I saw him strike down that beast. There has been no change in his state or his wounds. Plagued by obvious constant nightmares, and his troubling screams may have caused me to lose some of my hearing."

Sorren gave a light chuckle as he let the woman perform her work. He knew the Disciples of Grace were excellent healers, but rarely got to see their abilities at work.

"He did well for the city. I feel we owe him better than whatever malady ails him. Do you think you can help, M'lady?"

Sorren's grey eyes looked her direction, with genuine concern upon his face. Though, as he took in her soft elements and pale complexion, his smile returned to his handsome features with the thoughts of another potential conquest.

The young priestess gracefully gathered an item from a credenza just inside the church's sacristy. She returned holding a finely crafted box stained with a burgundy coat and twisted in fine leather wrap.

25

Alysia removed the robes of the unconscious man to examine his wounds, her face carrying fear and worry as his body appeared to be covered in bruises. She gazed back at Sorren to catch his different expressions and gave a deep smile back at him.

"I will do the best I can, Brother Sorren," she muttered.

"Aye, may Heir show you his appreciation for it as well. As I may wish to show you as well," he replied with a low growl.

"Thank you," she said, shying away from his comments, and back to her work. "You mentioned a beast. What did it look like?"

"Big, scaly, two horns that looked like they could impale any fortress. More teeth than any creature should realistically need, and an appetite to match." Sorren outstretched his arms in a manner to emphasize his words.

"Sounds like one of those Draconis, fortunate I've never seen one with my own eyes. You may want to hold his arms down." She then strapped the legs of the man to the table he lay upon.

Sorren nodded and held the savior's arms at his side. Alysia uncorked the bottle of alcohol and poured it over the wounds releasing a hiss, bubbling against the blood and grime. The man involuntarily flinched and groaned at the burning sensation, his muscles straining against Sorren's grip. She then quickly applied a blended salve of crushed herbs, the sharp scent mingling with the stench of blood.

Sorren began to utter a prayer to Heir. Alysia joined in with a prayer to her own god, Grace, that sounded more like an incantation than a prayer. She waved her hands over his body, as a light emanated from her hands and began to seep into his wounds, appearing to lessen some of the bruising and the finer cuts. Sorren continued his prayer, but disbelief shook him as none of his comrades had been able to use any of their healing magic to make this much of an impact. Either Alysia was better than anyone else whom had tried, or her god's magic could heal stronger than Heir's.

He felt his own prayer dim beside hers, the words hollow, the air still. Her magic soothed where his commanded, the light of Grace settling over the man like a memory answered. The wounds sparked softly, not in pain, but in recognition.

For a heartbeat, Sorren swore the air around them sighed, a whisper of something older than prayer had been waiting for this touch.

Alysia's eyes closed. "That should have mended more than this."

Sorren looked from her hands to the bruising still dark across the man's ribs. "Eh, did more than mine."

"Grace's light does not command flesh the way Heir's does," she added quietly to herself. "It reminds the body what it was before it broke. Something within him won't remember, or is choosing not to. I can dull the worst of it. Close what is small and left opened."

A small sigh escaped her, examining the bizarre condition. Another trickle of Grace's gift slipped from her fingers, drawn absently toward the bruising. "The deeper wounds are refusing—"

She gasped. "His eyes."

The man's eyes burst open revealing bright blue orbs and scattering their view quickly over the room. He seemed to still be out of it, Sorren tried to help him focus anyway. "Hey! Can you hear me?"

The man's eyelids fluttered open, revealing illuminating sapphire blue orbs beneath them. They darted wildly, unfocused as if searching for something. And with every few blinks his eyes grew brighter as if filled with a massive shockwave of blue mana before it dispersed with the next.

The man began to speak a foreign language, one Sorren and Alysia had never heard before. "Quid est fierna?" His voice was shaky, the dialect foreign, but the tone seemed like a question. His eyes were rapidly blinking as if he was trying to focus, and with every few blinks an emanating blue light filled his eyes.

"Easy, easy." Alysia soothed, hovering her hand over his chest as she channeled another pulse of mana.

Sorren thought back to one of his first missions he held once he was no longer a squire. He knew the fellow appeared familiar to him, but it wasn't until he heard his voice that it clicked for him. "Arlo? Arlo, you spoke the Shularian tongue the last we met, did you not?" The man on the bed tried to lean up towards him before he seemed to waver and fall back. Sorren glanced at Alysia.

Sorren's eyes narrowed as he studied the man's face, the lines of pain etched deeply into his pale features. Slowly, the pieces clicked into place.

"Arlo," he whispered to himself, the name familiar to his tongue. He tightened his grip on the man's arm with excitement. "It's been years, but I know this man. We worked a mission together, farmer's kids went missing, damn things turned out to be led by a hag coven covering as an orphanage. He spoke the Shularian tongue back then, was blonde too if I recall… What the hell happened to you?"

Arlo kept trying to shake the ringing in his ears, grimacing with every movement from the wounds scattered across his body. "Ubi lae saen? What is going *vi?*" His words appeared to be a blend of the foreign language he spoke previously and the common tongue. His face spoke of the pain the man obviously felt, pain that Alysia tried to soothe, but whatever his affliction was, it seemed beyond her. For a moment he continued to ramble in the mixture of languages, his foggy eyes cleared along with his focus. He clawed his way out of his nightmare, falling back to humanity.

"Where am I?"

CHAPTER 3

"Davenport, you're safe here in the Temple of Heir and Grace," Sorren assured, his smile wide and cocked. "How did I get here?" Arlo asked, wincing as he leaned forward, prompting Alysia to step in to inspect his wounds more closely. "Ah, a heroic tale, you don't remember?" he chuckled.

The name of Heir echoed faintly in Arlo's chest, but it carried no warmth. It was the other name, softer, that seemed to linger when Alysia moved about the room. The sound of it calmed the ache in his bones.

Grace.

"A'right, I arrived in Fall Lake just in time to see you smash a massive beast right into the ground, very heroically, I might add. Now, we need you to collect yourself and get us some information. I'm quite sure you know more than most of us do, currently anyway."

Arlo tried to focus on Sorren's words, searching his mind for any memory he could grasp. He lifted his hand and felt an unfamiliar weight pulling at it. "I'm sorry," he whispered. "I don't remember much, and I don't think this is mine."

The hammer pulsed once in his grasp, faint blue light brushing across his fingers as if testing him. The warmth faded the moment he doubted himself.

Hearing his words, Sorren lifted an eyebrow. He smirked to mask his unease.

"Seriously? Nothin' at all? The way you leapt from that tower was like nothing I've ever seen before. You're a fuckin' hero, mate. Might be a bigger one than Paladin Danladin himself." He jokingly smacked the arm of Arlo, sending a shock of pain throughout his body.

"You've also had this hammer in a death grip since I found you in that crater next to the beast." "Please, stop. I'm no... hero." Arlo let out another gasp of pain before giving up and letting his body relax on the makeshift bed. He closed his eyes and made an attempt to recollect what information he could.

"Last I remember was aiding a family, then I ran up the hill towards the shack I called a home. Anything else after that is still a blur, save for bits and pieces of oddities scattered throughout. I thought I had moved onto the next life," he added with a sigh. "Praise Heir that you didn't!" Sorren stated while giving exaggerated rhythmic beats to his white gilded armor. Beats that Alysia had not expected, nearly knocking a cup of water from her hands. "Well, you need to take it easy before ya try gallivanting about. If you're up for it, I would like to hear any and all details you got. Be good to have those oddities sorted out before ya see the King."

"They really do believe me to be some sort of hero." Arlo thought while effortlessly lifting the large warhammer up to get a better look. "After my mind went blank, I saw flashes, or visions of battles." "Visions?" Alysia and Sorren said in unison. "I don't know what they were, but it seemed like flashes of battles, or a war. Humans, Elfar, and other beings I've only read about in books and stories of past wars."

30

He took a deep breath in to move through the pain, while it was not as intense as it was when he first awoke. Pain continued to rack his body, making an attempt to get out of the bed before Alysia ushered him to stay. The more he thought about what happened the more he began to worry about the other inhabitants of the city. "And what of the others that attended the festival at Fall Lake? Are there other survivors?"

Burly hands rubbed through the short ebony hair of Sorren. "Eh, we are continuing to get some folks coming in needing aid here in Davenport, but almost anyone with half a lick of medicinal knowledge had ventured back to aid. While the city was officially completed, the... destruction caused some setbacks and there isn't a definite number of casualties. Alysia and myself have been assigned to watch over you, having a warrior of Heir and a priestess of the Gracemother at your disposal, you're a hot topic amongst the town." Sorren let out another bellowing laugh. "Guess I'll go let Brother Jason know you've woken. Get ya some rest friend, you won't be any good to anyone if you fall back into that deep slumber again!"

Arlo couldn't find what he thought was so funny, given the circumstances that he was in, and the idea that so many others had lost their lives. Yet he knew that followers of Heir, the God of War, were no strangers to battle.

"Yes, some rest would be nice. Forgive my memory in its current state, perhaps some sleep and a meal will do me good. And, I apologize, I know we met and worked together before, but what were your names?" Arlo asked, relaxing into the bed in order to find some solace from his pain.

"Sorren, Sorren Blaze. Protector within the Porters, a subsidiary of the Monastery of Heir's Reign." The tall man stated rising to his full form. He was built like a bull, but featured a clean baby face with chiseled features. Handsome and young, much to the folly of his conquests. He gave Alysia a wink.

"This here's Alysia, uh, I never caught your last name."

31

"Erudite, Alysia Erudite. He will be fine here Brother Sorren." She finished attempting to usher him out of the room.

"Your services shall not be forgotten by Heir or myself, I am sure. Nor your pretty face," Sorren added with a coy smile.

Blood rushed to the cheeks of Alysia, closing the door with an audible click behind him.

"Don't worry, he is in good hands."

Heavy footsteps rang out through the quaint fishing town. Rumors amongst the townsfolk spread regarding the nature of the attack, including wildly exaggerated talks of the creature itself. Many folks were gathered around the entrance to the town, where many individuals were preparing wagons and cargo crates for transport back to Fall Lake. Several small ships emergency docked along the river, pulleys sending cargo boxes to and from the ships.

The Porters, being stationed within Davenport, were leading the organization of the cargo onto the transport vessels. Several wolf-like creatures were seen among them, aiding in pulling the heavy weight of the cargo across the walkway. These creatures held a sleek muscular canine form, covered in thick fur but with an extended torso. Webbed forelegs, a dorsal fin on their back, and flipper like hindlegs aid in their ability to be swift on land, and within water. The Akhlut species is used heavily by the Porters, and fishers of Davenport to aid in travel and herding or retrieval of fish.

Sorren presumed Brother Jason would be found here amongst his other brethren. Upon arriving to the scene, he knew he was correct when he heard Jason's voice echoing throughout the dispersing crowd.

"The next ships are expected to return this eve, another cargo load will be prepped at dawn. Prepare the ship and leave within 15 minutes. Heir's strength be with you all." The Commander said with a clear directive before walking off.

Sorren watched on from a shaded patio, overlooking the clear water of the Caranora River. He knew this was a popular spot for Jason, and as predicted he went toward the very spot. Jason let out a heavy sigh as his back hits the patio wall. "Brother Sorren," Jason acknowledged Sorren's presence as he brought an ebony pipe to his lips to take a drag. "You know, the air is quite subtle today. If our tomorrows are not promised, we should truly cherish what we have today," he said with a somber, worried look on his face as he looked out over the meadow to the north. "How fares our guest?"

The larger, and younger of the two stood tall in order to give his report. "The hero of Fall Lake has awoken. His name is Arlo, but his mind is still foggy, and unclear. Much as we have noticed in his sleep, his pain seems to be unhealed, even with my own abilities and Sister Alysia's attempts. Honestly, it seems, unorthodox." he finished questionably, reflecting on the wounds he witnessed. "Even with healing from the Gracemother's clerics, his wounds still do not fully heal."

"I—" Sorren began, his brow furrowing, blood rushing to his face and his fist clenching tightly together. "Have to ask for an update on Fall Lake. This catastrophe angers me, I want to shed the blood of those responsible. Heir demands their blood." A tight grip was formed on his shoulder, releasing the red that filled his eyes. "Easy Sorren, we all have our parts to play. The King and his advisors are working out the details of what to do next. The Bladesingers are doing their part and researching what information they can. Their new commander, Crowley, is excellent with recon. We as Porters, must do our part."

He offered him a smile and a nod. "You perhaps may have one of the most important duties at the moment, the King is eager to meet this hero. I will let him know that he is awake, and we will plan a meeting once he is capable enough." Sorren relaxed his fist and nodded. He was thirsty, hungry, aching to get vengeance on whoever or whatever is responsible for letting that creature free. "Your words have always guided me true Brother Jason. Very well, let me go and check on our friend. Heir's blessing be with you brother."

Loud clanging from heavy footsteps filled the cathedral's walls. The door to Arlo's room burst open as Sorren's massive frame filled the doorway. A startled and sharp look from Alysia sent holes through Sorren, who gave her a wink.

"Sorry love, always gotta make my presence known, ya'know?" he said with a large laugh. "King's requesting Arlo's presence, came to see if he was awake or not."

Alysia shook her head and leaned over Arlo's bed, whispering to not startle him. "Arlo... Are you awake?"

Silence.

"Ya know, you can whisper into my ear like that sometime. Got a clearing about two hours east of 'ere that serves wonderfully for a picnic. Little private creek for some swimming after. Iffen you be interested M'lady." He grinned.

A sudden flash of blue lit up Arlo's eyes as he lurched upright in the bed, swinging the hammer with him. The strike barely missed Sorren's waist and sent Alysia tumbling to the ground. A deafening boom cracked through the room as the hammer slammed into the wall, blasting rubble and sparks of blue energy across the chamber.

Arlo shouted something in a harsh, unfamiliar tongue, his eyes wide, bright light spilling from their corners. He strained forward, the words tumbling out in a fevered rush until, all at once, his eyes fluttered and the light faded. He blinked rapidly, shook his head, and when he looked up again, only the deep blue of his natural gaze remained.

Sorren took a defensive stance, slowly moving towards Alysia to assist her in rising from the floor. "Sorry mate, didn't mean to startle ya." Sorren began to worry if Arlo could be trusted in front of the king, what would stop him from going into this possessed state and attacking. He brushed the idea from his mind when he assumed that the King's guards and likely the Paladin would be there to defend him.

Arlo rose from the bed, using the bed to keep himself from wobbling too much. His naked figure showed many signs of bruising, bruises that did not seem to heal themselves. His figure was well built. While not as tall or as muscular as Sorren. He appeared to work out frequently and be very toned, and at this moment Alysia's blushing red cheeks showed he was leaving nothing to the imagination.

"Hey, yo, we might wanna find ya some clothes." Sorren chuckled through his words.

Upon noticing his lack of clothing, he pulled the blanket from the bed to cover himself.

"I... apologize. I was having some strange dreams and your voice startled me. I don't have much money, but I can fix the wall."

"We will get that taken care of," she said shyly, avoiding eye contact with Arlo. "I'll go find some clothing that should fit you." Alysia hurried out of the room. "So friend, the King wants to see ya. Think you will be up for it tomorrow, he's got some questions for ya? Seems like you can rise to the occasion." His booming laughter echoed out through the halls. "Sure, I can speak to him, but I still don't remember any additional information," he agreed. Alysia returned a few moments later, offering some finely crafted silk trousers and shirt. Arlo accepted the clothing, while not a great fit. He was still appreciative of the offering. "Whenever he needs me to be there, I will."

CHAPTER 4

Davenport was only a small fishing town, but its proximity to the ocean and connection along the Caranora River allowed it to thrive. Streets of cobblestone echoed with the lively chatter of fishers, colorful fishing boats bobbed in the harbor, and adding to the town's charm. Many traders and fishers found homes here and supplied fresh fish from the sea to the south. A small, fortified manor for the King's highest and most important officials towered over the river below, decorated with the Lionhart sigil of a Lion's head centered on a gilded blue backdrop.

From the harbor one could still taste storm on the air, a faint bite of lightning that the river had carried south. Davenport kept working, but the chatter had a brittle edge, as if the town itself was listening for another roar heard round the world.

Guards accompanied by warrior-bred Akhlut were always stationed here, even when the building was empty. But now, the building was used to house the King and his advisors, assessing the next steps the Kingdom of Zenaria would take against the possible threat that was beginning to loom over them.

"Let them in," a voice commanded from the other side of the dining hall. The two men standing guard opened the door to see Brother Jason ushering Arlo and Sorren inside. Sorren gave a salute to his commander.

"Sergeant Sorren Blaze, presenting the hero of Fall Lake," Sorren said.

"At ease, Brother Sorren," Jason said in response, "I am Deputy Paladin Jason Wood, please follow me."

The men were brought to the head of the dining table, several other tables were in the room with a few empty mugs showing that others were previously there. This table was filled with cooked eggs and fresh fruit. Sitting on the other side of the table within a finely crafted and gilded chair was an elderly man that still appeared to be in great shape and health. White and blue robes lay beneath a fur lined royal cloak. An embossed golden crown sat upon his ash hair, silver beard adding to the aura of wisdom that surrounded him, and piercing emerald eyes looked over a parchment he was reading. His gaze barely lifted from the parchment, yet when it moved it cut with an edge. When it slipped to the warhammer at Arlo's side, a flicker of something colder than curiosity passed through the emerald eyes.

"I, Deputy-Paladin Jason Wood, am pleased with the honor of presenting his eminence, King Frederick Lionhart," Jason said as he took a bow.

"Sergeant Sorren Blaze, my king. And this man is the hero of Fall Lake, Arlo," Sorren said following in a bow before nudging Arlo.

"Arlo Devine, sir." Arlo followed.

"Please be seated," Said the deep voice of a man who stood flanking the King. His helmet and armor masked much of his body, but the diamond cross on his golden mantle gave the indication of whom he was, Paladin Danladin Ulrir, the second highest ranking official within the Monastery of Heir's Reign and commander over all the church's military strength.

Moments went by before anyone else spoke, Arlo looked around at the others to see what the next steps were, the king continued to read his scroll. The Paladin stood still like a menacing statue, Sorren held an impressive figure, but Arlo could see even he was awestruck by the sheer size and presence of the Paladin.

"I am told you are unwilling to admit to felling the beast. How did you come to possess such power?" The King demanded.

"And do not waste my time."

"I never said unwilling, I do not remember being the one to attack the beast. I remember that I was at a tower within the high-rise and the next I remember is a glimpse of me being in the air, falling towards the abomination," Arlo replied shifting in his seat to offset his rising pain. He still heard the screams, the monster's terrifying roar, cries and the smell of so much blood being spilled.

"Sir, I w..."

"Your Majesty," the paladin interrupted.

"Your Majesty," Arlo said, "I wish I had more. But, I only recall bits and pieces. I am a simple man born in Cyril, I was in Fall Lake serving in the construction of the city for the past few years. My family is of nothing noteworthy, both having passed away when I was only a youth." He felt the room decide things about him he had not decided for himself.

A servant, clad in a crisp blue uniform, took a flagon from the table and poured wine into the goblets for each man at the table, his movements swift and practiced. The faint jingle of keys at his waist hinted at his role as a trusted member of the King's staff. "Please eat," King Frederick waved his hands over the food within the center of the table, his tone commanding.

"And provide me with what information you do remember." The order sounded like mercy but landed like command. Sorren reached first out of habit. Arlo waited and felt watched.

Sorren dug into the food upon the King's urging, and drank excessive amounts of wine. Arlo began to explain what information he remembered on the people he was able to save, running towards his home, and then blacking out. Except for the blue light, then awaking to Sorren and Alysia. Frederick listened intently to the information shared, his expression unsatisfactory to the information given.

"And what of this blue light you saw? And these dreams?" Frederick asked, his emerald eyes feeling like they almost pierced through the man across from him.

"I don't know what they are, or were. I remember one of them, a man clad in armor, similar to yours." Arlo motioned towards the Paladin, "Standing over a woman with..." His voice trailed as he placed a hand upon the hammer leaning on his seat. "This hammer, in his hands."

The King's eyes narrowed, not in doubt but in measure, as if weighing a truth he always feared.

"I have an order for you Sergeant. And it is to be kept between those of us in this room, you escort Mr. Devine into the heart of Treycord Meadows. There is a tomb there, I order both of you to go and retrieve an amulet held within and bring it back to me."

"An amulet? Seriously?" Sorren said in a bewildered outburst. Was this truly the best assignment he could be given at a time like this? To fetch the king's jewelry. He almost felt belittled and humiliated and began to wonder whom he pissed off to be a babysitter and an errand boy instead of fighting in Heir's name, or even providing aid and comfort to those in Fall Lake.

Jason quickly snapped back at Sorren, who could feel the heat from the higher ranking three in the room. His look said everything a sermon could not.

Sorren stumbled with his words, swallowing the rest of his pride to let duty settle where anger had been. "I, uhm, mean, certainly my help could be better suited for aiding with the tragedy that occurred?"

"This is not trinket work," Frederick said, voice flat. "It proves what you are."

Arlo rose from his seat, which caused the Paladin to immediately take a step towards the table. "Your Majesty, I am no soldier of the Kingsguard, nor a member of the church," Arlo said, his tone irritated and certainly out of place in front of royalty.

King Frederick pointed towards the large warhammer at Arlo's side, "Looks like you already have a weapon, we will see that you gain armor as well," the king claimed the last drink of his chalice and rose to his feet. "Do not question my orders, boy, there is a larger plot at play here, and I *will* find out what it is. Elfar have crossed our borders. Twenty Salvar for each pair of ears. Bring proof, or do not return."

Arlo waited for someone to object. Sorren's face had gone hungry. Jason's eyes lowered. The Paladin did not move at all.

Each pair of ears.

The King and the Paladin quickly passed over to a side door, already opened by one of the servants. "Please enjoy the rest of your meal, I have other business to attend to. Brother Jason will see that you are well prepared," the king said before the door slammed shut.

Arlo stared at the door. He had woken into a command he had never sought, and already the hammer felt heavier.

Brother Jason smacked the back of Sorren's head, causing him to spit out a mouthful of egg and boar meat. "What were you thinking speaking out to the King like that? I expected better from you Sorren." He palmed his hand on his face and rubbed his eyes.

Sorren couldn't help but laugh his jovial laugh. "Not often I get to rub elbows with royalty, best to make an impression when you do." He continued to stuff his face with more of the over prepared food at the table. He gave Arlo a nudge when he realized that the man sat quiet and almost in a trance. "Say, he didn't tell us exactly where to go. You know the exact destination?"

"We will make sure that you do not leave without provisions. As for your destination, at the end of the Savage Run, is a single pink blossomed tree. The tree itself holds an illusion. Within your provisions will be a seal. Press it to the base of the tree to reveal the way."

"I am no guard, knight, cleric, or anyone of any importance. He wishes to send me to aid Sorren on this fetch quest. Everyone claims that I killed the beast..." Arlo began to say quickly.

"Easy, easy" Jason said, calming.

Arlo paid no mind to Jason and continued, "and now expects me to be a warrior and one of his fetch boys because I have this piece of metal and wood? Let's get this over with so I can go back to my life. Or at least what life I had before all this."

"Listen, Arlo, I understand your frustrations," Sorren said giving Arlo a reassuring look. "But we are all important to someone, I bet that family you rescued would certainly disagree with your sentiments."

"What Sorren says is true, we often do not see how important and critical we are to those around us. Let us eat, then we will gather whatever items you need." Brother Jason said.

The room seemed to breathe again. Sorren's jaw unclenched. Jason let the silence hold until Arlo's shoulders dropped with a heavy sigh.

CHAPTER 5

The clear blue sky glistened as rays of sun shone down on the new fall weather. The Lunamani Festival marked the end of the Lyorion calendar's year, a farewell to warm summer breezes drifting into crisp autumn leaves. Remnants of the twin moons' week-long eclipse still lingered, giving the sky a subtle purple tint. The weather was still warm, largely due in part to Davenport's coastal region that saw sun much of the year and rarely, if ever, saw snow. Thankfully, the weather was bearable for the two men, who were adorned in armor and traveling gear.

Arlo was not impressed by the gear, although he knew he would be more protected wearing the breastplate and greaves if something went wrong. Knowledge of the Elfar crossing into Zenarian territory was not anything new, and with the recent events seeming to be the work of the Elfar and their Lord Candurill Aevoridge, the armor was likely worthwhile if they were to be attacked. Other monsters and wild fierce creatures are known to reside within the Treycord Meadows, so preparing for the unexpected was wise.

As for the more hulking six and a half foot warrior of Heir, he was fighting internally with his own dilemma. Shaken by how everything was beginning for them, on one hand he knew to follow any order from his commanding officer, and especially from the joint leadership of the King and Archbishop. But on the other, he began to wonder why Arlo was sent with him, why put someone who is not a member of the church or the military on this mission? Sure, everyone believes him to have been the one to take down the beast, but why demand him to have come along? Something about the whole thing did not sit well with Sorren's stomach, especially after Brother Jason pulled him aside separately and told him, 'Watch Arlo closely, inform us of anything that seems different or unusual. And do not let the hammer be left behind.' He brushed it off and simply continued along their path.

Sorren could see the grimacing pain on Arlo, he kept pushing on, almost seeming to attempt to outpace Sorren when he could. "Yo, you good mate?" Sorren asked.

"Fine, thank you for your concerns," Arlo replied.

"Just makin' sure you're all right. We've been travelin' for quite a bit, we can set up camp before sundown hits," Sorren said, dropping his pack against a nearby tree. "This seems like as good a spot as any."

The two men set up their small camp, and shared some of the rations they had brought with them. The trip was estimated to only take about two days there, and two days back, so they provisioned enough food for the trip to avoid the need of having to hunt their own meals. As the sun set and the twin moons rose, the two sat together, Arlo kept quiet, and Sorren struggled to do the same.

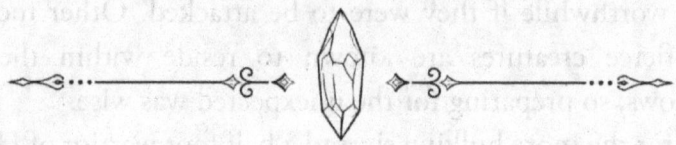

Finally, after some time Arlo said. "So you've known Jason for quite some time?"

Sorren perked at the beginning of conversation. "Brother Jason, is something like a mentor to me, he helped raise me when I was younger and led me through the path of the church. Taught me most of what I know, saved my arse a few times too."

"I am just struggling," Arlo admitted "Struggling to come to terms with everything that's happened. Of people claiming me to be, some sort of *hero*."

He shook his head and lifted his shoulders into a shrug. "Listen Arlo, I've heard tales of mortals becoming a conduit of something greater than themselves. I've seen some of the actions the Archbishop does in the name of Heir." His large fist patted the iron symbol of Heir, a perfect circle intersected by three straight lines that meet at a central circle. Within this inner sanctum, two diagonal lines cross, forming an 'X', often featuring a sapphire gemstone at the inner meeting points. "Maybe the hammer had something to do with it, maybe not. What I do know, is the people of Fall Lake and myself owe you a debt. Hell, maybe even all of the continent do. A mere man or not, Heir must have chosen you, but it's a bloody mystery, my friend. And I have no idea what to make of it."

Arlo gave a slight smile, perhaps this was the purpose he always sought out of his life. A hope for the future. "Thanks Sorren, if I recall correctly, the last time we met you barely held any rank, now you are Sergeant?"

Sorren nodded in agreement, "Aye, I am. The job you helped me on before got me through my trials. The gratitude of the girl's father we rescued from the Hag, and its head was enough to present me with my first official rank. Been doing deliveries and transports for the

Porters since, riding the waves along the coast. I've got a dream, y'know." He paused, gazing out into the night sky, watching as the twin moons barely overlapped each other. Luna, the larger of the two, gave a crimson glow, while Mani, the smaller and closer, cast an azure hue.

"I want to travel, not just locally, but plow waters untouched by men before me." His grey eyes sparkled with his dream, giving echoes of what seemed like oceanic waves splashing through, his own grunting pulled him back to reality. "But Heir hasn't yet seen fit to give me that chance."

"You are still young my friend, I've spent over 30 years seeking meaning in my life. Was the reason I came to Fall Lake. I've dabbled in every profession and trade that I could. I figure all those skills would be beneficial to the construction of the city." Arlo leaned back onto his bedroll, the pain was constant and numbing, but while he was constantly feeling it, he grew to find it manageable. Even simply laying on his bedroll seemed to mildly soothe the still aching bruises. "I think we should go ahead and get some rest."

Sorren agreed, "Aye, we should. Go ahead and get yourself some. I'll be up a little while longer and will keep watch. Hard telling what kind of beasties may come out lookin' for food."

The two found their comfort next to the small flame they kept stoked throughout the night. Sorren let Arlo get some extended rest, and only woke him up so he could get just enough to continue their travel. Much of the night was uneventful, a few howls and chittering of movement within the nearby woods. Just before daybreak, Arlo heard the faint sound of rustling, and what he thought sounded like laughter.

"Brenda, quit using your teeth!" Sorren shouted as fangs sunk his leg and began to pull him. Red blood began to fill over the teeth of the canine creature, Sorren looked to the flickering flame and watched as a hyena held a feral smile as it leapt towards Arlo.

Arlo came up with the hammer already moving, the first hyena sprang for his ribs. He turned on instinct, catching the leap against the hammer's haft instead of his chest. The impact jarred his arms. Blue light flashed across the weapon, bright enough to pain the beast's eyes.

The hyena recoiled.

The one on Sorren twisted harder, pulling him toward the dark beyond the firelight. Sorren grabbed his dagger and drove it down once, missing the skull and cutting only ear and fur. The hyena shrieked but did not let go.

"Stubborn little bastard," Sorren growled.

Arlo stepped after the second beast, but pain flared through his bruised ribs and slowed him. The hyena saw it. It lunged low.

Arlo dropped his weight instead of dodging. The hammer came down with a crack of thunder. Bone gave beneath the blow, and the beast collapsed in the grass.

Sorren finally found the skull with his dagger. The jaws slackened, and he kicked himself free.

Trickles of blue energy sparked along Arlo's figure.

"Aye, for someone who isn't a warrior, you sure know how to use that thing," Sorren remarked.

Arlo surveyed the area for any more of its pack, and when he was satisfied, he let the hammer fall with a sinking and audible thud. "I've had some combat training, just not to your extent," Arlo reached out a hand to aid Sorren to his feet. "You hurt?"

"Ah, nothin' I can't brush off."

"Are you sure? It is fine if you need to take some time."

Cracking his knuckles and his neck, he moved as if it barely fazed Sorren. Taking a cloth from his belt, he knelt down and cleaned the blood from the wound. "Easy, 'nough," he said before giving a quick prayer to his deity. Arlo watched as a small twist of mana and light coursed out from Sorren's hands, mostly clearing the puncture of the wound. "Not the best of healers, but Heir be with us that he does offer his chosen the ability. Even if it be minor."

"Fortunate, not many have even that small of a luxury," Arlo replied with a slight smile.

"It's mornin' already," Sorren said looking up at the slowly rising sun. "Let's go ahead and pack up and move along, in case any more of those beasts are nearby."

The two men agreed, and packed up their belongings. They opted to eat dried meat from their rations, saving them more time along the way. By Sorren's estimation they should arrive at the Savage Run just after noon. The hardest part of this encounter will be finding a single cherry blossom tree. Not native to the Treycord area, it would surely stand out among the rest of the local flora.

The Savage Run was named for the small river that runs off of Draylan Lake. During any amount of rain that comes in through the area causes the lake to flood, and the Savage Run takes on much of the excess water as a run off into the meadows. It's during this flooding that the waters move violently and unpredictably, often spanning and creating new run offs that don't last but often cause erosion. A village once existed in the area, which is where Treycord got its name. Unfortunately, the village was unable to survive the flooding and many of its settlers moved to other neighboring cities.

"Say, Arlo," Sorren asked hesitantly, "If we're going to be fighting together, I'm not one hundred percent convinced you aren't possessed or something. Honestly, I'm afraid we might have to fight to the death eventually," Sorren said worriedly.

Arlo, who had been traveling a few paces ahead of Sorren, stopped. "What do you mean?" he asked.

"Ah, just some bit of unease about this whole situation." Sorren scratched his dark hair, he was genuinely trying to find the right words to say. "Ya know, you've had a lot of oddities happening to you. Speaking foreign tongues, strange dreams, that blue light in your eyes."

"Blue light?" Arlo interrupted.

"Yeah, something when you start swinging, your eyes glow with a bright blue." Sorren put a hand on Arlo's shoulder and gave a slight squeeze. "The church is thinking you might be a blessing from Heir himself, they worry if it's for better or for worse though. Just followin' the King's orders and making sure we stay allies."

Arlo brushed the hand from his shoulder. "Is that what all of this is about? Seeing if I can be trusted?" Arlo scoffed at what Sorren said, one minute they are calling him a hero, the next they are not trusting him.

"I didn't mean to."

"I didn't ask to be seen as a hero, I damn sure didn't ask to go on a test to find some jewelry for *His Majesty*." Arlo mocked before turning eye to eye with Sorren, the smell of the jerky they ate previously still lingering on their breaths.

The larger man already had a hand on his sword, he wasn't trying to bring his concern to fruition. But Arlo seemed to be irritable by his questioning, and his leader's lack of faith with him. "Aye, calm down Arlo. I didn't mean anything by it," he assured while looking the man in his eyes, a flash of the mentioned blue light sparking over his eyes.

"This world needs *hope,* and that should be the focus right now. Let's get this amulet and get back so I can help rebuild what was destroyed in Fall Lake."

Sounds of rushing water were heard in the distance. "We should go." Was all that Sorren said, before Arlo brushed past him and towards the sounds.

With quickened footsteps, each stride a showcase of the urgency as they pressed onward along the water's edge, making their path to the 'end of the run'. Arlo attempted to rush, but after another half hour of walking, the pain in his body flared. He placed his back against a nearby oak tree. Sorren took the time to catch up to him, and hating the silence he spoke up. "I can lend some healing if you need it." Sorren offered.

"No, save it for when we are actually hurt," Arlo said with a wave of the hand. He had received healing from priests before, watching as broken bones were mended back together leaving behind only the slightest scars. The healing he received from the priests at the church did little for his overall condition. If Sorren's abilities were lesser than theirs, then it wouldn't heal these bruises and aches he was feeling.

A small collection of mountains were visible just above the wooded canopy northeast of the Run. They were both aware of the dangers of the Autumngar Wilds, the known collection of these mountains and the forests at their base. A path had been cleared through the wilds, connecting Davenport to Cyril in the north Zenarian territory.

Recollecting his brief stint as a traveling merchant, Arlo let a smile grace his lips. It lasted all of one travel from Davenport all the way to the center of the continent at a neutral settlement known as Traverse Crossing. The Crossing was known for being the central trading port for all of the territories in Shularix, and one of the only locations where they agreed to a truce. Nogmi innovations were on display, Dwarv weaponry, Elfar wood crafting, and whatever the Humans decided to stock. But this venture he was bringing some sort of artifact, or oddity to his "business partner", Gailen. Arlo hated it, the whole time traveling and he didn't feel rewarded or satisfied with the work, preferring to work with his hands and having a visible and tangible outcome to his work.

Fresh scent of pine resin, and a large crash of rushing water brought Arlo back to the present. He had been lost in his own thoughts and didn't even notice Sorren speaking to him.

"I find it strange that they want to hide this tomb with a blossom tree, not native to these parts for certain," Sorren grinned with his next thought, "Probably lure those bastard Elfar in closer." He was a warrior at heart, and his blade thirsted for a good fight.

49

"Cherry blossoms are more native to the Nogmi territory to the west. Never been myself, but I have heard tale that the Glitterwoods are an incredible sight," Arlo replied, his mind wrestling with the implications of Sorren's words. He had no personal fight against the Elfar, but if they were responsible for the attack on Fall Lake, were the ones they would encounter here at fault, or was it more of a pissing contest between the lords of the kingdoms.

"Maybe Heir will grace me to visit one day on my ventures, that's my dream ya know. My Da was a fisher, had his life taken by Daven Jones, the titan of the seas he called him." He patted a scroll case on the side of his pack. "Designed most of a ship, he deemed would be able to sail across the sea and find new land. Never got to finish his plans though, I've spent my free time finishing the design, it's something of a marvel I think, just needed to find a way to fund..." Sorren stopped talking and leaned forward, "Aye! Is that it?" he shouted, pointing forward towards a bright and peculiar sight, standing out from the remainder of the area.

The Savage Run roared, its tumultuous waters carving a path just a short distance ahead, the remainder of the running water finding its end somewhere beneath the land. The tree was a sight to behold, whoever cast this illusion was a skilled mage. Sorren's bewilderment at the beauty ahead of him caught him off guard from the mission they were given. He had seen many grand trees, the Autumngar Wilds held many tall wonders, but this one, maybe twenty feet tall, was in full bloom, the leaves coming from it appeared to be real, as Sorren was physically able to catch a falling pink heart shaped petal.

Arlo's heart swelled at the sight of the magnificent tree, delicate blossoms a symbol of hope, or possibly despair, on their continued quest. He pulled the warhammer from the hook on his side. He was told this was the key that would unlock it, how embarrassing and foolish it would be if this did not open the tomb claimed to be within this very spot. Eager to return to the familiarity of his ordinary life, he let determination burn within his veins, unknown to what lie ahead.

Arlo approached the tree, the weight of the hammer a tangible reminder of the mysteries waiting to be uncovered. He looked it over and took in its pristine craftsmanship, he knew the work that went into smithing, and this was finer than any work he had seen before. It was in this moment though, while looking over the perfect curve of the silver head, the glistening gilded circular accents, the reflective sapphire gemstone holding its central point.

Sorren's professionalism snapped back into place as Arlo moved past him, examining the hammer he still claimed to know nothing about. Overhead, his holy symbol caught the filtered light as sunbeams pierced the canopy and glistened down onto the blossom tree. Sorren's hand drifted to the artifact Brother Jason had given him. A backup, just in case Arlo's hammer failed to do... well, whatever it was meant to do. The Monastery was known for its cryptic instructions, especially when secrecy was paramount. Sorren suspected this was one of those times.

As Arlo lowered the hammer to the base of the tree, a palpable tension settled over them, the weight of destiny pressing on Sorren's shoulders. His pulse quickened as he attempted to take a step forward.

He felt frozen in place as the realization struck him. His eyes flicked from the symbol of Heir chiseled into the artifact's face to the hammer pressed against the blossom tree. Unaware that the path ahead would change their lives forever.

CHAPTER 6

The earth trembled beneath their feet, the roar of crushing waters grew, rising like a tide. A gust of wind swept through the clearing, a swirl of pink petals and a familiar blue aura of mana, enveloping the rocky face where the Savage Run ended. The illusion began to shift, the water did not disappear into a hidden cavern but continued beneath the earth, revealing a door etched with the Lionhart family crest. A singular black lion's head with a golden eye, and a blue backdrop. Above the Lionhart symbol rested the symbol of Heir. A pair of twin lightning bolts, a central warhammer aligning them, with a bright silver head, golden circular accents connecting into a central blue sapphire gemstone.

Beneath the carved hammer, nearly swallowed by age, one old word had been etched into the stone.

Elduun.

Sorren's breath caught. He had heard the word before in hymns old priests sang after too much wine, always in verses that were skipped when younger squires asked what they meant. He did not know the translation. He only knew the word did not feel like a name meant for mortals.

Sorren's mind raced with dawning realization. How had he failed to make the connection sooner? How could he have missed that the warhammer his *ally* possessed was THE warhammer known to his patron? And how did Arlo, someone who did not put his faith into Heir, come to possess it... Why not Sorren, or even Brother Jason, or the Paladin Danladin himself? Were they not suitable enough? He surged with envy, fleeting yet potent, as he grappled with the implications of Arlo wielding the holy weapon that his church only dared dream of. He could feel the joints and muscles in his hands clenching the artifact given to him by his superiors. He took a deep breath and placed it back into the leather pouch at his waist, amazed as the strange magic opened the tomb before them.

"I imagine this tree won't be the only thing standing between us and this amulet," Sorren remarked, stepping closer to Arlo, frustration pounding away within his chest. He did not like the secrecy that had gone into this mission so far, nor did he understand the full gravitas of what awaits them. But Sorren was sure of one thing, and that being near Arlo would propel him towards an unexpected future. Visions of wearing the golden mantle of the Paladin himself, the visions were enough to bring his expression to light.

"It seems that pleases you," Arlo said, a faint smile playing at his lips. "I trust in your abilities, Sorren. We should be prepared for what comes next."

The crashing waters hammered around the new entryway into the cavern below. Little light shone through the tomb, filling the proximity with damp old air and cobwebs untouched by many years. They proceeded carefully through the new passage, weapons readied in their grip. The immediate path inside was set with various stone panels, lined with the same insignia as the doorway. Darkness soon took hold as the two came upon a steep spiral descent.

The tomb closed in around him, its walls swallowed by darkness as the first scream echoed from the void. Arlo whipped his head around, scanning the darkness, his breath catching in his chest. Blood dripped steadily from the ceiling into moss covered pools of stale water, each drop slicing the silence like a warrior's blade. And with it came the sharp clash of unseen steel.

The hammer spun with weightless effort, swinging wildly toward a familiar roar that clawed the edge of his mind.

"Hope guides our way!"

The words escaped in a low whisper.

Again. Louder.

"Hope guides our way!"

The cavernous tomb erupted in a chorus of agony with the screams of men, women, children, shouting of terror overlapping in a rising crescendo that battered Arlo's senses.

'Save them!'

'Help me!'

'Stop this!'

'Arlo!'

The hammer pulsed in his hands. Blue, white and gilded light burst around him like a festival's grand finale. A towering figure cloaked in radiant gold flickered before his eyes, real, unreal, its form cast against the gloom as the hammer cracked into the stone floor with a blast that shook the very earth.

"Arlo!"

Sorren's shout was a distant thing, half-smothered by the storm raging in Arlo's head. He latched onto Arlo's arms, squeezing with all his strength. "Arlo, calm down!"

The hammer tore free again, a wild strike that sent a thunderous boom roaring through the tomb, blue sparks exploding in its wake.

Sorren stumbled back as Arlo's eyes blazed with unnatural light, words spilling from his lips in an ethereal tongue that clawed at Sorren's nerves.

"Fuck it," Sorren growled.

As Arlo wrenched the hammer back for another strike, aiming at a nightmare only he could see, Sorren lunged. He slammed into Arlo's side just as the hammer smashed downward.

The floor gave way beneath them.

And together, they plunged into the dark.

The two landed in a pool of stagnant spoiled water splashing a large portion of the water outward onto the surrounding stone floor. Sorren was the first to rise, noticing the area was lit by an eerie, familiar blue light emanating from the pool of water. It took him a moment to process the situation before he realized the light was coming from the hammer.

"Did we get him? The golden one?" Arlo asked, brushing debris and browned water from his armor.

Sorren stood flabbergasted. *Him? Gold one?* He was almost certain Arlo was losing his mind, seeing invisible people in the dark of these caves. Maybe this was a mistake, and the smell of spoiled air was to be the last thing he would ever experience. He always imagined he would go out one of two ways, mid swing as a legendary foe took him out... Or nuzzled between a set of breasts, his belly filled with the finest food and drink in all the lands, atop silk bedding. Arlo may count as the former, but he was filled with hopes and dreams, he wasn't ready to swim with *Daven Jones* yet.

"Sorry, fella. No one here but me and you." Sorren replied taking a look at his surroundings. "We got some insects over here though, none of 'em are gold though."

Arlo stood at full height, a half of a foot shorter than Sorren. Arlo's head swayed back and forth as he tried to collect himself, adjusting to the bright light in the darkness. "Thank you for the light, Sorren," Arlo said, nudging the hammer upward.

"Thank me? You did that somehow when you started swinging at me," Sorren chuckled back. "Almost took me out with that thing, ya did. Mumbling weird words to yourself. I was under the impression that you were possessed and going to kill me."

Arlo worried. This was not the first time he had swung at Sorren. If moments like this were to be expected, could he be trusted? No, that figure was almost too real. His skin appeared to be made of some sort of bronzed gold. And did it have?

It couldn't have, he thought to himself.

Arlo lost confidence in his understanding of the events that have taken place. But somehow, he felt that Sorren was not lying to him. That he did summon this light within the hammer, or at least brought out a feature of the weapon itself. Through the wrapped hilt of the hammer, and flowing all the way through its core to the central sapphire jewel, beveled into the center of a golden wheel. The light flowed outward, and Arlo could almost feel the light as an extension of himself.

"I apologize, again," he said with a sincere curl of the lips.

"For what? Bringin' excitement around? We may not know each other very well, Arlo, but I'm all for anything that reminds me I'm alive. A good fight, a good meal, or a pretty smile that gets me going in the loins." A half-cocked smile was enough to assure Arlo that his moment of confusion was not taken personally. His lack of clarity worried him more than it did Sorren. He was already not favoring the idea of being a pawn to others, and now it seems that all of this may be getting to him.

"I hope it's not in the same way as your ladies," Arlo said, patting his arm as he walked past. "Keep up."

Eerie blue light from the hammer was enough to guide the two through the area. While they managed to find a quicker way down, they were still unsure if they were on the correct path. And unaware if anything else awaited them ahead. Save for the handful of rats that scurried away from them.

The cavern's stagnant smell grew stronger, washing over them. Sorren's jokes about others dying down here did not sit well with Arlo. Who snapped back that if they weren't careful, they would be next. It shut Sorren up quickly, he hadn't even considered that. 'Certainly the King would send a rescue patrol to get them?' Sorren began to wonder before shrugging it off. He was brave enough and figured that between the two of them, they could smash their way out if needed.

"Hear that?" Arlo whispered back to Sorren as the sound of a light splash in water alerted them up ahead.

Sorren nodded, acknowledging the pool of water ahead of them. Though the light did not fill the entire room, the two could see that their path was only about twenty feet wide, and the outside of that path was filled with the same pool of stagnant, muddied water. Whatever they had heard must have come from beneath the thirty-foot bridge up ahead. A wave of curiosity and excitement washed over Sorren at the thought of his blade being thrust into whatever creature may lie ahead.

A few years back, fish men attacked him. They lived beneath the waters of Draylan Lake, just a short northeastern distance from him. Perhaps the fish men were what was ahead. None were known to be friendly creatures, often attacking anyone that came too deep into its massive waters. These creatures were called many names by the natives, depending on where you were from. With many of the humans calling them *Sea Devils* or *Sea Elfar*, other tales called them Draylani, and some Elfar stories he overheard one year during the Lunamani festival called them Muirshaen. He assumed that was just their word for them. Sorren preferred *Sea Devil*, or *Draylani* if he wanted to sound proper.

Still, he hoped it wasn't these creatures, always spotted in numbers, and while Arlo's hammer gave off a blue light, there was no strange luminescent blue lighting coming from the water, thankfully.

Something that made the creatures give off a unique but terrifying glow when they came up from the waters.

Arlo, on the other hand, forced himself not to get lost in his thoughts. The light splash had jolted him into a heightened alertness, his senses acutely tuned to their surroundings. The surrounding water seemed unnatural still, and Arlo couldn't shake the feeling of being watched, as if the cavern was poised to strike at any moment. He was certain that if something was lurking with them, it was likely beneath the bridge just ahead.

As they approached, Arlo squinted at the two half-height stone pillars, each adorned with glass ornaments at their tops. The sudden emergence of a massive, dark form from the water cut his inspection short. Arlo instinctively lifted his warhammer as it lunged towards them. The blue light from the hammer scattered in all directions, casting an eerie glow that illuminated the glass ornaments on the pillars, but also revealed the creature's presence, a serpentine mass coiling around the bridge.

"By the gods, what is that?" Sorren exclaimed, his weapon at the ready as he took in the looming threat.

Arlo's eyes widened with shock, his grip on the warhammer tightening as he braced for the impending clash. "Whatever it is, it's not here to welcome us."

The Drekaras, a monstrous serpentine predator, reared up before them, its jaws gaping wide to reveal rows of razor-sharp teeth. Its amber eyes locked onto them with a cold, predatory intent. With a swift motion, the creature coiled its body sharply around the wooden bridge, its large club-like tail swinging menacingly against the stone platform across the way.

Arlo and Sorren exchanged a quick glance, a silent understanding passing between them. As the Drekaras lunged forward, propelled by two powerful limbs, the two allies stood side by side, prepared to confront the looming threat in the darkness ahead.

CHAPTER 7

The Drekaras coiled, the wet slap of its scales against the stone reverberating through the cavern. With narrowed amber eyes, it lunged forward.

Arlo and Sorren were only a split second away from the massive jaws snapping shut with a deafening crack. It reared its massive body away from them and prepared another devastating lunge.

The bridge was even more dangerous. Arlo saw it as soon as the Drekaras moved. The planks were old, slicker from cave water, and too narrow for Sorren's wide stance. One bad step would send either of them into the black pool below.

The creature knew it too. It didn't rush them like a starving beast. It was herding them. Tail to the left, head to the right. It took more space than it needed, and then it lunged.

Sorren was the first to move, his reflexes honed by years of training. Narrowly escaping the jaws of the beast as he darted to the side, lifting his blade along its scaly side. The Drekaras hissed in pain, recoiling momentarily as its eyes became fixed on Sorren.

"Get its flank. Let's knock it off balance." Sorren shouted.

Arlo swung his warhammer in a wide arc, crackled sparks of blue energy arcing off the weapon with his swing. A narrow miss after its recoiled repositioning. Arlo followed Sorren's sidestep and took the flank of the creature, desperate to get an advantage on the creature.

Rocks flew towards Arlo as the bony tail met the illuminating pillar behind him. The creature's gaze still focused on Sorren, making them aware of the threat its tail carried. Sorren leaped for another strike as jaws descended onto him, the steel of the blade audibly clashing with the sharp exposed teeth that were only a breath away from claiming his hand. He struggled against the creature, his screaming echoing throughout the entire cavern as he pushed with all his might to finish driving the blade into the creature.

Sorren's feet separated from the ground as the creature's jaw strength was enough to lift the six and a half foot man from the ground. Sorren's pulse surged. Part of him relished the conflict, imagining the tale he'd spin later, if he survived. But he was almost certain the jaws and the teeth of the Drekaras climbed into a smile. A wave of excitement washed over Sorren as he felt the thrill of battle. The beast lifted him higher into the air and quickly, with ease, Sorren twisted midair and attempted to lunge at the beast one more time before it could claim him in its next bite.

"Hey! Put me down!" Sorren shouted.

"Deal with your end, I've got my own!" Arlo quipped back, fending off the relentless swings of the tail.

Arlo took just enough of a distance from the tail as it swung at him repeatedly. The pillar and platform they stood on taking immense damage and causing several rocks to fall and tumble down into the water below. An overhead strike met Arlo's hammer with a deafening crash of thunder. Arlo's footing gave way as he used the hammer defensively to block the strikes of the mace-like tail. The next strike he could plan accordingly and took a leap out of the way as the tail crashed down where he was standing moments prior.

Steel met the fleshy, forked tongue of the creature, and the blade sunk into the jaw. Sorren landed onto the teeth of the creature, piercing parts of his armor, both letting out an audible aura of pain. The creature did not hesitate though and snapped its jaws shut, only to be met with the head of Arlo's warhammer, knocking several of the teeth from its mouth and with enough force that Sorren found an opening to slide free from its mouth, several blood-filled holes adorning his breastplate. Once Sorren freed himself, Arlo released the hammer from the creature's jaws and let the jaws snap shut. Sorren's blade did not survive the vicious attack. All that remained was a jagged section of the blade and the hilt.

"Not again!" Sorren shouted, picking up what remained of the blade with one hand, the other clenching at his side, where the fangs pierced his armor.

The creature took no hesitation at Sorren's weakness, another desperate attempt to bite the warrior, only met with the blunt face of Arlo's warhammer. His focus unwavering, the weight of the hammer met the scaled head, causing the creature to twist and writhe in dazed agony. Seizing his chance, Sorren leaped onto the serpent's head, plunging the blade into one of its amber eyes. "Now Arlo! Hit it again!" Sorren called out breathlessly.

Arlo dodged an instinctive swing of the tail and used it to propel himself forward at the head again. His eyes were lit with the blue mana, the same mana emanating from the brightly glowing hammer. A thunderous crack echoed throughout the cavern as Arlo connected a second time, shattering the skull of the serpent. Shockwaves reverberated throughout the cavern, dislodging several loose rocks from the ceiling. The creature convulsed as its eyes grew dim and collapsed onto the platform, its tail hammering down one last time, shattering the remainder of the platform's edge as the rest of its body slumped down into the black water. The Drekaras lay motionless at their feet, its once mighty form now lifeless and empty.

The glow still pulsed faintly within Arlo's hands. He stared at the shattered skull, then at the hammer, he was unsure which frightened him more.

Sorren's laugh came fractured. He pressed one hand to his ribs, blood dark between his fingers.

"Well," Sorren said, breathing heavy, "that could've gone worse."

Arlo looked at the broken sword in Sorren's hand, the cracked bridge behind them, and the black water that swallowed the last ripples of the Drekaras.

"Not by much."

The two men shared a look, part relief, part understanding, before turning their eyes toward the far side of the bridge.

"You hurt?" Arlo asked, taking notice of the blood staining Sorren's armor.

"I've had worse." Sorren replied, a pool of energy gathered in his hand, placing it over the wounded area as the light filled the wound. The healing process always hurts more, he thought. While it was useful that followers of Heir possessed the ability to heal minor wounds, healing was less fun as the skin and bones mended back together.

"Fair enough."

Blue light from the pillars guided them across the bridge, with cautious footsteps of metal meeting the stone floor. Even when trying to walk quietly, Sorren's heavy footsteps were enough to alert everyone in Davenport.

The echoing ripples from the Drekaras served as a reminder for both to stay alert, as nothing else moved from the depths of the water.

Once they crossed the wooden planks, the blue lights lit against the wall ahead. Revealing the intricately carved stone ahead, symbols of Lionhart and Heir were joined by the symbols of the other five deities. A long pedestal was home to a white wooden casket, gilded with intricate symbols that sang with an elegant excess of riches known to nobility.

"Are we," Arlo took a worried look at Sorren, "supposed to open his casket?"

"Oh, well, I don't see any amulets hanging around." He shrugged, confused at what other options they had.

"This just keeps getting better." Arlo joked.

Sorren approached the resting place, his heart pounding with anticipation at what was inside. "Let's just get this over with."

With a gentle push, he used his weight to try lifting the lid of the casket. But nothing moved.

"Alright, maybe this isn't it?" Sorren wondered aloud, confused to their next steps. He saw no other containers, doors, or any other place that an amulet may rest in sight.

"Let me have a go."

Arlo kept one hand on his warhammer, and another on the lid of the grave. As his hand met the lid, a distinct click tremored inside, as the symbol of Heir centered on the wood, lit up the same blue as the surrounding lights.

He pushed the lid aside, letting light spill into the dark enclosure.

"Looks like your bark must be bigger than your bite," Arlo said.

"I loosened it for ya." Sorren chuckled, leaning over to look inside.

Lying alone within the tomb was a single amulet. No body, skeleton, or any other burial items resided inside. Save for the amulet resting at the end of a silver chain, gold surrounding an amber jewel.

This amulet was not as intricate and elaborate as the rest of the room would show.

"Guess this is it. I'll be the guinea pig," Sorren said as he brought the amulet to his eyes.

"What the hell does this have to do with me and the current situation?" Arlo said, curious but dissatisfied, that the King very well may have sent them on a quest for just a piece of jewelry.

"I dunno, but thanks, E... ard?" Sorren said, trying to make out the dusty nameplate. Handing the amulet over to Arlo so he could use the exposed cloth on his arm to clean it off.

"Eckerd Lionhart," they both said in unison, reading the now clean nameplate. "That's the name of..."

The amulet lit up in Arlo's hands, interrupting Sorren's words. "What the?"

Arlo held the amulet outward, ready to drop it at a moment's notice. A disembodied voice spoke out of the amulet.

"Fred, is that you, brother?"

CHAPTER 8

Silence hung between them as they stared at each other, both unsure what to make of the talking jewel glowing in Arlo's hand.

"Fred! Are you there, brother?" It called out again.

"I'm not Fred, my name is Arlo. King Frederick asked us to come and collect," Arlo paused, the absurdity of it all catching up with him. Certainly, a talking amulet was not the craziest thing he had encountered. "You."

The jewel's glow faded briefly, and Sorren believed they had only imagined the voice in his head. Startled when it spoke again. "That bastard doesn't even have the nerve to come back for me himself!" It gave out a crackling chuckle. "I knew he hated me, but at least have the decency to collect me himself."

The raspy voice rambled on like a toddler discovering speech. Arlo and Sorren continued to share confusion. Even in a world full of magic, a speaking jewel was peculiar.

"Anyway, I am Eckerd. Who might the two of you be?" The disembodied voice asked.

"Sorren, Sorren Blaze. Protector within the Porters. Pleasure to meet you, your nobility?"

"Just Eckerd is fine. Sitting at the royal table was never meant for me. Old Fred had all that royalty business taken care of." The voice's echo lit up as Eckerd mumbled undiscernible words. He seemed to like to talk to himself quite a lot, but if he was an amulet stuck in a dark and empty tomb, he may have had no one else to talk to. "So what about you, white hair and blue eyes?"

White hair? Last Arlo checked, his hair was blonde. He assumed the amulet could not see hair color... If it could see at all?

"Arlo Devine, no fancy rank or title."

"Well, for someone of no rank or title, that is quite an impressive weapon you hold there."

Sorren's eyes perked as Eckerd mentioned the hammer. Did he know anything about it? It would explain why the King sent them on this glorified fetch quest by an amulet's brother.

Lifting the hammer into the air, Arlo looked between it and the amulet. "What do you know of my weapon?"

"Ha! You don't even know what you carry? Its presence is intoxicating, even from here it leaves behind a trail of mana. I would love to see the face of the Archbishop when he sees *you* with it." His voice was filled with a joyous splendor that felt almost uncomfortable, and somewhat insulting to Arlo. "Whatever the reason, you are blessed with Elduun, the div—" The voice trailed off, "Wait, what is that? Dammit, I must go. Take me to Fred immediately."

"You must go? What the hell do you mean?" Sorren asked.

"No time. We must leave. NOW!" The voice echoed and pulsed. Then... nothing. Silence swallowed the chamber.

"Is this thing serious, Sorren?" Arlo asked, placing the amulet around his neck to keep it safe.

"I dunno, I mean, this place doesn't feel safe, especially with that serpent still laying there." His heavy boots met a rock that flew across the pathway, landing in the water beneath the dead beast.

"Maybe we should go ahead and..." The surrounding air grew heavy, a screech pierced their ears. An unknown force pulled at them, crushing them like a heavy weight.

Choosing to act first, their footsteps left only dust and tumbling rocks behind them. Their path became clear to them when they noticed a small section of rocks that led up the tomb.

Cold, wet stone awaited their ascent, stalling their movement and causing their boots to slip along the way. "Shit, it's back," Arlo said, taking a moment to look behind him.

One glimpse was enough, that the same figure he saw before was behind them. The sound of a pop being heard from deep behind them, and a glimpse of shimmering gold feathers.

"Don't let up Sorren."

"What the hell is it? I can't see anything behind us." Sorren replied, leaping across the pit they created earlier.

With a heavy thump on the ground, Sorren was able to make it across. The weight causing another portion of the ground to collapse.

"Shit, my bad!" He rang out, "Give it a running start."

Arlo took one more glance behind him, gripped the hammer as tight as he could and made a hopeful leap across.

He could see Sorren, his arm outstretched towards him, ready to catch his hand and pull him up. But the hand never came. As another gust of wind whistled through the tomb, and something pierced the back of Arlo's armor. He felt a cold chill run through his body as he slowly moved through the air, a tingling sensation filled his entire body.

Filled with silence, save for the sound of wings flapping in the distance. A piercing ring burst within his ears, silence quickly returning. Arlo blinked his eyes repeatedly, his vision blurry. At first he felt weak, then as the tingling sensation met his hand, wrapped tightly around the hammer, he felt energy, and strength returned to him.

"Arlo! Arlo! Take my hand." Sorren shouted, his arm reaching for Arlo's. It was almost like Arlo had gone unconscious again, he hung by a mere stone that began to crack, just out of Sorren's reach. He was worried that they both would fall again and then become prey Arlo believed to be behind them.

Moments went by, and just as the stone cracked and collapsed, Arlo looked up to him. His eyes narrowed, a furious blue glow spilling out of them. His hand met Sorren's and gripped it tighter than Sorren had ever felt before, the strength of Arlo right now hurt worse than the fangs of the Drekaras they had fought just a short while prior. Arlo began to chant in the strange tongue, and Sorren's unease deepened. Something in the cadence felt off, like a melody hummed just out of tune with the world.

Sorren grappled with the uncertainty of whether Arlo's actions were meant to cause harm, or if he was simply unaware of how strong he really was. Sorren struggled with the situation, contemplating leaving him here within the tomb, to deal with the believed threat and the strange entity of the amulet. His training and his conscience wouldn't allow him to continue with these unholy thoughts.

"Let's go! I'm not losing another man, not today!" Sorren shouted, feeling the strength of ten men as he pulled Arlo to the surface.

Arlo rose to his feet, his speed unmatched by any mortal man Sorren had encountered. He held the Hammer outward, gripping it with both hands and pointed it at Sorren. The chants grew faster, his voice deep and otherworldly.

Blue light gathering into the hand of Arlo, twisting, turning, and writhing as the power formed around his hands. Arlo appeared to be unfazed by whatever possession has befallen him.

That's it, Sorren thought.

"Arlo, something has possessed you," Sorren said leaning backwards towards the ground as the hammer came closer to him.

68

He could feel the blue energy, could hear it sparking off of Arlo's hands and down to the top face of the hammer. Bits of the energy crackling off the hammer, snapping against the ground and coursing through his body in tingling jolts.

Sorren found certainty that he was about to meet the same fate as the creature in Fall Lake. To be struck down by the weapon, that resembled his deity's own weapon.

A massive blast of blue sparked on the other side of the pit, Sorren's eyes took moments to catch up as he saw Arlo pointing the hammer away from them, his outstretched arm filled with magical energy. His ears deafened from the combined efforts of the energy and explosion, the cavern now rumbled beneath them.

"Sorren, we have to go. The tomb is collapsing." Arlo was already gripping Sorren's hand and pulling him effortlessly up to his feet.

"What the hell was that, Arlo?" Sorren asked as he got to his feet. He took a look back at the blast, the energy writhing in place, rocks falling and claiming the spot where they just were. He believed it to be in his mind at first, as he saw a golden figure one moment, and then gone the next.

"I don't know, but I'm not staying to find out."

"There! That's our way out!" Sorren yelled out.

Various forms of stone began to fall and collapse around them, traces and streams of river water filled the cavern. Light gave their path a destination.

"Almost there." The stones began to fall effortlessly, the light at the end of the tunnel growing dimmer with the entrance closing.

They ran faster than they ever had in their lives. Their feet aching, Arlo's body pulsing as every bit of his body, and the wounds already held writhed in agony.

The exit loomed ahead, a jagged hole barely wide enough for a man to squeeze through. Behind them, the roar of rising water grew louder, echoing off wet stone.

"Go!" Sorren barked.

Arlo didn't hesitate. He spun the hammer around, light coursing through its head. With a primal roar, he slammed it into the rock face.

The stone shattered at the impact.

Light poured in from the outside.

Brief.

Blinding.

They scrambled forward just as the thunderous collapse fell behind them.

The tomb sealed shut with a violent crash, entombing whatever remained within forever.

CHAPTER 9

The river carved its own path through the wild, untamed, uncaring and alive with purpose. The cave remained hidden from the world, not by the illusory seal it once held, but by the natural barriers now set to hide its secrets forever.

The afternoon air was thick with sunshine and the bite of a chilled breeze. Leaves swayed gently, but the quiet carried a weight, as if the forest held its breath. Several animals frolicked past, stopping to take notice of the two men resting along the shallow bank.

Sitting on a wooden log, the Porter removed his breastplate to inspect the bite from the serpent. His undershirt was stiff with blood, his own and the serpent's. The outward portion of the wound healed from his own magic. Still, he suffered some slight bruising.

His body ached, and whatever spirit had carried him this far was fading. But like always, he braced himself to push forward. First to rise, last to fall, that was the choice he made every day.

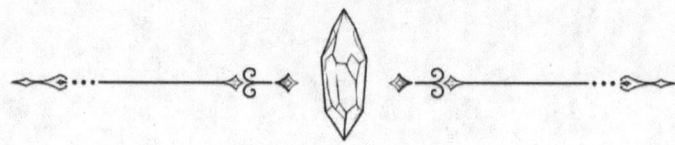

"Ready to get back?" Arlo asked.

"Hell yes," Sorren chuckled. "A warm bed. Sea air in my lungs. A tight body next to me, and most importantly, Mama Gretta's famous 'Seafarer's Delight'." Sorren smacked his lips together, his mouth watering just saying the name.

"Sounds interesting. I hope I get to try it," Arlo responded, ensuring that his pack was ready on his back and the amulet rested on his chest.

"You haven't had seafood until you had it. Fresh haddock, onions, carrots, leeks, and I don't know what kind of seasoning she uses. But no one else's stew can compete with it." Arlo could hear the joy in Sorren's voice. He was obviously a fan of food.

"This Gretta,"

"Mama Gretta," Sorren interrupted.

"Mama Gretta," Arlo repeated, raising a brow. "That the one you meant by the tight body?"

"No! In Heir's name, no!" Sorren said with a bellowing laugh. His heavy footsteps echoing within the area. "She's like a second mother. Been there since I first joined the church. Ever since my ma and da passed, barely hit the pubescent years when Brother Jason took me as squire and taught me the word of Heir." Like many chosen by Heir, Sorren had been taken in young. It was always up to the knight to choose his squire, some of which took on multiple at a time. Some were family members with promise and a strong bloodline, others were a gift or a familial trade to the church. But outside of those, the most frequent were orphaned children.

Orphaned children were common among the church, more commonly being taught the teachings of Heir or Grace, many of them being led by clerics of both churches.

"Sounds like you were one of the lucky few, not pressed to live within a non-religious orphanage. Left behind, sitting in rows while strangers judged if you were worth the trouble," Arlo said, trailing off.

"Aye, you could say that. But it pushed me down a path that wasn't my first choice. See, my Da was a fisher, and a damn good one at that. I still remember him now, always talking about uncovering new lands, the wind at his back, never staying in one place for too long," Sorren said, reminiscing about his past, and a future not given to him.

"Sounds like an interesting life he led. What happened to him?" Arlo asked.

"Claimed by the very thing he loved most. The sea. He always told me he would be the first to meet Daven Jones and live to talk about it. Unfortunately, he didn't." A deep, solemn sigh escaped the lips of Sorren. "Would love nothin' more than to have that life myself. He'd drawn up this grand design for a new ship, never finished it though. He wasn't the greatest engineer, but I took my hand at it and updated the design, been working on it here and there between my duties. Oh, I should show it to you when we get back." Sorrow fled to joy as Sorren spoke of his passion, something Arlo appreciated, as he had yet to find his own true passion.

"I would like that, Sorren," Arlo said with a sincere smile. "If you've got something worth dreaming about, don't let anyone take it from you, not even yourself."

"You think so? Most days I'm just living for whoever's barking orders, rarely for myself. If you ask me, they take themselves too seriously. I think it's why I like the Porters most. Constantly traveling, half the time being spent on some boat. It's not a terrible life. I regularly get to stick my sword in something new, occasionally getting to fight with my steel one." Sorren chuckled at his own joke. Seemingly very proud of that one. "Enough about me, while we are on the subject. Want to tell me about your dreams, Arlo?"

73

Arlo rubbed the stubble on his chin as they walked. Dreams and ideas of what he wanted to do next were common for him. While he was talented at many things, none of them really stood out to him, and he routinely changed careers after a short stint.

"I've tried a lot of things. But there's something about shaping timber into a home, it just felt real. Solid."

"Yeah, you mentioned working in Fall Lake during construction."

"Yeah. I liked the work, building, shaping something real. But it never felt like enough. I want what I do to matter. Give folks something solid, like a roof that brings hope during a tropical storm."

"Still got some things to figure out, huh?" Sorren said, looking up at the clear sky above. The twin moons peaked out over the horizon. As night approached, a decision had to be made. Continue through the night or find shelter and rest.

"Say, Arlo, you think we should rest..."

"Hold on," Arlo interrupted.

"Uh, okay, you see something?"

"That look familiar to you?" Arlo pointed towards one of the nearby oak trees. Buried into it was an arrow, fresh blood along the shaft and the ground meant someone was hunting something in this area.

Sorren lifted a charm attached to the fletching of the arrow. A silver leaf intricately etched with an Elfar symbol. A grin crossing his face. "Looks like some Elfar wandered where they don't belong." Knuckles popped with anticipation. Sorren's excitement grew at the thought of potentially getting some vengeance for what happened at Fall Lake.

"Something else happened here," Arlo's eyes narrowed, studying the brush.

"Agreed," Sorren acknowledged. "Bastards are normally more cautious when they come through these parts, not leaving a trace that they were even here." Sorren was familiar with the Elfar tactics, having fought with many of them over the years of his training. They normally were not this far south, but with the festival having just occurred, inviting Elfar into human territory may have been an excuse for them to dig deeper, whatever their agenda may be.

Arlo noticed the signs of underbrush being trampled, and broken branches scattered across the forest floor. The signs were clear, the Elfar were involved in some kind of conflict. Noticing the path leading northeast gave even further signs. Another arrow, broken and resting at the base of another oak. The disturbed forest floor, the arrows with the same charms, all painted a picture that a chase occurred here, of desperate resistance and determined pursuit.

"Those damn Elfar didn't leave a trail without a reason. They were after something, or someone," Sorren said, the sound of steel ringing through the air as he drew his weapon.

"If they were after someone, I will not leave them behind. Let's figure out what happened," Arlo said, his eyes filled with determination. The path ahead of them was littered with the unknown potential of Elfar danger. He couldn't shake the feeling they were walking into a trap.

With an accepting nod, Sorren tightened his grip on his weapon, muscles flexing as he mentally prepared for whatever was ahead. The silence of the woods was broken only by the distant chirp of a bird, the crunch of leaves beneath their boots. Sorren realized that his heavy thumping boots would not aid them in stealth.

Arlo led the way, his keen eyes scanned the ground for any further signs of passage. The path twisted ahead, treacherous and narrow, but the trail they left behind was unmistakable. Here and there, small splatters of blood marked their way, each drop a breadcrumb leading them deeper.

The air grew thick with an unsettling tension as they progressed further. Arlo motioned a hand to signal Sorren to stop, the tracks appeared to change, their steps deeper and more hurried. Markings of magic lay behind along the trees, embers burning away in the surroundings.

"Mages," Arlo whispered, his voice barely audible, Sorren relied on reading his lips to understand. "We need to move faster, and carefully."

Sorren nodded, his face set with a thirsty expression, eager to find his own form of justice. Together, they picked up their pace, moving swiftly but cautiously through the underbrush. The forest grew darker, trees casting long, ominous shadows in the fading light of day. They would soon lose most sunlight, the twin moons giving off the only visibility through the thick canopy above.

Arlo and Sorren quickly paced through the underbrush, their senses sharp, unwilling to miss any signs. The faint sound of conversation was heard ahead, the sharp and melodic cadence of the Elfar tongue. They paused, still hidden by the foliage and peered through.

Within the clearing stood a cluster of Elfar rangers, their towering lithe forms were draped in cloaks, that would normally meld into the forest. Bows slung across their backs, quiver filled with arrows, though some appeared emptier than others. The fletching resting within, gave away that these were the very same arrows that gave way their direction. In the center of the group, bound at the feet and hands with thick rope and carried by two of the rangers was a crimson haired woman. She appeared unconscious, her head covered by a rough cloth sack, although her vibrant hair spilled out and was unmistakable even in the dim light. She was nearly bare skin, a rough oversized cloak hastily thrown over her battered form.

Sorren's eyes narrowed at the scene of a potential damsel. "Damn Elfar," he muttered, taking a step towards them, his massive blade in hand. "We should take them out now, while we have the surprise."

Arlo shook his head and pulled Sorren back, his eyes fixated on the captured woman. "We don't know the whole story. Rushing in could get her killed. Let's play it smart and wait for our moment." Arlo's words were stoic, still brandishing a sense of determination as he analyzed the scene before him.

"Smart? These are our enemies, Arlo. The king himself declared them a threat."

Arlo's jaw clenched. "And what if she's not innocent?"

"We should spill their blood anyway, and if the girl gives us trouble, then same for her."

"We can't just slaughter them or her without knowing what happened. What if this is something bigger than we understand, and following them gives us valuable information?"

Sorren scoffed. "Why so cautious? I've fought these bastards before, you seen what they were capable of at Fall Lake."

"Not everything is black and white, there could be more at play here," Arlo replied, his voice steady.

Before Sorren could respond, the rangers began to move. Two of them raised the woman higher, adjusting their grips on the ropes, while the leader, a tall Elfar with silver hair and piercing grey eyes, issued quiet orders. The group started to move, leading their captive deeper into the forest.

Sorren growled, "We're losing them," tension radiating from his every muscle.

Arlo took a deep breath, weighing the options before them. Taking them now with the girl unconscious they could easily take her life before they had the time to react. He counted six, seven, including the leader, who never let his hand leave the pommel of his curved blade.

"We follow them, quietly. Wait for the right moment," Arlo said.

Sorren grumbled but nodded, his frustration evident. "Fine, but the moment things go south, I'm not holding back."

Together they shadowed the Elfar, keeping a safe distance but close enough to observe. Sorren took efforts to not let his oversized boots echo through the woods. The forest grew denser, removing much of the natural light from view. The rangers moved with practiced ease, barely making a sound and almost losing their tail as they navigated the terrain.

After what felt like an eternity, the rangers came to a halt in a secluded glade. The leader barked a command, and the group spread out, forming a perimeter. The crimson haired woman, still unconscious, was laid on the forest floor, her bound feet and legs making her appear even more vulnerable. The leader removed the sack from her head, revealing her face, pale, freckled and framed by the cascade of red hair. Her emerald eyes fluttered open, dazed and unfocused.

Arlo watched them closely as the leader approached her, speaking in the Elfar language he only knew pieces of. Something about a relic, or stone, unable to form a complete picture.

"We need to do something, now." Sorren whispered urgently.

"Almost," Arlo said, never taking his eyes off the clearing. "We move too soon, she dies."

Suddenly, the Elfar leader drew a dagger, holding it against the woman's throat. Arlo's heart pounded in his chest, they were running out of time. He feared what may befall her if they were unsuccessful at rescuing her. Her throat slit, blood spilt across the muddied grass, taken to Strathmore where she would live out an Elfar slave, or possibly given to the Elfar Lord Candurill himself as a human concubine. None of those things will happen, he told himself. Have *Hope*

"Sorren, circle around to the left, you take that one there, I'll lead from the right and have a go at their leader. On my signal." Arlo instructed, his voice calm despite the adrenaline coursing through him.

Sorren nodded, with a bloodthirsty grin. "Let's end this," he growled.

They moved silently into position, each step calculated and precise. Arlo watched, waiting for the right moment. Sorren's steps, the quietest they had been yet, their movements were seamless, so natural, you'd think they'd been fighting side by side for years.

The Elfar leader pressed the girl for answers, but she remained defiant, her green eyes flickering with a mix of fear and stubborn resolve. She spat in his face. The Elfar's lips curled into a cruel smile, and a backhand cracked across her cheek. Arlo knew they needed to act before things got worse.

"Now," Arlo whispered.

In an instant, they burst from the underbrush, weapons drawn. Sorren let out a battle cry, charging at the nearest ranger with a ferocity that took the Elfar by surprise. Arlo moved swiftly, his hammer flashing in the dim moonlight as he moved towards the leader.

The clearing erupted into chaos. The Elfar, though surprised, quickly regained their composure and fought back with skill and precision. Those closest to the fray drew their curved blades, igniting a hardened song of steel. Sorren emerged like a whirlwind of steel, what was left of his greatsword cutting through the air with lethal intent. The first Elfar he overcame with ease, the strength and pure power of the man overwhelmed the ranger's defense, and after several quick strikes, the man was knocked to the ground, his head cleaved in the opposite direction.

Arlo darted towards the center, intercepted by another ranger's arrows that clipped only portions of his armor, nothing punctured down to his skin. He felt slowed, the weight of the armor holding him back from his destination. The leader took notice of Arlo's approach, and lunged forward with the dagger, Arlo parried the strike and countered with the blunt force of his hammer. Sending the silver haired man to the ground, his dagger falling in front of the girl.

Amid the clashing of steel and shouts of battle, she remained gagged, but her eyes took notice of the knife on the ground in front of her. The crimson haired woman struggled against her bonds, attempting to crawl to her freedom.

Arlo quickly took the dagger in hand and cut through the ropes that bound her.

"Can you fight?" he asked, a sense of urgency in his voice.

Her emerald eyes locked onto Arlo's. "Yes," she said, voice hoarse, but strong. She took a separate dagger from Arlo's waist. "I can handle myself. Thank you."

Together, they turned to face the remaining Elfar, determination burning in their eyes. The fight was not over yet, but now they felt they had a fighting chance. And as Arlo and Sorren fought side by side with the crimson haired woman, they couldn't help but feel that this encounter was just the beginning of a much larger fight.

CHAPTER 10

The Elfar rangers recovered quickly from their initial surprise, their movements fluid and deadly as they formed a defensive circle around them. Orders barked in their native tongue as the rangers brandished weapons moved in.

Sorren was the first to engage, his heavy blade crashing down on the slender sword of an Elfar. The force of the strike staggered the ranger, giving Sorren the momentum to deliver a series of crushing blows. Each swing carried the weight of years of training and a seething hatred for the Elfar.

Arlo moved with precision. Parrying a thrust from one ranger, sidestepping another, and drove the head of his hammer into the second one's side. The blow launching the Elfar into a distant tree, collapsing into a heap. The Elfar immediately crumbled to the ground.

The crimson haired woman, sprang with a fiery grace, her dagger a blur as she struck out at the leader. The dagger was not enough to hold off the curved sword the Elfar called a windblade as its crescent curved guard used enough force to remove the dagger from her hands. With astounding dexterity she caught the blade with her other hand and found an opening in the leader's waistline, blood scattering as it cried out in fear. As if hearing the wind separating, she used the same dagger to deflect an arrow that seemed to be aimed past her and towards Arlo.

Sorren let out a triumphant roar as he sprang towards the second ranger exchanging blows with Arlo. "Come on, you bastards!" He shouted, his voice echoing through the glade. "Is that the best ya got?"

Arlo stepped out of the way of another blow, just in time to not be met by the end of Sorren's large blade. Arlo's eyes caught the red haired woman, she was holding her own, whomever she was, she was no stranger to a fight. He couldn't help but admire her strength and resilience. "Handle this one Sorren," Arlo said, moving in the direction of the leader.

The leader, now brandishing twin windblades, made another command as he moved into a readied stance. His feet spread apart, one sword over his head, the other in front of his waist.

"Got him." Sorren answered, attempting to sweep the ranger from his feet. He was met with a countered attack of the sword that bounced off the steel of his pauldron.

Rushing to her side, Arlo witnessed another archer loosing an arrow, the trajectory was aimed directly at the red haired woman. Instinctively, Arlo raised his hand in front of him, to stop the strike.

The woman's green eyes met Arlo's, a brief moment of shock took her face, and Arlo felt a strange stirring in his chest. He quickly pushed the feeling aside, and focused on stopping the attack from behind her. Sparks of electricity danced in his hand before firing off at the archer, the speed of the blast bursting in the face of the archer. The arrow launched wildly into the canopy above as the Elfar fell.

Her shock was brief, as the leader moved with blinding speed, his blades spinning as he attacked. She was able to parry one strike and

82

evade another, although the momentum was enough to push her back. Arlo inserted himself between them, blocking both blades with the hammer, narrowly missing his fingers on the handle. Arlo and the leader engaged in a deadly dance between the two while Sorren engaged the remaining rangers.

The leader's eyes narrowed, uttering curses of the Elfar language, but Arlo could tell that the man was determined to overcome. Arlo, with a surge of strength pushed back the leader and launched a relentless assault.

The woman sent her dagger flying into the back of a ranger, using the loose cloak on her back to shift him around, as two arrows were met into his chest. The man slumped to the ground, she stripped him of his bow and was already locked onto the other archer, setting multiple arrows flying and meeting their targets. Sorren nodded and shouted in excitement as he watched this mysterious woman's combat abilities.

Sorren roared and took the leader's flank. The leader's dance was enough to hold off both men for a moment, but the force of all three of them was too much. The woman sent an arrow into the leg of the leader, causing him to fall against the blunt side of the sword pressing him forward. Arlo swung the hammer and met the sternum of the man, cracking of bones echoing the forest floor.

His body slumped to his knees, his eyes wide with shock, before crumbling to the ground like a rag doll.

Their breaths were heavy, as the three attempted to catch their breaths. The glade was quiet now, fallen bodies of the Elfar scattered around them. Sorren took the cloak of the dead to wipe his blade, satisfaction sprayed across his face in the form of a bloody smile. What remained of the blade, following their battle with the serpent, was practically obliterated by the impact of the hammer.

The crimson haired woman stood a few paces away, the bow and a single arrow still clutched in her hand. Her emerald eyes met Arlo's again, and for the moment, the world seemed to stand still. Despite the dirt, bruises, and blood dripping from her lips, she was striking, her red hair a vivid contrast to the forest around them. "That was fun," she said solemnly looking over the dead.

"Are, are you alright?" Arlo asked, his voice softer and slower than intended.

She nodded, "Yes, thanks to you," she said, adjusting the cloak to cover her exposed skin more. "I'm Lucy," she said greeting them with a smile.

"Lucy," Arlo repeated, the name feeling strangely significant. "I'm Arlo, and this is Sorren."

"Aye, Sorren Blaze, pleasure to meet ya." Sorren interrupted, not even looking away from the fallen Elfar. He crouched beside one of the bodies and drew a short knife.

The first ear came away cleanly.

Lucy's smile died and immediately turned to worry. "What are you doing?"

"Proof," Sorren said, producing a cloth from his supplies. "King's order."

Arlo stepped toward him. "Sorren."

The warning in his voice made Sorren pause.

"They are dead," Arlo said. "That should be enough."

"For you and me, maybe." Sorren's jaw squared. "Not for a crown demanding justice. They did worse to us."

Lucy looked from the bloody cloth to Arlo. "And this is justice?"

"No," Arlo said. "Just proof of how frightened men become cruel."

Sorren looked away first, but he did not throw the cloth aside.

"Is there somewhere we can help you get to?" Arlo asked, offering a cloth of his own to her.

She accepted the cloth with a warm smile of gratitude. Her beauty was even more striking the cleaner it became. "I, don't know actually," she admitted with a low murmur.

"What do you mean? You must be from somewhere," Sorren chimed in.

"I would assume so, but I don't know where that is. I don't remember anything after I woke up in what looked like a battlefield. I felt something calling me this direction and was wandering, when I was attacked by that group."

"How long have you been wandering?" Arlo asked.

"Several days," she answered, then frowned like the words didn't belong to her. "I think. Time has been... strange. I remember waking. Walking. And sleeping when my body stopped obeying me."

"You've just been walking for days?" Arlo locked eyes with Sorren. "We are heading back to Davenport now, it's just to the south about a day's travel. You are welcome to come with us, perhaps someone there knows you?" They both wondered if the battlefield she mentioned was the aftermath of Fall Lake.

"Are you sure I wouldn't be a burden?"

"Ah, the more the merrier, Lucy!" Sorren joyfully chimed in.

She smiled and nodded to both. "Thanks, now I hate to do this to these guys after killing them. But I could really use some clothes."

Arlo took the tunic and a belt from one of the men and offered her privacy while she changed. It wasn't much but the tunic was long enough on the already tall Elfar that she was able to wear it more like a dress, using the belt to make it not look as flowing on her.

"I guess, this will do for now," Her laughter was playful and lighthearted.

Lucy adjusted the borrowed tunic and glanced toward the bundled cloth at Sorren's belt. Her smile faded, but she said nothing more about it.

"Do you boys have any food you can spare?" Lucy asked.

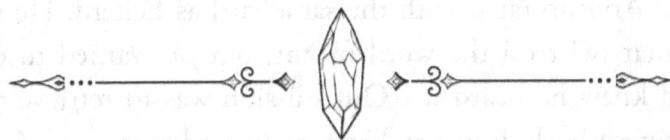

The trio decided to find a spot to rest as the night came closer. Lucy admitted she hadn't eaten anything more than some fruit she found along the path. The eerie silence continued much into the evening, something that made Arlo and Sorren feel uncomfortable and questioning of their current standings. They had already been attacked by hyenas, a massive serpent, and found and rescued a woman from Elfar rangers.

They opted to keep a lower profile, providing just a small campsite and offering to let Lucy sleep through the night, Arlo and Sorren vowed to swap shifts staying awake and on the lookout for any other possible creatures that may find them.

Close to the small fire they had made, Lucy ate the dried rations that Arlo and Sorren were sharing with her, taking small bites. Sorren sat in meditation, offering prayer to his deity, Heir. Arlo sat with his back against a nearby tree, his pain was visible as he massaged what he could, taking efforts to soothe the new and old bruising he had obtained.

Unknowingly, the amulet on Arlo's neck began to glow for the first time since the cave.

"Arlo," a disembodied voice called out, Startling Lucy enough to almost drop her dried meat into the flames.

"Who is that?" she called out, her eyes wide with surprise.

"Hello again, Eckerd," Arlo commented.

"Ah, hello to you as well, *friend*." The last word holding a slight curl to it.

"Who is Eckerd?" Lucy asked, growing nervous as she placed a hand on the Elfar dagger she had claimed.

Arlo raised the amber jeweled amulet, its golden tinge of mana swirling within and pulsating with every word Eckerd spoke. "A *friend*," Arlo imitated with the same curl as Eckerd. He wasn't sure what that twist on the word meant, but he wanted to ensure that Eckerd knew he heard it. "Our mission was to retrieve this amulet and bring it back, it just so happens Eckerd seems to," Arlo bobbled his head trying to determine the correct word for his explanation, "reside in it."

Eckerd's voice echoed softly from the amulet, "I sense you have made it out just fine and handled yourselves well."

"Great," Sorren remarked with a smirk, his eyes still closed. "Just when I thought we would get some peace and quiet." The irony wasn't lost on Arlo, Sorren normally leading most conversations with enough volume the Dwarv could hear him in the north. Even in his own meditation he was known to grunt, laugh, and mutter to himself loudly. Many of the Davenport patrons give a laugh when they hear the heavy beating of his weighted boots clanging throughout the town.

"We may have got ourselves into more trouble, some issues with the Elfar. What brings you here now?" Arlo said, wincing as he shifted to a more comfortable position.

"Ah yes, forgive me for not getting right to it. It's not often I get to talk to anyone... Well, I haven't talked to anyone in a long time." Laughter escaped from the amulet, startling each of them, talking amulets were not something you experience often. "I think the last conversation... Let me see, ah yes. I told Fred his wife Ambra had been..."

"Enough, old man. No time for old stories," Sorren said, still smirking and shaking his head. He was familiar with the elderly, having spent many years with Mama Gretta listening to fishing stories of her late husband, Jeoffrey, at least prior to his delusional and erratic behavior. A mission he got to accompany Jason on when he was still young into his squiredom.

"Okay, okay, forgive an old man's prattle. I sensed a dark presence nearby and merely came to investigate. Our golden friend's return was my first thought, but now that I am here, I can sense... That it came from this woman," Eckerd replied.

Lucy's grip tightened around her cloak, her green eyes narrowing. "What do you mean?" she asked, her voice still soft and steady despite her posture.

"There is more to your story than meets the eye," Eckerd continued. "Now that I am here, I do not sense the same presence that I once did."

Lucy looked away, her face a mask of guarded emotions. "I don't know what you're talking about. I don't remember anything prior to waking up in a crater in a destroyed city."

Arlo leaned forward, his interest peaked. "Lucy, is there anything we need to know? We can protect you."

She hesitated, her eyes flicking between Arlo, Sorren, and the amulet. Her emotions rampaged, anger, sadness, doubt. After a moment she sighed, her shoulders sagging in defeat. "I really don't remember, everything is just a blur. I saw a flash of blue, I woke up dazed and was heading this way. I don't even know how long I have been walking before those, Elfar you called them, started chasing me."

Arlo stood, wincing as his bruises protested. "It doesn't matter, we will help get you to Davenport, I have hope that we will figure out who you are. We leave at first light. For now we rest and recover. Get some sleep, I will take first watch."

Lucy nodded, her expression one of gratitude mixed with lingering fear of what the amulet meant by dark presence. "Thank you."

She settled down near the fire, wrapping herself tightly in the cloak. Arlo looked to Sorren. "You get some rest too."

"Don't mind if I do. Wake me if anything happens, and don't let something get my feet first!"

Arlo nodded, glancing at Lucy, her crimson red hair shining in the firelight like flickering flames. Something inside of him felt different as he looked at her, and he couldn't fight back the smile that crept onto his face.

As the night deepened, Arlo kept watch, the fire casting shadows around their campsite. The silence of the forest seemed to press in on them, but Arlo remained vigilant, his thoughts a mixture of concern and curiosity about the mysterious woman they rescued.

His eyes drifted to the amulet around his neck. The glow had faded, and Eckerd's voice was silent, but the weight of something larger hung heavily in the air.

From the corner of his eye, he noticed frantic movements and a voice softly speaking yet a sense of anger rose from it. He got up quickly, hammer in hand, and moved closer to the source, Lucy lay within the bedroll, thrashing back and forth, her eyes closed.

"Then strike me down here and now," she cried out in her sleep, her eyes filling with a red energy.

Arlo called out to her, yet her distress continued. He could feel her body giving off an immense amount of heat. Hotter than the flames she sat next to. He called and called and called to her but she did not calm. He began to worry, looking to Sorren, who slept peacefully and without any understanding to his surroundings.

Arlo took a deep breath, and cupped her cheek in his hand, saying her name one more time. Blue sparks, met red flames beneath his palm. Recognition, violent and unexpected. Arlo's eyes filled with blue before he could pull away.

Armor clad in white, blue, and gold stood tall over her, behind him blurred shadowed figures. Gripped tightly within his gauntlet, a pristine and elegant warhammer, fashioned with a golden encircled X and a sapphire jewel in its center. The hammer rested before her very eyes as she repeated, "Then strike me down here and now."

The hammer raised high into the air, and all she saw was the blue, mana filled eyes burned with anger before it swung down, and her eyes filled with blue.

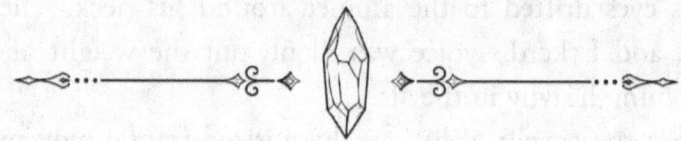

"Arlo," Lucy softly spoke out. Her arms tightly knit over his shoulders and around his neck. Traces of red mana dissipated, leaving behind tears of blood within her eyes.

Her warm presence was soothing, briefly he felt escaped from all of the pain he had become accustomed to burned away by her presence. His heart raced, as he came to the realization, their heads were touching, his hand no longer on her cheek but instead gripping her tightly against himself. He watched the red fade away, returning the emerald green orbs of her eyes. For a brief moment, he swore he could see a reflection of Lucy within her own eyes, covered in flames, before she blinked again. Her soothing, voice slipping on her strained heavy breathing that curled along his face and down to his neck.

"Arlo, you can let go," her voice finally making sense in his head, and letting her lay back down, taking notice of her rose freckled cheeks.

"I'm sorry, I'm sorry," he stuttered, realizing the inappropriate moment that was before them. His mind lost between the vision of the man wielding the same hammer he possessed. He witnessed this same vision during the attack on Fall Lake. Unsettled by what had happened, he was unsure why things have taken the turn they have. Who was she, who was the armored man, and how were the three of them connected. "You were tossing and turning, and I was just trying to make sure you were okay."

Her hair fell in her face as she shook her head. "I'm fine, thank you," she said with a smile, and placed her hand onto his cheek.

The same red flame met blue sparks, as she quickly pulled her hand back. "I'm going to go back to sleep, okay? You look tired too."

Arlo nodded, "Yes, it's about time for Sorren's watch." Standing to his feet, he offered her the same cloth he offered previously. "You have something on your face, I think you could use this."

Lucy cleaned her face off once more, and lay back down. She pretended to sleep until Sorren loudly took his post. She then buried herself within the cloak and looked at the same hand where flames met sparks. Mysteries continued to grow, more questions, few answers. One thing Lucy knew for certain, for the first time in days, she felt safe.

Those eyes. They were his. And yet... they weren't. They didn't promise wrath and obedience. They promised something worse. Something harder to bear.

Remembrance.

INTERMISSION ONE:
A SPOONFUL OF LORE

"Now, before we proceed further," I say, tapping my spoon rhythmically against the table's edge, "let me offer a little perspective. You see, stories are like a well-seasoned stew. Layers of flavor, each one stirred with care, best enjoyed one ladle at a time. And before we get to the next, let's take a breath and savor what's already come to light."

I lean forward, letting the firelight catch the glint of my favorite spoon, pinned proudly to my lapel. "By now, we've met our stalwart heroes. Arlo, burdened with a gift he never truly asked for. And Sorren, a man whose faith in his god and steel is tested more often than he'd care to admit. The two of them, walking forward together, each step drawing them closer to something neither of them fully understands."

I pause, giving the room a chance to settle with the weight of the words. "And then there's her. Lucy. Crimson hair. Emerald eyes. A fire in her veins. Wrapped in mystery, she walks the line between danger and something gentler. But who is she really? A spark of hope like the others? Or something darker that hasn't shown its face yet?"

Before I can muse further, a voice interrupts, warm and familiar.

"You just love dragging this out, don't you?" Forkner calls out from his seat near the hearth, raising his tankard with a grin that's all mischief.

"Ah, but patience is a virtue," I reply, my grin wide enough to rival the fire's glow. "Even the smallest pause can lead to the biggest truth, my friend. And while we're on the subject of introductions, perhaps it's time you gave them yours."

Forkner shrugs and sets his tankard down with a deliberate thud. The room quiets a bit as he shifts in his seat, stretching his stiff leg out onto the stool in front of him. "Well, if our gracious host insists," he says, always the performer when the moment calls for it.

"Ladies, gentlemen, and anyone hoping to call themselves adventurer," he begins, his voice carrying through the room. "The name's Forkner. Used to be a soldier. Used to be an adventurer. And... what was it you always call me, Spoony?"

"Hero," I say with mock reverence. "Though I've probably said it a dozen too many times for your liking."

Forkner chuckles, scratching at the grey along his jaw. "Hero's generous, but I've been called worse. I've fought in more battles than I can count, crawled through dungeons where the sun don't dare shine, and looked down the throat of more beasts than I'd care to ever see again. Got the scars to show for it, and the bum leg to remind me why I don't go looking for more. These days I'm content with the fire, the bar, and making sure Spoony here doesn't go off the rails with one of his stories."

"Which is a full-time job," Candy says as she passes by, eyes flashing like emeralds, her voice light but sharp enough to cut through the smoke.

Forkner grins. "Someone has to keep him honest."

I raise both hands, as innocent as a man with a pocket full of stolen tales. "Honest? Me? Forkner, I'm as honest as the day is long. Though some days are shorter than others, I'll admit."

The room chuckles, and Forkner shakes his head with a tired smile. "Let me leave you with this," he says, letting his voice settle into something quieter. "These stories Spoony tells... they aren't just stories. Not really. They're pieces of something bigger. You've got to listen for what hides between the cracks. That's where the truth tends to slip in."

He lifts his tankard in a silent toast. The others follow.

"Well said," I nod. "And with that, let us return to our tale."

Just before I continue, a quiet scuffle echoes behind me. Something small shifting in the shadows near the wall. I don't look, not directly. No need. Some friends deserve their privacy. Others, their mystery. Especially the kind that can pick locks, steal fruit, and still curl up like a prince when the night grows cold.

CHAPTER II

"Heir's lightning guides our path," Sorren prayed, taking the first step toward his home. An uneventful night, that was met with full clouds, darker than the waters of the tomb before. Echoing drums of thunder in the distance, feeding them of what was moving their way.

"What does that mean?" Lucy asked, her voice filled with curiosity.

Sorren glanced over his shoulder, his lips curling into a smile. Turning full attention, a large, gauntleted fist rest over the symbol on his chest. "A prayer to my deity Heir, the Arch-Paladin and god of war and lightning." The line sounded rehearsed, but his confidence and bravado still shone through.

"I see," Lucy said, processing the information. She turned the man bringing up the rear, his white hair flowing in the wind, covering the natural blue eyes. "Do you worship Heir too, Arlo?"

"No, I don't place my faith in a single deity. I find that all of them have their strengths and weaknesses, but many of the leaders of the churches, tend to be more talk than action." Arlo saw Sorren's eyes narrowing as he mentioned his own beliefs. "No offense, Sorren."

Stormy grey eyes lingered on Arlo. "*Why him?*" *he* wondered.

Realizing his stare, he released a bellowing and jovial laugh. Letting go of whatever thoughts weighed on him.

"Ah, none taken! You're entitled to your own beliefs and all."

Sorren continued forward, eager to not be met by the storm. Assuming they only had a few more hours before they were hit with the storm, he figured if they rushed, they could get about halfway through. With the skies still roaring and flashes dancing on the horizon, he doubted he'd stay lucky for long.

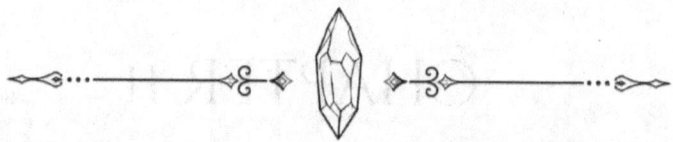

A short time passed, and the storm was unmistakable. The air was thick, the wind imposing on sparse foliage of the Treycord Meadows. Sorren's experienced senses at naval travel, embraced it, even if he knew they needed to stay safe from. The speed of the clouds and the grey and green contrast of the sky, spoke of the ferocity approaching.

Arlo kept a watchful eye on Lucy, making sure that she was able to keep up and not have any issues. Her steps were unsteady, her frame still frail, but she moved with a quiet resilience.

A startling crash exploding in the distance, causing Lucy to gasp unexpectedly. She felt the hair on her neck stand on end from the electrical build up, or her nerves, she wasn't sure.

"We should be on the lookout for shelter," Sorren advised, the tension he felt palpable. "This storm could be rough, we don't want to be caught out in the open when it hits." The sense of his normal self lessened, only put more worry on Lucy. She could remember what a storm was, but she could not recollect any storm she had ever seen or been a part of. Something that worried her, especially noticing how both men began to react.

"Over there!" The imposing storm brought back memories of hurricanes, floods, and an avalanche, each of which he had experienced. Eyes darting side to side, searching for the best place. Arlo pointed to a cluster of large boulders ahead, partially covered by vegetation. "That might offer some protection."

Making their way across the meadow towards the boulders, the wind picked up behind them, howling through the trees and whipping the loose clothes and hair around them. Wetness fell down their face, the first drops of rain beginning to fall, heavy and cold. The air thick, almost weighing them down as they ran.

"Is that all you've got?" Lucy shouted, her voice raw and shaken. A loud clap of thunder echoed through the surrounding area. The rain soaked them to the skin within moments. The grass beneath them becoming slippery, making their progress difficult. Crackling pops of lightning flashed above them, illuminating the area in a brief, eerie burst.

Now drenched in a cool summer rain, they reached the boulders huddling together to keep refuge in the small space they claimed, their breaths a ragged gasp. The storm unleashed its full fury around their sanctuary, wind howling like a pack of wolves, desperate to find their prey. But for the moment, they were safe.

"It seems none of us will need a bath after this!" Eckerd laughed.

"Funny, coming from the one who isn't getting wet," Arlo chuckled, shaking his head.

"A perk of being here, but not there," Eckerd's light tone replied.

Sorren settled against a rock, the rain beating down around them, only a small trickle of water flowing in through a crack in the rock face above. "Well, at least we are safe for now."

Lucy, tried to find comfort in their makeshift shelter. "Do you think it will be long?"

"Hard to say," Sorren replied. "Storms like this can be unpredictable."

"Try being the one without a body. It is much less thrilling, I assure you."

"At least you are dry! I'm soaked," Lucy laughed.

Sparks lit up the sky, deafening clap of thunder directly followed. Lucy flinched, and with a burst of defiance, and shouted, "Shut up!"

Arlo laughed, "Interesting way to deal with it."

"Everyone has their methods. I like hers," Sorren grinned.

"It helps," Lucy laughed, her voice tinged with nervousness. "Okay, how about someone tell a story to pass the time. Arlo?" she asked with a smile, forcing herself to be distracted from the storm.

Arlo smiled, though his expression was a mixture of tired and pained. "Sure, I've got a few. There was one time I was traveling to Bluefield, and find myself in the middle of a group of a bandit camp."

Sorren's eyebrow perked quickly, clearly interested. "This sounds good," causing friction in his hands, rubbing them quickly together.

Arlo began, "It was a few years back, prior to Fall Lake's beginning construction. I was hired to escort a merchant, someone else was hired to bring him from Bluefield, to our rendezvous. Traveled into the forest and waited for a short while at the rendezvous, after a few hours I grew worried and continued on for another couple miles. No recent signs of the wagon or anyone else for that matter. Storm rolled in, something like what we are experiencing now. Another mile, and boom, finally found him... Along with a half dozen bandits, and a leopard."

Another flash in the sky brought pause to Arlo's story. Waiting for the roar of thunder to pass.

"Azure Blossoms is what he was transporting. Crates of it too," Arlo continued.

"Ahh, that much Blossom would be worth a hefty amount," Sorren chimed in.

Lucy's face was marked with confusion, but she didn't want to interrupt the story. Seeking to find out the rest of Arlo's tale. "Go on."

"So the bandits had come out and surrounded the cart like a pack of wolves, from the appearance they didn't even see it coming. I watched briefly to see what they were going to do, heard them talking about taking the cart off his hands, the original escort started getting cowardly. I crept closer and decided to intervene."

"Intervene?" Eckerd chimed in, the rest of the group forgetting he was even still around. "You make it sound like you politely asked them to stop and leave."

"Not quite," Arlo laughed quietly. "I snuck up on their encounter, only to be surrounded myself by two more bandits that were following up as cavalry."

"Sounds like a fun situation to be in," Sorren commented, ever thirsty for another fight.

"It was... Intense," Arlo admitted. "I managed to disarm one, dodged the other. I felt like I was about to be overwhelmed, the merchant seemed eager to just give up and the rest of the bandits quickly took out the original escort. The other bandits moved in on me, and the merchant and everything went chaotic. But then, out of nowhere, a flash of lightning struck a tree nearby, setting it ablaze."

Lucy's eyes widened with intrigue. "Heir's lightning?"

"Not exactly," Arlo said. "Just a natural storm, much like this one. But it spooked the bandits enough for me to get the upper hand. I used the distraction to take out their leader, and the rest scattered."

"Lucky timing," Sorren remarked. "Or maybe Heir was looking out for you after all."

Arlo shrugged. "You know I don't place my faith with Heir. All I know is it was one of the closest calls I've had. Turned out, the merchant made the deal with the bandits and planned to use the escort to take the fall. Something about trying to get another batch after the first one disappeared."

"I bet I could take all of them," Lucy chimed in playfully. "Just like I can take you too!" She shouted out at the flashing sky, roaring once again.

Laughter filled the shelter as a kind distraction to their situation.

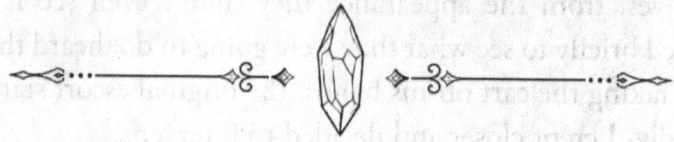

The mood settled as the storm continued to rage outside. Arlo rested against the stone face, lost in thought. The hammer lay across his lap, admiring the craftsmanship and details crafted into it. Glancing past the pouring rain, a figure of shadows moved, a single gold feather seemed to ignore the rain itself and fell gracefully throughout. Arlo gripped the hammer, as blue flashed in his eyes, when he saw clearly again both the figure and the golden feather were gone.

He brushed it off as his imagination when he heard Lucy speak.

"What exactly is Azure Blossom?" she asked, still curious of the story that Arlo told.

Sorren had sat in meditation, his eyes open and fixated on the storm. The charge of the storm sent a sensation throughout him that felt almost at home. The rhythm of the rain beating down into storm formed puddles. His eyes as grey as the rain, lit up at Lucy's question. "The Azure Blossom is a rare flower, it only grows up in Bluefield. Gets its name from the fields of blue flowers that grow there naturally. Highly valued for both its beauty and alchemical uses."

Lucy nodded, absorbing the information. "It sounds beautiful, have you ever seen one?" Looking at both Sorren and Arlo.

Sorren shook his head in disappointment. "Only heard stories. The merchants that do sell them, keep them under lock and key. So, unless you are in the trade or visit Bluefield, then you won't see them often."

Emerald eyes sparkled with a sense of wonder and curiosity. "Maybe one day, I'll get to see one for myself," Lucy hoped.

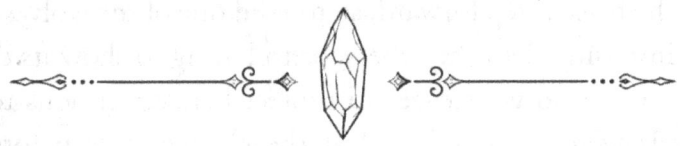

The worst of the storm had reached them, but a low growl pierced the steady rhythm. Sorren's body tensed, instinctively reaching for the weapon that was not his own. Arlo was on his feet within moments, hammer readied. Lucy turned to see a pair of glowing eyes ready to pounce at a moment's notice.

"Wolves," Arlo said softly. "They must be seeking shelter, same as us."

"Aye, but they can't have this one," Sorren said, the Elfar blade readied to cut through them.

For a brief moment, the two groups stared at one another. Multiple sources of eyes stood out in the storm, the growls becoming the focal point, as the rain was no longer the largest threat. Arlo and Sorren stood between the wolves and Lucy, prepared to protect her if the situation arose.

But the crimson haired woman was not ready for more bloodshed. Her eyes widened at the surprise of the pack surrounding them, but she quickly steeled herself. She pushed her way between the two men, "Let me handle this."

Before anyone could protest, she stepped out from the shelter, boldness shining through despite the beating rain. Her makeshift dress soaked once again, her steps slow and deliberate, her eyes scanning the darkness trying to get a sense for how many there were.

"Easy now," she said softly, her voice calm but held a deep commanding presence. "We're not here to harm you, you do not wish to harm us. We can share this space."

The wolves growled, their forms were barely visible through the curtain of rain. Lucy held her ground, her gaze unwavering. Her hands were raised in a gesture of peace.

As she took a step forward, so too did one of the wolves, larger and more imposing than the others, teeth baring to show its dominance. Sorren and Arlo were eager to protect her, yet curious to what her methods were. Sorren itched at the chance to leap forward, Arlo hesitant, wanting to watch the woman take her chance peacefully.

Lucy did not flinch, instead she knelt down to her knees, making herself smaller and less threatening. "We are all trying to survive this storm," she continued. "There is enough space for all of us."

The alpha wolf seemed to consider her words, its growls subsiding slightly. The wolf looked her over, then to Sorren and Arlo, almost as if it understood her. The tension in the air was palpable as Lucy slowly reached out a hand, the rain pelting away the dirt she was unable to clean off already. The wolf sniffed her fingers cautiously, the remaining wolves teeth baring, ready to pounce if their leader found the woman to be a threat. But to everyone's surprise, it nudged her hand with its nose.

Lucy smiled, a triumphant look in her emerald eyes. "See? We can share?"

Lucy slowly backed away, allowing the wolves to approach the shelter. The others watched in awe as the wolves settled down nearby, their eyes still wary but no longer aggressive.

"That was impressive," Sorren said, his voice filled with admiration and a touch of disappointment.

Arlo nodded in agreement, mesmerized. "You've got a way with words, Lucy."

She shrugged, trying to play it off yet her face still shining with her accomplishment. "Just doing what felt right."

The storm continued to rage, but the mood inside the shelter shifted. A sense of camaraderie, an understanding between the humans and the wolves. Arlo shared some of their remaining food with the wolves, offering some pieces of dried meats as a further peace offering.

One of the wolves carried a pup by the nape of its neck. The pup was not too young, but seemed to be struggling to walk, blood seeping out of its leg. It was apparent now they were trying to find shelter for their young. A few members of their pack appeared to be of the same litter as the injured pup.

Lucy slowly approached the pup, her heart aching at the sight. "Poor thing," she murmured, reaching out her hand.

The wolves growled, their hackles raised, warning her to stay back. Lucy hesitated, but the need to help overwhelmed the fear of the wolf pack. She took a deep breath and moved closer, her eyes filled with empathy.

"I just want to help," she whispered, more to herself than the wolves.

She did not know where she came from or what lived beneath her skin, but she knew this much. Fear did not have to be answered with teeth. Pain should not be left alone just because it belonged to something that could be dangerous.

As her fingers gently touched the pup's fur, a strange warmth spread from her chest to her fingertips. Red light began to fill her emerald eyes, flickering like flames. She gasped, feeling a surge of energy she was unfamiliar with.

The wolves sensed the change and snarled, their eyes alert. Arlo and Sorren were ready to intervene, Eckerd mentioning for them to stay calm. Lucy's focus remained on the injured pup. Red mana flowed from her hands, forming into tendrils of flame-like light that wrapped around the pup's leg.

The pup whimpered, but Lucy's touch was gentle, her intent pure. "It's okay," she said softly, her voice trembling with the effort to control the magic. "I'm here to help."

The mana pulsed, almost as if it had a life of its own, and the wound on the pup's leg began to close. An audible pop within the leg, the bone setting back into place caused the rest of the wolves to be ready to pounce at a moment's notice. The blood stopped flowing out, the torn flesh knitting itself together. Lucy's eyes widened in awe and fear, the red light casting eerie shadows on the walls of the shelter.

For a moment, the wolves' growls were louder, their stance aggressive. But as they saw the pup's injury heal, the hostility lessened. The alpha, watched Lucy cautiously, its growl fading to a low rumble.

Sorren and Arlo exchanged looks of astonishment. Sorren's hand tightened uncomfortably around the Elfar blade, unsure of what to make of the scene. Arlo, however, took a step forward, his eyes locked on Lucy.

"Lucy," he said quietly, his voice filled with a mix of marvel and concern. "What's happening?"

"I... I don't know," Lucy replied, her voice barely a whisper. The red light slowly faded, leaving her hands shaking and burning. The pup, now fully healed, stood on its feet and nuzzled her hand, a grateful whimper escaping its throat.

The alpha wolf stepped forward, sniffing at the pup and then at Lucy. Its eyes held a mixture of suspicion and gratitude. Finally, it lowered its head, a gesture of acceptance.

Lucy let out a breath she hadn't realized she was holding, her heart pounding. "I just wanted to help," she repeated.

Arlo placed a hand on her shoulder, his eyes softening. "And you did, Lucy. You really did." When his hand touched her shoulder, the last ember of her magic slipped into him by accident. His pain eased for a moment, not vanished, only quiet like a room after shouting.

She gasped, a brief vision flashing before her eyes as she heard distant screams. She turned to look at Arlo, the red of her eyes fading back to emerald. Strangely, her cheeks were adorned with bloodied tears.

The wolves, now more at ease, settled around the humans, their bodies providing warmth against the storm's chill. Arlo gently wiped the blood from Lucy's cheeks. The pups played roughly, coaxing Sorren into their playful banter of loose bites and roughhousing. Lucy

sat quietly, awaiting the storm's end, unsure of what to make of her
newfound abilities.

CHAPTER 12

Once the storm finally came to rest, the trio emerged from their makeshift shelter, drenched but relieved it was over. The wolves had already dispersed, once a light drizzle remained. Sorren stretched, a roaring growl rumbling from his chest signaled their march back. The sky calmed, the grey of the dark clouds fading away to reveal the natural blue above.

The landscape was vast, with the sky above a brilliant, cloudless blue. The air carried the scent of wildflowers that dotted the horizon. Tall grass swaying gently in the breeze, creating a soft and musical sound.

Arlo spent the camp hours quiet yet restless, his eyes rarely leaving the storm around them. Worried that the golden figure would return once again. Its purpose was unknown, and Arlo was certain it had something to do with either the amulet, or the hammer.

Lucy took a different approach, admiring the rolling hills of the meadow. She skipped and jumped around in muddy circles. Her carefree dance beneath the sun showed little concern for the mud. She basked in the sunlight, and both Arlo and Sorren couldn't help but admire her relaxed and joyful demeanor.

"Alright, Davenport here we come!" Sorren shouted, joining Lucy in her joyful play. Heavy footsteps splashed the puddles beneath his feet, marching along the path with his head held high. They had trouble along the way, but they were damn sure much closer to being done with this mission, and Sorren was ready to kick back and enjoy a night at home.

"Look at that," Arlo said, pointing to a distant hill where a herd of wild horses grazed. The arch of a colorful rainbow setting in behind them. He couldn't resist a smile when he saw Lucy run ahead to look at them, eyes glistening with wonderment.

"It's amazing how peaceful it is here," she said softly, kneeling to a cluster of flowers, with butterflies passing between petals.

Arlo caught a subtle shift in her demeanor. The way she tilted her head, the sparkle in her eyes. It all seemed more intense, more captivating. Was it the sunlight playing tricks, or was this more of the secrecy hidden behind crimson hair and emerald eyes.

Flashes of blue light illuminated the area, casting stark shadows against the cobblestone streets. Mutilated bodies lay scattered, their forms twisted in agony. Shredded flesh adorned the walls of the nearby buildings, painted in a tapestry of blood and despair. Amidst the chaos, anguished screams of a child echoed over and over again, clutching his dying mother as she whispered her final prayers to the gods, her son's tearful pleading blending into a whisper against the distant roar of an unseen horror.

Another flash revealed fleeting images of men and women meeting their end, faces frozen in terror as a monstrous creature, colossal and armored with thick scales, unleashed its primal fury. Tears mingled with blood and viscera, marking the grim aftermath of its rampage. In the middle of this carnage, a stone tower loomed.

At the tower's crest stood a shadowy figure, a hand resting on their shoulder with a weight of unspoken responsibility. Pain seared through every touch, echoing the hopes and prayers that reverberated through the chaos.

"Please, let her find success as a jewel smith," a voice pleaded in desperation.

Soot covered hand gripped the other shoulder firmly.

"Keep these people safe," urged another, the burden of responsibility weighing down.

Ribs ached beneath gentle hands, each touch leaving behind an imprint of sorrow and despair.

"She deserves to live."

Youthful hands pleading at the legs, grasping for hope amongst the devastation.

"Someone, anyone, help us."

Each touch,

Each plea,

Dissolved into wisps of blue mana, swirling and pulsating with aching intensity. The unbearable weight of sorrow surged as the blue light flashed once more, searing its visions into the depths of memory.

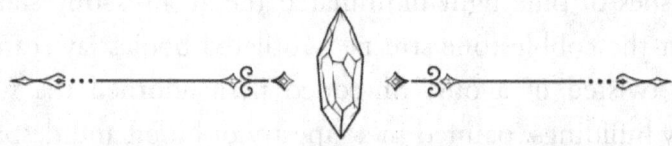

"Arlo? You all right back there?" Sorren called, noticing his lagging pace and heavy breathing.

Arlo stumbled slightly, his heart racing as the vision subsided. He looked up to see Lucy and Sorren a few steps ahead, unaware of his disorientation. He shook his head, trying to remove the imagery of disaster.

"Yeah, just… remembering," Arlo replied, forcing a smile though his entire body ached. His shoulders, his rib, and his knee burning with a pained burden. He quickened his step, fighting through the pulsing wounds of his body. He shook his head once more, shaking the vision that still haunted the edge of his thoughts as he followed in tandem.

The sky had darkened, and now they traveled on the outskirts of Davenport, fields of crops stretched out on either side of the path, tended by farmers who waved as they passed. Distant sounds of children's laughter carried on the breeze, adding to the warmth.

Lucy eagerly waved back at the farmers, admiring the harvest the farmers would soon be bringing to market. Her pace had slowed slightly, if only to stay near Arlo and ensure he was truly well. But the biggest shock and heavenly smile came when she got sight of an Akhlut on a farm playing with a young boy and girl.

The outskirts of Davenport were finally within reach. Sorren's mouth watering at the idea of Mama Gretta's heart stealing meals. His pace quickened, putting a good distance between him and his companions.

"None of this seems familiar to you?" Arlo asked, interrupting Lucy's admiration.

She shook her head, her voice perky but stained with a sorrow of disappointment. "No, unfortunately. But getting to see all of these wonderful things, did you see those cute kids and their adorable animal?"

"I did, and I am quite envious of you right now," he admitted.

"Oh, why is that?" she asked. Twisting her body to face him, her head tilting up to look into his eyes. Her narrowed eyes glistening with the rays of the setting sun on the horizon.

His throat tightened, his heart seeming to freeze. His eyes tracing the dotted freckles along her face, painted intentionally on the canvas of her skin. All was lost, no worry about the king's quest, no fear of looming war. For a moment, even his pain was gone as he took what felt like an eternity tracing her features into his mind. The woman proved herself already to be dangerous, how little he knew.

"Well?" her voice was coy, her posture inviting, leaning closer to him. The sunset in her eyes almost seemed to hold a flame within, the ripples of embers forming into a womanly shape.

"I... Uhm, I'd love to be able to experience all of these things for the first time again." He got out, his throat swollen as he was lost in her.

She let out a soft heavy breath, her movement so fluid it seemed someone else took her place. Her playful giggle, led into skipping along the well traveled path ahead. "Come on Arlo, we're going to lose Sorren."

Arlo's chest fell as he remembered to breathe. No other woman had ever stirred him like this. There was something about Lucy, a mystery that drew him in, a presence that felt comforting and familiar, and something that made him feel vulnerable yet strangely alive.

"You good my boy? Thought you were going to lose yourself." The voice of Eckerd called out.

"Yeah, I think I will be."

"Good, just don't get yourself in over your head."

⸺⸱⸱⸱⸺◆⸺◆◈◆⸺◆⸺⸱⸱⸱⸺

The setting sun cast a golden glow over the bustling town, while the sky above shifted in a dance of colors. The blue and red moons, Luna and Mani, rising on the horizon created a spectacular display within the evening sky. Now just past the semi-annual festival and its accompanying eclipse, Mani was prominent in the sky, casting a soft crimson hue across the landscape, blending with the deepening blue of Luna to paint the sky in shades of purple. The atmosphere was charged with a mix of excitement and unease, as if the heavens themselves were still adjusting to the change in season.

The town was alive with activity, the streets filled with people going about their evening routines. Wagons made their final trips into the city from Fall Lake, their wheels creaking under the weight of tension that lingered in the air. Children ran through the streets, their laughter a stark contrast to the hushed whispers of the adults around them.

Arlo, Sorren, and Lucy navigated through the crowd, the air thick with whispered gossip. Their arrival had not gone unnoticed, as vendors called out their wares, trying to make the last sales of the day, while townsfolk shared news and rumor.

"Did you hear about the monster that attacked Fall Lake?" a woman whispered to her companion, her voice barely audible. "Supposed to be enormous, with scales like armor and eyes that even the dark seemed to fear."

"Yeah, and I heard the Elfar were involved." Replied her companion, a man wearing a worried expression. "They've been all over! Even heard some have been spotted around Stagwood. Up to no good, I know it."

A man nearby asked, shaking his head. "That's nonsense, it was the Draconis, I bet. They're coming for us all!"

The trio continued to make their way through the crowd, the gossip becoming too common to ignore.

An older gentleman chuckled sarcastically, joining the gossiping group. "Ha! More like an inside job if you ask me. There is always someone looking to stir up trouble for their own gain."

Another voice chimed in, "The Porters say they are increasing patrols, but I don't feel any safer. What can they do against a monster like that?"

"Nothing if the size of that thing is what they say it is. Hey look at that." A man pointed towards the docks. "Who is that stepping off the boat? Looks like someone important."

A small cargo boat adorned with the banner of Heir had docked. As they approached the docks, the trio noticed the commotion surrounding the recent arrival.

Arlo narrowed his eyes, trying to get a better look at the figure disembarking from the boat. "I can't see enough from here. Think it's someone from Fall Lake?" he asked, glancing at Sorren.

Sorren shrugged, "Not quite up the ladder enough to be told any specifics yet. It's a Porter vessel for sure."

"Let's go find out," Lucy said eagerly, tugging at Arlo's sleeve as she pulled him along through the growing crowd.

A man stepped off the boat, flanked by gilded armored knights. A commanding figure whose presence alone demanded respect. His attire, a white and blue robe adorned with intricate gold trimmings indicated his connection as a high-ranking cleric of Heir. Despite being slightly heavyset, the man carried himself with grace and authority, his short white hair and beard displaying aged wisdom from years of dedicated service to the church.

Sorren nudged Arlo, nodding towards the man. "That's Archbishop Dolph Celestino," he said quietly. "He leads the kingdom alongside King Frederick."

Lucy's eyes flicked towards the Archbishop, her expression curious but cautious. "He looks... Formidable," she said softly, noting the aura of power that surrounded the Archbishop.

Sorren nodded, "He is, the king has slightly more power over the government matters, but the archbishop holds sway over all things religious. Not to mention his incredible abilities and accomplishments as a cleric that led him to his position."

Behind the Archbishop, several medical personnel and soldiers of Heir were helping wounded individuals off the boat.

Arlo scanned the faces of the injured, searching for a sign of familiarity within the group. Each bandaged figure stirred a mix of relief and anxiety. Making a mental note to send a letter later. His unnatural behavior sparking a notice from his companions.

"You alright, Arlo?" Sorren's voice pulled him from his thoughts and intense gaze.

"Yeah, just… thinking," Arlo replied, his gaze lingering on the last of the injured being tended to. "I need to check on someone."

Lucy, noticing Arlo's solemn expression, stepped closer. "Someone important?"

Arlo hesitated, not wanting to burden them with his personal worries. "A friend," he finally said, "Sabil. She runs a tavern east of Fall Lake."

Lucy nodded understandingly. "Oh, I hope she is alright."

"Me too," Arlo whispered, a flicker of concern evident in his eyes.

In the quiet moment that followed, Lucy's gaze shifted, a smile masked a thought that crossed her mind.

Continuing their walk through the town, they absorbed the sights and the sounds. Whispers of the Archbishop's presence spread like wildfire among the townsfolk. Many people attempted to shout questions and requests at him, his guards stopping every attempt through. People ran up asking for Heir's blessing or healing, others bombarding him with questions to the state of Fall Lake.

The guards spoke for him, ushering all of them away from the Archbishop and demanding all of them to put in a formal request with the mayor and all would be answered in due time. Many of the citizens were displeased with the approach and several more whispered rumors again.

The streets became narrower and more crowded as they approached the town center. Tension in the air palpable, the townsfolk's unease evident in their hurried movements and hushed conversations. The looming threat of what may come weighed heavily on everyone's mind.

Nearing the market square, the smell of roasted meat wafted through the air. Mingling with the scent of blooming flowers from nearby stalls. Despite the underlying tension, life in Davenport continued.

Vendors held various wares, fishers with their daily catches of glistening silver fish laid out on melting beds of ice. Net makers showcased intricately woven nets of varying sizes. Some were patched and weathered, worn by years of use, other held promising durability against the tumultuous seas. Hand-carved figures of wooden sea creatures, painted in vivid colors. Herbalists and apothecaries displaying potions and remedies, stalls filled with dried herbs.

One vendor stopped Arlo in his tracks, offering what he claims to be his finest brew that would put the color right back into his white hair. Arlo was held with confusion as he believed his hair to still be blonde as it was prior to the events of Fall Lake. Yet to realize how his physical appearance changed along with the events.

"Did you see that?" a woman exclaimed, pointing towards the main street. "A whole contingent of knights, and they look serious."

"Hopefully we will hear from the king. He's been cooped up in his palace for days now," an older man said.

A young man stopped, a pack of belongings on his back. "I'm not waiting around. I heard whoever attacked Fall Lake is on their way here next."

"Don't be ridiculous," another man scoffed. "It's just rumors. The Porters will keep us safe."

"Safe? Hah!" an elderly woman interjected. "The Porters can't even keep the peace in the market. What chance do they have against real threats?"

Sorren felt a rage building up inside of him as he listened to the people's words. Had the king not addressed them yet? Surely he wouldn't have waited this long to attempt to calm the citizens. Just as Sorren went to speak, Arlo caught his shoulder. "Not the time."

Sorren sighed, quickening his pace as the familiar sight of Mama Gretta's tavern came into view. The warm glow of lanterns and the inviting aroma of home-cooked meals promised a brief respite from the ongoing troubles that lay ahead.

Arlo, however, couldn't shake the feeling of unease. The vision that haunted his thoughts, the presence of Archbishop Dolph, and the worry of what the amulet might yet reveal added to his growing sense of impending conflict.

CHAPTER 13

The welcoming embrace of the tavern was a stark contrast to the rest of the town. Adorned with plenty of fishing knickknacks and decorated with crab cages, anchors and netting, the inside was even more warming. With tables made from repurposed wood, likely from old boats, and the smell of seawater filled the air.

A woman walked around the establishment, pouring drinks and serving food. A tall, robust woman with a heartwarming smile and salt and pepper hair eagerly smiled as she saw the trio enter.

"Sorren, it is great to see you, young lad. Please have a seat anywhere you three like." Her words were quick as she served other patrons, but the welcome was still warm.

"This place seems incredible," Lucy said, her eyes wandering between the patrons, the decorations, and Mama Gretta.

"One of my usual stomping grounds, you can say. Mama Gretta's been nice to me, decent enough Heir fearing lady. She insists I get a taste of luxury when I do get to spend time off duty," he chuckled lightly with a wink, "Though, the rooms whenever I need them do help quite a bit."

He leaned back in one of the wooden chairs, lifting the front legs from the ground, and used the fourth chair as a stool. His heavy muddied boots spoiled the seat.

"So, the 'Mama' part is more than just a nickname," Arlo joked, taking a glance over to the boot occupied seat.

Lucy chuckled as Sorren slid his feet onto the freshly cleaned floor.

Mama Gretta made her appearance known by placing three mugs onto the table, already filled with a dark purple liquid. "Sorren, it is so great to see you again. And with company, no doubt, who are your friends?" she asked while embracing Sorren in a tight embrace.

"Miss Gretta, this is Arlo and Lucy. They've been helping me on a quest from the king himself." Sorren beamed pridefully.

The woman's eyes sparkled with warmth as she looked over both Arlo and Lucy. "Welcome, both of you. Any friends of Sorren are friends of mine," she said bringing Arlo into a hug first, followed by Lucy.

"And my, what beautiful hair you have, darling. I've never seen someone with hair as vibrant as yours."

Lucy returned the embrace and blushed. "Thank you, Miss Gretta. What a fine establishment you have here."

"Thank you, dear. It was my late husband's vision, I just helped bring it to life," she said with a smile. "Now, here is some wine to get you started, imported fresh from Cyril."

Sorren held his drink up to cheers with the other two. Arlo followed suit, motioning for Lucy to do the same.

"Aye, to Mama Gretta!" Sorren cheered as the three clanged their mugs together, the whole establishment joining in on the cheer. "Miss Gretta, we will take three of whatever you got left for the night, an extra tip if it's Seafarer's Delight. And extra toast if you don't mind." The woman let out a raspy chuckle before nodding and moving to the back to prepare the meal.

"Sorren, I don't have any money to pay for the meal," Lucy added.

"Ah, don't worry about it. Arlo and I can take care of you," he said with a bellowing laughter.

"As you remember I woke up without any belongings, I don't have any Salvar either. I kind of woke up to you and Alysia, nothing on but this hammer in my hand." Arlo added. "Probably should go back and see her soon."

"Who is Alysia?" Lucy asked quickly, her voice threaded with disappointment.

"A local healer, she treated some of my wounds when Sorren brought me here," Arlo responded, taking a large drink from his mug.

"Oh," she said in relief. "Were you hurt badly? I know you were in pain when we traveled." she asked, looking over his exposed skin.

"It's strange really, no medicine or magic have healed these wounds. They almost seem, unnatural. But..." He seemed to linger off.

"Yeah, we brought him here to Davenport because we think he is the one who took out that beast. He was the only one we found who survived in that area, we didn't see anyone else there." Sorren explained, "Several of Heir's knights tried to use their magic, Brother Jason himself even tried too. We brought him here hoping one of Grace's priestesses could help," he said, taking down his drink in one gulp.

"Grace? Why does that sound familiar?" Lucy asked, trying to think.

"Goddess of Creation herself, and wife to Heir. Her healing magic is the best in the world. We thought certainly one of them would be able to fix him." Sorren looked back at Arlo, his grin fading. "Alysia helped. Took the edge off it a bit. Closed what little wounds would listen. But the deep ones stayed, whatever is wrong with him seemed to like her healing, but wouldn't accept it."

He looked around for a bartender or Mama Gretta.

"I'm gonna get us some more drinks, be back soon."

118

As Sorren walked away from the table, Arlo turned to Lucy, his eyes searching hers. He leaned in, lowering his voice.

"Why did your magic help me?"

Lucy tilted her head, a playful smile tugging at the corners of her lips. "Excuse me?" she asked, her voice light and teasing.

Arlo's eyes searched hers, his confusion mingling with curiosity. "Back in the woods, you used magic on me, and the pain vanished. It hasn't happened with any other magic."

Lucy leaned closer, close enough that her voice hid behind the tavern noise. "Why do you have his eyes?"

It sounded like flirtation at first. Then Arlo saw the fear behind it.

"Whose?" Arlo's confusion deepened, his pulse quickening.

A flicker of something foreign crossed Lucy's face. Her green eyes flared to a fiery red for a heartbeat. "I don't know why my magic helped you," she said, her voice a seductive whisper. "And I don't know why you have the same glowing sapphire eyes as my dream."

Arlo felt a chill, shivering at her proximity. He glanced down to the hammer, its intricate design glinting in the dim light. "It might have something to do with this," he murmured.

Lucy's gaze followed him to the hammer, but only briefly. Her eyes snapped back to his, intense and unwavering. "I will find out." She whispered with a dark promise.

Heavy footsteps approached, breaking the tension. Mama Gretta set three mugs and bowls of stew onto the table with a clatter, as Sorren plopped down onto the seat again.

"Oh, it looks lovely, thank you, Mama Gretta!" Lucy's voice was bright and cheerful again, her demeanor shifting as if a switch had been flipped. She smiled warmly at the woman, but Arlo's unease ate away at him, as if she had changed, if only for a moment.

"Thank you again dear, you three enjoy and let me know if I can help with anything else." The woman said, serving another patron at a nearby table.

Arlo watched Lucy as she shifted in her seat, her movements fluid. It was as if a different person sat before him, her secrets unknown to the world, and possibly even herself.

The three dug in, engaging in casual conversation about the taste of the food. The Cyrillian wine was a common favorite among many, a sweet flavor that held a heavy bite at the end. The stew was in fact 'The Seafarer's Delight' as Sorren called it, and certainly lived up to its name. The fresh caught fish was excellently accented by the remaining flavors of the stew, and a great companion to the wine.

"Daven Jones' Locker, why do they call this place that?" Lucy asked, after Sorren mentioned the name of Gretta's establishment.

"Well, her husband was a big fisher, a friend of my Da even. Naturally he spoke of the tale of Daven Jones, the ancient titan of the sea. Few have survived from it, and the few who claimed they have, are most likely full of it," he said between bites of fish and carrots. Bits of stew flying across the table as he used his hands to tell his story. "The name was a tribute to the very legend itself," he leaned in closer so as not to speak so loudly and interrupt the other patrons. "But I tell ya what, he lost his mind he did. She found a hidden room her husband kept, worshipping the beast even. She let Brother Jason and I know, and so we investigated. Good thing she found it in time, as he already had plans to sacrifice her to the very creature."

Lucy let out a gasp, engaged entirely in the story. "No," she mouthed.

"Yes ma'am, had talked her into a boat ride he did. Followed him out there and sure enough he drugged her. Had both of her feet weighted to an anchor and flipped the boat." His voice was filled with sadness and relief. "We pulled her out and she would go on to be okay, but when we went to pull him out... His body wasn't there."

"I feel for the woman, any children?" Arlo asked, genuine in his curiosity of Gretta's standings.

Sorren shook his head grimly. "No, at least none by blood. Many of the youngsters come around to help her out. That's how she got the 'Mama' moniker. So, there we were, Brother Jason and I, diving into the depths of the sea with his akhlut Azu, searching for any sign of Gretta's husband. The water was murky and cold, the kind of chill that seeps into your bones and makes you wonder if you'll ever feel warmth again. We didn't find anything, I headed back up to be with Gretta, Jason and Azu were gone for what felt like an eternity. We thought something happened to them when they finally made their way topside." Sorren let out a heavy sigh before pointing to a wooden framed box nailed to the wall.

"That there is all they found. His grandfather's knife, passed down to him, we continued to search for hours that turned into days. Looking in shifts in the surrounding area, no sign of him at all. Eventually we had to come to terms that he wasn't going to be found."

Arlo listened intently, his gaze shifting between his two companions. "And Gretta? How did she take it?"

"She was devastated, of course," Sorren replied, his voice filled with empathy. "But she also felt relief in knowing the truth, even if it meant losing her husband in such a tragic way. From that day on, she vowed to run this tavern with all the strength she could muster, keeping her husband's memory alive in every dish served and every story told."

Lucy nodded, thoughtful on the story of Mama Gretta. "It must have been difficult for her, losing someone she loves to a secret like that."

"It was," Sorren agreed, "but Mama Gretta is a strong woman. Always emerging stronger than before from any hardship she has faced."

Arlo glanced around the tavern, noticing the nods of respect and admiration from the other patrons who seemed to hold Mama Gretta in high regard. "It's fascinating the atmosphere in here is such a stark contrast to the rumor mill outside. You wouldn't know that anything has happened in recent days. She's built quite an establishment and obviously a bigger reputation," he remarked.

"She's earned every bit of it too." Sorren replied with a smile.

A fresh round of drinks clanked down. Mama Gretta's twinkling brown eyes scanning the table. "Enjoying yourselves, I hope?" she asked warmly.

"We are, Miss Gretta," Lucy replied eagerly with a grateful smile. "Thank you for the wonderful meal, I love how lively the people are." She took another drink into her hand, feeling an unfamiliar warmth over herself as she swayed along to the minstrel's music.

Gretta chuckled, her voice carrying the warmth of a crackling fire. "Anytime dear, it is only a small reprieve that I can offer them."

Lips curled into a smile on Arlo's face, hearing Mama Gretta's words. "Hope," he whispered to himself. It was comforting, knowing that there were still others who even during the darkest of times would still be willing to spread hope in the world. He couldn't help but feel a sense of belonging in the cozy tavern, surrounded by warmth and companionship. Despite the uncertainties and dangers that awaited them outside these walls, for now, everyone felt hopeful and safe in Mama Gretta's embrace.

Another round of drinks eventually made their way to the table, and each of them continued to feel their sense of comfort with time. Sorren wandered off to other tables, reminiscing on an anecdote from his days as a squire, his eyes gleaming as he chatted with whatever woman happened to be at the table.

Lucy, feeling the music, or possibly the wine, joined several impromptu dancers, rallying several patrons into a fun dance routine. Drinks continued to arrive, and the dancers' moves became increasingly exotic and unique with time, drawing a larger crowd.

Arlo sat back, enjoying his time reflecting and listening to the stories told by Sorren and several others around the room. Each time Sorren was mentioned or glanced at, he was with another woman, their identities blending into a parade of different faces, brunette, blonde, redhead, all captivated by his charm. He chimed in with his own tales and thoughts whenever it pleased him. Yet, his eyes were always caught by the same twirling flame among all the other patrons. Vibrant crimson hair tossed and turned with each smooth, swaying movement. Occasionally, his eyes were met with emeralds within the flames, and in those fleeting moments, the flame's movements took on a seductive grace that left him breathless.

"Look at them go!" someone yelled from the crowd, their voice filled with admiration.

The room's energy shifted, laughter and chatter melding into the rhythm of the dance.

Arlo's gaze remained fixed on the flame, the world around him blurring into a background of muted colors and sounds. Every spin, every sway, drew him deeper into the moment, a subtle magnetism that held his gaze.

Lucy's movements were fluid, each step a perfect blend of precision and spontaneity. Her body moved in harmony with the music, her skin glowing under the dim light of the tavern. Arlo couldn't look away, he was entranced by grace and energy that radiated from her like a wild flame.

Arlo felt a curious blend of detachment and connection, his mind wandering between the present and distant memories, all while anchored to the engaging red flame across the room. He couldn't tell if the warmth spreading through him was from his drinks, the enchanting dance, or the green eyes that seemed locked onto his, but he didn't care. The moment was perfect, a fleeting slice of magic that pulled the two of them into a separate world.

The night wore on, and the music began to wind down and the dancers dispersed. Lucy, her movements slowing, eventually made her way back to the table, her cheeks flushed and her breath coming in soft pants. She collapsed into her chair with an exhausted but content sigh, her eyes still sparkling from the adrenaline.

Two keys were placed on the table by Mama Gretta bringing both of them back to the present. "Here you go, dears," she said, sliding the keys towards each of them. "Sorren took care of your tab and paid for two rooms for the night. Side by side, just up the stairs."

Arlo nodded his thanks, his eyes still lingering on Lucy as she pushed herself to her feet, swaying slightly. "Thank you, Miss Gretta," taking the keys and helping Lucy steady herself.

Together, they made their way up the stairs, Lucy leaning on Arlo for support. Her breath warm against his neck, sending a shiver down his spine with each exhale. His hand rested on the small of her back, guiding her gently. The climb felt longer than it was, each step an eternity of shared glances and lingering touches. Their footsteps echoed in the quiet hallway, a soft rhythm that seemed to match their beating hearts.

When they finally reached their rooms, he took the key to her room, his fingers brushing against hers as he unlocked the door. She leaned in closer, her hand resting on his chest for balance, her touch igniting a small flame that turned into a jolt of electricity that coursed their entire bodies. The moment caught his breath, and he found himself lingering, reluctant to let the connection slip away.

"Does that happen with everyone?" she asked.

"No."

"Good," her voice was soft. "I think I would be jealous if it did."

For a moment, the world stood still. Hearts fluttering, a strange sense of connection you only find when you've known each other for an eternity. He reached out and brushed a strand of hair from her face, his fingers sparking along her skin. She leaned into his touch, her eyes half-closed.

The moment was abruptly shattered by a drunken patron stumbling down the hallway, loudly asking, "Hey, Is this my room?"

The spell was now broken, Lucy and Arlo pulled back, both of them with reddened cheeks. Arlo cleared his throat and took a step back, motioning the patron to his room. "I should go," he said awkwardly.

Lucy leaned against her doorframe, her smile laced with a touch of disappointment hidden behind a smile. "Good night, Arlo."

CHAPTER 14

Arlo lay restless much of the night, tossing and turning in the comfortable tavern bed. Yet, something deeper gnawed away at him. Every time he drifted toward sleep, his mind filled with voices. Cries, pleas, and prayers each a haunting reminder of lives cut short and hopes ended.

His wounds felt as if he were being pulled down, weighted by a burden that rested on him. With every blink he saw their last breaths, the family left behind, the lovers awaiting their return, the empty shops that would never flip their 'open' signs again.

Sometimes he wished he was able to be as carefree as others, to not want to find something, anything that gave him purpose in life. He believed this was what he got for spending his life searching for a calling. But was it really this?

Amid all of the voices and faces that were embedded into his head, not once had he seen Sabil's. He had hope that she was alive, still running the tavern as Mr. and Mrs. Percy had taught her to do when they adopted her. He knew he must get the letter out and make sure his friend was okay, she was likely worrying about him as well.

He took the time to acquire a quill and parchment and began to fashion a letter to let her know that he was okay. All he wanted was a sign that she was okay in return.

Sealing it, he placed it into the drawer of the wooden desk within the room, and made another pass at sleeping.

The down pillow was refreshing after their nights under the stars. The linen sheet, carried a soft cool breath of the sea. But above all, the one thing he was most eager to have off of him was the bulk of the armor. It was the most uncomfortable for him, while he respected those who put their lives on the line wearing them.

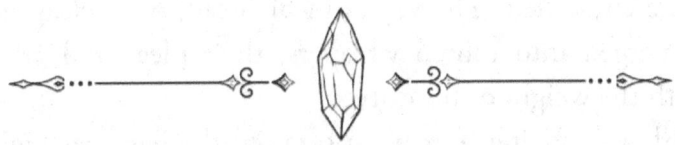

Arlo lay in the silence of the tavern room, the weight of his thoughts pulling him deeper into the recesses of his mind. The night air hung heavy around him, filled with the faint scent of wine and the distant chatter of what little nightlife remained within the city. His body, troubled from the events of the past few days, found little release against the constant noise of his thoughts.

In his solitude, his mind summoned memories with vivid clarity, the soft freckled skin and fiery crimson hair that defined Lucy. A tender smile tugged at his lips as he traced the contours of her image in his thoughts, each detail etched with an intimacy that transcended mere recollection. Her mesmerizing emerald eyes burned with an intensity that seized his breath, a reflection of otherworldly flames that danced with untamed fury.

Hatred etched lines upon her face, as her gaze penetrated his soul with a ferocity that chilled him to the core. Her lips moved, absent of audible words, yet they unleashed torrents of flames.

From her back, broken and bone-like protrusions jutted outward, each tip a crimson luster of fresh blood that dripped into dark, ominous puddles upon the ground beneath her. Shadows gathered around him, silent sentinels that stood as allies against the fiery woman that threatened to consume everything in her path.

His fingers tightened around the familiar grip of his hammer. No longer in just his trousers, he now wore immaculate blue armor that told the story of many battles. Mana swirled in brilliant blue, encasing the head of his hammer in a cocoon of pulsating energy that sparked off in every direction as bolts of lightning.

Before him lay a battlefield of devastation, charred bodies strewn like broken burnt statues, each a testament to the unimaginable fury that she embodied. The voices in his head, once clear and distinct, now merged into muted whispers, their pleas and cries drowned beneath the weight of his duty.

With a steadying breath, Arlo raised the hammer high above his head, muscles aching to release justice upon her. Mana pulsed with raw power, an ethereal glow that illuminated the darkness around him, a beacon of strength against the wildfire that was the woman. His heart pounded in rhythm with each pulse, at first he thought his heart hastened to match it, but as he brought the thoughts to his mind, the mana was a pawn at his fingertips, something he now mastered.

He swung the hammer downward, a brilliant arc of blue erupting from its head, a torrent of mana unleashing in a blinding light that seared the night sky. The air crackled with energy, an earth-shattering scream echoing through the depths of his being, a primal cry that reverberated through the very fabric of reality.

Lucy's eyes snapped open to the sight of intense blue eyes hovering over her, hands gripping her shoulders with a steadiness that contrasted sharply with the chaos of her waking nightmares. She was drenched in sweat, her body trembling uncontrollably from the remnant of her dream. The air around her crackled with residual energy, a tangible echo of the mana that had surged through her.

Arlo's voice pierced through the haze of her terror, his concern in his voice as he called out her name. She flinched at the sound, her vision still clouded by haunting imagery that plagued her sleep. Blinking away the last traces of mana, his blue eyes softened into Arlo's familiar face, seated beside her on the bed.

Her throat felt raw, as if the flames from her dream still burned within her. She struggled to regulate her breathing, each breath a labor of effort to claim control over her trembling body. Red mana, remnants of her intense emotions, seeped from her eyes, staining her cheeks with its fiery presence before fading into the reality of blood.

Mama Gretta appeared at Arlo's side, a comforting presence in the midst of Lucy's turmoil. She offered a mug of water, her soothing voice grounding her to the present. Lucy accepted the mug gratefully, the coolness of the water washing away the remnants of her fiery rage.

"Easy dear," Mama Gretta's gentle voice said, "You've been screaming for longer than a siren's song."

Lucy nodded weakly, her fingers tightening around the mug as she tried to steady her trembling hands. The memory of the primal cry of her scream etched into her memory. It felt more than a nightmare, a reminder that something lurked within her.

Arlo's presence offered her a semblance of comfort, his hand still clasped on her shoulder to anchor her to reality. She searched his eyes, finding brief solace within. The concern etched across his face, a silent promise of protection that eased her heart.

Gretta exited the room quietly, ushering the other patrons who came to investigate back downstairs.

"I…" her voice was hoarse, each word a struggle of tightness that lingered within her throat. "It felt so real."

Arlo squeezed her shoulder gently, his voice a soothing song of understanding. "I know," he whispered, "but you are safe now."

Lucy couldn't shake the vivid reality of the images in her mind. Flames that consumed her, a darkness of death and destruction that threatened to swallow her whole. She closed her eyes, willing herself to push back the memories from her fragile mind.

"I saw…" Lucy hesitated, her voice barely a whisper against the silent room. "You… the hammer… mana… but it wasn't you. You just… have his eyes."

Concern crossed Arlo's features. He was familiar with the scene of the blue figure standing over a woman who looked exactly like her. The charred bodies, the blood, and flames were etched forever into his memory also. But he had no answers, only more questions.

"I saw something too," he said. "Not all of it. Enough to know you are not making it up."

Lucy's fingers tightened around the mug. "That supposed to make me feel better?"

"No," he admitted. "But maybe it means neither of us have to be afraid alone."

She looked at him then, searching for the line between the man in front of her and the blue-eyed figure from her dreams.

"You keep saying things like that," she whispered, "and I almost believe you."

"I'll take that as a start."

A faint smile touched her face then disappeared.

"Do you want to talk about what you saw?" he asked.

She shook her head quickly. "Not tonight."

A moment later, Lucy took a deep breath, trying to steady herself. "It's just… everything feels so… overwhelming. The dreams, the visions, you… I don't know how to make sense of it all."

"It's a lot to take in," Arlo agreed. "But you don't have to go through this alone. I'll be there if you need me."

She felt sincerity in his voice, and smiled at him with shining eyes of gratitude. "Thank you, Arlo. That means more to me than you know." The comfort of his words easing the turmoil within herself. "I'm so tired," she admitted, her voice a soft whisper as her eyes became heavy.

"You should get some rest, I'll be right next door if you need me," he said, starting to rise from the bed, but Lucy's hand shot out, gripping his hand firmly. Jolts shot out through both of them, a warm flame kindling as their fingers touched and intertwined. "Can you… stay?" her voice broke around the question. "I don't know why, but you make me feel comfortable when you are close. And I don't want to be alone with myself."

Arlo looked down into her eyes, his heart aching at the vulnerability he felt from her. He nodded, settling back down on the bed beside her. "Of course, Lucy. I'll stay as long as you need."

He drew the blanket higher over her shoulder, then lowered himself to the floor beside the bed.

Lucy watched him through tired eyes.

"I said stay."

"I am," he rested his back against the bedframe without releasing her hand. "Close enough to reach. Far enough that you never had to wonder why I stayed."

Lucy sighed in relief, squeezing his hand. His warmth and the steady rhythm of his breathing slowly lulled her into a state of calm. She knew the nightmares may return again, but with Arlo by her side, she felt a new sense of strength and security.

Lucy's breathing gradually steadied, her grip on Arlo's hand slowly loosening as she slipped into a peaceful sleep. He watched her for a few moments before adjusting himself to the floor. Every move he made, her fingers wrapped around his briefly, even in her sleep filled state she wasn't letting go.

The room was quiet, the sounds of the tavern quieting, his focus fell to the rhythmic rise and fall of Lucy's breath. Arlo's thoughts wandered, reflecting on the bond that had grown between them. He felt a deep responsibility for her, a fierce protectiveness that went beyond mere friendship. Every touch a feeling of relief he longed for.

It was strange, he had been ready to be done with everything when they first set out for Treycord Meadows. Even after finding the amulet of Eckerd, whom he remembered he left in his own room, he still wanted to be done with the mission and back to his normal life. But since he had met her, he had rarely thought about going back to his so called normal life, where he felt he lacked purpose. But a newfound drive had filled him, a drive that despite the chaos, he wanted to see through to the end.

As the night grew deeper, Arlo found himself drifting into a light doze, his body finally succumbing to exhaustion that had been eating away at him. Another warmth fell over him, easing the pain along his body until it was no more than a blurred memory. His body had almost gone limp, as Lucy's hand released his own, it fell to his bare shoulders. Warm red mana seeped from her hands and relieved Arlo of some of the pressure he had been feeling. He did not question it, nor did he let it intrude on his thoughts any further. The moments of peace would be taken and cherished.

And so, he dreamt of beautiful skies and enchanting mountain tops, fields of magnificent blue flowers that went on for miles.

CHAPTER 15

Sorren woke with his head pounding and the room spinning slightly as he tried to orient himself. The first thing he noticed was the unfamiliar ceiling above him, wooden beams crisscrossed in patterns he was unfamiliar with. He groaned as his mind pieced together fragments of the previous night. The next strange thing he noticed was the warm body next to him, a woman's arm draped across his chest.

He turned his head slightly, taking in the sight of her dark hair spread out across the pillow, her dark skin glowing softly in the morning light. She was slightly plump, her curves accentuating a sensual allure that made Sorren's satisfied grin spread across his face.

"Well done, Sorren," he congratulated himself under his breath, carefully lifting the arm and slipping out of bed. He winced as the movement made his head throb even more. He glanced around, taking in the modest furnishings of the room. Nothing about the room jogged his memory of where he was at first.

Then it clicked. He had been here numerous times, in this very room of the tavern. He remembered the particular creak in the floorboard near the window, and the small crack in the mirror's frame from a boot that was thrown at him once. His grin widened, memories of past conquests flashing through his mind.

The blanket had not done her modesty many favors, so Sorren did the noblest thing he could manage. He looked at the ceiling, congratulated himself for nearly three seconds of restraint, then found his trousers.

He slipped back on his boots, he cast one last glance at the sleeping figure, caught more skin than manners allowed. He nodded in triumph and quietly made his way out.

The hallway was quiet, the sun's light casting a soft glow through the small window. Sorren took his leave down the stairs, each step cautious to avoid the known creaks that would signal his departure. He entered the common room, now empty save for a few early risers. He didn't see either Arlo or Lucy amongst the crowd and assumed they both probably slept great after the week they have had.

Crossing the room, he didn't see Mama Gretta, but one of her employees cleaning up from the nightly activities. A young woman with curly hair and an apron stained with the morning's work. A sweet girl, married to another Porter, pretty too, yet Sorren respected her husband enough to never charm her. The woman glanced up and gave Sorren a nod of acknowledgement. He managed a smile in return and headed towards the stairs on the other side of the room, leading to the rooms he had intended for Arlo and Lucy.

He climbed the stairs two at a time, eager to get on with the day and present their findings to the King. He placed his hand on Arlo's door, and not bothering to knock he burst through the door only to find it empty.

"Huh," he said scratching his head. "Where the hell did he go?"

He turned back into the hallway and looked around when he heard a voice come from the room. He returned, noticing the majority of Arlo's clothing and armor neatly tended in the corner of the room. His boots sat cleaned next to them.

"Sorren?" A voice called out.

Sorren was certain he was hearing things, or had finally drank too much the night before. His head was still clinging to ache of the morning hangover when he continued to scan the room. "Arlo?" Sorren called back to the voice.

"No, it's Eckerd." On the credenza of the room hidden behind a couple books Mama Gretta kept in these rooms, was the light glow of the amulet. Sorren placed it in his hands.

"Eckerd, ya know where Arlo went?" Sorren asked.

"I do not. I expected him to be here in the room. But I've called out to him most of the night, to receive no response."

"Huh, I thought you were able to see or something from where you are."

The voice paused for a while before speaking again. "An echo, consider that I see an echo of where you are. When nothing is happening, I cannot sense anything. Your abrupt entrance into the room though, that left an echo."

Sorren shrugged, knowing the amulet could not directly 'see' him. "Alright, let's go check on Lucy and see if she knows where he is. Sly dog may have already tried to make a move."

Sorren made his way back to the hall, this time equipped with the amulet in hand. He knew the room designated for Lucy, only a few steps away. He hesitated briefly, and softly knocked. If Arlo wasn't in the room with her, he would feel guilt for waking her.

Inside, Lucy stirred at the sound, blinking her eyes open to find Arlo still sitting on the floor next to her, his presence a comforting aura. She turned her head toward the door, her voice still groggy with sleep. "Come in."

Sorren opened the door and peeked inside, his grin widening as he saw Arlo leaning against the bed, rapidly blinking his eyes to straighten his vision.

"Morning, sleep well?" Lucy asked indirectly.

"Pretty well, yeah." Arlo groggily got out.

Sorren chuckled, stepping inside and closing the door behind him. "The right answer is, next to you, who wouldn't?"

Arlo's cheeks turned a shade pinker as he glanced at Sorren, then back at Lucy. "Uh, good morning Sorren," he greeted, trying to hide his embarrassment behind a smile. "We should head to the palace soon shouldn't we?"

"Aye, last night I had a message delivered that we would be returning this morning," Sorren said, looking around the room, noticing the remnants of their stay. Displeased that he didn't see clothing ripped and torn across the floor, he could tell Arlo was a more decent man than he was. "I can head down and get us some breakfast cooking." Sorren left the room, loud thumps accompanied by creaking floors that surprisingly didn't wake the entire establishment.

"Sounds like a plan," Arlo winced, rising to his feet as Sorren left the room. The pain had returned to him, wracking his body as if he had been struck by the hammer a dozen times over. He glanced down at his arm. A new bruise had formed beneath the skin, deep blue at the center and fading purple around the edges.

He had heard that magic took its toll. Exhaustion. Fever. A trembling hand after too much channeling. This felt different from anything he had ever witnessed before. It did not feel as if he had spent something. It felt as if something far too large had passed through him and his body was proof of the survival.

Chatter caught his attention from behind him as he turned back to the bed, removing his hand from the newfound bruising.

"Did you say something?"

Lucy, wide-eyed and confused, looked around the room. Her bare shoulders pressed against the headboard, the sheet of the bed held around her collarbone. Her freckles continued down her shoulders and to her arms as an accent to her smooth skin. "I didn't say

136

anything. You okay?" she asked, a mysterious glint in her eye as she tilted her head slightly, her eyes grazing from his bare waist, up his defined abdomen, along his chest and finally into his eyes. It was a dangerous gaze, one that Arlo could feel his heart pounding away, louder and faster than Sorren's boots on Miss Gretta's freshly swept floor.

"Yeah, yeah, I am fine. I'm gonna go get ready now." He stuttered the words and let one last glimpse back at her as he left the room and returned to his own. He say on the bed that was declared his, though he had not used it. Lifting his hand, he could still feel the sense of power the mana manifested in his grasp. It was strange for the first time in his life feeling the mana in his control like that, an intense jolt of electricity that poured through him when he felt the initial arousal of the magic. Blue jolts that he sent sparking up his own arm, he had felt like a child with a new toy.

He saw the mirror against the wall, placed over the dresser for someone staying to get a glimpse of themselves before heading out upon the town. He did not recognize himself anymore. His once blonde hair draped down to his shoulders was now void of color, a blank white like a canvas that awaited paint, almost a sense of purity he thought, but he wasn't a pure person. A beard had started to grow in, the fine hairs manifesting the same color as the rest of his head, he normally preferred to be freshly shaven and hold a clean look but he was not displeased with his current look.

His eyes were always blue, a sky blue that his father said reminded him of Arlo's mother. One of the few memories he could remember of his father, and only a brief painting had been made of his mother and father that the orphanage destroyed when he and Sabil had acted out. But even from the picture, he could tell he shared a look with her, a beautiful woman with golden hair, bright smile, and sky colored eyes. Yet something was different about his eyes now, he still held the same sky colored blue, but the closer he looked the deeper the blue got, the same color as the mana he was now able to manifest.

"Let's go, Arlo." He whispered to himself. Taking one last notice of the bruises that spotted his body, he noticed several along his shoulders, at least one on his bicep, several along his chest and ribs. With every glance he saw a flash of a vision, a person, murmurs of their words before they died. He shook his head to bring himself back to. Gathering his clothing from the days prior and putting his boots back on. He had taken the time to clean them the night before, and to keep his clothes neatly together, a habit he picked up from the orphanage where they would be punished for not taking care of their belongings.

He was dissatisfied to say the least, the armor had been ruined, the clothing soiled no matter how hard he attempted to clean them. A meeting with royalty and he looked like he had lived the streets for years. He took the rest of his belongings and geared up to meet Lucy in her room. As his fist was about to knock on the door, the gentle creak of the rusted hinge sounded and brought the two of them face to face. Lucy smiled and said, "hey, I was just coming to get you."

Sunshine poured through the window behind her, igniting her fiery hair into a display of brilliance. The light, a picture frame to display her elegance. He still couldn't help to be mesmerized, even when she still wore the ill-fitting Elfar clothing as a dress. He knew they would need different clothing before they met with the king.

"Let's... Let's head down then, don't want to keep Sorren or the King waiting," he said.

"Aye! Courtney, food's looking good. Mama Gretta's teaching you well, ya? Looks, brains, and can cook, my kinda lady." Sorren eagerly shouted to the employee. A large tray of fried eggs, bacon, fresh fruits, and the morning's baked bread were laid out on the table.

"She has," the young woman answered, placing utensils next to each other. "She also has been teaching me how much of a flirt you are."

Footsteps were heard behind the woman, as Arlo and Lucy approached the table. The woman poured two cups of a pulpy liquid, an off orange color.

"This looks amazing," Lucy said. Peeking over the woman's shoulders at the food around the table. Sorren hadn't waited for them, and had already broken the yolk of his eggs and taken several gooey bites.

"Why, thank you." The woman said before disappearing to the kitchen area.

The three sat and enjoyed their breakfast. Sorren attacked his food like a wild dog, crumbs of bread and bacon scattering across the table. He soaked his bread in the yolk, small drips splashing off his plate and onto a mat beneath it. His eating was loud, much like his boots, and every bite piled high that you would think was his last.

Arlo, on the other hand, cut his food into small, precise pieces, savoring each bite as if he was trying to stretch out the enjoyment of flavors. Occasionally glancing at Lucy to see how she was managing.

Lucy ate with a mix of hesitation and curiosity, her actions reflecting her struggles. She seemed to rediscover each food with every bite, pausing occasionally to examine a piece of fruit or slice of bacon before eating it.

"This juice is interesting," Lucy said, sipping at the pulp filled drink. "What's it called?"

"It's a local blend," Sorren replied, "Different citrus and a bit of honey."

"Do you like it?" Arlo asked, his voice gentle as he patted food from his mouth.

Lucy nodded slowly, her eyes distant, some sense of similarity yet the juice was so foreign to her. "Yes, it's... different. I think I like it."

Finishing their breakfast, Sorren leaned back in his chair, patting his stomach. "A'right, we've eaten like kings, now let's go see one."

Arlo nodded, but then paused, "Hold on, Sorren. If we are going to meet the king, we should at least look presentable."

Sorren looked down at his own attire and shrugged. Stains of blood, his own and others, dirt, grime, and more. While the ladies may enjoy a man who isn't afraid to get dirty, the king would be a different story. "You might have a point."

Lucy, still adjusting to her surroundings and unfamiliar with the town looked between both men. "Do you think we can find a place to get clothes quickly?"

Arlo smiled reassuringly.

"Yes, there's bound to be a shop nearby. This town has always had good merchants."

Sorren was the first to rise to his feet, and led the group out of the tavern. He was a few paces away, and was rambling on about something that neither Arlo nor Lucy could hear. The two shared a look and decided to follow him. The morning sun was bright, casting a warm glow over the cobblestones as they made their way through the market. Stalls were set up with various goods, and the smell of fresh bread and spices filled the air.

Several street merchants had already begun setting up their carts and offered them 'the finest deals' on their merchandise, but many of them were lacking in the clothing department. Sorren finally stopped and pointed over to a quaint shop with a neatly painted sign that read "Lara's Fine Garments."

Entering the shop they were greeted with the soft rustling of fabrics and a faint scent of lavender. A middle aged woman with squinty eyes and a small smile approached them, her black hair pinned back, and her posture commanding yet welcoming.

"Good morning! How can I assist you today?" her voice was melodic, and she moved her hand over her wares with a grace of someone who took pride in her craft.

140

Arlo stepped forward, eyeing some of the garments within immediate view. "We are seeking appropriate attire for a meeting with the royal family. Nothing extravagant but..." Sorren brushed past Arlo, interrupting him. "Something that speaks of dignity and respect. And something that is well fitted to my arms." He excitedly added, flexing to show the mountainous shapes of his arms.

Lucy giggled, watching Sorren interrupt their comrade with his ego filled display. Arlo let out a heavy sigh as he knew Sorren was going to take this too far. He knew very well that many of the Heir knights liked to show off, and Sorren was definitely one of them.

The woman's eyes sparkled with interest, and likely the conquest of a large sale. She looked each of them over, mentally dressing them over in her mind. She lifted a finely crafted wooden measure, adorned with intricate markings surrounded by her own name, and began to take measurements of each of them.

"Follow me, please," she ordered, leading them to the back of the shop, rows of delicately crafted garments were displayed. Sorren immediately gravitated towards a burgundy tunic with golden embroidery.

"This one here, oh it's calling my name," he said with an ear to ear grin.

Lara chuckled, her laugh light and infectious. "Good choice, dear. That tunic has seen many successful negotiations."

Arlo sifted through the various fabrics, eyeballing a couple that caught his eye, but ultimately he deemed too haughty for his taste. Robes that seemed to be light and well fitted, something someone would wear to inspire courage and hope, he disregarded it whenever Lara told him the cost. Whether he liked it enough or not, he was indebted to Sorren and wouldn't dare overspend. Instead he chose a more subtle, yet still elegant in its simplicity, blue tunic with silver accents. "That will do nicely," Lara nodded approvingly.

Lucy looked through the selection, her fingers brushing over the fabrics until she found a sapphire blue dress that caught her eye. "This is lovely," she said, lifting the dress off the rack.

Lara smiled warmly, "that dress is exquisite. Would you like to try it on?"

Lucy nodded with a wide smile and followed Lara to a fitting room. She slipped into the dress and stood before a large, ornate mirror. The gown was low cut and tight around the waist, giving a lift to her chest and exposing much of her shoulders and neckline. A slit down the leg coming from the hip exposed plenty of bare skin beneath it. As she admired the sapphire gown, her vision began to blur as she twirled. Her reflection in the mirror shifted, revealing a field of blue flowers that stretched endlessly with her standing in the center. In the midst of the flowers behind her, a golden figure appeared, its radiant presence startling her. Above her, along the canopy of the vision, an armored figure quickly drew into view. Its eyes bearing the same sapphire blue as the dress itself. She gasped and stumbled back, the vision fading as quickly as it came.

Lucy braced herself against the door, breathing heavily, she quickly changed out of the sapphire dress. "I don't think this is the right one for me," she said, handing it back to Lara.

The tailor looked concerned but understanding. "Of course, dear. Perhaps a different color or cut might suit you better? One less revealing?"

Lucy nodded, still shaken by the vision. She looked through the dresses again, her hand shaking as she selected a rich red dress. She tried it on and felt a sense of warmth and confidence. "This one feels right," she said, smiling softly at her reflection.

Lara's smile returned. "Ah, that dress was inspired by the moon Mani herself. I think it will be perfect for you."

As they admired their choices, Lara moved with efficiency, measuring and making quick adjustments and noting the changes needed for each outfit. "I'll have these fitted for you right away. Please, have a seat and make yourselves comfortable."

Lucy sat down, still visibly shaken. Arlo noticed and sat beside her. "Are you alright, Lucy?"

She nodded, but her eyes were still distant. "I... It's nothing," she said, hiding her worry behind a smile.

Arlo placed his hand on hers, his touch sending a reassuring jolt throughout her body. He blushed and quickly pulled it away, trying to hide his embarrassment as he saw her physical reaction. "We're here with you. You're safe."

Sorren stood nearby, glancing over more of the fabrics while counting several coins of Salvar from his pouch. "After this, we can head straight to the king. Afterwards maybe I can show you around town more, if'n I don't get stationed baby sittin' the two of ya again." He laughingly joked.

Within an hour, their new clothes were ready. Lara returned with the garments, and presented them to each of them to put on.

"I must say, the three of you look quite dashing."

Sorren adjusted his tunic, giving a mock bow. "How do I look?"

"Like you might actually impress someone for once," Lucy teased.

Arlo chuckled as Sorren's mouth gaped briefly. Finally at a loss for words. "Let's go then. The king awaits."

Sorren placed the agreed amount of Salvar onto the counter, a little extra as a tip. Lara watched them with a proud smile as they left the shop.

The city bustled around them. Many of the Kingsguard and Porters were out and about within the city. A stark contrast to each other's missions, as the Kingsguard themselves did not directly answer to the church, but were the military force led by the king's General, Darion Marquez. The sun had risen high in the sky, strikingly later than they had realized it to be. Despite his large breakfast, Sorren's stomach began to growl.

The grandeur of the palace was enough to cause Lucy to freeze in place. She had not been able to see it the previous night and was certainly amazed by it as they made their way to the outer walls. The palace was not terribly old, built in the hard years after the Cleaving, when Frederick Lionhart had barely become of age and crowned King. Nearly a century had passed since then, yet the man still walked, ruled, and fought with a strength that brought more worship to him than doubt. The guards at the entrance eyed the group cautiously but allowed them to pass after Sorren presented his credentials.

As they began walking through the ornate halls, a familiar voice shouted from behind them. "There you are! Do you know how long I've been looking for you?"

Jason stormed towards them, his expression a mix of relief and frustration. "The king wants to see you, now. He's been waiting all morning."

CHAPTER 16

King Frederick's throne room was a grand hall, adorned with rich tapestries and intricate carvings, each telling a story of the kingdom's storied past. The air was thick with tension as Arlo, Lucy, and Sorren made their way through the hallways of the palace. Their new attire did little to ease their nerves.

As they approached the throne room, two guards clad in polished armor opened the heavy doors, revealing King Frederick seated on his throne. His expression was one of deep contemplation, lines of worry etched into his face. The archbishop, Dolph Celestino, stood beside him, a stern look of disapproval fixed upon his features. Paladin Danladin stood to their left, his eyes scanned the newcomers with suspicion.

Sorren was the first to step forward, bowing deeply. "Your Majesty, we bring news of our mission," he began, his voice steady and respectful. Arlo and Lucy followed, offering their own bows of respect.

Frederick's eyes flickered with interest. "Rise," he commanded with a heavy voice. "Speak your news."

Sorren straightened his posture, his gaze steady on the king. "We have found an artifact, an amulet that we believe holds the spirit of Eckerd Lionhart, your brother." Arlo stepped forward, lifting a gilded amber jewel amulet from his neck and presented it to the king.

The soft glow of the amulet led the entire room to fall silent. The guards tensed, and Paladin Danladin positioned himself protectively near the Archbishop.

Eckerd's voice emerged from the amulet, whimsical and mischievous. "Well, well, if it isn't my dear brother. Still brooding, I see. Or sense."

The king's eyes widened, a mixture of relief and annoyance settling on his face. "Eckerd? How can this be real?" he demanded, his voice shaking slightly.

The amulet grew a bright amber color, Eckerd's voice rang out again, lighthearted with a touch of bitterness. "Ah, Fred, always the pragmatist. It is a long story involving a bit of old magic and a lot of time. Let's say, you left me in quite a predicament, a bit like being buried alive, but with less dirt and more magical confinement. Not exactly…"

Frederick's face tightened with frustration. "This is no time for jokes, Eckerd. We are on the brink of war, and your flippancy is not welcome."

"War, you say?" Eckerd's tone shifted to a more serious note. "Then you shall need all the help you can get. It seems like you found some capable allies already." His tone lightened again. "Even if one of them does look like he's spent a few too many nights at the tavern."

Sorren smirked but remained silent. Dolph stepped forward, his eyes narrowing as he looked between the amulet and the three who presented it. "This reeks of witchcraft," he hissed. "A voice from beyond the grave? It's unnatural." Turning to Frederick with his staff pointed toward the amulet. "You claimed your brother passed years ago, and had the tomb built to hold his body."

Eckerd laughed. "Oh, Dolph, always the skeptic. Relax, there is nothing to fear. He could not have buried me because I am not dead, although he wished otherwise."

Arlo, growing impatient, stepped forward. "Can we quit this bickering and actually listen to what Eckerd has to say?"

The king and Dolph both turned their gazes towards Arlo, surprise evident in their expression. Dolph's eyes narrowed, and he took another step forward, his staff pointing accusingly at Arlo. "And who do you think you are, to speak so boldly in the presence of your leadership?"

Arlo held his ground, meeting Dolph's gaze without flinching. "I am no one, just someone the king sent to retrieve his amulet brother. And if I may add, we need to hear what hope Eckerd has to offer."

Sorren joined in, his voice steady. "Arlo is the hero of Fall Lake. If anyone deserves to be heard, it's him."

Lucy began to shift uncomfortably, feeling the weight of the room's tension and the scrutiny of the king's court.

"Hero?" Dolph whispered, eyeing Arlo up and down judgingly, lingering on the hammer at his side. "You claim to be a hero, yet it was Heir who intervened. The boy merely wields a replica of Elduun, and now we should praise him? He should be lucky Heir spared him when lightning struck the beast."

"Dolph," Frederick's voice echoed the halls with a brutal twist of the word. "Let us hear what Eckerd has to say. But know this, trust is earned, not given, even for the King's brother."

The amulet glowed brightly as Eckerd's voice ringing out, more serious than before. "As I said, you will need formidable allies. Allies that I can provide, if I am rescued from the island known as, The Gauntlet."

"The Gauntlet," Jason said, stepping forward. "Those waters surrounding it are treacherous, filled with rocky paths and larger threats that our current ships cannot handle. We would need a vessel large enough to be unaffected by these dangers."

Dolph interjected, his sneer of displeasure spreading. "Designing and building such a ship is not a quick or easy task. We have more pressing concerns with the threat of war looming."

Eckerd replied, his voice a steady melody. "Building this larger vessel could be beneficial in this coming war. Transport of larger amounts of supplies and troops up and down the coast. Said ship could hold many purposes when you attack or defend from the sea. Imagine how much more effective the Porters could be if they were not just errand boys."

Frederick's interest was piqued at his brothers proposal. The need for a larger vessel that would aid in fending off larger threats of the sea was something he had others working on with no concrete solution. "You speak of allies and furthering our developments. You have been gone quite some time brother, perhaps you have lost the measure and cost of time, material and an engineer to design said ship, this would take ages just for this one goal. Tell us who this ally is, and we will determine if it is worth this development."

Sorren took a single step forward, expecting to have one of the royalty scold him for doing so.

"Your majesty," he said, forcing his shoulders square, "I have not come emptyhanded. I have been working with a Nogmi engineer on a larger vessel. Not just drawings. The keel is laid. Frames are up. Lower hull is started."

Dolph's sneer sharpened. "You expect us to believe you have hidden a warship under a tarp?"

"No," Sorren said, clearing his throat. "I expect you to believe I have hidden an unfinished mistake with potential."

A few uneasy looks were shared among the room.

Sorren continued before anyone could stop him. "My Da, my father, started the design years ago. I changed it after joining the Porters. Alf changed it as well, but he says it will survive the sea further than any vessel he has seen before."

Frederick did not smile. "How much of it exists?"

"Enough to save us time, but not enough to save us work. The bones exist."

"How long?" the king asked.

Sorren took a breath, his heart ready to burst from his chest.

"A month to put her in the water? Probably another week to truly trust her."

Dolph scoffed. "You don't sound confident."

"Wood, steel, sailcloth, labor, pitch, rope, mages to help with heavy lifting and sealing, and every shipwright you can spare. Give me that, and we launch her in a month."

Frederick's gaze stayed on him. "And without those things?"

"Then she remains my father's dream, my embarrassment, and your brother stays stuck where he is."

Silence fell over the room again, calculation instead of pure dismissal.

Frederick finally stood.

"Bring the engineer, bring me the plans. Then take my shipwrights to this hidden hull of yours."

Sorren bowed deeply, hiding nothing of the relief in his face.

"Yes, Your Majesty."

"And Sorren," Frederick added.

Sorren looked up at once.

"If this vessel fails, it will not only be your dream that sinks."

The smile left Sorren's face.

"Aye, we won't fail."

Dolph's skepticism was palpable, the concern of following a disembodied voice to a dangerous land was reasonable. "And who

149

should captain such a vessel? Someone experienced and trustworthy no doubt, we could have a Reigner here in no time to do so."

Jason raised his hand and took a bow, "If I may, Sorren has proven his worth in every other way. His determination, accolades and accomplishments I believe make him a fitting candidate. As a Porter, he is already trained in naval training."

Paladin Danladin, silent for much of the encounter finally spoke, never moving from his location. "Jason speaks the truth. Sorren has shown much promise over recent years, his determination and success in this task would demonstrate his ability to lead and captain this vessel… as a Protector of Heir."

Frederick gave a slight nod, "Sshow me you have the plan and I will see to it that you have the resources needed."

Sorren bowed deeply, hiding the grin on his face. He felt the moment to be surreal, a dream that he expected to be pinched awake from. But it was no dream, but a reality, he would be given the opportunity to build the ship his father only dreamed of.

Fred's eyes turned to Arlo and then Lucy, his gaze scrutinizing her. "And who is the third among you? Why is she here as well?"

"My name is Lucy," she said awkwardly.

Arlo took a step forward to assist her. "Your majesty, Lucy awoke alone in the crater. She holds no memories of the event at Fall Lake or her prior life. We rescued her from a group of Elfar that we encountered near Savage Run."

"No others survived from the crater, save for the two of you? And you have found each other as company, rescued from the hands of the enemy?" Dolph eyed both heavily, the tension in his face spoke the truth of his distrust. Dolph began to storm forward, his staff presenting itself pointed towards Lucy. "She is but a spy from Candurill himself, let us see what her memory truly holds."

Arlo placed one hand firmly on Lucy's shoulder, her heart beginning to race. His other hand rested on the pommel of the hammer, ready to draw it at a moment's notice. "Enough, Dolph.

This is enough of you and your tyrannical judgments." The miracles Dolph had performed were legendary, known amongst anyone in and out of Zenaria. Arlo likely stood no chance, but he would not sit idly by while Lucy was attacked, not again after the vision they shared.

Arlo's remark to the Archbishop left everyone in shock and awe. Silence once again ruled the throne room. The only sound that was heard was the slow steps of King Frederick who paced towards Arlo and Lucy.

Danladin stood ready to draw his sword, his eyes locked on Arlo, but held his position, waiting for the king or archbishop's command.

Sorren stood shocked, unable to fathom Arlo's boldness towards both King Frederick and Archbishop Dolph.

Jason moved to place a calming hand on Arlo's shoulder, an attempt to de-escalate the situation, but Arlo shrugged him off.

What felt like an eternity passed, as everyone in the room watched Arlo and Dolph stand face to face.

"Dolph." Frederick ordered, the Archbishop staying in place. Frederick intervened in front of Dolph and looked both Arlo and Lucy over. "Tell us what you both remember from the events in Fall Lake. If you are allied with the Elfar, you will find a death quicker by telling us the truth."

"I told you already," Arlo growled. "I don't remember much at all."

Arlo's eyes lost focus, the pain of a thousand needles settling in, his wounds wreaking havoc across his entire body.

Blue flashed before his eyes as he witnessed several mages, Hume, Dwarv, and Nogmi, all sending orbs of mana weaving through the air, bursting like fireworks against the monster's hide. His eyes flashed again to visions of bodies strewn along the ground, blood-covered hands as a woman held her young.

More mages appeared in a fiery blaze, these ones of Elfar descent. The Elfar blasts were connected with nearby structures, and from his eyes he watched as a building began to topple onto a man, frozen in fear.

Another flash and he was walking alongside a family, not just walking, but leading them somewhere. He looked around at the devastation caused by the monstrosity. Victims wounded, blood spread across the cobblestone, buildings trampled and scorched. His walk became a run, the children he was escorting left behind, repeating his name over and over again.

"Arlo"

"Arlo"

"Arlo"

"Arlo."

Visions faded away, brought to the present by a subtle voice. The pain fading from Arlo's body as a gentle touch to his back melted away his pain.

The gaze of the room set on Arlo, realizing that he had lost focus around him.

"So you don't remember anything at all?" Dolph asked.

"Small bits, truthfully," Arlo began. "I know that I was in Fall Lake. I saw the creature running into the city. Mages attacked it, but none of their spells fazed it and steel did not penetrate it. I did, I think, witness Elfar attacking buildings and people. Collapsed one right onto someone, there was no way he made it out alive."

"Elfar mages attacking Fall Lake, combined with the reports of other attacks on Cyril after the Elfar enslaved the Dwarv last year? I told you, Frederick, that inviting the Elfar to Fall Lake was a terrible idea, even if it is tradition," Dolph snapped towards the king.

"You know I had my reasons, Dolph," Frederick said, his sudden turn causing the guards in the room to react without hesitation. "Any other items that you remember or anything you wish to note about the event, or are we done here?" Frederick asked hastily, taking a stern look back at Arlo and Lucy.

"Nothing else that I remember, sir," Arlo added to end the conversation.

Frederick's gaze softened lightly as he motioned towards Sorren. "You will both join Sorren and his crew. We will see if your memories return and we will see where your loyalties lie."

Dolph let out a low growl, his eyes gleaming with suspicion and disgust. He clenched his staff tightly, his knuckles white with tension. Without a word, he turned on his heel and stormed out of the room, his robes billowing behind him.

Frederick now turned to Sorren. The loud slam of a side door shaking the candles in the room. "You have your mission. Retrieve the blueprints, gather all the information you need, and bring the Nogmi engineer here. Return by sundown."

Sorren nodded and then bowed. "Thank you, Your Majesty. We will not fail you."

Frederick continued, "When you return, Danladin will escort you to the engineers in town. They will work on this vessel under your supervision. This will be taking valuable resources from other matters, rebuilding and tending to the wounded of Fall Lake, and preparing our defenses. Do not let this be for nothing."

INTERMISSION TWO:
A NOTE OF OPPORTUNITY

I tap my spoon against the edge of the table. The room's light is soft, but the fires having been rekindled by our dear friend, Forkner. My words hung in the air for a moment, drawing the attention of those gathered.

I lean forward through the creaking of my old chair. "In this moment, I would like to reflect on something peculiar. Opportunities, how they come to us wrapped in the most unassuming packages, like a meal served without a garnish. But make no mistake, it is the substance that matters. It's what is inside the moment that holds the potential to change everything."

A soft clink of glasses pulls my attention for just a second. Someone, likely Candy, moves quietly along the room's edges. She's quick, almost invisible when she chooses to be, but I catch a flicker of green as she slides a drink onto a table and moved back into the shadows. It's what she is best at, after all. Observing, listening, understanding. Candy has a knack for seeing what others miss, noticing the smallest sparks in the darkest corners.

"Opportunities don't always announce themselves. Sometimes they're subtle, a whisper instead of a shout. Other times they look like nothing more than an ordinary person with an extraordinary will. And when we seize them, when we dare to take hold of what's offered, even if it terrifies us, we find something remarkable... Sometimes we even find ourselves."

I take the spoon in my hand, spinning it between my fingers before placing it on the table with a flamboyant display. "Now, let us continue. Watch for the sparks, the whispers, the notes played softly amidst the chaos. The faintest of melodies can carry the weight of change, and that brings us to a new individual, one who may just fit this very idea."

A green-haired figure moves past me again, collecting an empty glass with swift hands. She pauses briefly, meeting my eyes with a knowing glance before vanishing into the shadows once more. A small smile touches my lips, lost is where I would be without a crew. "Now then, let us meet this new opportunist, and see where the next note in this tale takes us. Shall we?"

CHAPTER 17

Arlo, Lucy, and Sorren walked through the bustling streets of the city, their destination the outskirts where the river's edge met an old dockyard. The sun hung high in the sky, casting a bright, warm light over the cobblestone paths and the shimmering water. The scent of salt and fish permeated the air, mingling with the distant sounds of hammers striking metal and the creak of wooden ships bobbing.

Moving away from the heart of the city, the grand architecture gave way to more utilitarian buildings. Warehouses and workshops lined the streets, doors wide open to reveal craftsmen and laborers hard at work. Sorren led the way, calling out to several individuals, but stopped for none. Lucy and Arlo followed closely behind, taking in the sights and sounds of the industrious part of the city. Tension from their previous conversations still weighed heavily upon them.

Eventually, they reached the outskirts, where at the end of the dock rested a massive warehouse. Old property of someone in the city where Sorren was able to purchase it for a reasonable fee a year ago.

A large, sturdy building that once had been a hub for commerce in the cities earlier years. The imposing structure loomed ahead, dwarfing the surrounding buildings, its wooden doors reinforced with iron, stood ajar, inviting them into the dimly lit interior.

Inside, the scent of sawdust and metal was thick in the air. The hull of the ship dominated the space, a colossal framework of timber and steel. Two Nogmi moved about with purpose, their movements synchronized as they continued to saw wood in tandem. One of them stood just a little over three feet tall, standard size among the Nogmi, a full greyed beard that hung down to his plump belly, and his hair stuck straight up for at least a foot under his headband. His skin was tanned, at least what could be seen beneath the grease and sawdust covering him. The other, a slightly taller and lankier Nogmi with a long face that resembled a wooden plank, had a strange contraption with a wheel in place of one of his legs.

"Wicket and Willy Fizztop!" Sorren called out to them.

Both men looked up, continuing their eerily united movements, they let the saw drop to the floor, narrowly missing Willy's good foot. Arlo and Lucy shared a look as the two men ran to Sorren and embraced him. Their voices were exact opposites, Wicket's voice was deep and full of bass, while Willy's voice was much higher, and his speech more drawn out.

"Look who's back!" Wicket boomed, his voice far too large for his body. "It's been too long, Sorren! We've been waitin' for you to see what we ruined."

"Aye! We've made some good headway since you left," Willy chimed in, his higher pitched voice dancing through the air as he rolled around Sorren.

Sorren grinned despite himself and knelt to embrace them both. Even on one knee, he still towered over the Nogmi. "It has been three days."

"Three busy days," Willy corrected, rolling a neat circle around him on the little wheel that replaced one of his legs.

"Three dangerous days," Wicket added.

Sorren's grin weakened, he regrated everything he said to the king already. "Dangerous how?"

Wicket and Willy looked at each other.

"The stern," they said together.

Sorren shut his eyes. "Alf said the stern was fine."

"No, he said the stern would float," Willy said.

"Briefly," Wicket added.

"Where is Alfonze?"

The two Nogmi shared a look, grinning with jagged broken teeth and pointed in opposite directions. "Alf?" they said in unison.

"He's around somewhere, said something about needin' a 'pee break'," Willy said.

"And a stiff drink too." Wicket added.

"We'll wait for him then," Arlo said, "My name is Arlo, we are here to help however we can after we finish our business."

Wicket and Willy glanced around Sorren. "Ya need a pee break too?" they asked.

Arlo's mouth was caught agape, he was familiar with Nogmi, having met them several times. They were a short statured species, about half the height of Arlo, although they looked fairly human, they were often known to have exaggerated features and never hold back, be it from a drink, words, or an idea.

Willy rolled over next to Arlo and reached his hand out to Lucy. "My, my, my, and who might you be?" he asked, eyebrows raised and his crooked smile attempting to be flirtatious.

Lucy couldn't help but smile at his attempt, barely able to hold in her laughter. "I'm Lucy, it's nice to meet you."

Wicket barged over, knocking into Willy. Both rolled along the floor and knocked into several metal tools that were perched atop a pile of wood.

"I'm okay." Both men shouted. The room erupted into laughter as they watched the two bickering brothers clamber to get up and back to their feet.

"You boys in here slackin' off again?" An unfamiliar voice came from across the room. Walking in with a dramatic flourish, hair sticking out in all directions and his moustache cut into two different shapes, bushy and long on one side, shorter and droopy on the other. His crooked teeth peeked out with his wide smile, and his old hat, looking like it had been blown up at some point, sat askew on his head.

"About time you showed up, thought you were skipping out on our work," Sorren said jokingly.

"Well, well! Looks like the boss finally showed!" Alfonze declared, taking a heavy drink from his hat. "So what brings you by, thought ye' were headin' off ta Fall Lake for a while."

Sorren's large hand rest on the shoulder of Alfonze, guiding him and the others into the 'office' of the warehouse. The room barely had a place to sit, piles of debris and trash littered around the room, an oak table sat along the far wall, quill and ink lined neatly beside it. In the center of the table was a large parchment, markings over various pieces of it, the design showed a massive ship.

The details aligned with the framework just outside of the room. It very well could be the grandest ship created, and there were only four of them working on it.

Alf was caught up to speed on the situation, a request from the king himself to finish their vessel. Alf couldn't believe it, his mind was racing with the possibilities of what could be done with the king's fortune and additional hands.

"Fantastic news! An all we gotta do is find his brother? Should be easy 'nough." Alf said with a crackling laugh. "And I get ta meet the fancy king himself. I better get my good pants on."

159

Alf ran out of the room, shouting at his brothers to pause their work and clean the place up. The brothers scrambled, clinging and clanging as they moved items to and from.

"Sorren," Arlo said, stopping him as he went to leave the room. "Let's give them a few minutes to get things in order," he said, gesturing towards a couple of crates they could use as makeshift seats. "We need to talk about the king and archbishop."

One of the crates creaked and cracked as Sorren forcefully sat on it. He paid it no mind, leaning the crate backwards and balancing on it. "Aye, I suppose so. What about 'em?"

"I don't trust either of them." Arlo admitted with a low grumble.

Sorren snorted. "A whole lotta balls you got talking to them like ya did. I ain't ever seen anyone talk like that to them, and those that I heard about were met with imprisonment."

Lucy sat elegantly on her crate, her eyes distant as she stared off. "For those who call themselves leaders, they spoke so disrespectfully. Had Arlo not said something, they wouldn't have liked what I had to say."

"You lot might want to watch your tongue out in public. People worship both of 'em." A loud bang echoed on the stone flooring as his crate met the ground. "I'm not saying you weren't right, just be careful."

Arlo sighed, rubbing his temple. "You are right, but why are they cooped up in their palace? Why aren't they out here in the streets calming and leading their people?" he questioned, looking Sorren in the eyes. "Rumors are going to keep spreading, and someone needs to give the people *hope*."

"But they have so much other things to worry about," Sorren countered, leaning forward on his crate.

"That gives them no excuse," Arlo said. "As you said, the citizens worship them. Has he even left the safety of his walls? You heard the people last night, filled with rumors and the King hasn't said a word."

160

Sorren frowned, considering Arlo's words. And the state of their current affairs. "What are you getting at?"

Arlo straightened himself, his eyes lighting a brilliant blue. "Leadership is more than just holding a title. Real leadership is working beside the people, not ordering them from behind walls. The King and the Archbishop should be out here, showing strength, providing guidance, and giving hope to the people who need it most right now."

Lucy smiled and nodded in agreement, she let her loose stare drop and admired Arlo's conviction. "Actions speak louder than words. The people need to see their leaders standing with them, not hiding away."

Sorren sighed, leaning back on his crate again. "You make a valid point. Just be careful. I would hate to see us all get locked up in the brig for it."

"We don't need to speak against them," Arlo said, his hand gripping tightly around the hammer. Something about him felt different, seemed different than when Sorren knew him before and now it appeared more evident than before. "We need to lead by example. Show the people that they are not alone, that there are those willing to stand with them. We're not just building a ship here, we are building hope."

Sorren nodded slowly, his frown fading into a brilliant smile. He and Lucy shared a glance, moved by Arlo's words. "Aye, you're right."

Sorren leaned back again, the swaying crackling of the wooden crate beneath him gave wonder to how long it would take to break apart. "You know, building this ship, it's been a dream of mine. My father started the design, and I've been fortunate to meet Alf and his brothers to help me continue the work. The idea of me creating the largest vessel Zenaria has ever put to sea, one that can travel the ocean without fears… I'm not gonna lie, it's exhilarating."

Arlo smiled, the tension easing in his face. "And it's not just a ship, Sorren. Believe in what this can be, a symbol. A symbol of what we

161

can achieve together, of the hope and strength we can inspire in others."

Lucy nodded, "I don't remember what other ships look like, except for those we saw at the dock. But if this ship is what you say it is, it could be something that symbolizes the future and what future boats use as a goal."

Sorren quickly stood up, the impact of the crate slamming into the ground again causing it to collapse beneath him. "Enough jabbin' our jaws then. Let's get to it. ALF!" he yelled out through the door of the office space.

Lucy lifted herself from her seat, and smiling at Arlo said, "Do you always have big speeches like that?"

Arlo waved his hand, allowing her to go first out of the door. "No, not at all. I try to avoid an audience."

She chuckled softly, her eyes sparkling. "Well, you're pretty good at it. It's kind of cute."

Arlo's cheeks flushed slightly, following closely behind her. "Thanks, I think."

Rumors continued to buzz in the air like mosquitoes to the swamp. The recent attack on Fall Lake was still the talk of the town. But more whispers of Elfar involvement were on everyone's lips. The introduction of the Archbishop into the town gave more fuel to the belief that dark times were on the way. But new rumors have begun to surface, as word quickly spread of the King's latest decree behind closed doors.

A group of townsfolk gathered near the market, discussing the large order for wood placed at the sawmill. "Why do they need so much lumber?" One man wondered aloud. "They planning to build a wall around us, to protect us?"

"I heard it was for a ship, something big enough to take us all away from here." His companion replied.

The group kept quiet, although it was apparent the rumors continued to bother them. Especially when they were heard to be called out by a few of them as a suspicious or new group. A few streets prior to the palace, the group was alerted to a ragged man standing above them. His wild eyes darting about, his hands carving frantic shapes in the air as he preached to anyone who would listen to him.

"The end is near!" he shouted, his voice cracking. "The prophecies speak of this time, of the darkness that will consume us all!" His fingers lingered as he pointed to Lucy. "Draconis have risen, devouring the world, send it back to the nothingness it once was!"

Some in the crowd scoffed and laughed, while others listened with a mix of fear and curiosity. Several children began to cry in fear of the man's words.

"The gods have forsaken us, left us to rot and fall victim. The king hides upon his throne, and the bishop prays to the ones who do not heed his call." The man's eyes lingered over the party, before being grabbed by the arms by several guards in the area.

"Alright, Carver, no one needs to listen to a drunk's blasphemy. You're coming with us," One of the guards barked.

Lucy paused, watching the scene before her unfold. "Another doomsayer," Sorren told her, shaking his head. "There is always someone predicting the end of the world."

"It's unsettling," Lucy said, her eyes fixed on the man and her hands clasped against her chest. "Drakaros, why does that sound so familiar."

Arlo thought back to the need for someone to take charge and let the people know what is happening. Otherwise these doomsayers would scare the people enough with their blasphemous ideology. "Draconis, are creatures of immense power and size. They appeared a little over 100 years ago and have been seen as more frequent, towering creatures with scales harder than stone. I've not seen one before, but the beast in Fall Lake appeared like the descriptions I have been given before, except that one did not have wings like the others."

The street preacher struggled, but the guards were unrelenting. "You can silence me, but the legion has already begun their fight and all will be consumed."

The crowd dispersed, the excitement of the spectacle fading. But the voice of the crowd only brought more panic amongst the crowd. Arlo turned to his companions, his face grim. "Whether he is right or wrong, it is clear that fear is spreading."

Lucy nodded, glancing back at the preacher being hauled away. "Let's hope the King gets more concerned with leading his people through these times than silencing voices."

Sorren's jaw tightened, the preachers words lingering in his mind. "If there is truth to what he said, we need to be prepared. This ship might be more important than I realized."

Alf, who had been uncharacteristically quiet, finally spoke up. "Then let's make sure it's the best damn ship anyone's ever seen. If the world's gonna end, let's go down with the ship!"

"Something like that," Lucy chuckled.

Alf continued on ahead, glancing back to the others. "You lot gonna keep standin' there with your hilts up your arse? I ain't paying ya for nothin'."

"You aren't the one paying anyone!" Sorren shouted to Alfonze, rushing to catch up with him.

Arlo looked to Lucy, letting her lead the two of them. They followed along a short distance behind Sorren and Alf, who were exchanging playful banter.

"I forgot to thank you, about last night," Lucy said, her voice soft and sincere.

Arlo glanced at her, a small smile playing on his lips. "For what?"

"For staying with me after my nightmare," she continued, her eyes meeting his. "I just appreciated having someone there with me."

Arlo's smile widened, "Anytime, moments of peace are hard to come by. I'm glad I could be there."

Lucy lowered her gaze briefly, "These dreams about the man in armor. It always feels so real, then I wake up and there is just... so much negativity." A smile crossed her lips as she continued, "But you're the bright spot in all of this, I can't help but find it easier to handle with you around, and I have hope that we will figure this all out."

Arlo chuckled, trying to lighten the mood. "I guess that makes me your beacon of hope."

"Maybe it does," Lucy laughed quietly. "Let's catch up before they forget about us."

CHAPTER 18

The room was dimly lit, shadows clinging to the corners, reluctant to retreat from the meager light of the flickering candle on the bedside table. The air was heavy, the scent of herbs and the faint mustiness of the old wooden walls that had stood the test of time and devastating storms. Nyla sat quietly by her mother's side, her tall frame folded into the small chair, her hand gently gripping Ana's frail fingers.

Ana's breathing was labored, a struggle against the force that drained her life away little by little. Her dull curse bound eyes, once vibrant and full of life, met Nyla's gaze, full of pain and determination.

"Mother," Nyla whispered, her trembling voice barely a mouse's squeak as she pulled her own blue-tinted white hair behind her ear. "You should rest more. I can get you some water or… or maybe the herbal tea Sunny brought last time."

Ana's weak smile tugged at the strings of Nyla's heart. "My sweet girl... You've done more than enough."

"But I do worry," tears filling around blue specked purple eyes. "You're all I have, Mother. I can't lose you."

Ana's grip tightened, an attempt at a show of strength to defy her weakened condition. "Nyla, listen to me," but her labored words proved otherwise. "The world is full of people who wouldn't understand... Who wouldn't accept you. You cannot leave here."

Nyla nodded, but her heart continued to waver and eat away at the love she felt for her mother. Her mother's words were, repeated to her any time Nyla got adventurous or begged and pleaded to go out. But Ana almost always refused, opting for other less traveled area by the people of Zenaria. But Nyla had seen her mother's condition worsening with each passing day, no matter how hard she tried to keep her comfortable.

Ana's breath grew more ragged, her body convulsing slightly as the curse flared up. Panic surged through Nyla as she quickly grabbed a vial from the nearby table, its contents a mixture of herbs and the little magic she could muster. She held it to her mother's lips, urging her to drink.

"Please, mother, this will help." She frantically uttered over and over again.

Ana obeyed, swallowing the bitter liquid with a grimace. Slowly, the convulsions eased, and her breathing steadied. Nyla let out a sigh of relief, but the fear lingered, gnawing at her mind. She hid a tear that fell from her face.

As her mother drifted into an uneasy sleep, Nyla remained by her side, watching the rise and fall of her mother's chest. She knew this was only a temporary solution, that the curse would continue to consume Ana until there was nothing left.

After what felt like hours, Nyla stood and quietly slipped out of the room. She needed air, a space to clear her mind and collect her thoughts. Her mother's side used to be that place for her, many years ago before the curse had taken its hold on her. The small cabin they called home was nestled deep in the forest, hidden away from prying eyes. It was the only world Nyla had ever known, a world of shadows and secrets, but never the world she wanted.

She stepped outside, the cool night air brushing against her skin like a gentle caress. The twin moons' light filtered through the dense canopy above, casting red and blue patterns onto the ground. Nyla walked slowly, her thoughts heavy with the weight of her mother's condition.

A small clearing was her destination, a place she often came to when the walls of the cabin felt too close, too confining. Here, she could be alone with her thoughts, away from the fear and the worry that plagued her every waking moment. The thoughts of leaving terrified her. She had lived in seclusion her entire life, sheltered from the dangers her mother had warned her about. And yes... the idea of finding a cure for Ana, of freeing her mother from the curse, was like a beacon in the darkness, calling to her.

"You can't do this," she whispered to herself, trying to quell the rising tide of determination in her chest. "Mother said it's too dangerous."

But even as she spoke the words, she knew her resolve was crumbling. She couldn't just sit by and watch her mother waste away, not when there might be something out there that could save her.

Sunny's words echoed in her mind, "Stay with your mother and keep her comfortable, I will be back tomorrow with more medicine."

If she left now, Sunny would be back by morning, and he could watch over her mother while she was gone. But a doubt crept into her mind, where would she even go? She had never been into the cities, only heard stories and tales about them from the books Sunny would bring by.

It was then that she remembered Sunny's words, about how the King's ships in Davenport were always stocked with the finest medicines and potions, magical artifacts, and rare ingredients. She knew Davenport was to the south, she and Sunny had been out hunting a few miles south when he showed her the path that he said led directly there.

That was it.

If there was any place to start looking, that was the one.

Nyla shivered, the enormity of what she was considering sent a shock of fear throughout her entire body. But fear alone wasn't able to stop her, fear was what kept her in place in the cabin, at her mother's side accepting her mother's fate and not finding a permanent solution. She had to try, even if it meant stepping into the unknown, into a world that would likely see her as a target.

"I have to do this," she said aloud. "For Mother."

Nyla glanced back at the cabin, the only one she had ever known, where her mother lay sleeping, unaware of the choice her daughter just made. She swallowed hard, her heart ready to burst from her chest with the thought of leaving her mother behind, even for a short while.

But it was the only way.

"I'm sorry, Mother," she whispered into the night, as if the wind could carry her words back to the cabin. "But I can't just watch you suffer."

Nyla let out a determined breath and turned from the clearing, heading back to the cabin to prepare for her journey. She didn't know what waited beyond the forest, only that staying meant losing her mother. That truth carried her forward.

CHAPTER 19

The grand entrance to the Palace of Davenport stood before them, its towering walls and ornate carvings reflecting the might and wealth of the kingdom. The sound of their footsteps echoed against stone as Sorren, Alfonze, Arlo, and Lucy all approached, wonder filled glee lit Alf's smile as he stood awestruck by it's beauty.

As they neared the palace doors, they were greeted by a tall, imposing figure clad in gleaming armor. His presence was awe inspiring, and as striking as the shining steel he wore, every piece meticulously polished to perfection. The golden mantle representing his command and rank within the church. His eyes held a stern look, and while he did not move in the slightest, the group knew he was well aware of their approach.

"Paladin Danladin," Sorren saluted with a professional tone, "As requested by His Majesty, I have brought the plans for the proposed ship and my trusted engineer Alfonze Fizztop." He nodded from the

Paladin to the rest of the group, each of them giving a salute back. Although Alf's needed a little bit of work.

"I will ensure that His Majesty is made aware of your arrival. You will be escorted to the naval engineers on site, who will review your plans to ensure their integrity." Without hesitation or awaiting a response, Danladin turned on his heel, leading them through the massive doors of the palace.

The group walked in silence, their footsteps muted by the plush red carpet that lined the corridors. They walked through a series of winding hallways, each turn revealing more of the palace's grandeur. Finally, they reached a set of heavy wood doors, which Danladin pushed open with ease, revealing a large, bustling chamber.

Inside, the room was filled with engineers, craftsmen, some of which whom gathered around a massive table covered in blueprints of various designs. The atmosphere was charged with energy, the sound of animated discussions and the rustling of parchment filled the air. All of it abruptly stopped when the Paladin entered the room.

"Here we are," Danladin announced as he stepped aside to allow them to enter. "I will let the King know you have arrived, and return for you when he is prepared for you."

Once again, without hesitation or wasted words, the Paladin turned on his heel and left the room.

As Danladin exited the room, the group was left standing at the threshold of the chamber. The engineers and craftsmen inside eyed them with a mixture of curiosity and skepticism. Sorren took a breath, puffed his chest out, and strutted forward. He had faced battles and challenges before, but this, convincing Davenport's finest minds that their ship design was not only feasible but the work of legends, was a different battle.

Alf, on the other hand, seemed completely unfazed. His awe of the Palace and the Paladin have already been replaced with an eager grin as he approached the massive table alongside Sorren. The Nogmi looked like a child in a candy store, eyes darting from one design to another.

"Now this is what I'm talking about!" Alf exclaimed, his eyes scanning the detailed drawing with childlike excitement. "Some fine work you all got here, yes indeed! Although… a few tweaks wouldn't hurt."

"Aye, I agree with ya, mate," Sorren said sharing the eager surveying of the works on display.

A few of the engineers exchanged skeptical glances, their expressions a mixture of disbelief. Several began to scurry and cover their designs. But the oldest among them, a grizzled man with a stern face and a trimmed beard, stepped forward, crossing his arms over his chest.

"You must be Sorren," the man said, his tone laced with a hint of condescension. "I hope you realize what is at stake here. This isn't some backwater project, the King wants a ship that will speak legends around the entire continent. You can show us what you have, but don't be upset when we have to fix it."

Alf didn't miss a beat. With a flourish, he began to unroll his own set of blueprints on the table, his confidence worn proudly. "Oh, I'm well aware of that, my good man. That's why Sorren and I started this project in the first place! She's already a beaut, got the hull built, took me and me brothers months to do by ourselves while Sorren had his duties. Go on, take a gander, I may be a Nogmi, but I promise it's sized for ye' Humans and us alike!"

"That's right, Alf and the rest of 'em have been hard at work. You won't find a better crew than those three." Sorren reassured.

Whispers ran through the room, several individuals looked over the parchment giving their opinions and sharing it with each other. The design was unlike anything they had ever seen before, Nogmi ingenuity was something that they were fairly unfamiliar with. Their skepticism waned, replaced by genuine interest and curiosity.

A younger man with sharp eyes the color of open sky, pointed to a section of the blueprint. "This design... it's very ambitious." He remarked, glancing at Alf. "You say the hull is already complete?"

Sorren stepped forward, seeing his opportunity to help in the pitch. "Yes, near our shipyard by the coast. We've kept it under wraps, but it's ready for inspection. We need your expertise to finalize the procurement of materials and we need helping hands willing to expedite the remaining build."

The younger engineer studied the blueprints for a moment longer before nodding slowly. "This is unlike anything we've worked on before. The balance, the weight distribution, it's all so precise. Although several elements seem unnecessary and unconventional. Here, for instance." He tapped a section near the midship. "Extra bracing along the inner hull and these staggered bulkheads. Why place them here, where they will complicate construction, instead of reinforcing the keel or bow?"

Alf's eyes sparkled as he leaned in closer, his voice taking on a more serious tone. "Unconventional? Perhaps. But that's what makes it special, don't you think?"

Sorren placed a hand on Alf's shoulder and leaned in with him. "This isn't some ordinary Porter ship, boys, we're building something that will sail into legends. Trust us, every detail has been accounted for. I know he doesn't look the part, but Alf knows what he is doing."

The room buzzed with more discussions, several naysayers had already removed themselves from the discussion. But several others continued to study and analyze every last detail of the design.

The older man stroked his beard thoughtfully, then nodded. "All right, let's see what you've got. If this ship's as good as you say, then we've got work to do."

They all worked side by side, discussing the ins and the outs of the design, Nogmi engineering techniques being discussed with the Humans gave new insights into ways they could reinforce structural design. They continued assessing how much more material they would need, and the number of hands they would need to complete it. Some of the engineers already had mages, that aided in their crafting, which made it much easier to work on more dangerous or unreachable areas.

Arlo and Lucy watched on giving their input here and there. They felt mostly out of place, but were impressed by the knowledge in the room. But as a couple hours passed, they grew uninterested in the foundational workings and debates between the engineers.

One of the engineers had questioned the structural integrity of a particularly bold choice. Alf's explanation seemed to drag on when the door to the room burst open again.

"You see," Alf had explained moments before, his hands waving to emphasize his point, "it's all about balance, like walking a tightrope while juggling flaming swords, your Auntie Mertle, all while wearing your skibbies. You might think it's risky, but if you get the balance exactly right, it's a remarkable sight! And trust me, thi-"

All eyes were on the door, as Paladin Danladin, burst into the room. His clanging armor interrupting any conversation presently occurring. "The King will see you now, follow me, Professor Bertrum included."

The older engineer among the group was surprised at first to hear his own name be called out. But nodded in agreement, lining up with Sorren, Arlo, Lucy, and Alf to join the King's chamber.

The group followed the Paladin through the winding corridors of the palace, the echoes of their footsteps mingling with the distant hum of activity from within the walls. Arlo brought up the rear, his thoughts heavy with considerations of the proposed path before them. He glanced at Sorren, who appeared confident and held himself high. Arlo could see the admiration for the Paladin in the younger man's footsteps. Alf, was still buzzed and amazed at the excitement from the other engineers and continued the conversation with Bertrum as they walked. Lucy on the other hand, wore a troubled look. Her gaze lost in the distance. He picked up glances over her shoulder as they occasionally turned corners or passed a niche.

He wasn't alone in his thoughts, but now was not the time or place to discuss with her either. King Frederick did not seem like a man who liked to be kept waiting, 'spoiled,' Arlo thought to himself. But the King's faults spurred more thoughts in his mind, of the people of Davenport, Fall Lake, Cyril and the rest of Shularix. How many loved ones were lost in what felt like an eternity ago, yet was only several days. Venturing to the remembrance of the people just outside the palace, speaking of ill omens, and apocalyptic events. How many lives were cut too short, how many families devastated, how many now without homes. The weight of their struggles were carried with him as he walked the hall, and he knew this was a moment when he had to speak his truth.

A set of intricately carved wooden doors marked their arrival, Paladin Danladin pushed them open with a swift, practiced motion, and just like he did earlier made his grand appearance. They were not in the same room as before, instead this chamber was grand, with soaring ceilings adorned with tapestries depicting the history of the Zenarian leadership. One side held the faces of royalty past, the other of the former Archbishops and Paladins. The blank spaces waited to be filled whenever a new member of the kingdom's line took their place. The King himself stood near a large window, his gaze enamored by the horizon where the river and land met the sky. He turned as they entered, his expression calm and emotionless.

"Your Majesty," Danladin announced, bowing deeply before stepping aside to allow the group to enter.

King Frederick nodded in acknowledgement, his gaze sweeping over each of them before settling on Sorren.

"You've brought the plans for the ship?" he asked, his voice steady but carrying the weight of expectations.

"Yes, Your Majesty," Sorren replied, ushering Alf to step forward and present the rolled blueprints. "We've made significant progress, and with the help of your engineers, we believe we can complete the project in just over three weeks, if manpower and material are provided."

The King took the blueprints, but before he could unroll them, Arlo cleared his throat and stepped forward. All eyes turned to him, including the King's who raised an eyebrow at the unexpected interruption.

"King Frederick," Arlo began, his voice firm and respectful, "before we delve into the details of the ship, there's something else I need to address, something that concerns the people of this land, especially those in Fall Lake."

The King's expression shifted slightly, curiosity replacing the initial surprise. "Go on," he said, gesturing for Arlo to continue.

Arlo took a deep breath, steadying himself. "The people… they're suffering, Your Majesty. They've faced loss, destruction, and uncertainty, and they need a leader they can see, one they can trust. They believe that you're hiding behind these walls, leaving them to fend for themselves. I've heard them, seen the fear in their eyes. They need to know that someone is willing to stand for them, not just in word, but in action and presence."

The room grew tense as Arlo's words hung in the air. The Kingsguard and Danladin each reacted in unison as if practiced in the event that one would speak outwardly to their king. Their weapons were ready to be drawn to defend or apprehend Arlo as soon as the time came.

Lucy shifted uncomfortably, Sorren nodded at Arlo's words with surprise and admiration. But the King's gaze hardened on Arlo as the gravity of the words ate at him. Time stretched as Frederick stared at Arlo. It was hard to tell if his face held anger, or disgust.

Frederick placed the blueprints onto a nearby table and approached Arlo. Danladin adjacent to the king as the distance faded. Arlo's heart raced, and although he felt like he was sweating from ear to ear, he held the gaze against King Frederick, neither man willing to back down.

Lucy felt a roaring flame building inside of her, her foot moving forward to stand by Arlo before Sorren's arm intercepted her path. She looked up to him, only to see his head shake slightly. Alf and Bertrum both took a step back, not wishing to be caught in whatever cross-fire was ready to start.

Arlo's conviction did not waver. His blue eyes were met by the King's, they stood eye to eye, peering into the depths of each other's souls.

"You speak boldly, Arlo," the king said, ending the silence, his voice carrying an edge of caution. "But do you understand the weight of what you're saying? I have responsibilities, a kingdom to protect. The decisions I make are not always understood by those who do not carry the burden of rule. And yet you speak to me like I am unaware of the state my kingdom is in."

Arlo nodded, the pain in his body deepening, as whispers rose in his head. Hopes. Dreams. Cries. Pleas. He stood in the battlefield as all around him was destroyed by the monster, he heard their screams, he heard their begging, he heard their wishes.

"I do understand, but the burden is not yours alone to bear. The people, Your People, are strong, but they need guidance. They need to see that there are others with them, especially now. The ship is important, yes, but without the faith of your people, even the greatest ship will sail on troubled waters."

The room fell silent again. Frederick and Arlo's eyes did not separate as the King, as if weighing the truth of his words against the mantle of responsibility. "We stand on the edge of a war, and we don't even know who the true enemy is. Candurill and the Aevoridge family are likely behind it, but that creature was of Draconis descent. I know it. The weight of this responsibility has settled on me since my father's passing eighty years ago. You stand before your King ready to claim his rule as being insufficient, acts of treason are met with imprisonment, and in some cases... beheading. Guards."

At the mention of their names, the guards immediately surrounded Arlo, whose grip tightened around the hammer resting near his feet.

"If this is the cost of speaking, so be it."

Lucy let out a gasp, her eyes narrowing and slowly fading from emerald to a fiery crimson.

Sorren felt a chill crawl up his spine as the King's command echoed through the hall. Arlo stood his ground, defiance etched in every line of his face, his grip tighter around the hammer's hilt yet he did not draw it... yet. The air between the two men crackled with unspoken tension, a war of wills fought in silence. Sorren could see the storm brewing in Arlo's eyes, a flash of blue, ready to break and spark outward as he had witnessed before.

"Hand over your weapon," Danladin declared, his voice firm and unyielding.

Arlo's jaw clenched. "You think this will save you?" His voice was low but carried the weight of a thunderclap. "Do you really believe that hiding behind walls and orders will protect your people? The enemy is already at our doorstep. While you sit here planning, they are preparing to strike. Your people need a leader, not a coward who trembles at the sight of danger."

The words hung in the air like a sword over the king's head. Sorren felt his heart pounding in his chest, torn between loyalty to the crown and his deity, and the undeniable truth in Arlo's words. He could see Lucy out of the corner of his eyes, her breath coming in short, sharp bursts. Her hand twitched, and to Sorren's horror, a small flame flickered to life in her palm, barely noticeable, but undeniable.

A thin line of blood trickled down her cheek in a crimson tear. Sorren's mind raced. This wasn't the Lucy he knew. Something darker was surfacing, something she had kept hidden, and this moment was only fanning the flames within. Panic flared in his chest as he struggled to decide what to do.

Danladin's gaze flicked to Sorren, his eyes sharp as the steel of his massive sword. "Sorren, keep her back."

The order snapped Sorren into action. He stepped closer to Lucy, placing a hand on her shoulder. "Lucy," he whispered, his voice trembling with urgency and worry of what was to happen next. "You have to calm down."

But she was unfazed by his words. Her gaze locked onto the king and the guards surrounding Arlo. Her breaths were growing more erratic, less stable, the flame in her hand growing with the flames in her eyes. Sorren tightened his grip on her shoulders, and could feel the heat radiating from her. "Lucy, please."

Her eyes snapped to his, and for a moment he saw the wild fear there, and confusion, and what he thought was the shape of a flaming figure turning away deep in their depths. Then the flame in her hand dimmed and flickered out of existence. The blood continued to trickle, but her breathing began to slow. She blinked, as if waking from a nightmare, and the darkness in her eyes receded.

"Sorren… Arlo…" She breathed, her voice barely a whisper.

Sorren exhaled a breath he hadn't realized he was holding. He turned his head to look at Arlo and guided Lucy away from the situation. "We have to stay out of it." He told her, feeling more directed at himself than anything.

The tension grew even more as one of the guards moved forward, their weapons drawn, and aimed at Arlo. "Hand over the hammer," one of them barked with authority.

Arlo hesitated, his eyes flickering between the guards and the king. His grip hurt around the hammer's hilt, the pain as strong as the strange bruising that plagued his body. Whispers continued to flow within his head, voices, pleads, cries, and wishes. The wood beneath the hammer began to creak under the pressure as a small crack began to form. Arlo let go of his grip and waved his hand forward towards it.

"You are still making a mistake," Arlo said with a quiet intensity.

Frederick's jaw tightened and his eyes hardened, ready to order the guards to drag Arlo away. Yet he did not speak. Something in the room held his tongue.

"This weapon isn't just a tool, but a symbol of strength we need to face what is coming. If you take it from me, you're not just disarming a man… you're disarming hope."

The guard sneered, reaching out to take the hammer. But as his fingers wrapped around the handle, his expression changed from confidence to confusion. The hammer refused to budge. The guard grunted, pulling harder, but the hammer seemed to fuse to the ground, immovable.

Another guard stepped forward, then another, each attempting to lift the hammer, and each failing. Disbelief spread among the faces of the guards as more and more joined in, each trying to raise the weapon in unison and separately.

Danladin's eyes narrowed as he watched the scene unfold. "Enough!" he barked. Shoving the guards aside and stepping in front of Arlo, "What witchcraft is this, Arlo? Stop whatever trickery you are playing at!"

Arlo's gaze remained steady, unyielding, and held the presence of a calm intentional storm. "There is no trickery here, Danladin. If you can't lift the hammer, ask yourself why."

The king's face twisted in frustration. Turning sharply to Arlo, his voice a low growl, yet a spark of something else shifted in his look. "Lift it." He demanded calmly.

Arlo did not hesitate. He reached down, his fingers closing around the hammer's hilt. The weapon rose as if it weighed nothing at all. He held it aloft, the metal glinting in the torchlight, a silent challenge to the king and his court.

The hall fell into a stunned silence. Even Danladin, seemed at a loss for words. Finally after what felt like an eternity, the king spoke, his voice devoid of its earlier harshness and now replaced with a newfound respect. "It seems that Heir himself favors you, Arlo," he said, his gaze still locked onto the hammer. "Perhaps there is more to your words than I first realized."

Arlo lowered the hammer, but his grip on it remained firm. "This isn't just about me, Your Majesty. It's about the people, your people. They need more than a king who issues orders from behind his walls. They need someone who will stand beside them, bleed with them, and be a beacon that they can rally behind."

Frederick's expression softened slightly, the weight of his crown felt less like a symbol and more like a stone on his head. He looked around the room, at his guards, at Paladin Danladin, and finally back to Arlo and his friends. "You speak of things that are difficult for a king to hear, but necessary all the same. You are right, Arlo. The people need to see their king not as a distant figure, but as one who is willing to share their struggles."

He turned to Danladin, who nodded in silent agreement. The paladin's earlier hostility melted away, replaced by a curious and hesitant respect.

"Thank you, Your Majesty. Together, we can give the people hope, and with that hope, we can face whatever darkness is coming."

Frederick nodded in return, the faintest hint of a smile on his lips. "You have my word, Arlo. We will face this together."

The tension in the room eased. The guards lowered their weapons, but the unease remained in their eyes. No one there would forget what they had just seen.

Sorren let out a sigh of relief, releasing his hand on Lucy's shoulder. She had calmed down, the flicker of flames in her eyes fully extinguished, though the blood on her cheek remained a stark reminder of the momentary loss of control. Arlo moved next to them, and offered to wipe the blood from her cheek.

The king straightened, his regal demeanor returning. "Let us direct ourselves to the matters at hand first. I will change my plans and leave for Fall Lake tomorrow morning, Arlo, Sorren, Lucy I would like for the three of you to join me as I address the people of Davenport before my departure. Danladin, will you spread word through the city that I will have a declaration tomorrow morning, and for all to be in attendance at the docks." Danladin nodded, his gaze lingering on Arlo briefly before he turned to leave the room.

"Now, let us look over this vessel, and the plans you have." His voice holding a newfound resolve. The group followed the king to the large table where Alf and Sorren's plans were spread out. The engineer, who had been nervously watching the entire exchange, joined in the explanation of the ship and what changes they have decided to make. The king listened intently, nodding occasionally, his expression growing more determined and pleased at what he was hearing.

Finally, after thorough explanations, the king nodded. "This will do," he said. "I have already ordered material, we will begin construction immediately. Sorren, Alfonze, you will have the backing of our engineers and laborers to build this ship, some of our mages that are still on hand can assist where needed." His look landed on Arlo, "Tomorrow morning, I will make a public declaration, a promise to our people. I want each of you to stand with me when I do, together we will bring the town together in an effort to build the finest vessel the world has seen."

Sorren exchanged a glance with Arlo and Lucy, sensing the shift in the king's demeanor. They had sparked something in him, Arlo specifically, something that he hoped would change the course of their future. The conversations continued for a short while, working out some of the finer details, Sorren mentioning that he even had already planned a regal cabin meant for anyone of authority or importance that the king found appreciated and pleased with.

But the night grew closer, and the group dispersed, Arlo felt a weight lifting off of him as they left the halls of the Palace, and joined back to the fresh air of the water, the sounds of seagulls squawking nearby, and the hustle and bustle of the towns nightlife. But while the weight of his thoughts and desire to see the kingdom be led as it should be, his body ached him even more so.

They led their way back to the vessel and the storage space where Alf and his brothers began to discuss the changes that would be made and the new order of things as the engineers would assist them. The rest of the group, looked to the evening and night and sought to claim a room at Mama Gretta's.

The inn and tavern was bustling, as usual with this time of night. Plenty of individuals seeking to lose the struggles of their daily lives for a moment of reprieve if only for a short while.

Sorren, ever the social butterfly, found himself naturally drawn to the lively atmosphere of Mama Gretta's. With a grin that could charm the scales off of a Draconis, he mingled effortlessly among the patrons, exchanging flirtatious banter and rounds of drinks with anyone that was up for a good time. It was his way of unwinding, of grounding himself in the simple pleasures of life amidst whatever turmoil he was put against.

Arlo, however, was not in the mood for revelry. The weight of the day's events pressed heavier on him. He had spoken his mind to the King, and perhaps made a difference to the people of Davenport, and Zenaria as a kingdom. But he knew there was more to come, and for whatever reason he was thrust into the middle of it with the hammer. "I think I'm going to turn in for the night," he said, his voice quiet. He gave Sorren a brief nod, knowing his friend would be just fine without him. Lucy, who had been quietly enjoying her food and drink and observing the festivities around her, hesitated but followed Arlo's lead.

"I'll head up too," she said, her voice barely audible above the lively tavern. There was something in her tone, a hint of unease that Arlo didn't miss. They made their way upstairs, the noise of the tavern fading as they ascended to the quieter, more secluded rooms. When they reached the hallway that led to their rooms, Lucy paused, turning to Arlo with worry on her face.

"Arlo," she began, her voice shaking, "I... I'm worried about everything that is going on. With what we are getting into with the King, my missing memory, the dreams I've been having. I've had them every night and they get more and more vivid, and I just don't know what to do." She pulled at her arm with the other, doubt pouring on her face as she looked down to the floor. Arlo saw the worry in her voice, in her eyes, but he was unsure of what to do for her, as he was in the same position. Everything continued to get deeper and heavier, how long before they were flooded with responsibilities not exactly their own but they were forced to claim because it was the right thing to do.

"I'm right here, Lucy," he reassured her, placing a comforting hand on her shoulder. "If anything happens, if you need anything, just call for me. I'll be there." A small spark of blue hidden to the naked eye sent a calming chill throughout her body.

She nodded, a small, grateful smile tugging at the corner of her lips. "Thank you, Arlo. It means a lot to know that you're here."

They parted ways, Lucy entering her room while Arlo stepped into his own. He closed the door behind him and took a deep breath, trying to shake off the lingering tension of the day. He needed to clear his mind, to focus on what lay ahead and what exactly his part was in it. He wanted to try something, to find a way to possibly do all of those things at once.

He settled onto the floor, legs crossed over each other, while he was never one to meditate, he wondered if it would help him attune with everything. So he centered his thoughts on the hammer that lay in his lap, and cleared his struggles from his mind.

The room around him faded away, replaced by a vast field of blue flowers that swayed gently in an unseen breeze. The air was charged with energy, mana freely flowed around him pulsing in rhythm with his heartbeat. He could feel it, the raw power within him, sparking outward in tendrils of blue lightning that danced across the field.

He made attempts to call it, to control it, wielding it around his fingertips, then within his entire hand, then up his arm. The strength it possessed was new to him, yet felt so natural all the same. Uncertainty filled him next when he witnessed a figure of gold in the distance, its form indistinct but radiating an aura of strength. Arlo tried to focus on it, to draw closer, but as quickly as it had appeared, the figure began to fade leaving behind a tendril of gold that faded away into a purple mist.

He reached out, trying to hold onto his vision as the scene around him began to shift, the blue flowers wilting and the sky darkened with storm clouds. Buildings grew around him, and people of different descents lined the streets in festivity. He was back in Fall Lake, the revelry around him fading as the shadow of a monstrous figure loomed over the buildings. The sound of people calling for help filled his ears, a desperate chorus he couldn't shut out.

Arlo began to run away from the creature, witnessing sparks, flames, and debris being tossed around him. Bodies lay lifeless on the ground surrounding him. He saw a family ahead. He recognized them, a woman and her two children. His mouth moved, but no sound came as he tried to call out to them, grabbing them by the hand to lead them to safety.

The scene shifted again, Arlo's feet continuing to run as if he was not even controlling them anymore. He followed a blue tendril, leading up the hill to where his small cottage way. The beast causing wreckage throughout the city and leading its way towards him. He ran, their hopes and prayers snagging in his chest like barbs. Everyone he passed tried to speak, then blurred and vanished, leaving only the ruin the Draconis-like creature made of them.

The scene continued to change as he climbed a tower, following the tendril of blue mana. While he felt like he was following it... at the same time he felt as if he was the one guiding it. His feet burning as he ran up the spiral staircase of the lookout tower, something designed to be a focal point to lookout on the new city of Fall Lake, to look out on the lake and see the small towns that were across it. But as he made his way to the top, there was only one sight he was given. A devastating view, the city entirely destroyed, he watched and looked over the various pieces he had aided in building. The castle walls, the residential district, an area a friend of his claimed for his smith house, all of it left behind as burning rubble. The cause, centered upon the town, its eyes locked onto the one building left standing, the same one Arlo now stood upon. The creature ran, and Arlo could feel the presence of the blue mana around him, he could feel it sparking up his legs, his torso and arms, and could feel it encompassing his entire being, the strength of raw energy within his hand, and as the creature came closer he was ready to pounce. But as he pounced the scene shifted again, the sky now an ominous red.

Bodies littered around him, as he stood tall, the hammer high above his head. A woman, crimson red hair, emerald green eyes, and two blackened stumps on her back kneeled before him. Her eyes filled with a dark intent, the woman screamed a piercing scream that pierced him to the core.

The scream tore him out of the vision. His eyes snapped open, breath ragged, and only then did he realize the sound was not in his head. It was coming from the next room. Lucy's room.

Without hesitation, he bolted to her door, bursting into the room to find her thrashing in her bed, tears streaming down her face as she cried out in terror.

Her voice was dark and otherworldly but as he leaned over to calm her as he called out to her, her eyes were filled with dark flames and she looked him directly in the eyes. "Ripping my wings away won't stop anything."

"Lucy, I'm here."

Her eyes quickly faded, the thrashing ended, but her breath was still ragged as she tried to process her surroundings. When she saw Arlo, she broke down, sobbing uncontrollably. "It was horrible, Arlo," she choked out between sobs. "There were people... so many people... and they were all dead because of me. And that figure, the one in armor, he was there again with the hammer in his hands."

Arlo's heart sank at her words, a cold dread sitting in the pit of his stomach. He held her close, whispering soothing words as she cried into his shoulder. "It's not real, Lucy. Just a nightmare. Whatever it is, we will face it together, okay? You're not alone."

She nodded, her sobs gradually subsiding as she clung to him. After a few moments, she pulled back, wiping at her tear-streaked face. "I'm sorry, Arlo. I didn't mean to wake you."

"Don't apologize, I'd rather you wake me than go through this alone."

"Thank you," she whispered with a shaky smile of gratitude. "I don't know how I would get through this without you."

"Get some rest Lucy, I'll be right here if you need me."

She nodded, lying back down as Arlo tucked the blankets around her. He stayed by her side until her breathing evened out, the tension finally leaving her body as she drifted back to sleep. He sat beside the bed, his mind heavy with the thoughts of the visions he had seen and what she had told him. He couldn't shake the feeling that there was something more, something he was missing.

He stayed by her side until her breathing evened out. Only then did he let his eyes close. And the echoes of his vision slipped in after him, waiting.

CHAPTER 20

First light of dawn broke over the horizon, slowly bathing the docks of Davenport in a warm, golden hue that reflected off the gentle waves lapping at the shore. The morning air, crisp with the promise of a new day, carried the unmistakable briny scent of the sea mixed with the earthy aroma of wet wood from the docks. Seabirds circled above, their calls echoing like a chorus welcoming the dawn. Already, the town was a hive of activity, with fishers hauling in their early catches, merchants setting up their stalls, and children chasing each other through the cobblestone streets, their laughter a brief respite from the tension that gripped the town. Yet despite the hustle and bustle, there was a sense of collective anticipation, as all eyes were slowly drawn to the raised platform in the town square, where King Frederick would soon address his people. The sunlight caught on the royal banners that flanked the platform, their vibrant colors a sharp contrast to the somber mood that lingered in the air, a mood as heavy and unyielding as the thick morning fog that had yet to fully dissipate.

The devastation at Fall Lake was fresh in everyone's mind, the memory of that horrific day etched into their hearts. There was an unspoken fear in the air, a shared anxiety that clung to the people like a shadow the same as it had the past week.

As the crowd continued to gather, the king's entourage made their way to the platform. King Frederick, his regal bearing as imposing as ever, was flanked by his Kingsguard, each one a towering figure in gleaming armor. Archbishop Dolph, with his cold and calculating gaze, walked beside the king, his presence commanding respect and fear in equal measure, a factor that was only increased as the stoic Paladin Danladin stood tall behind them both.

Among them stood Lucy, Arlo, and Sorren, each bearing their own burden as they approached the platform. Sorren was calm and collected, wearing his finest armor that gleamed in the morning light, each polished plate a testament to his superiors that he was ready to stand with the kingdom's most prominent figures.

Lucy however was less at ease. Her eyes sharp and alert, darting amongst the crowd, catching every movement, every shift in demeanor, and look, seeking for anyone familiar in the crowd. But aside from her own predicament, she felt out of place, like a pawn in a game she did not fully understand, sure the emerald dress that had been given to her caught the attention of many individuals of the crowd and would have anyone ready to listen to her authority.

Arlo on the other hand, felt consumed by burdens. His heart was heavy with the knowledge of what was to come, each step toward the platform felt like he was sinking deeper and deeper into something he was not ready for. He was pleased in a way, that the king had listened to his words and chosen to stand before his people in such a public display, but with every eye in Davenport now turning toward them, he could not shake the unease that twisted in his gut, that some inevitable, and unseen fate was swiftly approaching. The weight of responsibility bore down on him, and though he tried to hide it, the tension was evident in the stiffness of his shoulders and the tightness of his grip on the hammer.

As they approached the platform, the crowd fell into a hushed silence, each of them clinging to the outcome that was coming. The king ascended the steps, a grave expression placed upon his face as he faced the masses of people. Many of which were no native to Davenport, but refuges of Fall Lake and the surrounding area that fled the area for one reason or another.

King Frederick raised his hand, and the silence screeched to a halt. Breaths held in anticipation that would only be set free whenever their leader finally spoke. He stood and looked over the crowd, his people. His voice was clear and powerful, crawling over the assembled crowd with the authority of a man who had ruled for decades.

"Citizens of Davenport, faithful followers of the Zenarian monarchy," he started, his voice serious, "we find ourselves on the edge, burdened by the sorrow of the calamity that occurred in Fall Lake. The lives lost, the immense devastation, it weighs on us all. And yet, we cannot allow despair to take root in our hearts."

He paused, allowing his words to sink in, his gaze sweeping over the crowd. The people listened intently, their faces a mixture of hope and sorrow. Whispers amongst the crowd filling the area with doubt.

The first cheer that answered him was small. Then another rose. Then a dozen more. Arlo watched the sound move through the square until it soon became no sound at all, but immense pressure. Frederick straightened within it. The years on his face did not vanish, yet something in him sharpened, like the faith of the crowd had found armor beneath old skin and fastened it tight around him.

"Know this," the king continued, his strengthened voice silencing the crowd once more, "those responsible for this heinous act will be brought to justice. My heart goes out to the families who have lost loved ones, for they were my own brothers, sisters, sons, daughters, mothers, and fathers alike. And I swear to you, by the gods, and by my honor as your king, that I will not rest until those who perpetrated this atrocity have been avenged."

The crowds whispers spurred once more in response, collective grief finding a voice in the king's words. But there was something else there too, a lingering doubt, fear that through the king's words would not be enough to protect them.

"We are a people forged in the crucible of adversity. Our history is one of resilience, of standing strong in the face of overwhelming odds. A century ago, my father fought his final battle at the end of the Hassien war. I was only sixteen when the Cleaving took him from us and placed the ruins of our kingdom on my shoulders. We lost families. We lost homes. We lost sister kingdoms. Our hopes were dashed, our country was broken, and through unity we took the ashes of three kingdoms and stood together. Through that unity, Zenaria endured. Through that belief, we rebuilt. This new threat will be faced the same way, together, united in our resolve and unyielding in our pursuit of justice."

Many of the members of the crowd cheered at the King's words, while others stressed their concerns. They lost the city to one monster, how would the other cities hold if another of these beasts strikes again.

The people wanted to believe, thirsting for safety, but the weight of the recent tragedy had shaken their faith.

"This new ship we are building," the king pressed on, his voice firm, "is more than just a vessel, a symbol of our determination. It represents our commitment to defending our lands, to standing against those who would seek to destroy us. This ship will be the mightiest we have ever constructed, a strength in our dark times."

The crowd responded with scattered applause, but the energy was short lived, many of the naysayers were eager to stress their concerns. Their doubts were not outweighed by the king's words, as they held onto the shadow of fear over them.

From the back of the crowd, a voice rang out unexpectedly, but bolstered either by the quiet as the king went to resume his speech, or through the strength of the words themselves. " What good is a ship if we cannot protect our people? We need more than promises, and floating wood, more than symbols! We need action!"

The king's eyes narrowed as he searched the crowd for the outburst. The crowd cheering to their fellows words. The Archbishop stepped forward after waiting for his moment. He had seen the growing discontent in the crowd, felt the tension that crackled in the air like a gathering storm. Now, as he stepped forward, his cold eyes swept over the people, measuring their fear, their anger, their desperation.

"My children," Dolph began, his voice smooth and commanding, "do not let your hearts be clouded by doubt. Heir and his fellow gods watch over us, and their will is clear. This tragedy is a test, a trial of our faith, of our strength as a singular people. And we must not fail."

His words carefully chosen, each one plucked to soothe the crowd while subtly reinforcing their alliance on the church. The people were still shook from the king's speech, but listened in the low speak amongst each other.

"The king has spoken true, our hearts broken for those who took their final breaths at Fall Lake." Dolph continued, his tone shifting to one of grave sincerity. "But know this, the church stands with you, working tirelessly to provide aid, to heal the wounded, and to bring comfort to the grieving. We are not idle in this time of crisis. Heir is with us all."

There were nods of agreement in the crowd, but the underlying unease remained. Each speech, spoke to a different person but they were not all united, nor swayed and eased at their words.

"And yet," Dolph's voice took on a darker edge, "we must be vigilant. There are forces at work in this world, dark and malevolent forces that seek to destroy all that we hold dear. The Elfar, and possibly the Draconis, they are our enemies, lurking in the shadows, high amongst their mountains, or deep within their woods, and they are waiting for the moment to strike."

Fear and anger rippled through the crowd at the mention of the opposed forces. The air grew more volatile, whispers and cries more desperate as the wildfire of gossip spread.

"These are the times that try men's souls. But we must not give in to fear. Instead, we must place our trust in Heir himself, in his fellow gods, in the divine order of Zenith that has been established. Through our faith, we will find the strength to overcome any obstacle, as Heir provide us the miracles and ability to overcome."

The crowd's mood shifted, their fear and anger mingling with desperation for something to believe in. Dolph saw it from miles away. "Let us not forget, that we are not alone in this struggle. The church stands with you, as does the crown. Together, we will face these challenges, and we shall emerge stronger for it!"

The crowd's response remained uncertain, fear not fully extinguished. Dolph decided to press his words more, he needed to give them something more, something... or someone to rally behind.

"There is one among us," Dolph announced, his voice taking on a note of triumph, "who has already proved his valor in the face of this great evil. One who has been graced by Heir himself, gifted with the power of Heir to strike down the beast at Fall Lake and saved countless lives."

Echoes of words spread through the crowd, whispers from survivors of the one whom leapt from a tower and downed the beast. Many believed it to be just a legend, some believed it was the Paladin himself. Their interest was piqued, their rumors made official, soon they would be given a face and a name.

"Arlo Devine," The name was spoken with a deliberate weight, and Dolph's gaze locked onto Arlo, who stood among the king's entourage. "Step forward."

The Archbishop's words hung in the air, each syllable seemingly stretching time itself. Ripples of chatter echoed throughout the onlookers, an undercurrent of unease. Arlo's name fell like a hammer, shattering the fragile silence that was constantly waiting to be broken.

Arlo's heart pounded in his chest as the eyes of the crowd turned toward him. He hadn't expected this, hadn't wanted this. The leap at the beast at Fall Lake had been a desperate act of survival, to aid the cries of the people around him, it was no bid for glory. And yet here he was, being thrust into the spotlight, his deeds laid bare for all to see.

Reluctantly, Arlo stepped forward, feeling the weight of the moment pressing down on him. He opened his mouth, hesitation taking over soul, words caught in his throat. For a moment, doubt ate away at his confidence, all of the people of Davenport, for all he knew the entire kingdom, stood before him. Waiting, and ready for what he has to say. But as he met the expectant eyes of the people, he found a spark of resolve.

Lucy and Sorren exchange a glance, a silent conversation passing between them. Lucy's brow furrowed, confusion and concern flickering in her eyes as she searched Sorren's face for answers. Sorren was already calculating, the wheels of his mind turning as he tried to decipher the archbishop's true intentions. Was this a trap? A test? His gaze held hers for a moment longer, offering her a smile and a nod, what little reassurance he could muster.

Faces within the crowd were etched with fear, desperation, disbelief, and a faint glimmer that they were searching for something just a little bit more… He knew he could not walk away now, these people needed something more to believe in, something to rally behind. And right now, that something was him.

He took a deep breath, voice quiet at first as it broke through the impenetrable wall of hesitation, the pounding of his heart ready to escape his chest louder than any words he had. But his voice grew stronger, louder, with every word.

"I'm not a man of gods, and I don't pretend to have the answers to the darkness that has befallen us. But I do know this, hope is not

194

something that can be given to us from above. It's something that WE forge in the fires of our shared struggles, in the face of our greatest fears. It is born from our will to fight, to stand together, to refuse to let darkness consume us."

The crowd was quiet, hanging on his every word. Arlo felt a shift in the air, he wasn't quite sure yet what it was. "Hope is not a thing to be given," he repeated, more softly now, "but a thing we create, a flame we kindle in our hearts, and it is that flame that guides us and bonds us together."

The looming fear seemed to fade away as the crowd began to nod, pleased whispers, and joyful agreements.

"When I stood before that beast, I wasn't thinking of glory or victory. I was thinking of the people who needed someone, who needed their neighbors, friends, family. The people that needed at least one person to stand with them and act. It wasn't some divine power that gave me strength, but *Hope,* hope that we could still make a difference, that there will always be a future worth living for."

Confidence swelled within his chest, bolstering his voice. The people's words clinging to every passionate word, his speech was filled with conviction that he hadn't realized he possessed. He began to walk amongst the stage, the people rallied with him.

"Hope isn't just a word, it's a weapon. It's the light you find that pushes back the darkness, strength that lifts us when we're beaten down. Hope binds us together, makes us stronger together, forging us to be more powerful together."

King Frederick's smile was a mask, carefully practiced as any king should be in not displaying his true thoughts and intentions. Archbishop Dolph held a similar masked smile, a bead of sweat betraying his nerves, fingers tightened around his staff, knuckles whitening as he fought to keep his composure.

King Frederick kept his practiced smile, the kind every king wore when the crowd chose a new favorite. Archbishop Dolph's looked the same at a glance, but his eyes had gone flat and measuring.

This wasn't how he'd meant it to go.

Arlo's words kept rolling, and with each roar of approval from the crowd, Dolph could almost feel the scaffolding of his careful plans shift. A hero of the people was useful, so long as he remembered who held the reins.

Dolph's fingers tightened on his staff until his knuckles went white.

'We'll have to be careful with this one', he thought, and the smile on his lips never moved.

"We're not just survivors," Arlo declared.

"We are fighters, builders, dreamers. We are the hope that refuses to be extinguished, a fire that refuses to die out. And as long as we stand together, as long as we hold onto that hope, no darkness can conquer us."

He paused, his eyes sweeping over the cheering crowd, meeting their gazes one by one. He was filled with energy at this point, something stronger than the pure raw mana he had learned to harness the night before. This feeling was more intense, yet he felt connected to every man, woman, and child that stood before him. His pain had faded away, the bruises subsided as he stood energized with the people of Davenport.

"Remember this, we are the light in the darkness. We are the hope that endures. And together, we will stand tall."

Arlo raised the hammer high into the air, a bolt of lightning cracked through the sky, striking the weapon with a blinding flash. The crowd gasped, then erupted into cheers, their voices a roaring wave that echoed across the docks, and what felt like the entire world. The spark of lightning had not just struck the hammer, it had struck their hearts, igniting a flame of hope that burned brighter than ever before.

Arlo stood upon the wooden platform, the hammer still raised as he stood as a symbol of hope before the crowd. Their energy surging around him as remaining crackles of lightning sparked off along the ground. Unknowingly to himself, he had begun to become something more than just a man. He had become a symbol, a beacon of hope in a world that desperately needed it.

And the words he had spoken,

"We are the light in the darkness, we are the hope that endures. And together, we will stand tall."

Those words would be remembered, repeated, and passed down through generations, a rallying cry that would spread for many years to come.

King Frederick stepped forward, his expression one of pleased surprise. He placed a hand on Arlo's shoulder, his voice filled with approval but only quiet enough for the two to hear. "You've given these people hope when they needed it most. And for that, you have my thanks."

The king turned to the crowd, his voice strong and commanding. "Let that day be remembered! Not just a day of tragedy, but as a day of hope, of unity, of strength! We will rebuild, we will fight, and we will emerge victorious!"

The crowd's cheer roared in response, fear, doubt and despair washed away by the tide of hope that surged through them. They had their king, they had their hero, and now they felt that they had a future to fight for.

The ship carrying the king set sail, the cheers of the crowd echoed across the water, carrying with them the hope that had been reignited in their hearts. Arlo watched the ship disappear over the horizon, his mind racing with the weight of what had just happened. As people and faces that he would not soon forget approached him. Thanking him for what he had done. Offering him praise and reward for so strongly showing an act of blind faith.

Dolph's ploy had backfired, in a way. He had thrust Arlo into a position of power and influence, but it was clear that the archbishop had not anticipated the strength of the response. The people now looked to Arlo not just a shero, but as a leader, a role he never wanted, but could no longer refuse.

The crowd began to disperse, the king's vessel sailed off towards Fall Lake. Dolph returned to the church to provide healing to the remaining wounded. Left behind was Arlo, Lucy, and Sorren who had begun to head to the warehouse where Sorren's ship was stored, their journey through being approached by many of the residents and refuges giving their thanks. Several survivors of Fall Lake approached him, tears in their eyes, thanking him for his sacrifice for what he had done.

"Best damn speech I ever heard, who knew you had that in ya," Sorren said with a massive grin.

"It was truly inspiring," Lucy added, "I don't know that Dolph meant to put you in that position, but I think it was what the crowd needed. You're a natural leader."

"Aye, that he is."

"I'm no leader," Arlo added, "Just a man who did the right thing."

As they approached the warehouse, the sound of hammers striking metal and the murmur of voices echoed through the open doors. The scent of sawdust and fresh timber filled the air, mixing with the salty breeze that drifted in from the harbor. Inside, a small army of engineers and laborers were already hard at work, their efforts focused on turning the skeletal frame of the ship into a vessel worthy of the voyage ahead.

The structure dominated the center of the warehouse. The skill of the three Nogmi brothers was well on display and many of the engineers seemed pleased at the actual progress they were beginning work on. The framework was sturdy and reinforced, but much remained to be done. The masts were yet to be erected, the decking needed to be laid, and the interior quarters were still a chaotic tangle of beams and questionable scaffolding.

Sorren's eyes swept the entire area, his face a mixture of pride and excitement. "We've got a long way to go, but with help like this we'll have her ready in no time."

"Afternoon, lads and lassie!" came a booming voice from somewhere above. Arlo and Lucy looked up to see Alf perched upside down, his lopsided grin and dangling hat making him look like a jovial acrobat.

"Alf," Sorren called back with an eager grin and a wave, "how's progress?"

"Steady as she goes!" Alf replied, pulling himself upright. "We've got our plan set, the crew's all geared up and ready to knock this beauty together. Just waitin' on the magic folk to show, and we'll be right as rain in the Roxstone."

Arlo couldn't help but smile at the Nogmi's infectious enthusiasm. Despite his eccentric appearance and carefree attitude, Alf had surely shown his talents at shipbuilding, and his brothers were just as skilled in their own right, even with all of their quirks.

Lucy's eyes sparkled with determination. "Looks like you could use an extra set of hands! Where can I pitch in?"

She ran up to one of the Wicket brothers, who was busy overseeing a group of laborers. She grabbed a few unfamiliar tools and began to make herself useful, despite her lack of expertise. The sight of her earnest effort brought a hearty laugh from the crew.

"Well, if it ain't a sight for sore eyes," Wicket chuckled, shaking his head. "Just mind those tools now, lass. They might be tricky if you're not used to 'em."

Willy, the lankier brother, glanced up from adjusting a complex mechanism. "Looks like we've got ourselves an eager beaver," he said with a grin. "Don't worry, we'll find a spot for you."

The atmosphere in the warehouse grew even more lively as Lucy joined in, her efforts bringing a new energy to the work. The others laughed and began to pitch in, their camaraderie and shared purpose making the task ahead feel less daunting.

"They really know what they're doing, don't they?" Arlo said.

"Best in the business," Sorren confirmed. "If anyone can get this ship ready in time, it's them."

Arlo nodded, appreciating the effort and skill that was going into the construction. "We'll need to make sure everything's perfect. The gauntlet isn't the kind of place you get a second chance, and we have to ensure this beauty will survive much longer after that."

Alf had made his way down to join them, clapping Arlo on the back. "Aye, lad, you've got that right. But don't you worry, we'll have her ready to take on anything the gauntlet can throw at her. Now you boy's gonna lolly gag around or dip your toes in and get dirty?"

CHAPTER 21

The door to Daven Jones' Locker creaked open, and the trio of Arlo, Sorren, and Lucy stepped into a whirlwind of cheers, claps, and laughter. The tavern had always been a lively place, but tonight the energy was on another level, as if the air was charged with the buzz of celebration. The roaring fire in the hearth cast a warm glow over the room, making the wooden walls gleam around the old fishing nets and other worn fishing paraphernalia.

As soon as they entered, the noise level surged, and Arlo found himself at the center of it. The townsfolk of Davenport crowded around him, their faces alight with admiration and gratitude.

"There he is!"

"The Hero of Fall Lake!"

"He's even got the hammer with him!"

Voices rose from every corner of the bar, a chorus of shouts and calls.

"Let us see the hammer!" another voice cried, more joining in, eager to catch a glimpse of the weapon and its wielder.

Arlo was overwhelmed by the attention, but managed a sheepish grin. He lifted the hammer slightly, just enough for the crowd to see, and the room erupted into applause. People pressed in closer, each one wanting to shake his hand, pat his back, or simply express their gratitude.

"You've given us hope, my boy," an older man said, his voice thick with emotion. "We thought we were going to lose everything, but you've shown us these dark times won't last."

Arlo nodded, the man's words weighing heavily on him. He wasn't sure how to respond to such praise, but the sincerity in the man's eyes left him humbled.

Sorren, sensing Arlo's discomfort, clapped him on the shoulder with his familiar arrogant grin. "Well, looks like you've got enough admirers for a lifetime, my friend. Don't let it get to your head."

Lucy chuckled softly, her eyes twinkling with amusement. "You're practically glowing with all this attention, Arlo."

They finally made their way to a small table near the hearth. A few more people approached, shaking Arlo's hand and offering him drinks. The barmaid who brought their ale beamed at him as she set down the mugs.

"This one's on the house," she said with a wink before disappearing into the crowd.

Arlo took a long drink from his mug, trying to steady himself amidst the overwhelming gratitude pouring in from all sides. Sorren, leaning back in his chair, raised his drink in a mock toast.

"To the hero who never seems to get tired, not even after a day of hard labor," Sorren said with a teasing grin. "What's your secret, Arlo? Endless stamina?"

Lucy giggled. "Maybe he's got more energy than we thought, huh?"

Arlo nearly choked on his drink. "It's nothing like that," he protested, trying to maintain his composure. "Just... a lot on my mind, I suppose."

"Sure, sure," Sorren replied with a wink. "But seriously, you don't look like you've been working on the ship all day like we have. I feel like I've been run over by a wagon, and you're sitting here like it's just another day."

Sorren wasn't about to let it go. He leaned in closer with a wicked grin. "A lot on your mind, or a lot of ladies keeping you up at night? With stamina like that, your lady friends must be incredibly happy."

Lucy's giggle turned into full-blown laughter, and even Arlo had to smile despite the embarrassment.

"You're impossible," Arlo muttered, shaking his head.

"Just making sure you're not keeping all your talents hidden," Sorren replied, raising his mug again. "To the most well-rounded hero I know."

Arlo groaned, but couldn't help laughing along with them. "Let's just focus on the ship, alright?"

Sorren smirked, clearly not finished with his teasing. "Speaking of hidden talents, did you notice that brunette checking you out on the way in? She couldn't take her eyes off you. I bet she's already planning her move."

Lucy's laughter faded slightly, her expression shifting to something more guarded. "Oh, really?" she said, trying to sound casual but failing to mask the edge in her voice. "I didn't notice."

Arlo glanced at Lucy, sensing the change in her tone, but before he could say anything, Sorren chimed in again.

"You're a regular heartbreaker, Arlo. Saving towns, building ships, and now catching the eye of every lady you pass."

Lucy took a sip of her drink, her eyes flickering to Arlo for a moment before she focused on her mug. "Well, I guess being a hero has its perks," she said, her voice light, but her smile did not quite reach her eyes.

Arlo, now fully aware of the tension, felt his own smile falter. "It's nothing," he said quickly, trying to defuse the situation. "I'm just here to help with the ship, that's all."

Sorren finally noticed the shift in mood and backed off with a chuckle. "Alright, alright, I'll give you a break. But don't be surprised if that brunette comes over later. You've got quite the reputation now."

Lucy's forced smile eased slightly, but there was still a hint of something more in her gaze as she looked at Arlo. Before the silence could stretch too far, she sighed and leaned in closer.

"You know, it's not just the ship that's been a challenge today. I think the real struggle for everyone has been trying to keep up with the Fizztop brothers and their nonstop antics."

Sorren's laughter shook the table and drew a few glances from nearby patrons before the rest of the bar went back to its own noise. "I've never seen a group of men more confused and terrified at the same time. Wicket and Willy have them running in circles with their Nogmi methods. I thought one of them was going to pass out when Willy started explaining his advanced pulley system using his leg as an example."

Arlo grinned, grateful for the shift in conversation. "But you have to admit, progress is being made. The ship's coming along faster than we expected."

Sorren's expression softened, and he nodded. "Yeah, it is. For the first time in a long while, I feel hopeful about what's coming. We're building something here, something that's going to make a difference."

The night wore on, and the energy in the room pulsed even stronger. The cheers and laughter were relentless, the warmth of the fire mixing with the heady scent of ale and roasting meat. Sorren and Lucy were pulled into conversations with various patrons, each eager to share a drink or a tale with the Hero of Fall Lake and his friends.

In the midst of it all, a familiar figure entered the tavern. Brother Jason's presence was a calm contrast to the lively atmosphere. He navigated through the crowd with ease, his eyes searching until they landed on Arlo. With a warm smile, he approached the table where Arlo sat, a wooden box tucked under his arm.

"Evening, Arlo," Brother Jason greeted, placing the box on the table. "I've got something for you. Consider it a token of appreciation from His Majesty that he wanted to keep in your hands."

Arlo glanced at the box, a sense of unease prickling at the back of his mind. "What's this?"

Jason's smile widened, but there was seriousness in his eyes. "Just something the king thought you should have. Take it to your room before opening it. Not something most others would want to see."

Arlo nodded, curiosity overlapping with caution. He reached out and took the box, feeling the weight of it in his hands. "Thank you, Jason. And thank the king for me as well."

Jason nodded, his expression softening. "I will. There's more news too. The king has arranged for your stay at Mama Gretta's to be fully covered. Anything you need, food, clothing, whatever it may be, just let me know and it'll be taken care of. Same goes for Sorren and Lucy."

Arlo's eyebrow rose in surprise. "That's... generous."

"The king doesn't forget those who've done right by the kingdom," Jason replied with a knowing look. "And you've done more than most. Now, if you'll excuse me, I've got a few other matters to attend to."

As Jason turned to leave, Sorren appeared at Arlo's side, a pint of ale in hand and a grin on his face.

"You look like you've seen a ghost, Arlo. What did the good brother have to say?"

Arlo hesitated, glancing down at the box in his hands. "Just a gift from the king. Something personal, apparently."

Sorren's eyes lit up with curiosity. "Mysterious. You gonna open it?"

"Not here," Arlo replied. "I'll take it upstairs later."

Sorren shrugged, his interest already fading as he was swept back into the revelry by a group of laughing patrons. Lucy, noticing the exchange, watched Arlo with a curious glance, but before she could approach, a group of young men moved in, clapping Arlo on the back and offering him drinks.

As the tavern continued to buzz around them, Lucy found herself drawn away from the crowd and toward a quieter corner of the room. Her gaze landed on a lone woman seated there, nursing a drink with a far-off look in her eyes.

Lucy approached the table slowly. "Mind if I join you?"

The woman looked up, her expression tired but polite. "Of course not. Please, sit."

Lucy took a seat across from her, noting the weariness in the woman's eyes. "Rough night?"

She chuckled softly, a hint of sadness in her voice. "Just a long one. Sometimes it feels like the weight of the world is on our shoulders, doesn't it?"

Lucy nodded, her gaze drifting back to the lively crowd behind them. "Yeah. It does. But I've found that it helps to share that weight with others."

The woman smiled, an empty smile that still tried to be kind. "Wise words. And I suppose you are right. Alysia Erudite, by the way."

"I'm Lucy... uh, just Lucy," she replied somberly, as she tried to grasp at the frayed edges of her history again.

"Hello, Just Lucy," Alysia said with a faint smile, trying to lighten the mood. "You seem familiar somehow."

Lucy's heart skipped a beat at the words, hope sparking at the possibility of a connection to her forgotten past. "Familiar? Do you think we might've met before?" she asked, her voice full of quiet anticipation.

"I'm not sure," Alysia said slowly. "It's just... there's something about you." Her gaze lingered on Lucy's eyes, then, almost subconsciously, on the line of her shoulders. "You remind me of someone, but I can't put my finger on it."

For a heartbeat, something like recognition flickered across Alysia's face. It was there and gone before Lucy could name it. Beneath it, Alysia felt something deeper, a quiet warmth that hummed under Lucy's presence, the same way the world felt when her prayers to Grace were answered.

Lucy's gaze softened as she sat closer to Alysia. "I don't remember much about my past," she admitted, her voice dropping. "All I remember is waking up in the same crater in Fall Lake where the beast was. I've been trying to piece anything back together ever since. When you said I seemed familiar... I wondered if we might've crossed paths before."

Alysia's eyes widened slightly at the mention of memory loss, and she leaned in closer, her tone gentle. "That's a heavy burden to bear. Same as Arlo, in his own way. Especially since he never wanted that kind of life."

"So you know Arlo?"

"You could say that. I met him when Sorren brought him to me after the attack on Fall Lake."

"To you? Why would they do that?"

"I'm a cleric of Grace," Alysia said, taking a sip of her drink.

"Grace? She's one of the gods, right?"

"You are correct. Grace is the goddess of creation, and her followers dedicate their lives to healing, nurturing, and growth."

"She sounds wonderful. Maybe I had some connection to the followers of Grace?" Lucy said hopefully.

"It's possible. We believe in the potential of every being to create, transform, and grow, much like the world itself. Grace was the original creator of this world many years ago." Alysia reached into her purse and took out a coin etched with two six-pointed stars and three circles intertwining them. "Here. You can keep this, if you ever feel like you need something more to guide you."

Lucy smiled and accepted the coin, listening intently to the words Alysia shared about Grace, her heart racing as she felt a strange familiarity with the teachings. "I... I don't know if I was ever one of Grace's followers," she said, barely above a whisper. "But hearing you talk about it, it feels like something I should remember."

Alysia reached out and placed a comforting hand on Lucy's arm. At the touch, that quiet inner hum flared for an instant, the same way it did in the holiest moments of worship. Alysia hid her reaction behind a gentle smile.

"Perhaps Grace's light still shines within you, even if you cannot remember it," she said. "If you ever wish to learn more about Grace, or need someone to talk to, I'd be happy to help. You can usually find me at the Seabound Church. It's a little busy right now, with everyone we're helping from Fall Lake, but if I can find the time, I will make time for you."

Lucy smiled, the warmth of Alysia's gesture easing the tension in her chest. "Thank you, Alysia. I'd like that. Maybe talking with you and learning more about Grace will help me find some answers."

Alysia returned the smile, her eyes twinkling with kindness. "I hope so."

As Lucy drifted back into the crowd, Alysia watched her go, her thumb tracing the edge of her coin of Grace.

"Not yet," she murmured under her breath. "You're not ready to hear it yet."

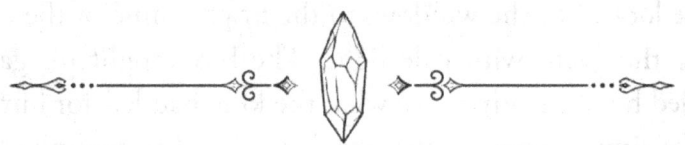

Arlo climbed the narrow stairs of Daven Jones' Locker, the din of the tavern gradually fading behind him as he made his way to his room. Whatever the walls were made of, they allowed little noise from below to pass through and offered a quiet, more settled space. When he reached his room, Arlo closed the door behind him, shutting out what sound remained and the world for just a moment. He placed the box on the small table by the window, took a deep breath, and sat on the bed next to it. He leaned forward, running his hands through his white hair.

This quiet was what he was used to. This was what he sought after a long day of work, the same as he had done many times in Fall Lake.

Just as he told everyone, he was no one of importance. He had never held many jobs for long, finding them unfulfilling or empty once they were done. But he found the most reward when he worked in Fall Lake. He was involved in many different fields, offering his hand wherever it was needed. Carpentry, masonry, hauling, whatever work was required. He held enough knowledge to do most of it, but never felt like an expert in any.

His mornings had been filled with a quick breakfast, then work from sunup to sundown. Always the first to arrive, always the last to leave. It left him with little free time the past couple of years in Fall Lake, but he had enjoyed the work nonetheless. And he was only a few hours' travel from his childhood friend and fellow orphan, Sabil Percy, who worked at her adoptive parents' tavern on the trail from Cyril down to Davenport. He spent his rare off days with her and helped around their farm to stay occupied.

Now he was here with a new label as "hero" thrust on him without warning. But that was just like the rest of his life. Always wandering.

He looked to the window, to the bright shine of the twin moons filling the room with pale light. The box caught his gaze, and he decided he was ready to see what the king had left for him.

The simple wooden box, unadorned and unassuming, seemed to pulse with a quiet weight. He hesitated, feeling the pull of whatever lay inside. It felt like his brief peace would break the moment he opened it.

Inside, nestled in a bed of dark cloth, lay the amulet of Eckerd. The artifact gleamed faintly in the dim light, its intricate designs swirling like captured lightning trapped in amber. Arlo reached out, his fingers brushing against the cold metal, and instantly he felt a presence stir within as the amber jewel began to glow softly.

"Ah, Arlo," came a deep, resonant voice that felt like the words of an aged wise man spilling out from the amulet itself. "To what do I owe the pleasure of your company this evening?"

Arlo smirked, a low creak rolling from the bed as he leaned back onto it. "I just needed a quiet moment, Eckerd. Frederick left for Fall Lake this morning. Held a big speech where Dolph thrust me into the spotlight."

"Dolph," Eckerd's voice dripped with mild disdain. "He did not go back with my brother?"

"I don't think so. He was still helping around the church with the injured and wounded. Brother Jason brought the amulet to me, wanted me to hold it for safekeeping."

"Well, I'm glad to be in the company of good people then. I bet Dolph was not too thrilled when you rallied the people, eh?"

"I think it was meant to make me look bad, but someone had to do it. Neither he nor the king were doing anything. They needed someone to look up to." Arlo took a slow breath as he thought through the way the day's conversations had gone.

"Aye. My brother once knew the exact words to rally the people. I think he, like many others, lost himself along the way. It all started when Ambra left him... Never mind. Not the time or place for stories."

"Left him?" Arlo asked. "I thought the news that spread said she passed away."

"Ah, yes. That is what was said. But between you and me, that is not what happened. For all we know, she could have passed by now. Perhaps another day, my boy." The voice echoed with a faint smile. "How do you feel about becoming the Hero of Fall Lake?" he asked, turning the subject away.

"It's... strange. I didn't ask for this, or want it. But I also cannot walk away from it now. It's like the more I try to find some peace, the more the world seems to demand from me."

"The world," Eckerd lingered on the word, "has a funny way of latching onto those it sees as strong. It will push you and test you until you either break or become something greater."

Arlo let the words sink in, his fingers tracing the edge of the amulet. "You've been through this before, haven't you?"

"Oh, many times," Eckerd replied with a sigh. "And I watched my brother struggle with the same thing. He was barely an adult when the title of king was thrust upon him. But the burden is no lighter just because it has been carried before, or because you've been trained to handle it since birth. You will find your peace and wield your strength into something new." Arlo's quiet sigh carried through the connection as clearly as any word. "Tell me, how goes the ship? Fred last told me he was going to fund it, but he did not speak with me before leaving. He is always less forthcoming with information."

A faint smile crossed Arlo's lips as he dwelled on the events of the day. "It's coming along well, actually. Faster than I expected. Sorren's Nogmi engineers have their own... unique methods, but they're remarkably effective."

"Good," the disembodied voice said quietly. "A strong ship for a strong purpose. You will need it for what lies ahead, I suspect."

Arlo nodded, though a sense of unease lingered. "I've been hearing things when others are around me. It's overwhelming sometimes. I feel like I'm being stretched too thin, like I'm losing myself in all of this."

"That, Arlo, is the curse of those who care too much," Eckerd said, a note of empathy in his voice. "But it is also your strength. Do not let it consume you, but do not shut it out either. You will need to find a balance. If you do not, the weight will crush you one day."

Arlo sighed again, feeling the truth of Eckerd's words. "Easier said than done."

"Isn't it always?"

"Unfortunately."

"Just remember, my boy, you are not alone in this. Even if it feels that way, you have allies, both seen and unseen. Draw strength from them, and from yourself."

"Thanks, Eckerd. That's basically what I said to the people of Davenport. They needed that hope, and I think it worked. It brought us together."

"Remember, Arlo. You are stronger than you think. Do not let the world tell you otherwise."

Arlo nodded and placed his hand on the box to close it. "Thanks, Eckerd. We will talk again soon. I need to head back down for now though."

With a soft click, Arlo closed the lid of the box, sealing the amulet inside once more. He sat for a moment, letting the quiet of the room settle around him, before standing and heading for the door. The noise of the tavern began to seep back into his awareness and, with a deep breath, Arlo steeled himself to rejoin the others.

CHAPTER 22

Stepping back into the lively tavern, the noise and energy hit Arlo like a wave. The warmth and camaraderie of the room were comforting. He wove his way through the crowd, offering nods and polite smiles, but his mind was still half-occupied with his conversation with Eckerd.

He was almost at the bar when a group of people approached him, their faces a mix of emotions that Arlo could not immediately place. They were haggard, worn from travel and hardship, and their eyes held a depth of pain that made his heart skip a beat. As they drew closer, the noise of the tavern seemed to dull, as if the world narrowed to just this moment.

One of the men, older with graying hair and deep lines etched into his face, stepped forward. His voice was rough, tinged with the weight of grief.

"You're the one, aren't you? The one who fought the beast at Fall Lake?"

Arlo nodded slowly, the tension in his chest tightening. "I am."

The man's eyes bore into him, and for a moment Arlo felt a flash of something that bordered on anger.

"We lost everything," the man said, his voice low and tight. "Our homes, our families... everything was destroyed when that thing came. My wife, my daughter..." His voice broke, and he had to pause, his hands trembling as he balled them into fists.

Arlo swallowed hard, guilt and sorrow welling up inside him. "I'm so sorry," he began, his voice thick. "I—"

Before he could finish, the man's expression shifted, softening as tears welled up in his eyes.

"But you... you tried to stop it. You did more than anyone else could do. If it wasn't for you, none of us would have made it out alive."

The change in tone caught Arlo off guard, and he blinked, trying to process the sudden shift. The man reached out, placing a rough hand on Arlo's shoulder.

"Thank you," he said, his voice barely audible. "You gave us a chance."

Arlo was about to respond when another member of the group, a woman with a scar that ran across her entire cheek, stepped forward and grasped his hand.

"You're our savior, Mr. Devine," she said, her voice trembling along with the tears in her eyes. "We don't have much left, but we have our lives. My children survived, thanks to you."

As she shook his hand, Arlo felt something strange. A surge of energy pulsed through his body, making his breath catch in his throat. His vision blurred for a moment with a blue lining, and when it cleared, the world around him shifted.

Suddenly, he was no longer standing in the tavern.

He was back at Fall Lake. The smell of smoke and ash filled his lungs. He saw the woman he had just spoken with, laughing with a small child at her side. The image burned bright and warm, then in an instant flames engulfed the buildings. Screams echoed in the air. The child was gone, replaced by a crushing sense of fear and loss.

Fall Lake faded away as quickly as it had come, leaving Arlo gasping for breath. He barely had time to process it before the next person stepped forward and shook his hand.

Another surge of energy. Another vision.

This time he saw a young man standing proud before his family's farm, only to watch it torn apart by the beast's rampage. The fear, the helplessness, the desperate hope that someone would save them, all of it washed over Arlo like a tidal wave.

One by one, the refugees came forward. Each touch of their hands brought another flash of their deepest fears, their greatest hopes, their most painful memories. It was overwhelming, the flood of emotion threatening to drown him as he experienced their anguish firsthand.

By the time the fifth person let go of his hand, Arlo's knees were shaking. Sweat beaded at his temple despite the cool tavern air, and his grip on the hammer had gone slick.

A faint crackle of blue danced across his fingers as the last vision snapped away. A tankard on the nearby table buzzed, its metal rim jumping with a sharp tink before settling.

"Are you alright, lad?" one of the refugees asked, frowning. "You've gone pale."

"I'm fine," Arlo lied.

He tried to steady himself, but the onslaught of visions left him reeling. He could hear the voices. He could feel their pain as if it were his own. The wounds of his body ached until they became excruciating. And then, just as he thought he could not take any more, something else began to take shape.

The tavern around him faded once more, and in its place, a towering figure emerged from the shadows of his mind.

The figure was golden, its radiant form both majestic and terrifying. Wings stretched out wide, casting a shadow that seemed to swallow the world around it. The air grew cold, and Arlo felt a deep, primal fear clamp down on his heart.

The golden figure loomed larger. Its presence was suffocating, its eyes glowing with an unnatural light. Arlo's heart pounded in his chest as the figure's gaze locked onto him, piercing through him with a force that left him trembling. The wings unfurled even farther, and the space around Arlo warped, the noise of the tavern fading to a distant echo.

For a moment, it felt as though the figure was about to reach out and pull him into its grasp. The weight of its presence was crushing, the darkness at its back closing in. Panic surged through him as he tried to react, to do something, anything, to fight against the terror that swallowed him.

Then, just as quickly as it had appeared, it was gone.

The golden light dimmed. The wings receded. The suffocating presence lifted.

Arlo blinked, and the tavern rushed back into focus. The noise of the crowd, the warmth of the fire, the rough hands of the refugees still gripping his shoulders, it all returned in an instant and grounded him back in the present.

He stood there, shaken and unsure of what he had just experienced. The refugees continued to thank him, their words barely registering as he tried to make sense of what had happened. The golden figure, the towering wings, the bright, cruel eyes. It was the same presence that had haunted them back in the cave, the same ill omen that seemed to follow him wherever he went.

Lucy had seen it too.

Arlo took a deep breath, trying to steady himself. Whatever the figure was, it was no friend. It was a threat, a shadow that loomed over him and everyone around him. The visions had passed, but the fear lingered, a cold knot in his stomach that refused to loosen.

He forced a smile as people continued to approach him.

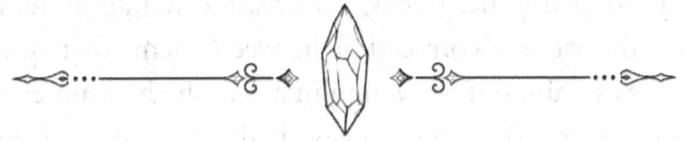

Meanwhile, across the tavern, Sorren found himself caught up in the rowdy atmosphere. He had been pulled into a game of dice with several patrons, his boisterous laughter blending with theirs as he rolled the bones across the table. The outcome did not seem to matter much. Whether he won or lost, Sorren was clearly enjoying himself.

One of the patrons, a stout man with a scraggly beard, clapped Sorren on the back.

"If you play dice as well as you swing that sword, we're in for a long night, my friend!"

Lucy had continued her conversation with Alysia, listening to more of the teachings of Grace and letting Alysia vent about the struggles she faced as a healer. After a while, she glanced across the room, and her eyes landed on Arlo.

He was standing with a group of refugees, but something was off. His posture, the slight sway in his stance, the way his gaze seemed distant and unfocused. Her heart tightened with concern.

"Excuse me, Alysia," Lucy said, rising from her seat. "I think something's wrong with Arlo. I need to go check on him."

Alysia nodded, her eyes following Lucy's gaze. "Of course. We can continue our conversation later."

Lucy moved quickly through the crowd, her eyes fixed on Arlo. But as she approached, another woman swooped in beside him. Tall, with auburn hair and a coy smile, the woman placed a hand on Arlo's arm. Her body language was clearly flirtatious. Far too close.

Lucy's heart dropped, a sharp pang of hurt cutting through her. From where she stood, it looked like Arlo was leaning into the woman, his hand coming up to rest on hers.

Lucy stopped in her tracks, her breath catching in her throat. She had felt the strange connection between them, that quiet pull she could not explain, but this stung in a way she had not expected.

They weren't together. They had never even spoken about anything like that. She had no claim on him.

But the sight still cut, sharp and stupid and unfair, and the worst part was knowing she had no right to feel it.

She quickly turned away, blinking back the sudden rush of emotion. It was not her place to feel this way, she reminded herself. She couldn't even remember who she truly was, let alone who she might have meant to someone in the past.

But the hurt lingered, refusing to be dismissed so easily.

Lucy made her way back to the table where she, Sorren, and Arlo had started the night. The laughter and cheers of the tavern continued to swirl around her, but she felt strangely disconnected from it all. She sat down, staring at the empty glasses in front of her, trying to ignore the tightness in her chest.

She could still see Arlo from the corner of her eye, but she forced herself not to look directly at him. Instead, she focused on her breathing, trying to steady herself, trying to push away the jealousy that gnawed at her.

As Arlo regained his focus, the world around him seemed to snap back into sharp relief. The noise of the tavern returned, the clamor of voices and clinking glasses pressing in on him. But there was something else. An unfamiliar pressure on his arm.

He blinked, trying to fully clear his vision, and found himself staring into the brown eyes of a woman he did not recognize.

She was tall, with auburn hair that cascaded down her back in loose waves. Her smile was warm and inviting, and there was a glint of something playful in her eyes. She leaned in closer, her hand still resting on his arm, her voice low and smooth.

"You know," she began, "I've heard a lot about you, Arlo. The Hero of Fall Lake, slayer of that beast. Quite the story."

Arlo's thoughts were still muddled from the strange visions, but he managed a polite smile. "It's… been quite a journey."

The woman's hand slid down his arm, her fingers tracing a line to his hand.

"I bet you've got some incredible stories to tell," she said. "Maybe you could share a few with me over a drink. I've got a table in the back. A bit quieter. A lot more private."

Arlo hesitated, still trying to shake the lingering weight of the earlier visions. A fog of disorientation clung to him. Something felt off. He glanced around the room, his gaze searching for familiar faces, something to ground him.

Before he could respond, the woman stepped closer, her hand tightening around his.

"Come on," she coaxed. "You deserve a break after everything you've been through. Let me help you relax."

Arlo gently but firmly removed her hand from his. "I appreciate the offer," he said, trying to keep his tone kind, "but I'm afraid I'm not really in the mood for that tonight."

The woman's smile faltered for a moment, but she quickly recovered, tilting her head as if considering him from a new angle.

"Maybe another time, then," she purred, leaning in to whisper close to his ear. "I'll be around."

As she walked away, Arlo felt a mixture of relief and confusion. The encounter had pulled him fully back into the present, but the strange visions and the golden figure still lingered at the edge of his mind. He needed to get a grip on whatever was happening to him. He needed to understand why these moments kept coming.

Turning his head slightly, he caught sight of Lucy across the room, sitting alone at their old table. She was staring down at the empty glass in front of her, her shoulders tense, as if she was holding something back.

A pang of guilt hit him. He had not meant to ignore her or anyone else, but whatever had just happened had shaken him more than he wanted to admit. He could see the hurt in her posture, the way she kept her gaze fixed on the glass instead of looking around.

Something about it tugged at him, and he found himself moving toward her before he had fully decided to do so.

As he approached, he noticed the way her eyes flicked up to him, then quickly away, as if she didn't want him to see whatever she was feeling. But something was wrong. Whether it was the aftermath of his strange experience or something else entirely, the tension was clear.

"Lucy," he said quietly as he reached the table. "Mind if I sit?"

She glanced up at him, her expression carefully neutral, though something in her eyes remained guarded. After a moment, she nodded and gestured to the seat across from her.

"Sure," she replied, her voice steady but holding a hard edge. "Have a seat."

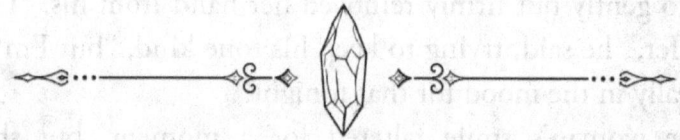

Lucy and Arlo sat in awkward silence. Arlo shifted in his seat, unsure of what to say next, when Sorren approached with a blonde woman on his arm.

"Well, my friends, I'm calling it a night," Sorren announced with a wink, clearly pleased with himself. "I'll leave you two to whatever plans you might have."

Arlo raised an eyebrow, but before he could respond, Sorren leaned in closer and lowered his voice.

"Arlo, take care of Lucy, alright? She's good people." Then, with a cheeky grin, he added, "But if you two decide to share some more drinks, or anything else, just remember to be responsible."

Lucy shot Sorren a pointed look, but there was a touch of humor in her eyes. "Goodnight, Sorren," she said.

"Goodnight, you two," Sorren called over his shoulder as he led the blonde woman toward the stairs, leaving Arlo and Lucy alone at the table.

Lucy watched him go, then turned her gaze back to Arlo, her eyes searching his face.

"He's something else, isn't he?" Arlo asked.

Lucy smiled, though a faint shadow remained in her gaze. "He's a character, that's for sure."

"Arlo, can I ask you something?" she said softly.

"Of course," he replied.

Lucy hesitated, glancing away for a moment before meeting his eyes again. "You seemed... distant before you came over here," she said, her voice laced with concern. "Is everything alright?"

Arlo hesitated, running a hand through his hair. "I'm fine. I guess I was just caught off guard by the swarm of people that were approaching me."

Lucy's voice dropped. "What about that woman? You seemed to be getting pretty close to her."

Arlo blinked, caught off guard by the question. He shook his head, a faint smile tugging at his lips. "She came on a bit strong, that's all. I didn't know how to react, and honestly, I was just trying to keep my balance. It was nothing."

Lucy studied him for a moment, then her shoulders eased. "I believe you," she said finally, her tone sincere but still holding a touch of vulnerability. She let out a small breath of relief. "It's just... I don't know. It's been a strange night."

Arlo nodded, understanding her unease. "It has been. But I'm here, Lucy. Whatever's bothering you, you can talk to me."

Lucy's eyes flickered with something like relief. She took a deep breath before speaking again.

"Actually, there is something. I feel comfortable with you, Arlo. More than with anyone else. And I was wondering..." She hesitated, biting her lip as she looked down at her hands, then back up at him.

"Would you stay with me tonight? In my room, I mean. I just…" She trailed off, searching for the right words. "I just feel safer when you're around."

Arlo nodded without hesitation. "Of course, Lucy. If that's what you want, I'll stay."

Her expression brightened slightly, though a hint of uncertainty lingered in her eyes. "Thank you," she said quietly, a small smile playing on her lips. "But, um, just to be clear, you'll keep to your side of the bed, right? Unless you're planning on being a gentleman with a lot less self-control than I thought."

Arlo chuckled, the tension between them easing. "I promise, Lucy. I'll be the perfect gentleman."

She let out a soft laugh. "Good," she said, her smile widening. "Because if you can't, I'll have to kick you out."

Arlo grinned at her playfulness. "You won't have to worry about that. I'll stay where I'm supposed to be."

They agreed to call it a night and made their way up the stairs to their rooms. As they reached Lucy's door, she paused and turned to look at him with a mix of gratitude and something deeper.

"Thank you, Arlo," she said softly. "For staying. It means more to me than you know."

Arlo looked deeply into her emerald eyes, his voice just as soft. "I'm glad to be here, Lucy. I wouldn't want to be anywhere else."

He watched as she walked into her room and shut the door. He waited a few moments before heading to his own room to change. When he returned, Lucy was already under the bedding, the dim light casting a warm glow over the room that made her crimson hair shine in the night's pale light.

Arlo quietly slipped into bed beside her, keeping to his side as promised. As he settled in, he could feel the weight of the day's events begin to lift, replaced by the simple comfort of being close to someone he cared about.

"Thank you, Arlo," Lucy murmured, her voice already heavy with sleep. "For everything."

For the first time since Fall Lake, sleep came without screams. Between them, in the narrow space they had promised to keep, something small and bright settled in. Too quiet to name, but strong enough to keep the dark at bay.

Far above the tavern's roof, unseen through the clouds, something golden turned its gaze toward Davenport and waited.

CHAPTER 23

The woods near the Autumngar Wilds were dark tonight. Nyla hadn't looked back since she left her mother behind. She knew Sunny would care for her, but worry gnawed at her all the same. What if she left... and something happened? But what if she stayed... and watched her mother fade away? The unfairness of it all pressed down on her. Why her? Why did she have to hide because her father was Elfar, because her pointed ears and icy white hair made her "different"?

It had never made sense. Why she could not walk the streets with the other children. Why she had to stay cloaked, allowed outside only when darkness or snow concealed her glow. She was taller than others her age. Her mother had told her that height came from her father's people, but that was nearly all she ever said about him. The silence around her father felt like its own kind of shame.

Earlier that evening, she had seen a faint scatter of lantern light far off along the road. Wagons, most likely. People. Hope tugged at her for a heartbeat, but fear tugged harder. Humans staring. Humans questioning. Humans deciding she was wrong. Rather than risk it, she turned away from the road and cut deeper into the trees, alone.

The shadows thickened as Nyla moved deeper into the forest. The dense canopy overhead blocked most of the moonlight, leaving only the pale glow that slipped through the leaves to guide her. She hadn't looked back, but the weight of her decision stayed with her. Her mother's frail, sickened form lingered in her mind, chilling her worse than the cold.

Sunny would help. Sunny always helped. But what if even that was not enough?

Nyla pushed the thought away, focusing on the path ahead. She had to keep moving. Had to find something that could help. But doubt stalked her like a second shadow. What if she failed? What if she wasted precious time and her mother suffered because of her?

The frigid air bit at her skin, slipping through her cloak. She clenched it tighter, but the shiver that ran through her was not from the wind alone. The silence of the forest pressed in around her. No birds. No insects. Only her own footsteps crushing leaves beneath her boots.

Then the rustling started. Soft at first. Harmless. But it grew, heavier and deliberate.

Nyla froze.

Sunny once told her that when a forest goes quiet, it is already too late.

Movement flickered in the corner of her vision. A shadow gliding between trees. Panic surged through her veins. She spun toward the sound, but the shifting darkness made her eyes lie to her.

Her breath hitched as she reached instinctively for the dagger at her waist, her fingers trembling.

Then she saw them.

A pair of glowing eyes in the brush.

A low growl rolled through the air.

The beast emerged from the dark, hulking, matted fur hanging in clumps, teeth bared and glistening. Saliva dripped from its jaws as it fixed its gaze on her.

Nyla stepped back, but her legs felt rooted to the forest floor.

The creature lunged.

She barely lifted her dagger before it slammed into her. They hit the ground hard, its claws ripping across her arm as she struggled beneath its weight. Pain exploded up her limb and she cried out, thrashing, fighting, her dagger shaking in her grip.

Hot breath washed over her cheek. Saliva dripped onto her skin.

In a desperate strike, she slashed upward. The blade carved a line from the beast's brow, across one eye, and down its muzzle. It lurched back with a wounded yelp. Nyla seized the moment, shoving it aside and scrambling to her feet, blood running down her arm.

The beast hesitated only a moment, growling as blood trickled over its ruined eye and down its muzzle, before lowering itself to pounce again.

Nyla's breath came in short, panicked bursts. She could not take another hit. She would not survive it.

With a burst of adrenaline, she ripped off her cloak and hurled it at the creature, the fabric tangling around its face. While it shook and clawed at the obstruction, she ran.

Branches tore at her cheeks. Roots nearly sent her sprawling. She did not look back. She did not dare.

Behind her, the beast crashed through the underbrush, furious and relentless. Its growls chased her through the trees.

Blood slipped from her fingers as she clutched her wounded arm, spattering the forest floor in a thin, staggered trail. She angled away from the faint orange glow of the distant road, fleeing deeper where no one would see her and nothing could recognize her.

She ran until her lungs burned, until her legs trembled violently beneath her. At last she stumbled into a small clearing and collapsed against a tree, gasping.

The beast was nowhere in sight.

But the fear remained lodged in her chest.

Nyla clutched her bleeding arm, pain throbbing hot and cold. She had nearly died. Her journey had only just begun and she had already come so close to its end.

Tears welled in her eyes.

What was she thinking? She could barely handle one wild beast. How was she supposed to save her mother? How was she supposed to find an answer when she did not even know what she was looking for?

The forest loomed around her, dark and uncaring. Far off, somewhere she could not see, wood splintered and something vast bellowed, but Nyla pressed her hands over her ears and curled tighter against the tree.

She felt small. Helpless.

Like a lost child crying for someone who was not coming.

Alone in the vastness of the wilds, Nyla buried her face in her hands and wept.

CHAPTER 24

The next few days blended into a relentless flurry of activity as Arlo, Sorren, and Lucy immersed themselves in the shipbuilding project. The construction site was a hive of movement, the clamor of hammers, the hum of machinery, and the occasional shout of orders filling the air. The massive frame of the ship began to show visible progress each day, though the work was straining and the hours long.

In the midst of the ship-focused whirlwind, Arlo and Lucy decided to share a room, finding solace and comfort in their decision. This led to the return of Arlo's room to Mama Gretta, who welcomed the change. Their new shared space, though modest, became a quiet refuge amid the chaos. Arlo continued his meditation practice, now a daily ritual, and this helped him make progress in his control over his newfound mana abilities. The focused practice allowed him to harness his powers with greater precision, although he still had a long way to go before he truly understood them.

The people of Davenport had come together in remarkable unity. Many of the residents pitched in and helped with the building of the ship where they could, even if it was only offering meals for the workers or a change of clothes. The entire community had been rallied by Arlo's impassioned speech, giving each of them purpose. Many who were not needed at home began to rotate their time and efforts into rebuilding Fall Lake.

As the end of the first week approached, progress was significant, but the team faced a new challenge. A shortage of specific lumber, vital for the final stages of the ship's construction, became apparent. Arlo brought the issue to Brother Jason's attention, having expected a shipment a day or two prior.

The situation grew more tense when Archbishop Dolph Celestino was drawn into the discussion. As Jason and Arlo presented the problem to him, Dolph's response was swift and uncompromising. He assigned Arlo the task of locating the missing lumber, insisting that Arlo go alone. The tension between the two climbed to an immense level, with Jason stuck in the middle of it all.

"You are the Hero of Fall Lake, after all," Dolph declared, his tone dismissive. "This should be nothing for someone of your caliber."

Arlo's frustration was plain. "Just because I did one thing does not make me your hero to call on whenever you have a problem. I do not work for you."

Dolph's eyes narrowed. "We do not work for you either. We are providing a great deal for this project. The least you can do is search for the caravan with the wood supply you need. Our resources are stretched thin as it is."

"You have Porters aiding in the transport of this caravan. If something happened to them along the way, my going alone may not help the situation."

"As I told you already, those Porters sent to escort the merchant were the only ones we could spare."

"All I am asking for is a few men or women and horses to hasten the travel."

"And I am telling you that we do not—"

"Enough," Brother Jason finally said. "Quit bickering. Arlo, I will go with you."

Dolph scoffed at Jason's response. "He cannot take our Deputy Paladin as well."

"I am not asking for permission, Dolph. I am going with Arlo. We will look into this together and find out why the caravan is missing," Jason added, "We will be back before you need to leave for Fall Lake."

"Thank you, Jason," Arlo said with a nod. "That is all I was asking for."

"So be it," Dolph said. "I have other matters to attend to." He turned away, leaving Arlo and Jason behind.

The morning light began to creep over the horizon as Arlo and Jason prepared to depart, the cool air carrying the promise of a sunny day ahead. They had risen before dawn, moving quietly through the streets of Davenport to avoid waking the others. Lucy and Sorren had offered to accompany them, but Arlo assured them he would be fine, insisting that they needed to stay and oversee the shipbuilding project. With the horses secured and the wagon loaded, they were ready to leave.

Azu, Jason's loyal Akhlut, rested in the back of the wagon, his keen eyes already scanning the surroundings. The creature was a formidable presence, a hybrid of powerful aquatic and terrestrial traits. His body was sleek and muscular, covered in a smooth black and white coat reminiscent of an orca, with a stark contrast between the deep, inky black silky fur along his back and the pure white smooth underside. His head, broad and strong, bore the distinct markings of a wolf, with piercing blue eyes and powerful jaws filled with sharp teeth suited for tearing through both fish and flesh. His rounded, triangular ears were always alert to the sounds of his environment.

The journey through the lush green countryside started quietly, each man lost in his own thoughts. The path ahead wound through rolling hills and patches of dense forest, the trees growing thicker as they moved further from the coastal town of Davenport toward the wooded town of Stagwood.

Finally, it was Jason who broke the silence between them. "You know, Sorren speaks highly of you," he said, his tone neutral.

Arlo glanced over, not surprised by the comment. "I think Sorren speaks highly of most."

Jason nodded, keeping his eyes on the road ahead. "He thinks you are a good man. Someone who can be trusted in anything, especially in a fight. That is not something he says lightly, I promise you."

Arlo shrugged, unsure how to respond. "Sorren is a good man too. Young and naïve at times. But were we not all."

"That he is." Jason hesitated at first, his next question hanging between them. "Any more memories about Fall Lake?"

Arlo hesitated, the memories of that night still faded and unclear. "I do not know for certain," he admitted. "I have been meditating daily and have made some of my memories clearer, but the others still feel jumbled. I can remember most of what happened before I ran up the tower. The cries and tears of the men, women, and children I tried to save before that monster got to them." His voice held a quiet sadness as he spoke, the weight of that day never fully leaving him.

"He also mentioned that you have mana abilities," Jason said with a glance over. "That is new as well?"

"Yeah," Arlo nodded. "I have been practicing, trying to get control of it. It is... strange."

Jason's face softened, and for a moment the stern Paladin gave way to a more sympathetic companion. "We have all got our battles, Arlo. Sometimes it takes a while to figure out what we are fighting for."

They fell into another silence after that, each man drifting back into his own thoughts, sharing the occasional remark about the land or a familiar landmark as it passed. As the day wore on and the sun climbed higher in the sky, they drew closer to Stagwood. The terrain grew more rugged, the forest denser, with towering trees casting long shadows over the road. The air grew cooler, a stark contrast to the coastal warmth they had left behind.

Azu, who had been lying quietly in the back of the wagon, suddenly perked up, his ears twitching as he sniffed the air. A low growl rumbled in his throat, and his hackles rose. Something was not right.

Jason immediately noticed the change in his companion's demeanor. "Azu senses something," he said, his voice tense. He pulled the reins, slowing the horses to a stop.

Arlo gripped his warhammer tightly, his instincts ready to take over. "What is it, boy?" he asked, knowing he would not get an answer he could understand. The creature's growl deepened, his eyes fixed on the thick brush just ahead.

The two men dismounted, leaving the horses and wagon behind as they cautiously approached the area where Azu was staring. The underbrush rustled, and the faint scent of decay wafted through the air.

They emerged into a small clearing. The sight that greeted them sent a chill down their spines. The remnants of the caravan were scattered across the ground. Broken wagons. Shattered crates. Splintered wood everywhere. The unmistakable stench of death hung thick in the air. The bodies of the Porters and the merchant who had accompanied the lumber were strewn about, their faces twisted in terror and pain.

Closer to the road, a second set of marks cut across the trampled ground. Deep claw furrows crossed over a lighter set of tracks, smaller and longer-striding than the Porters' prints. In a few places, dark drops stained the dirt and veered away into the trees, as if someone had run while bleeding.

"Someone else was here," Jason murmured, frowning at the thin trail that led away from the wagons. "Someone who was not part of this caravan."

Arlo knelt beside one of the bodies, his expression grim. "They did not stand a chance," he muttered, examining the deep, savage wound on the merchant. "Whatever did this, it was no ordinary animal."

Jason's eyes swept the trees that ringed the clearing. Some trunks were splintered, bark torn away where something huge had slammed through. "This was an ambush," he said, his voice low. "But by what?"

Before Arlo could respond that they should not wait around to find out, a loud rustling came from the edge of the clearing. The forest split open, and the creature stumbled into the light. A bear's shape stretched too far, forced into angles a body should never hold. Its fur was matted and patchy, with strips torn away to show ropey muscle beneath. Across its face, a fresh, angry gash ran from brow to jaw, one eye clouded with blood where some blade had struck it before.

Its remaining eye glowed a sickly yellow, not with hunger, but with the awful awareness of something that was never meant to live this way.

The twisted sight of the creature left no doubt in their minds. This abomination was what had felled the caravan.

The abomination roared, a guttural, gurgling scream that sent a shiver down their spines. It charged toward them with a thunderous speed that did not match its massive size. Arlo and Jason had only seconds to react.

The creature lunged forward, its massive jaws snapping inches from Jason as he dodged to the side. The ground trembled beneath its weight, and the stench of decay filled the air. Arlo raised his warhammer, adrenaline surging through him, ready to counter the beast's ferocity.

"Watch the eyes," Jason shouted, his voice steady despite the chaos. He darted to the side, studying the beast's movements. The creature swung its claws, each swipe a raw show of its unnatural strength. Jason ducked, narrowly avoiding a strike that would have cleaved him in half.

Arlo swung his warhammer, aiming for the creature's flank, but the beast anticipated his move. It sidestepped with unnatural speed, its claws slicing through the air and catching Arlo off guard. The force of the counterattack sent him sprawling backward, crashing into a tree trunk. Pain shot through his body as he struggled to regain his footing.

"Get up," Jason shouted, his voice cutting through the chaos. He kept his eyes locked on the creature, his movements mirroring its as it circled him. With a swift motion, he lunged forward, thrusting his sword toward the beast's throat. The creature snarled, twisting away from the blade, its maw snapping inches from Jason's face.

Arlo lay sprawled on the ground, his vision swimming in and out of focus. Pain radiated through his body, the remnants of the wounds from Fall Lake flaring back to life vigorously. His mind filled with flashes of visions and voices. The roar of the battle pressed in on him, the sound blurring into a tangle of strange voices, growls, and the clash of steel against claw.

He blinked hard, trying to clear his vision, but all he could see was the creature looming over Jason, a dark silhouette against the mottled sunlight filtering through the trees. Arlo's breath came in ragged gasps as he struggled to push himself upright. The world spun, and each movement sent sharp jabs of pain through his ribs and shoulders, a grim reminder of the burden he carried.

"Arlo," Jason shouted, his voice strained as he tried to urge him to his feet. "Get up."

Arlo clenched his teeth, fighting against the waves of agony that threatened to drag him back down. His fingers dug into the earth, clawing for leverage as he pushed against the grassy ground. The rough texture scraped his palms, grounding him even as the creature's roar echoed in his ears. He could feel the vibrations of the beast's movement nearby.

He had to get up.

He drew in a deeper breath, the scent of blood and decay filling his lungs, mingled with the sharp, fresh smell of the forest. With each breath, the pain sharpened, his body screaming in protest. It had not stopped him yet. It would not stop him now.

Arlo's legs trembled beneath him as he managed to shift his weight onto one knee, the ground cool against his skin. He fought to ignore the pulsing ache in his chest. The memories of Fall Lake surged through him. He clung to the faces of the people he had saved, and to the ones he had not. Their hopes pushed back the weight of their loss. They drove him forward, igniting a flicker of determination deep within.

The world was not waiting, and neither was the beast. Arlo did not rise because he was ready. He rose because someone needed him to.

With a final surge of effort, Arlo pushed himself up the rest of the way, bracing his body against the rough bark of the tree. His vision sharpened as the creature came fully into view, its claws glinting menacingly in the afternoon light. Jason stood before it, sword poised, but Arlo knew he needed to be part of this fight. He gritted his teeth, forcing himself to focus, summoning every ounce of strength he had left.

Arlo watched as Jason pressed on, refusing to back down. But the creature, relentless in its fury, caught Jason off guard, slamming its massive paw into him. The impact knocked him to the ground, the breath driven out of his lungs. The beast loomed over Jason, its foul breath washing over him as it prepared to strike.

In that moment, Jason seized his chance. With fierce determination, he stabbed upward, driving his blade into the creature's clouded eye. The beast howled, a horrific sound that tore through the clearing, but it did not relent. Blood streamed from its ruined eye as it raked its claws down Jason's arm. The deep gash bled freely, but Jason gritted his teeth and stayed focused.

Arlo's heart raced as he took in the scene. Azu, too, had been knocked back, struggling to regain his footing, but the creature was fixated on Jason. Arlo felt the pressure of the moment, the urgency to act. He forced himself to concentrate, feeling the warmth of the mana within him, yet it slipped away, elusive as smoke.

"Focus," he whispered to himself, shaking off the dizziness that threatened to cloud his mind. He envisioned Lucy's face, her calm presence anchoring him in the chaos. With each breath, he cleared a bit more of the noise, reaching for the magic that simmered just beneath his skin.

The creature lunged again, claws poised to finish Jason.

Arlo's eyes snapped open, a sudden surge of power igniting within him. He thrust his hand forward, channeling every ounce of energy he could muster. Lightning crackled across his skin, an electric blue glow lifting the hairs on his arms.

With a roar that mingled with the storm building inside him, Arlo unleashed a bolt of lightning. A sharp wind burst outward, whipping leaves and debris away from him. The bolt shot forth and struck the beast with blinding brilliance, sending it staggering back. In that moment, his eyes blazed with an unnatural blue light, calmer than before but no less fierce.

As the creature tried to regain its balance, Arlo did not hesitate. He charged forward, warhammer raised high. The ground beneath him seemed to hum with energy. He brought the hammer down with all his might, summoning a second bolt of lightning to crackle from the weapon and slam into the beast in one final, devastating blow.

The abomination collapsed, its limbs twitching once before going still.

Breathing heavily, Jason wiped sweat from his brow and glanced at Azu, who had settled beside him, panting but ready if needed. "You did it," Jason said, his voice full of tired gratitude.

Arlo stood over the fallen beast and nodded, his heart still pounding with a mix of adrenaline and sorrow as he scanned the surrounding area. The blue light in his eyes faded, the remaining sparks dispersing into small threads of static.

"Yes," he said quietly. "But unfortunately, they did not."

He looked at the scattered remnants of the caravan, the heavy fog of combat and death pressing down on the clearing. Each lifeless body told a story, and the sight pulled at his chest. These were only a few more whose hopes and dreams he would carry with him.

Jason wiped the ichor from his blade, his eyes moving over the gruesome scene. "We cannot just leave them here," he murmured, his voice low and full of regret.

Arlo nodded, his gaze drawn back to the fallen men. "They deserved better. We should give them a proper burial."

Azu padded closer and nudged against Arlo's side, sensing the somber mood. The creature's defeat felt hollow in the face of the loss that surrounded them. Arlo rested a hand on Azu's sleek head, drawing strength from the hybrid's steady presence.

"It just feels wrong, does it not?" Jason said quietly.

"It does," Arlo replied, his voice heavy. "They were here, fighting for their lives, and now..." His voice trailed off.

Jason looked around the clearing, searching for a way to turn the grief into action. "Let us make this right. They deserve peace."

"You alright?" Arlo asked as Jason bent to move one of the fallen men.

"Yeah. That thing just got me a little too good. I will be fine," Jason said. He paused, then added, "And you?"

"I will be better when we get this shipment back and we have a warm bed to sleep in. Let us do this together, then." Arlo offered a small smile.

They set to work, the men moving in quiet solitude. Azu kept a watchful eye, alert for any sign of lingering danger as they gathered the bodies. Each one felt like a personal loss. Jason spoke each of their names, their rank, and how long they had been with the church. He would not say it aloud, but guilt gnawed at him. He had been the one who assigned these men to this task.

As they arranged the bodies side by side, Arlo paused, his expression solemn. "What if this happens again? What if we cannot save them next time?"

Jason met Arlo's gaze, his own heart heavy with the weight of the question. "We cannot carry that burden," he said. "We do what we can, and we fight for those who cannot fight for themselves. That is all we can do."

"Yeah," Arlo sighed, letting Jason's words settle. "I guess that is true."

The two men worked in silence, their thoughts intertwined, the sadness of the moment settling around them like a shroud. As they finished laying the bodies to rest, Arlo felt a calm wash over him, as if honoring their sacrifice helped quiet the turmoil inside.

Once their somber duty was finished, they turned their attention to the scattered wood. They loaded as much of it as they could onto the wagon. The night crept closer, casting long shadows as they prepared to make their way back to Davenport. They would not make it back before nightfall, but they would make it late into the night.

For now, that was enough.

CHAPTER 25

Arlo and Jason trudged through the winding streets of Davenport, the weight of their grim cargo leaving their conversations few. The bodies lay in a makeshift cart, wrapped in tattered blankets, remnants of lives from another kind of monster's attack.

"Just over there," Jason gestured toward a small chapel, its weathered wood illuminated by the rising moons. "They'll be honored here."

Together they guided the cart to the chapel's entrance. A lone villager stood by, his face shifting from curiosity to shock as he realized what lay beneath the blankets.

"May Heir's grace guide them," he whispered quietly.

Arlo exchanged a solemn glance with Jason.

"I'll see to it that they're properly taken care of," Jason said, his voice low but steady.

Arlo nodded, stepping back as Jason took the lead, gently lifting the blankets to reveal the faces of the fallen. He took a moment to speak with the grieving townsfolk, offering what comfort he could, while Arlo hung back, his own heart heavy with the weight of loss. He had witnessed too many lives lost, and each face felt like a bruise on his soul.

Once Jason's task concluded, their next destination was the warehouse where the long-awaited lumber was needed.

"We'll finish here, then I'll head back to the temple," Jason said.

"You've got a way with those abilities of yours," he added, nodding toward Arlo's still-bruised hands. "I didn't know you could channel that kind of magic. You really saved us back there."

Arlo shrugged, a faint smile breaking through the weariness.

"Just did what had to be done. Couldn't let anyone else die today."

Jason clapped Arlo on the shoulder.

"Thanks for having my back. I see why Sorren likes hanging around you."

"Anytime," Arlo replied warmly.

They arrived at the warehouse late into the night and unloaded the lumber in silence. No one was there to greet them, but Arlo knew that Alf and the rest of the crew would be relieved to find it waiting come morning. After a few words of thanks, the two men parted ways.

Arlo headed toward Mama Gretta's, hunger gnawing at him. The thought of a warm meal and a cold drink beckoned him like a siren's call. The tavern's inviting glow shimmered in the evening light, and as he approached, the sounds of laughter and clinking mugs spilled out, wrapping around him like a familiar embrace.

He wondered if Sorren and Lucy would still be up, if they had waited for his return. Either way, he was ready to see his friends, dull the edge of the suffering from the lives lost, and fill himself with whatever was quickest on the menu.

Inside Mama Gretta's tavern, the atmosphere buzzed with energy, laughter mingling with the scent of roasting meat and baked bread. Two patrons stood at the center, voices raised in an intense argument over a trivial matter, something about a fishing net. The crowd swelled around them, blocking the view of most patrons, faces animated with excitement as they watched the scene unfold.

Mama Gretta, her hands on her hips, stepped forward, her presence commanding yet motherly. "Now, now, lads! Save it for the fishing nets, not for each other!"

A booming voice echoed from the back of the tavern.

"I've got money on Ron!" Sorren shouted, laughter woven into his tone.

A smile crept onto Arlo's face as he weaved through the mess, the familiar chaos washing over him. The argument broke up, patrons dispersing, allowing him to slip into the room's heart. He found an empty table near the roaring hearth, a staple for them almost as if it was reserved for them, the fire casting a flickering glow on the wooden walls.

"Bowl of stew and some ale, please," he ordered the passing server, leaning back in his chair, exhaustion creeping into his bones.

Just as he closed his eyes, savoring the heat from the fire, a loud thump that echoed like a victory cry brought him back to reality. Sorren appeared at the table, two mugs in hand and a grin on his face. "Good to see ya back," he said, sliding a mug toward Arlo.

"It's good to be back." Arlo laughed, raising the drink in thanks. "It was fine. Mostly quiet and nice weather. Had some trouble, but we were able to retrieve the lumber. Couldn't have done it without Jason."

Sorren settled into a chair, leaning forward. "You know he's a great man. Glad you got ta see it yourself."

Arlo nodded, appreciating the bond Sorren shared with Jason. "He does seem like a good soul."

Before they could delve deeper into their conversation, a steaming bowl of stew and a frothy tankard of ale arrived at their table, the aroma rich and inviting.

"Seen Lucy?" Arlo asked, glancing around for her familiar red hair.

241

Sorren shrugged, taking a hearty swig of ale. "Yeah, she went up earlier. Probably asleep by now."

Arlo savored the warmth of the stew, the hearty broth a welcome comfort after the day's toll. He relished the taste of spices mingling with tender meat and fresh vegetables, letting each bite linger on his tongue. Sorren leaned back in his chair, a satisfied grin on his face as he listened to Arlo's contented murmurs.

"Alfonze is optimistic about the ship," Sorren said, picking up his mug again. "He thinks we could have it ready before the next full moon."

Arlo nodded, excitement bubbling within him. "That would be incredible. We'll need to make sure we have a crew and equipment prepared too then." He downed his first drink in one go, the ale burning a warm trail down his throat.

"Easy there, hero," Sorren laughed, raising an eyebrow. "You can't go stumbling around like a drunken sailor. That's my job!"

"Just celebrating a bit," Arlo replied, a grin spreading across his face as he started on another mug of ale. "We've faced worse, right?"

"True enough," Sorren admitted.

Arlo took another swig of his drink, the bitter taste mixing with the warmth in his stomach.

As Sorren finished his own drink, he glanced around the tavern, scanning the bustling patrons. The lively chatter faded into background noise, allowing Arlo to lose himself in his thoughts. He thought of Lucy, her vibrant energy and the way her laughter danced in the air. The memory of her comforting presence lingered, and he felt an urge to seek her out.

"I think I'll go check on Lucy," Arlo said, pushing back from the table, his heart racing slightly at the thought of her.

"Sounds good. I'll grab another drink and catch up with you later," Sorren replied, already drifting toward the bar.

With that, Arlo stood, his meal finished, the remnants of his drink still swirling in his mug. He headed toward the stairs, each step feeling heavier with anticipation. He was nervous. If she had already gone to sleep without him, then he worried her nightmares would return. She had said that sharing a room with him helped, and after that first time she had not had them again.

Arlo approached the shared room, a soft glow spilling from within. He hesitated at the door, feeling a flutter of anticipation. Slowly, he pushed it open, the creak of the hinges barely audible over the tavern's distant chatter. The room felt still, the air thick with unspoken words.

His gaze landed on the bed, the sheets rumpled but empty. Disappointment curled in his chest.

"Lucy?" he called softly, but silence answered.

He glanced around, searching for any sign of her presence. The wooden furniture cast shadows, but there was no hint of her. His heart sank a little more. Maybe she had gone back down to the tavern, he thought.

As he turned to leave, a draft brushed past him, catching his attention. He glanced down the hallway toward the balcony, curiosity igniting within him.

He moved toward the open door, the cool breeze swirling around him, a whisper urging him forward. He stepped outside, the night air invigorating and soothing against his skin.

Lucy leaned against the balcony railing, the twin moons casting a light of red and blue over her. She wore her nightclothes, but Arlo recognized the loose tunic as his, hanging over her shoulders.

"Want some company?" Arlo asked, stepping closer, his voice barely above a whisper.

Without a word, she turned and enveloped him in a warm embrace, her arms wrapping tightly around him. A sharp pang shot through his side, a reminder of his earlier injuries, but he held back a grimace, unwilling to break the moment.

"I was worried," she murmured against his shoulder, her breath soft and fragrant, a blend of wildflowers and the night air.

"I'm fine. Just had to deal with some… logistics."

Her hair brushed against his cheek, and he inhaled deeply, captivated by the sweetness of her scent.

"I thought maybe another monster had come back for you," she teased, stepping back slightly to look at him, her eyes sparkling with concern masked by playful banter.

He chuckled, a genuine laugh that eased the tension in his chest. "If it had, I'd be bringing it back as a trophy."

"Now that's a story I'd like to hear," she said, tilting her head, a playful glint in her eyes.

He came to stand beside her, resting his arms on the railing as he watched the moonlight dance on the surface of the water, a comfortable silence enveloping them.

They stood side by side, leaning against the railing, watching the moonlight dance on the water in swirls of red and blue. The night stretched on in a kind of endless peace.

"So, how was your day?" he asked, glancing at her out of the corner of his eye and breaking the silence.

Lucy's eyes lit up, a spark igniting within her. "You wouldn't believe the antics those Nogmi brothers got up to while working on the ship!" She laughed, her excitement bubbling over. "Wicket accidentally spilled a barrel of tar everywhere! You should have seen Alf trying to chase him down to get it cleaned up. He slipped and ended up face-first in it!"

Arlo chuckled, picturing the chaos. "And I thought Jason and I had our hands full. What else happened?"

"Oh, and Willy decided to fashion a makeshift slingshot out of some old rope and a plank," she exclaimed, clapping her hands together. "He was trying to hit a seagull, but instead he launched a whole bucket of nails across the yard. Everyone ducked for cover like it was a battle."

Arlo couldn't help but laugh, her enthusiasm infectious. "I can't imagine how that ended."

"Let's just say there was a lot of yelling, but in the end they were all covered in laughter, though Alf was furious about the nails. He was chasing Willy around with a broom, yelling about safety," she said, her voice filled with joy. "I swear, it felt like I was in a play."

As Lucy spoke, Arlo felt a warmth unfurl in his chest, her laughter mixing with the night air. He leaned closer, intrigued by her animated storytelling.

"And how about you?" she asked, tilting her head, her gaze lingering on him. "Did you manage to keep Jason out of trouble?"

"More like the other way around," he replied, his tone playful. "He was busy with logistics, and I got to know Azu a little better. That creature is impressive. Strong and clever, just like you."

Her cheeks flushed at the compliment, a shy smile spreading across her lips.

"You think I'm clever?" she teased, leaning in slightly, their faces inches apart.

"More than you know," he murmured, his heart racing. The air between them crackled with tension, each word lingering like a promise.

"Arlo..." Lucy began, her voice low and inviting, but then she sighed, breaking the spell. "I'm tired. I think I'd like to go to bed."

He nodded, a hint of disappointment washing over him but understanding the need for rest. "Yeah, let's get some sleep."

They stepped back inside, the room dim and quiet. As Arlo moved to unbuckle his armor, Lucy's gaze lingered on the bruises visible beneath the straps.

"Let me help you with that," she offered, stepping closer.

He hesitated but eventually gave in, allowing her to unfasten the buckles. Each piece of armor clinked as it hit the floor, and when she finally pulled off his shirt, he caught her gaze.

"You've been through a lot," she said, tracing the bruising and cuts along his body.

Arlo felt exposed and vulnerable, but he trusted her. "It's nothing I can't handle."

For a brief moment, the world around them faded, and Lucy's breath hitched. Arlo's physique was striking, each contour and muscle defined beneath his fair skin. He wasn't overly muscular, but the detail in his tone stood out, his body a testament to strength and resilience. She blinked, catching herself before the blush crept up her cheeks.

"Wow," she managed, forcing herself to look away, a hint of fluster creeping into her voice. "You're... um, quite fit."

"Thanks," Arlo replied, a touch of shyness in his own demeanor as he rubbed the back of his neck. "Just comes with the territory, I guess."

Lucy took a breath, shaking off the moment. "Let me help you relax. I can give you a massage; it might help with the pain."

"Are you sure?" he asked, concern flickering in his eyes.

"Absolutely," she said with a reassuring smile. "Just sit down."

He sank into a chair, the weight of the day settling heavily on his shoulders. As she placed her hands on his back, a soothing warmth radiated from her palms. The moment her fingers pressed against his skin, small red droplets of mana seeped from her hands, dancing like embers in the air.

As the red mana met the blue ribbons that spiraled off his bruised skin, they intertwined, creating a beautiful, shimmering effect that enveloped them both. The merging of their energies eased the burden of pain that clung to Arlo, the tension in his muscles unwinding with each passing moment.

"Earlier, when we found the caravan..." he began, his voice low, drifting into the memory as Lucy continued her gentle massage. "We ran into trouble. Some sort of beast attacked them. I could feel the fear in the air. It was like the weight of the world pressed down on us."

Lucy listened intently, focusing on the rhythm of his words and the connection forming between them as they shared this moment of vulnerability.

Arlo sat in the chair, the weight of his earlier encounters beginning to lift as Lucy's hands worked their magic on his back.

"It was chaos," he continued, his voice soft, the memories flooding back. "The creature burst from the trees, and the men were caught off guard. I could hear their fear, feel it even."

Lucy pressed her thumbs deeper into the knots of tension, her fingers dancing over the bruises that marred his skin. "And then you fought it off like the hero you are?" she teased lightly, a playful lilt in her voice.

He chuckled, but the sound was laced with a hint of sadness. "I didn't feel like a hero. Just a man trying to keep his friends alive."

With each stroke, Lucy's touch melted away the remnants of his burdens, the exhaustion that clung to him like a shroud. He felt himself sinking deeper into the chair, his thoughts drifting away from the chaos of battle to the warmth radiating from her hands. The room felt smaller, their connection tightening like the strings of a bow, taut yet exhilarating.

"Just a man, huh?" she said, a teasing note threading through her words. "Seems like you're downplaying it a bit. I'd say you're more than that."

He caught her eye in the mirror across the room, a flicker of mischief sparking in her gaze. For a moment, he lost himself in the depths of her green eyes, their vibrancy pulling him in like a tide.

"Maybe," he muttered, suddenly self-conscious under her scrutiny. The warmth of her fingers and the rhythm of her touch had coaxed a sense of calm that he had long forgotten. The chaotic memories faded, replaced by a gentle pulse of intimacy, one that neither of them dared to define just yet.

As Lucy's hands glided lower, her playful demeanor persisted, her fingers brushing against the contours of his shoulders. "I think you should give yourself more credit. Not everyone could face down monsters and still come out standing."

He felt a smile tug at the corners of his mouth, her flirtation a sweet distraction from the burdens that had plagued him for so long. "And what would you know about facing monsters?" he replied, attempting to keep the banter light, ignoring the shiver that her closeness caused him.

"I have my own battles," she said lightly, her voice softening, yet the tease lingered in her tone. "But I suppose we all do, don't we?"

Arlo nodded, the room growing quieter as their conversation faded into a comfortable silence. The connection between them hummed, a secret melody known only to the two of them, leaving the air thick with unspoken promises.

As Lucy finished the massage, her hands lingered for a moment, warmth radiating between them. Arlo leaned back, savoring the lingering sensation of her touch, his mind clearer now, free from the weight of recent events.

"I appreciate that," he said, a soft smile gracing his lips. "But now I should probably change before we settle in for the night."

Lucy nodded, her cheeks tinged with a faint blush. "Right. I should probably."

"Actually," he interrupted, a playful glint in his eye, "could you turn around? Just for a second?"

Her brow raised, but she complied, turning her back to him. Arlo quickly unbuckled his belt and stripped off his trousers, the fabric pooling at his feet and causing a slight ruffle in the air. The cool air brushed against his bare skin, sending a shiver through him, but he felt liberated without the heavy weight of armor.

"Okay, you can turn back now," he called out, pulling on a clean pair of trousers. He kept his shirt off, feeling the freedom of the night air against his skin.

Lucy turned, her gaze flickering over him before she quickly averted her eyes, a shy smile creeping onto her face. "Looking... comfortable."

"Gotta let the skin breathe after a day like today," he replied with a chuckle, easing onto the edge of the bed. He felt the bed shift as Lucy settled in beside him, the sheets cool against his warm skin.

They lay on their sides, a comfortable distance apart, yet as the night pressed on they mutually crept closer to each other. Silence and the darkness of their dreams finally gave them restful sleep.

CHAPTER 26

The past week had flown by in a flurry of demanding work and long hours. The ship took shape in the old dockyard, craftsmen working day and night under the watchful eyes of Sorren and Alfonze. Materials arrived day after day, the streets bustling with laborers hauling timber, sails, and iron.

On this particular day, Arlo, Lucy, and Sorren found themselves strolling through the lively streets, the sounds of laughter and conversation swirling around them. They had just dropped off a shipment of supplies at a nearby tavern when Sorren glanced up at the sky, noticing the clouds gathering ominously.

"Looks like we might get some rain," he said with a frown.

"Not just rain," Arlo said, feeling a strange charge in the air. "Something feels off."

Lucy glanced at him, concern flickering in her eyes. "What do you mean?"

Before he could answer, the air shifted. A thick fog rolled in, swallowing the streets and shrouding the townsfolk in an eerie haze. The laughter faded and was replaced by an ominous silence.

"What the?" Sorren began, but his words fell flat as the fog grew heavier, swallowing them in its grasp. Silhouettes of citizens shifted into distorted and strange shapes. Then, without warning, a figure emerged from the shapes and cut through the fog, bathed in an unsettling golden light that gave color to the mist around them. The figure moved slowly and with purpose.

"Stay close!" Arlo shouted, grabbing Lucy's arm as the trio instinctively huddled together.

The golden figure broke free from the thick fog, its skin a polished bronze, gleaming beneath the muted sunlight. Intricate golden armor adorned parts of its body, reflecting the light in dazzling patterns. But the being's wings were what truly stood out to them. Enormous feathered wings unfurled behind it, electricity arcing between the feathers.

The fog transformed, swirling into a tempest of gold that sparked static all around them. Arlo reached for his hammer, but he had left it behind at Mama Gretta's. Sorren also reached for his sword, but found nothing there. They were unarmed, having grown comfortable with their presumed safety on the streets of Davenport. Their eyes were struck by the immense size of the being and the fear it produced. With a sudden, powerful beat of its wings, the figure shot upward, its wings carrying its weight effortlessly as it hovered above them.

Bolts of lightning shot out of its hands faster than any of them could react. The cobblestones it struck cracked and shifted as the energy flew past them. The being pooled another ball of electrical mana into its hand and readied another strike.

"Get down!" Sorren yelled, but Arlo was already moving. He did not have his hammer, but he did have something else. A power he barely understood but could no longer ignore. Cerulean mana surged through him, and without thinking, he stepped in front of Lucy, his hands extended outward instinctively, his eyes pouring with mana.

A shimmering blue shield formed around them, energy arcing in the air between them and the relentless assault from above. Arlo's body began to strain, voices began to fill his mind, his teeth gritting as bolt after bolt crashed against the shield, then dispersed into nothingness. Everything else faded away. There was only the shield, only the mana that coursed through his body.

Arlo's mind was locked on the bubble of blue energy, voices deafening his ears to anyone or anything else around him. The pains of the burdens he was slowly accepting aggravated him as he let out a massive growl. Blue enveloped his entire vision before slowly fading away. His eyes were freed now, blurry but no longer blocked by the blue mana as before.

Lucy and Sorren were nowhere to be found.

Arlo found himself walking through a magnificent room. The stones beneath his feet were cold, and ahead of him loomed six massive statues, each one depicting a figure he could not quite make out. He blinked, attempting to bring the view into focus, but the details remained out of his reach. At the end of the hall stood a throne, glittering with what he thought were jewels, though the colors all bled together in a wash of blue.

A voice called out to him, distant yet commanding.

Drop the shield.

Suddenly, Arlo was back in the streets, the roar of the storm returning in full force. The shield faltered, but before he could react, a wave of molten flame shot past him, heading straight for the golden figure. The warmth was familiar, comforting, and in that moment he recognized it.

Lucy.

Her flames were relentless, each passing second causing the wave to grow larger, her body shivering at the use of her own magic. Shrieking cries echoed through the area as Lucy cried out in pain.

Her body was burning up, every use of her abilities leading her to bloody tears and raw agony.

But Lucy was not going to stand by and let this being attack her friends. She fought through the pain and held on until she felt the resistance end on the other side. She let the flames die down, but stood her ground with heavy, ragged breaths.

She did not stop. Even as her voice broke into ragged screams, she stood firm, her flames an undying defense against the figure. With a final push, she unleashed a torrent of fire that blazed with her ferocity, the likes of which none of them had seen before. The golden figure paused, as if it was considering. Then, with a single beat of its wings, it soared into the sky, breaking the storm and pulling it along with it.

Arlo and Sorren glanced at her and felt as if they were in the presence of someone, or something, else entirely. The fiery mana that pulsed around her like a beating heart had taken shape. Two red curls of mana flanked each other on her forehead. Twin embers had pushed out of her back.

Arlo's breath was heavy, his body aching in constant pain, and he quickly fell to one knee. He couldn't shake what he saw. What was that? Why was he in a throne room? What was going on with Lucy?

Lucy felt the pain of her magic taking its toll. The flames dispersed and her hands were left aching in scorched pain. Her eyes were stained with streaks of tearful blood. For a moment she held herself strong and tall, a majestic sight, with the crimson aura surrounding her, her emerald eyes slowly breaking through. But her body began to falter, her knees trembling before giving out beneath her.

Arlo was quick and was able to get his arm around her waist to hold her steady. Her body was hot, extremely hot to the touch. She looked up into Arlo's eyes as the red mana almost appeared to walk away within her emerald eyes. She smiled and let a simple whisper leave her lips before she fell into a rest.

"Malik."

"Malik?" Arlo and Sorren both said in unison.

"We need to get her to Alysia," Arlo said, his voice filled with worry. He lifted Lucy into his arms, despite the fatigue threatening to overtake him.

"Agreed, let's hurry before that thing comes back. You got her?" Sorren asked, taking notice of Arlo's own fatigue. "You don't always have to carry the weight alone, you know."

Arlo shook his head, already moving in the direction of the church. "I'll be fine. Let's hurry, before that thing decides to come back."

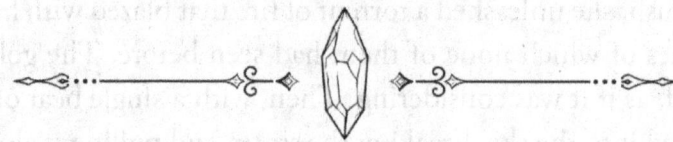

The doors to the church burst open hastily as Sorren held them for Arlo and Lucy. Sorren led them toward the infirmary, passing several clergy members and priests in the middle of their own daily duties. As they entered the busy infirmary, the sight of the remaining wounded from Fall Lake settled in, striking an ache into their hearts. Barely any beds remained, but as they caught sight of Alysia they immediately headed toward her.

Alysia turned from her work, her eyes sharply locking onto Lucy in Arlo's arms. The sight of the crimson-haired woman, limp in his grasp, sent a shock of urgency through her. Without a word, she motioned for a place to lay Lucy, her hands and the hands of several other healers already glowing with white or blue mana, eager to use whatever magics they had on her.

"What happened?" she asked as she began to examine Lucy, running her hands over the scorched skin.

The tips of Lucy's fingers were blackened and blistered, her palms swollen.

Sorren leaned against the stone wall, his eyes fixed on the window in expectation for trouble to come barreling through at any moment. "She had… uh, trouble with her magic," he said. "It got away from her."

Alysia did not glance up, but she heard the hidden tone behind his words. Instead she focused on Lucy, her magic weaving through the damaged skin, repairing the blisters and burns inch by inch. Alysia stopped briefly as she noticed something strange she had never seen before, but continued on without acknowledging it or drawing attention to it.

Arlo let out a deep breath. His body screamed with fatigue he had not realized he was feeling. He was fixated on watching Lucy's face. She stirred slightly under Alysia's touch, her eyelids fluttering open, revealing her deep green eyes.

"Arlo?" she whispered.

"I'm here," Arlo said softly, leaning in until he was only inches from her face. "We are safe now, thanks to you."

Lucy's fluttering gaze drifted between Arlo, Sorren, and Alysia, struggling to piece together the fragments of her memory. "What... happened?"

"You pushed yourself too far," Arlo replied, brushing fallen strands of her hair that blocked her face. "You used too much magic."

Sorren stepped forward, crossing his arms. "But you did well," he said, a smirk tugging at his mouth. "You stopped the flames and the figure. We're still standing thanks to you."

Lucy's eyes flickered, his words barely registering as exhaustion pulled her back under. Her lips curved into a faint smile.

"She's lucky she didn't do more damage to herself," Alysia said, dismissing the other healers away. She continued to run her fingers along Lucy's hands. The white glow of her healing magic deepened to a red. It was Sorren who caught it this time, and Alysia's questioning look, as her mana appeared to be pulled by Lucy's red. The mana repaired the lingering burns on her skin. Burns like this normally required patience and precision and were best not rushed, but whatever magic lay within Lucy appeared to have a mind of its own and a desire to heal itself.

"She'll be fine. She just needs time to rest." This time Alysia glanced to Sorren and then to Arlo. "What really happened?"

Arlo exhaled a full breath, a flood of relief washing over him as he heard Alysia's claim to her health. His eyes never left Lucy's face, and he remained quiet as he pushed out every other sound around him while the world carried on, unaware of any danger that may have passed.

Sorren remained by the window, his posture relaxed but still alert and scanning for any additional oddities. "We were attacked in the streets," he said with only a glance toward Alysia.

"Attacked?" Alysia said, surprised and rather loudly. She caught herself and repeated more quietly. "Attacked?"

"Yeah, we were attacked by some winged golden figure with bronze skin. Believe it or not…"

"Sorren, are you saying you were attacked by a Deva?" she asked, now fully distracted from her duties to Lucy. Sorren's first silence crept on in almost a confirmation. "Sorren?"

"Yeah, I think so. Right before Lucy passed out, she said his name… Malik." Sorren's voice was low and grim, and he had to make sure no others were listening before he spoke again.

"Why were you all being attacked by Heir's Deva? By the Gracemother, how did you even survive it?" she asked, amazed at the fact that they were still alive.

Sorren lifted his arms and shrugged, then pointed toward Lucy's hands. "Arlo shielded us, and then Lucy let hellfire loose and they left."

Alysia let go of Lucy's hands and wrapped them in a linen cloth. She took one more glance at her skin, amazed at the amount of healing that had already taken place.

"She will be fine," Alysia said, looking toward Arlo. "Whatever magic she has inside of her fused with my own and healed her hands enough. Her palms are still reddened, fingertips still have some blistering. She should keep them wrapped with the ointment I've applied to them and she will be fine within a day or two."

"Thank you," Arlo whispered. "I'm going to stay here with her for a while if that's okay."

Alysia nodded, taking away the soiled medical tools. As she rounded the corner to dispose of them, a strong arm met her shoulder, stopping her in place.

"Alysia, can you keep this between us?" Sorren asked, leading her to a quiet place.

"Of course," she replied.

"Something hasn't been right since I brought Arlo from that crater. Lucy also claims to have woken up in that crater. Something just doesn't..." His voice trailed off before Alysia continued for him.

"Feel right? I understand what you mean. There is something different about both of them. Something raw, but powerful."

"Exactly. It worries me what role they both actually play in all this. Especially if they are being... hunted." He leaned in to say it quietly.

"I wish I had more to tell you. The books I have read only speak of the Devas as existing and give little more detail," Alysia added.

"Yeah, I've read 'em too. Devas are the hand of the gods. Malik being Heir's enforcer. Which doesn't help me with the feeling that they've come to take back Heir's hammer."

"It does seem strange, and they both possess an immensely powerful sense of mana within them. When I used my mana on Lucy, it was as if her own was taking mine on, as if it made it its own."

"Like a parasite?"

"Something like that."

"Oof," Sorren sighed. "Leaves me with a lot to think about. And makes me worry about everyone's part in what is actually going on. Anyway, sorry about the trouble. I'll check back on them later."

CHAPTER 27

Sorren stepped into the nave of the church and crossed the threshold. Many worshippers had begun to gather, and prayers murmured throughout as they called to their gods. His heavy boots clunked against the floor as he consciously tried to lighten his steps so he would not disturb anyone in the area.

He glanced back one more time, considering Lucy's state and her brief outbursts that had almost come true. He tried to ignore what would have happened if she had used her mana against the Kingsguard only a few weeks ago. Brushing the thoughts from his mind, he turned toward the library. The wooden doors groaned against the force of him pushing them open. Inside, the view of leather-wrapped books crept into sight. Many of the volumes had been crated in preparation for transport to Fall Lake, where the new grand chapel had been built and was fortunate not to have been destroyed during the attack.

His fingers trailed along the worn spines of many of the religious tomes. He was seeking answers, or at least more information. His studies did not go into detail about the Devas, instead focusing on the gods themselves, primarily Heir.

Skimming the titles, his eyes stayed focused. Many of the titles were familiar, detailing legends of the gods and the history of their land, but nothing that he believed related to Malik, the Deva of Heir.

Frustration washed over him until a particular title caught his eye. The book was bound in cracked, weathered leather, its title barely legible.

The Celestial Hierarchy: A Compendium of the Divine

Sorren's lips curled into a grin as he believed he had found the one. He pulled it free, the weight heavy in his hands, and the history stored within the book felt heavier still. The pages were fragile, yellowed with age, and gave off a musty scent of ancient wisdom. His eyes darted over the script, taking in detailed descriptions of the celestial order. The book spoke of angelic beings, divine warriors and protectors, and even included a brief description of the Devas but did not go into detail.

"Dammit," Sorren cursed under his breath, snapping the book shut with a sharp thud that sent dust spiraling into the air. He placed it back upon the shelf and moved to another section of the library, his jaw clenched with frustration. If Malik had crossed paths with them, there had to be a reason. He felt it was his responsibility to learn what he could about him, to see what he wanted.

His fingers hovered over another row before landing on a smaller, less ornate book. The title was written in faded gold but caught his attention all the same.

The Warriors of the Divine: The Deva

Sorren's pulse quickened, hope stirring inside his chest as he carefully pulled the book from its place and opened it quickly. This book felt less cared for than the previous one, its pages much more worn, and he saw smudged markings and blurring of words that he felt could become a problem. The pages themselves were filled with illustrations of powerful celestial beings, figures armored in radiant light, their eyes blazing with the strength of the divine. And then, in the middle of the book, an entire section dedicated to Malik himself. Their golden hair framed a stern face, eyes that glimmered with the heat of a sun. Malik appeared tall, almost as if their semi-humanoid shape had been elongated and stretched.

The text detailed Malik's role as the enforcer of Heir's will, his protector, and also his judge. Wrathful when crossed, merciless against those who defied the order he was sworn to protect. Sorren's heart continued to race as the Deva's responsibility became more clear. Malik was not just a guardian, but the embodiment of judgment, swift and unyielding.

"So you are both the shield and the sword," Sorren thought to himself. If Malik viewed Arlo or Lucy as a threat to Heir's balance, then was he acting as a protector or a punisher?

His thoughts raced back to the claim of the hammer that Arlo wielded. Was he in fact truly wielding Heir's own weapon? All of Heir's followers knew of the hammer, and its name was etched into the previous book under the section of Heir himself.

Elduun.

"It's just trying to take back the hammer?" Sorren said to himself, continuing his research.

The air in the library felt colder as Sorren flipped to the next page. There, hidden among the stories of Malik's legendary battles, were accounts of his interactions with mortals. Sorren's fingers trembled slightly as he read of those who had wielded magic tied to Heir. Some had been guided by Malik, others… destroyed by him.

Sorren strained his eyes, trying to read the smudged text that came next. Names mentioned of those who came before were illegible and left as a mystery to Sorren, and possibly the rest of the world.

"I need more," he said, scouring the shelves for any other information he could find. Each book he pulled held some tidbit of information, yet none of it seemed to hold any answers about Malik or Arlo and Lucy's place. He continued to flip through the pages, each purpose of each book offering a glimpse, but everything Sorren had found so far rested in history long past and gave little detail. It read more as if the reader already knew the details of the Devas.

The only thing he knew at this point was that Malik, and the other Devas, had not been seen since the Hassien War, and the gods even further than that. His hand rose and rubbed his scalp as he dove deeper into his memories, seeking and searching for more information.

"Come on, Sorren, think, think," he repeated to himself over and over again.

His thoughts were interrupted by the soft creak of a floorboard behind him.

Sorren's hand instinctively went to the dagger at his belt as he turned, grey eyes narrowed in suspicion. He was greeted not by a threat, but by the hunched figure of an elderly man. Sorren recognized him as the temple's librarian. Silver hair was barely visible beneath a tattered hood. Sorren knew he was one of the oldest living amongst the people, and also knew he had recently taken time off from his duties due to his age catching up to him.

The old man gave a small, friendly smile as he approached, his cane tapping lightly against the floor.

"Forgive me for startling you, young master," the librarian said, his voice gravelly and ragged. "Anything this old man can help you with?"

Sorren relaxed, although his unease lingered. "I'm looking for information on the Deva of Heir, Malik."

The librarian raised a bushy brow. "Malik, you say? A rare topic in this day. So few know what he has actually done for our people."

Sorren hesitated. He wasn't sure how much to reveal. On one hand, he wanted to trust the old man wouldn't go blabbing about his search to Dolph or any other officials. But he had little other choice, and it seemed the man had more information on Malik than any of the ink he had read to this point.

"I found this book," Sorren said, raising the book for the man to see, "but it's old, and it doesn't mention more recent events."

The librarian stepped closer, adjusting his glasses so his eyes could scan the title. "Ah, yes, *Warriors of the Divine*. Written several hundred years ago." The man paused and took a deep breath, taking a seat on a bench nearby. "Come join me. If you are looking for events after the Hassien War. Well, I lived through the end of it, believe it or not, and we heard many tales of the Deva and Malik."

"The last known event of Malik occurred at the very end of the war. He and the other Devas fought the Titans and Colossi over many years, each battle ending in a stalemate until the day of the Cleaving."

Sorren took a seat next to the man. He hadn't even thought to ask the librarian until now, and he felt silly for not having done so.

"So Malik was there, alongside the other Devas, fighting to protect the gods' chosen from the wrath of the Hassien army. Those titan born were determined to overthrow the god born of Shularix and take this land for theirs. Malik's role was to protect us and execute those who threatened Heir's people. Many say he fought fiercely, but he was injured during the battle with Shular, an injury that never fully healed."

Sorren's eyes widened, feeling so close to the information he had been searching for the entire time. "Injured? How?"

The librarian tapped his cane against the stone floor, his voice dropping to a near whisper. "A wound dealt by Shular himself when he performed the Cleaving."

Sorren's confusion was evident on his face as he tried to piece the events together.

"After Malik knew Shular was dying, his arrogance took hold and he turned his back on the titan, leaving himself vulnerable. In an act of desperation, Shular used his final strength to try to slay Malik as

262

well, and he molded the northern mountain peaks to pierce Malik. Little did Shular and Malik know that their actions would cause a catastrophic change to the entire world. This event caused a separation in the land as Shular's body molded into the earth itself, causing the lands to separate, the sea level to rise, and the next few days to be filled with tidal waves, flooding, earthquakes, and the loss of lives immeasurable. And thus, it was Malik who caused the Cleaving inadvertently."

"They don't teach the story like that when we are young."

The man smiled with a shake of his head. "No, no they don't."

"So why tell me now?"

"My final days are numbered. What a shame it would be to let knowledge of our past go to waste."

While Sorren himself already knew the answer, it didn't sit well with him, and a chill ran down his spine. "But if Malik's been gone for so long, why is he showing up now? Why would he suddenly—"

"That, my boy, is the question, isn't it? What could possibly draw a Deva back after a century of silence?"

Before Sorren could respond, the old man pulled from his robes a slender and undecorated tome. "Perhaps this will help you in your search. Do not share the contents of this book with just anyone else, but this book may contain some... less flattering accounts of the gods' and church's dealings with the titans and their kin. You may find what you are looking for here."

Sorren accepted the book with a nod of thanks, although his mind seemed elsewhere. An uncomfortable prickling sensation crept up the back of his neck. He glanced around the library, suddenly aware of how quiet it had become, how the shadows seemed to loom longer than they should.

Am I being watched?

His eyes darted toward the far corner of the room, where the dim light barely reached. For a moment, he thought he saw movement, just a flicker, like the shadow of someone slipping away. He blinked, his heart racing, but the space was empty.

He turned back to the librarian to find he was gone. Eager to move past this point, Sorren remembered that he had other obligations to attend to as well. He would keep hold of the book he had been given and try to find answers later. They were days away, after all, from the ship, his ship, being ready.

CHAPTER 28

Lucy began to toss within her bed, her awareness slowly rising. Sunlight shone through the window, casting light on the curtained walls surrounding her. She blinked, bringing her surroundings into focus until her eyes landed on Arlo, seated in a chair beside her. He watched her quietly, leaning forward with a relieved smile.

Her hands, wrapped tightly in layers of bandages, twitched with discomfort as the memory of their fight with the golden figure flashed into her mind.

"Arlo?" she rasped.

Arlo leaned forward, his voice gentle with concern. "How are you feeling?"

Lucy's gaze dropped to her hands, trying to fully piece together the details of her memory. "Why… why are my hands like this?" she asked almost to herself, not even registering his question.

Arlo hesitated at first, his smile fading. "You used your magic during the fight. But you pushed yourself too far, Lucy. And you passed out afterward."

The weight of his words didn't settle with her. Instead, flashes of fire, the heat of mana surging through her, and the burning sensation in her hands came rushing back. A golden figure, a sense of overwhelming power, loomed in her memory, but every time her mind grasped to reveal the details, they slipped away.

"We fought someone," Lucy said distantly. "I remember a figure, golden, powerful. I remember acting and then everything... exploded out of me. And then my dream..."

"That was Malik," he said, with a heavy significance on the name. "Or a version of them, at least. They appeared out of nowhere, and we barely managed to hold them off."

"Malik..." The name rolled off her tongue as if it belonged there. "That name seems so familiar, I think..." Her voice trailed off as she held her bandaged hands against her temple. More memories dropped back into focus: the battle, and eventually her dream.

"According to Sorren, Malik is a Deva of Heir. But Malik hasn't been seen in Lyorion for at least a hundred years. And now, suddenly, they are here when everything started at Fall Lake."

"What do they want?" she whispered.

"We don't know. Sorren mentioned that Malik is the judge of Heir, that they appear whenever a threat to Heir shows up. I don't know if it's the beast in Fall Lake, the hammer, or..."

"Me?" she whispered even quieter, leaning forward into her memories. "I had another dream, and Malik was in it. I was running, leading people against... Heir and Malik. I remember their smile, then so many were dead and I was left standing..." She hesitated before continuing, reliving the memories of her dream that felt lifelike. "And then I was falling, or maybe..." Her voice faltered as the sensation of that fall lingered around her, the ground rushing up toward her, the wind pressing against her.

A knock interrupted her as Alysia entered the room. "Good morning, I hope I am not interrupting."

Lucy shook her head, glancing away as she stayed lost in her thoughts.

"No, it's fine," Arlo answered.

"I just came to change the bandages and look at Lucy's skin. Happy to see you awake. Are you feeling well? Any pain?" Alysia asked, preparing some ointments and new linens as she spoke.

"I'm fine," Lucy replied absently, lost in discerning her vivid dreams from the fragments of reality. As she sat there, a strange sensation washed over her, like an itch she couldn't reach. Not from her hands, though they did feel odd beneath the bandages. It was something deeper, a discomfort she couldn't quite place but that left her feeling like she was missing something.

Alysia carefully unwrapped the bandages around Lucy's hands. As the final layer came off, she gasped softly, her eyes widening in surprise.

"Lucy..." Alysia whispered, inspecting her skin with awe and confusion. "Your hands, they're completely healed. There isn't even a scar remaining." She quickly turned Lucy's palms over, studying them closely. "I've seen plenty of burns like this before, and they don't heal like this. Not this remarkably quick."

Lucy glanced down at her hands, flexing her fingers. The skin was smooth, unblemished, as if the burns had never happened. But instead of relief, that same nagging sensation grew stronger, the feeling that something was missing.

A light balm was applied to Lucy's skin, more out of routine than necessity, before Alysia rewrapped her hands. "If you continue like this, you should be able to leave by tomorrow," she said, still full of wonder.

Lucy nodded, but her thoughts drifted elsewhere, to the strange hollow ache that had been there since she'd woken up in the crater. It was stronger now, perhaps from the use of her magic she wasn't fully aware she contained. But the hole she felt wasn't just from her memory, but from herself entirely.

The harbor was alive with activity as Davenport's citizens gathered to witness the return of King Frederick. Banners in the kingdom's colors fluttered high above, and the soft voices of the crowd rose as time pressed on. Children sat on their parents' shoulders to catch a better glimpse of the approaching ship, while vendors shouted food and drink at the growing crowd.

Sorren and Jason stood at the forefront of the gathering, their armor polished to a shine and their posture rigid, reflecting the formality of the occasion. Both of them flanked the main path leading from the dock to the city's cobbled streets, eyes fixed on the horizon where the ship was expected. Behind them, the people of Davenport waited in eager whispers of anticipation.

The King's ship came into view, cutting through the water with elegance. As it docked, the gangway lowered, and King Frederick descended with his Kingsguard. Clad in a deep blue cloak embroidered with silver, the King moved with confidence. His crown caught the sunlight, sending glares across the dock.

The crowd instinctively parted as the King stepped forward, his gaze sweeping the dock in greeting of his people. He approached Sorren and Jason, who both greeted him with a bow. As the King reached them, he gave a nod of acknowledgement, offering a slight but firm smile to the two Porters.

"Rise," King Frederick ordered, his voice clear and steady. The two men stood, and he wasted no time. "Walk with me," he said, motioning for them to follow as he moved through the crowd, offering nods and waves to his people.

The town erupted into cheers as he passed, banners waving in the air, and children ran alongside, eager for a glimpse of their ruler. Sorren and Jason kept pace beside him, their minds already shifting to the task at hand. The festive atmosphere of the harbor was a contrast to the King's solemn air, which went unnoticed by the people, but not by Sorren and Jason.

Through various points of calm, the King was able to make conversation with the two Porters, seeking an update on their current standings.

"The ship is nearly complete. We've made significant progress and are ready to transport it to the launch site and make final adjustments," Sorren said confidently.

Frederick's face lit up for the first real time, but there was forced restraint behind his excitement. "Remarkable. I knew I could trust you, Sorren. The work you've done is nothing short of admirable."

Once they were within the palace walls, Frederick's demeanor changed. While he still seemed to be happy, there was something eating at him inside. "Where are Arlo and Lucy?"

"Arlo and Lucy are both recovering. Lucy had an accident that put her out for a few days, but she's improving. Although she has been put off from directly lifting and working entirely on the project, she has helped in other ways. She and Arlo left earlier to visit the launch site and make sure the construction there is going as planned."

The King's expression flickered, something unreadable passing over his face before he nodded, satisfied. "Good. I've something important to tell you all and would like for them to be here when I do."

Jason, who had been silent up until now, cleared his throat. "I'm sure they'll be back soon, Your Majesty. Is everything okay?"

"Yes, everything will be fine. Some information has come to light, and I plan to address it with all of you first before we announce it to the town. Let us plan the feast the night before launch. I think it is only right that we are able to celebrate this grand accomplishment together, but we'll speak more soon."

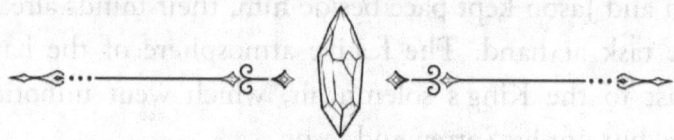

Arlo and Lucy walked along the southern edge of the continent, where the new dock stood proudly against the sapphire waters. The air was calm, with a subtle cool breeze that kept the warm air from being unbearable. The dock stretched out into the sea, its planks freshly laid and secured, waiting for the ship that would soon take them on their journey to find Eckerd.

A cool breeze rolled off the ocean, carrying with it the gentle scent of salt water. The dock was only the start of the expansion of Davenport, as the engineers had already been discussing improvements and future efforts to build more vessels like it. One day they imagined much of the city would stretch the entire path to the dock, lines of vessels this size, and some imaginably larger.

Lucy glanced back at the structure as they walked further down the coastline. "The dock looks perfect. You think it'll hold up after we set sail?" she asked.

"It'll do more than that. Once it's done, this dock won't just be for one ship. There are plans for a whole shipyard here one day," Arlo said with a touch of pride.

They reached a spot on the sandy beach where the grass met the sea, the ground sloping gently toward the shoreline. Wild Akhlut pups played nearby, sleek black and white forms splashing through the shallows as their mother kept watch. The sight was calming and untouched by humanity, with years of natural beauty bursting from the entire area.

Lucy dropped down onto the soft sand, leaning back on her elbows as she let the sea breeze wash over her. She watched as a dolphin leapt up from the waves in the distance, its graceful arc sending droplets of water glittering in the setting sun.

"It's beautiful here," Lucy whispered so as not to break the serenity.

Arlo took a seat beside her, his gaze sweeping across the ocean. "It is. And quiet. No hammering, no shouting. Just the sound of the waves. Feels like everything's how it's supposed to be."

She smiled softly, tracing the horizon off in the distance. "Why don't more people live out here? Seems like... paradise."

He shrugged, the corner of his mouth twisting upward. "Some do, but most stick to the cities. Easier to buy what they need rather than hunt or fish for it. Plus, there's safety in numbers."

Lucy turned toward him, a teasing spark glinting in her eyes. "Is that why you lived in Fall Lake? Didn't fancy yourself a fisher?"

Arlo laughed and shook his head. "No, if I had my choice, I'd live in a place like this. A quiet home, not too big, not too small. Just enough."

She leaned closer as curiosity began to fill her. "Just enough for what?"

Arlo's gaze softened, his tone becoming more thoughtful. "For me, a wife... maybe a few kids. Enough space to build with my own hands, fish for what I need, hunt when I have to. Close enough to town to get supplies, but far enough away to not be bothered."

Lucy's playful smile shifted. "Sounds perfect. A place for the kids to run wild, explore, and grow up free."

Arlo nodded. "Yeah, free to be themselves, away from all the noise and politics."

She shifted her focus back out to the ocean, watching the waves reflect the golden light of the sun. She lost herself for a moment as she traced her mind for any other remembrance of her past. Memories of the past month washed over her with tinkling imagery she couldn't piece together, all of it leading to moments that were just out of reach.

"That kind of life and freedom sounds nice. But I think you'd get lonely out there, living that quiet dream."

He chuckled, leaning back on his hands. "Maybe. Could always use some company to keep me from getting too lazy."

"Oh, you wouldn't be lonely for long. I'd make sure of that. Storm Lucy would come and liven up that quiet little life of yours, whether you like it or not."

Lucy let out another laugh, tossing a handful of sand playfully in his direction. "You would get tired of me real fast. I've been known to make some noise."

"I'll take my chances," he said, brushing the sand from his arm.

The two of them sat in silence, watching the Akhlut pups wrestle just up the shore. The wind rustled gently through the grass, and waves crashed along the beach line. Lucy absentmindedly traced patterns in the sand with her finger, her thoughts far away.

Arlo was the first to stand, breaking Lucy's trance. "Come on, we should head back before the sun sets," he said, offering her a hand with a warm smile.

Lucy looked up at him, her playful smirk returning as she took his hand. "You just like bossing me around, don't you?"

He laughed as he lifted her to her feet. "Someone has to keep you in line."

Lucy let out a mocking laugh, shaking her head as she brushed sand off her clothes. "You're lucky I let you. I could make things a lot harder for you, you know!"

"I'd like to see you try," he said lightly as they began to walk up the beach.

The breeze teased Lucy's hair into soft waves around her face. She gave him a sideways glance. "Don't tempt me, mister. I have plenty of ways to make your life difficult."

"Oh, really?" he said, taking a few quickened steps ahead and continuing his walk backwards. "You going to sabotage the ship?"

She gasped dramatically with a hand over her heart, sand dispersing around her feet as she stomped her foot. "How dare you even suggest that! I'm deeply offended."

"Just saying, you'd make a dangerous enemy."

"Maybe I'm already dangerous," Lucy teased with a playful poke to his side. "You'll just have to be careful around me."

"Oh, I'm plenty careful," Arlo replied with a low voice as he turned to walk beside her once more. "Especially around you."

Redness rushed to her cheeks, a small smile spreading across the corners of her mouth. She bumped his shoulder lightly with her own. "Careful, huh? I'm not that scary."

"Scary? No," Arlo said, his voice even softer. "Just... unpredictable."

They slowed their steps as they reached the edge of the shore, standing there for what felt like an eternity before either of them said anything.

"You know," Arlo began, "it's so peaceful out here."

Lucy nodded, her gaze still focused on the line of the horizon off in the distance. A gentle unknown, a dangerous welcoming. "Yeah, I could get used to this. Being away from everything, just... taking in a breath of fresh air."

"Exactly," Arlo said quietly, glancing at her now. "It's like for once, I'm not rushing onto another job or fighting some metaphorical battle. I just get to be... here."

Lucy turned, her emerald eyes matching his gaze. Her heart skipped a beat at the sudden softness in his voice and the heart-piercing gaze that only furthered her blush. "That's a rare thing for you, huh?"

"Rare," he agreed, tracing the details of her face, noting every freckle's placement that only accented her beauty. A brief pause came next, quiet, intense magnetism that pulled their bodies closer together. "And... kinda nice."

The sound of the ocean faded to the background as the world narrowed to just the two of them. Their eyes were inseparable; even if they wanted to break the connection, neither of them would. Lucy's pulse quickened, a warm charge holding them locked in place. Her breath caught as Arlo stepped just a little closer, his hand brushing against hers, accident or not, it felt like a jolt coursed through her entire body, sending a chill that made the hairs on the nape of her neck stand. She glanced down at their hands, a flicker of surprise at how natural it felt, how right it seemed.

Arlo noticed it as well, but neither of them moved away. The closeness, the quiet tension, it wasn't the first time, but it felt like the beginning of something they weren't quite ready to name.

Lucy cleared her throat, "You would need help with that quiet little life."

"How so?"

"You would build the house too square, wake everyone before dawn, and says its building character."

"That doesn't seem like a bad thing to me. Sounds practical."

"It sounds unbearable."

They both laughed. "So what would you do?"

"I would put flowers where you said flowers did not belong. Teach the children terrible songs. Let them get muddy—"

"The children?"

Lucy's cheeks colored at her own words.

"The imaginary ones," she said quickly. "For your imaginary quiet house."

"Right." Arlo looked toward the water, his smile stayed. "Those ones."

The silence that followed was not empty, filled with things neither of them had the courage to touch.

Lucy brushed sand from her hands and stood. "We should go before Sorren thinks we were eaten."

"He would be offended he was not invited to fight whatever ate us."

They laughed, and together they started back.

CHAPTER 29

The sound of the ocean gave way to the hum of Davenport's streets, the buzz of life returning as they approached the outer reaches of the city. As they reached the outskirts, a figure came into view just ahead of them. It was tall, broad-shouldered, and moved with the familiar stride of heavy footsteps that were signature to their very own friend Sorren.

"Well, well, well, look who finally decided to show up," Sorren called out, his voice carrying easily over the sounds of the city behind him. "Thought you two got lost or something."

Arlo shot him a glare, but it was hard to hide the grin tugging at his lips. "Nice to see you too, Sorren."

Lucy raised an eyebrow as they neared him. "What, were you worried about us?"

Sorren let out a booming laugh and gave them a devilish grin. "Nah, I was just trying to track you two. Thought I might find you getting into trouble… or… something else." he finished with a wink.

Lucy blushed instantly, her cheeks warming as she exchanged a quick glance with Arlo. "Oh, please," she said, her voice half-mocking as she tried to hide her embarrassment. "Don't you have more important things to do than look for us? Like build a ship?"

Sorren gave them both a playful look, his smirk growing as he saw the effect on Lucy.

Arlo coughed, clearing his throat in an attempt to play it cool, but Lucy's blush deepened further. "Nothing like that," Arlo shot back. "We were just… enjoying the view."

"Sure," Sorren said with a knowing grin. "The view."

"Shut up," Arlo muttered, shaking his head, though there was a playful hint in his voice. Lucy, on the other hand, couldn't stop herself from laughing softly despite the heat still blooming in her cheeks.

Sorren glanced at the two of them, his smirk settling into something more relaxed. "Anyway," he said, changing the subject, "the King's been asking about you two. Says he's got some news and wants to make an announcement later. Figured it must be important if he's calling for both of you to be there too."

Seriousness settled over Arlo's demeanor. "News? What kind of news?"

Sorren shrugged. "Didn't say much to me, but whatever it is, it's big enough to gather a bunch of officials and us before it's announced to the public. Everyone's meeting up at the castle soon. Thought I'd better come drag you back before you missed it."

"Sounds serious. You think it's news about Fall Lake?" Lucy asked.

"Serious enough," Sorren agreed. "So, come on. Let's head back before the King thinks you've run off together to avoid him."

Arlo sighed, running a hand through his hair as he fell into step beside Sorren. "Always something, isn't it?"

276

"Hey," Sorren said, flashing a quick grin. "At least I found you before things got… too interesting."

Lucy rolled her eyes, though a smile tugged at her lips. "You're insufferable."

"That's why everyone loves me," Sorren teased back, earning a half-hearted swat from Lucy as they began their walk to the city palace.

The grand hall of Davenport was filled with many members of the city's leadership. Discussions of politics, families, and forced smiles were abundant. Brother Jason and Paladin Danladin both stood flanking the chair of the Archbishop himself, the Just Throne, while members of the elite Kingsguard stood flanking the Lion's Throne, the seat of the King. Sorren marched in, head held high, boots stomping with attention as he made his rounds to the individuals in attendance. Arlo and Lucy instead forced themselves into a more secluded area of the room, opting to find some place alone and away from the political intrigue.

It wasn't long before the doors flung open and King Frederick and Archbishop Dolph were both announced into the room. King Frederick took his place upon his throne, waving for all in attendance to be seated or quiet down. The stern look upon his face, the padding below his normal robes, the faint strain in his posture, he acknowledged several, including Arlo, with a nod.

"Thank you all for coming," he began. "The news I bring today is not easy, nor is it welcome. But we must face what lies ahead head-on."

Silence settled over everyone in the room, speaking only through shared looks that grave news was coming. Frederick rose to his feet, standing with his head held high, his eyes scanning the faces of the people.

"I have received word that the last few free Dwarv settlements of Hlandaheim have fallen. The forces of Candurill and Syrussul, leaders of the Elfar and the Draconis, have now laid claim to what remains of the northlands. This alliance between these two forces... they are calling themselves the Draconis Legion."

The hall collectively gasped at the hard-hitting news, trying to process what it meant, what was at stake, what they would need to do next.

"For years," Frederick went on, "the Dwarv have fought valiantly to hold their territories against the Elfar advances. A few strongholds remained free, Revnastad among them. We do not yet know what lies of Hibora's frozen climate, but it would be my assumption that the Draconis would also see to its submission."

Silence maintained itself within the room, save for the shifting of armor and clothing as the weight of the announcement sank in. The Dwarv, proud, strong, and resilient, had been at war with the Elfar for years as they sought to expand north. Their intentions had always been unclear, and motivations seemed to simply be to feed Candurill's ego.

Fear, anger, and disbelief were woven throughout the faces around the hall. This new alliance was the embodiment of two of the most powerful forces on Shularix, and now they were joining forces to conquer the north. It was only a matter of time before they moved west to the Nogmi, and south to the Zenarian Kingdom. Another attack like Fall Lake? The Draconis are large, massive, fierce creatures. Protective scales, massive wings, and many of them able to breathe fire from their mouths.

Whispers now filled the room as Frederick took a brief pause. Sorren, who had made his way over beside Arlo and Lucy, let out a low growl. "I'd love to stick my sword into either of those bastards."

The Archbishop stood and raised his hand, clearing the noise from the room. King Frederick began once more, "We must prepare. We cannot afford to be caught off guard when they inevitably look our way. The ship is nearly complete, and with it we need to prepare ourselves for the future. The development of this ship is about forging alliances, gathering strength, and ensuring we have the means to resist if the Draconis Legion arrive."

A man stepped forward, dark-skinned and sharp-minded. Felix had a reputation for being quick-witted and idealistic, which likely led to his promotion into his position. "Your Majesty, with all due respect, we're talking about the Draconis Legion laying claim to the north, uniting two of the most dangerous forces known to us. If they've already sent one of their creatures to test our defenses, who's to say they won't send more? We need to fortify, not just here in the capital, but across the entire nation."

While he spoke calmly, anxiety and concern were evident in his voice. Felix wasn't one to panic, but his understanding of the magnitude of what they were up against was clear. He glanced at the others within the room, gauging their reactions to his abrupt interruption. "If they come south, we need to be ready. The beast that attacked Fall Lake showed us what they're capable of, and that was just a single attack. We have to better our defenses."

Archbishop Dolph rose, standing next to King Frederick, their entourage shifting around them in both defense and deference to let them have the floor. "We must have faith," he said in an expertly calm resolution. "Heir will guide us through this storm. The Draconis Legion may have power, but their power comes from destruction, from darkness. We stand for something greater, something just. We defend our people, our homes, and we do so with the zeal of Heir on our side. We must remember that in times of war, it is not just strength that carries us through, but our faith in the divine."

Voices began to scatter about as the onlookers spoke amongst themselves. Several gave acknowledging prayers to Heir, while others seemed unmoved. They were, after all, faced with monstrous beasts and united enemies.

Commander Illana, the head of the Kingsguard, was next to speak. She was a tall, imposing woman, with silver armor that shone around the lionhead symbol on her chest. Her hair was short and well kept, only encouraging her no-nonsense command. "Faith is important, Archbishop," she agreed with a steel voice. "But faith alone will not stop the Draconis Legion. We need strategies, defenses, expert soldiers ready to lay down their lives for their brothers and sisters of Zenaria. If the north has already fallen, then it is only a matter of time before we are next. We need to act now. High General Darion would agree, if he were here."

The mentioning of the High General quieted the room once more. Then another man stepped forward. He was elderly, Lord Henric, his family having spent many years as members of the Zenarian nobility, and always one member of the family appointed a seat at the Davenport council. "Commander Illana, you speak of war as though it's on our doorstep. But we're too far south to be their immediate concern, are we not?"

"That is the point. We need able and willing bodies to defend our borders. Tell me, Lord Henric, the Draconis have terrifying wings and fly at incredible speeds. Do you think they will just take us one city at a time, border by border? We need to have every location we have capable soldiers prepped with scalebane ballistae."

"Much good that did in Fall Lake, that bea—" Henric began to raise his voice before being interrupted.

"Enough!" King Frederick cut in. "I understand the severity of our situation, but we will maintain level heads."

Another man spoke up after Henric took his seat, a local advisor to Davenport not born of nobility, but having earned his place among the council, a stout man by the name of Gregory Baelor.

Baelor rubbed his hands together nervously, continuing the conversation. "Lord Henric has a point. Our settlements along the southern coast have always been safe from the troubles of the north. The Draconis have never shown any interest in pushing this far. We should strengthen our defenses, yes, but we must also consider the possibility that this Legion may not even look our way."

Tension spurred throughout the room, several individuals beginning their own discussions, each rooted in their own point of view. The room split into those who saw the Draconis as an immediate threat, and others who clung to their faith and ideals that the southern lands would remain untouched.

Arlo and Lucy sat quietly at their table. Lucy's fingers began to tap nervously on the wood. The possibilities of what this war would bring caused her to dwell into a dark place within her mind. Arlo had taken notice and placed his hand onto hers in an attempt to ease her.

Sorren, who had strangely remained quiet through much of the conversation, moved to the center of the room. His heavy boots echoed throughout the hall, the sound overcoming the voices that continued to grow in the room. "This isn't a question of 'if'," he repeated until the room quieted once more. "It's when. I would wager the Draconis Legion isn't interested in holding territory, they want control. They will come south, eventually. And when they do, if we haven't prepared for that inevitability, we will fall just like the Dwarv settlements." He glanced around the room, taking in everyone's faces, their worry and concern. His confidence didn't waver as he stood in the middle of some of the most important people in his nation. "Some of you may not have seen the devastation I saw in Fall Lake. I was fortunate enough to arrive after someone heroically took it down. If they have more creatures like the beast that attacked Fall Lake, we won't survive by bickering like we are."

"Bold words, from someone who will be setting sail and leaving us behind in only a few days, young man," Lord Henric responded solemnly. "Perhaps we should all get on this ship of yours and leave this place behind."

Sorren's fist tightened, and as he went to speak, another familiar voice spoke first in an attempt to bridge the divide. Brother Jason stepped forward from his place among the royalty. "We cannot afford to argue amongst ourselves. We need to show our strength, not just to our own people, but to the Legion as well. If we are united, if we stand together with faith in Heir and our strategy, we can weather this storm. But it requires all of us doing our parts, working together, and not pulling apart."

The tension in the room simmered down, though the unease, and the disdain on Lord Henric's face, lingered.

"Faith in Heir saved us from the struggles of Fall Lake. With his awareness of the Draconis threat now known, our faith in him will continue to protect us from the darkness that approaches," Archbishop Dolph said, followed by several acknowledging prayers among the crowd.

It was then that King Frederick, standing with his arms folded, spoke again gravely. "This is not about whether or not they will come south. They will. The question is how we respond. And we need more than faith, more than defenses. We need a true symbol, a rallying point for the people to look to in these dark times."

Arlo sat with his hand still on Lucy's, their touch an attempt to soothe each other from what they knew was coming next. Arlo's heart was racing as visions of Fall Lake were brought back to him.

Running blind, sweat pouring down his face and burning his eyes. He saw bodies dropping, being eaten, crushed, stomped. The beast was massive, scales that appeared impenetrable even to the few ballistae mounted on several guard towers. Arlo could hear his own voice, barely audible against the cries of the people pleading for help. Pleading for hope that all of this would end.

A foxlike creature that he followed up a hill and up a tower. Death surrounded their paths. But their faces were etched into his mind, their voices a harrowing cry that seemed to lead both him and the fox. He ran up the tower as their faces joined him, whispers, cries for help, prayers unanswered. And when he reached the top, he was met with an endless sight of those who had passed, each of them speaking of their hopes and dreams, before melding into a blue light that stood out in front of him. He saw the creature coming forward, its tormenting eyes set on the tower he stood in. He had one foot on the window of the tower, his eyes marked the blue light of the voices and faces and he leapt.

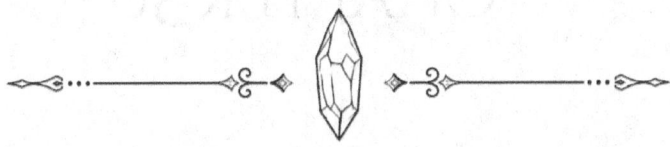

"The people need something to believe in, a symbol of something greater, of strength, of resilience," Frederick's voice said softly. Arlo tried to focus his eyes as he looked around the room, making eye contact with both Sorren, who gave him a nod, and Lucy, whose silent worry was processing the gravity of the situation. War wasn't some distant idea, it was real, and it was here.

As Arlo rose to his feet, his mind still in a foggy haze, he heard the King's words but did not register them at first. His eyes cleared, and everyone in the room was locked on him, waiting for his response.

"The people need something to believe in. Will you be that symbol, Arlo?"

CHAPTER 30

The weight of the King's words hung heavy in the air. Arlo felt the gaze of the chamber resting on him. Expectations pressed down on the lingering wounds from the day of the attack, as if everyone believed he somehow held the answer to all of their problems. His heart pounded, and for a moment he stared down at his hands, at the calluses formed from work and effort, not war or battle.

He felt rushed, like he needed to provide an answer to make everyone else feel better, regardless of how he himself might feel. The visions returned, not as thorough as before, just faces and voices of people. Some he recognized from Fall Lake, others he had never met. He sat there in loss as the wracking pain within his body continued to pulse and bring fresh agony with every beat of his heart.

Lucy's hands met his this time, pulling him back into the room. This was not the first time he was asked to be this symbol for them. He still was not sure how he was supposed to bring them answers.

But as he met Lucy's gaze, he felt the pain and concern fade. A deep breath settled his mind, and words finally began to form.

"I appreciate your confidence in me, Your Majesty," Arlo said softly, his voice growing with every word. "But let me be clear about something. I am not a fighter. I am not a symbol or some chosen hero. The people do not need a man holding a hammer to follow. What they need is leadership that guides them, a community that stands together with them."

He lifted his head and looked around the room, addressing every person present as he rose to his feet before ending his gaze with Frederick. "I did what had to be done at Fall Lake. Not because I am some chosen one, but because it was the right thing to do. And that is all I want. To do the right thing."

Several of the council members began to whisper quietly to each other, not expecting this defiance to the King's request. Arlo's frustration rose. He knew what they were asking, and deep down he understood the weight of the situation, the need for what they wanted from him. But that did not make any of this easier.

"I did not ask to be in this situation," he continued, more passionately. "I did not ask to hold that hammer, and I sure as hell did not ask to become some puppet for people to use whenever they need a symbol of hope. I have spent my life trying to do what is right, but I will not be manipulated into becoming something I am not."

Dolph took a step forward, interjecting. "No one is making you into anything, Arlo. We are simply…"

Arlo cut him off, his frustration finally breaking the surface. "No one? Are you serious, Dolph? You already made me into something. You already paraded me as the Hero of Fall Lake. You did not ask. You did not give me a choice. You just shoved me into that role because it was convenient for you."

Dolph's expression faltered, his composure slipping. "That was to inspire the people. You…"

"No," Arlo interrupted again, more forceful than before. "You did it because you needed something to rally behind. You needed to give them something when they were scared. And now you are doing it again. Do you think I do not see what is happening here? You are trying to use me because I downed the beast, because I just happened to be the one to survive that night and somehow wielded the hammer."

Arlo walked away from the table and turned to the entire council. "I am not some weapon you can wield when things go wrong. I am not some figurehead you can parade around for morale. I am just a man trying to do what is right for everyone, and I will not let any of you turn me into a pawn in this game. I will not let anyone own me."

The air in the room was tense. The guards' hands were ready at their weapons, the council members holding mixed reactions. Some uncomfortable glances, some anger, and others stunned silence. Even King Frederick, who had spoken with such confidence earlier, seemed momentarily taken aback.

Dolph's face tightened, his gaze glued to Arlo. "We are not trying to use you, Arlo. The people need…"

"They do not need me," Arlo countered sharply, his frustration boiling over. "They do not need a man holding a hammer to be their hope. They need leadership. They need you, the King, this council, to actually guide them through this. To protect them, to keep them safe, to make the hard choices. That is your job, not mine."

Arlo took a deep breath, trying to calm the storm in his chest. He turned back to King Frederick, his gaze steady and determined. "I am not saying I will not fight, or that I will not speak to the people if it means protecting them. If it means doing the right thing, then I will stand and do what needs to be done. But I will not be your puppet. I will not be at your disposal. I fight on my own terms, because the people deserve more than a symbol. They deserve real hope. They deserve to believe in themselves, in each other, because that is real hope."

A long pause followed. Arlo questioned himself, wondering if he should say something else or sit back down. Was he about to be dragged away for disrespecting the leadership? But his words had cut through the council, undeniable in their truth. In reality, no one knew what to say next.

Dolph was the next to speak. "You were given that title because the people needed something to believe in. We do not have time to adjust everyone's moral compass when there is a war at our doorstep. Do you think this is about you? This is bigger than you, bigger than all of us."

Arlo's eyes began to burn with defiance, just as his frustration had begun to calm. "The people do not need to be lied to, Dolph. They need leadership, not a false hero. If you wanted a symbol, you should have been it. You and the council should have stepped up. Instead, you forced that mantle onto me because it was safer and more convenient for you."

"Enough," Dolph growled, his patience snapping. "You dare speak to me like this? I demand he be imprisoned." His hand slammed down on the table next to him, making the entire room shudder. His holy knights began to move at his command. "Your Majesty, this insolence cannot be allowed. He undermines the authority we have built."

Arlo did not flinch, but the tension in the room thickened as Frederick raised his hand, commanding silence and stopping the knights in their steps. "Dolph," the King said evenly, "he has his right to speak his views."

The Archbishop's face flushed with rage, his nostrils flaring. "You choose him over me?" he hissed, barely containing his fury. "After all we have built together, Fred? You side with a boy over your partner? Do you forget who stands beside you in matters of the church?"

The King's gaze did not waver. "I choose to hear him. That does not mean I stand against you, Dolph."

Dolph's eyes flashed with betrayal as he glared at Arlo. "This is a mistake," he said angrily. "You will regret this, Fred." With that, he stormed out of the room, the heavy door slamming behind him with a deafening thud. Paladin Danladin followed close behind.

Arlo's chest was tight, but he did not back down. He looked around the room, meeting each of their eyes, waiting for any of them to speak. Lucy moved to his side, silently reassuring him that he was doing the right thing. Sorren had lingered by the door, his eyes clouded with thought, watching the exchange in silence.

"I will not be a puppet for anyone," Arlo said quietly but firmly, locking eyes with the King. "I will fight for the people because it is the right thing to do, not because someone says I should. I will stand for them, but it will be on my terms. The people need more than a symbol. They need hope, unity, and leadership from all of you, not just from me."

King Frederick nodded. "You have made your point, Arlo. And I respect that. If you choose to stand for them, you will do so on your own terms."

With one last glance at the room, Arlo turned. Lucy moved in step behind him. As he reached the door, Sorren stood watching his friend with lingering hesitation. As Arlo left the room, Lucy turned to give her only input to the room. "The people deserve more than just a symbol, King or a god. They deserve to believe in each other. That is what gives them hope."

Sorren held the door for his friends. Hesitation and duty warred in his chest. Arlo glanced back at him one more time, and Sorren shut the door behind them, staying in the hall.

As the heavy door clicked shut behind Arlo and Lucy, the tension in the room lingered like smoke from a smoldering fire. The faces around the room were tight with unspoken thoughts.

King Frederick, maintaining his composure, folded his hands before him, his eyes fixed on the door before turning to the others. "What was said today needed to be heard."

Jason adjusted his posture, reflecting both concern and faith within his eyes. "Arlo speaks the truth. We cannot ask someone to lead when they have not yet found their path."

Commander Illana's gaze remained fixed on the King. "I agree that forcing Arlo into this role would be a mistake," she said firmly. "But the threat remains. What happens when the Legion comes? When the next attack strikes and we are all still hesitating? We need to act now and not wait for him to find himself when lives are at stake."

Her gaze flickered around the room, ending on Sorren, who stood still beside the door, arms crossed over his chest. He had wanted to leave with Arlo, but something held him in place.

Felix, who had been pacing since Arlo's exit, spoke next with animated hands. "Illana is right. We need something more concrete, something we can count on. Hope and faith are fine, but what about real, tangible defenses? What about the next wave of Draconis beasts? We must act now, and not wait for them to tear another city apart."

Jason stepped closer to Felix. "Faith does not mean inaction, Lord Felix," Jason replied. "But we must recognize that no wall, no sword, no army can stand alone. The people look to Arlo because he struggles as we all do. The people see him and know they are not alone in their fight." He glanced toward the King, seeking confirmation. "Faith must guide us, but so must wisdom."

Felix rubbed his face, clearly frustrated from the events of the night. "Faith will not stop these beasts from tearing apart another village. Look at what happened to Fall Lake. How long before it happens again? If not here, then somewhere else."

"We recognize all the threats," the King replied. "Arlo's reluctance is a challenge we must face, but imprisoning him or forcing his hand will not serve us. He is not our puppet whose strings we can pull."

Felix opened his mouth to respond, but a sharp look from Illana silenced him. She was not finished.

"What if we gave him time?" she asked. "Let him work through his own hesitation, but we must also prepare in the meantime. We need contingencies, more than just faith in Heir. We need tactical readiness."

Her words were direct and practical. She was not known to dabble in spiritual affairs, having always focused primarily on action, preparation, and control.

King Frederick sighed, drumming his fingers lightly on the table. "You speak with reason, Illana. But our resources are already stretched thin."

Lord Henric's voice carried dismissal. "I still do not see how any of this is our problem." His fingers tapped impatiently on the armrest of his chair as he eyed the others. "We are far too far south for the Legion to reach us. This is more of a Cyril problem, is it not?"

The room turned to Henric, disbelief passing through them. Commander Illana's lip twitched in disgust. "You are a fool if you think that," she said coldly. "If the Legion is this bold, they will strike wherever they can, and Davenport is far from safe."

Henric scoffed. "Let them come. We will handle our own."

"It is exactly that arrogance that has led to past civilizations falling," Illana shot back, leaning forward in her seat, her voice sharp as her sword. "Your walls will not hold against beasts like the one that attacked Fall Lake. Like Arlo said, we need to be united in this fight."

Jason nodded. "Faith will guide us, but we must work together in all things. Strength comes not from one corner or one city, but from the whole."

Sorren felt a cold knot twist in his stomach. As Jason spoke of faith and Illana spoke of tactical strength, his mind wandered. He had always believed that Heir's path was the righteous one, that there was an order to the chaos of the world. But now, watching the council debate, watching the weight of expectations placed on Arlo's shoulders, something continued to gnaw at him.

It was not that he doubted Heir. He had never questioned the god who had guided him his whole life. But he had begun to doubt the people who claimed to speak in His name. Watching Dolph's fury, the King's carefully measured words, and the council's conflicting motivations stirred something deep within him. Could it be that the path forward was not as clear as he once thought?

Illana's sharp voice pulled Sorren back into the conversation. "We need to secure our defenses now, not later. I can rally the guards, but we will need more than swords to fight these beasts. We need alliances, mages, something more tangible than hope."

Felix snorted. "Agreed. And let us not pretend this is not creeping us toward war. If the Draconis Legion can send a creature like that, what else do they have in their arsenal? We need eyes on the borders."

"They are already on the borders," Sorren finally muttered, his voice gruff as he unfolded his arms, eyes still distant. "And we are here debating symbols."

Illana's eyes cut toward Sorren. "You have something to add, Sorren?"

He hesitated for a moment. "I just…" Sorren trailed off, catching Jason's eyes, searching for answers in his mentor's calm face. "I have never questioned faith. Not once. But something feels off."

The room quieted. Even Illana and Felix stopped their bickering as they listened to him.

"It is natural to feel that way, Sorren," Jason said. "We all have moments where the path is not clear."

Sorren grunted, shifting his weight uneasily. "It is not the path I am worried about. It is the people who claim to know it." His voice grew rough, scraping against the air like a blade against stone. "We have always preached about Heir's justice, about truth. But here we are, twisting those words, pushing them onto people like Arlo. He did not ask to be Heir's chosen, yet here we are trying to make him fit that mold. That sound like truth to you? Like faith?"

The room's eyes widened at the questioning of faith.

"We speak about unity under Heir, but what happens when the people claiming to speak His words twist them? What happens when faith turns into a tool to bend men to someone else's will?"

Jason exhaled slowly, his face a mixture of sadness and realization. "Sorren, I understand your concern. Truly, I do. But we are not bending men to our will. We guide them, help them find their strength."

"Are we?" Sorren's voice was low, but challenging in every way. "Because from where I am standing, it looks like we are deciding for them what they should believe, who they should follow. We are putting Arlo on a pedestal because it is convenient for us. Not because he is ready, or because it is his choice."

Jason's usually calm demeanor faltered for the briefest of moments as he searched for his next words. "Faith," he said slowly, "is complicated. It is not always clear-cut. We do the best we can with what we know and sometimes…"

"No," Sorren cut him off. "Sometimes we do not. Sometimes we twist it. And maybe we have twisted it so much that we cannot see the real truth anymore."

Jason's silence was answer enough.

Sorren's eyes narrowed, a deep frown pulling at his lips. "You have always been my mentor, Jason. I have followed Heir's light because you showed me the way. But now? Now I am not so sure. Not about Heir, but about us. About what we are doing in His name."

Jason opened his mouth to respond, but no words came out. His silence cut deeper than any rebuke ever could.

Sorren looked around the room, his heart pounding in his chest. The King watched him with unreadable eyes, Felix looked uncomfortable, and Illana appeared ready to charge into battle no matter the cost.

Jason's silence hung between them all, an understanding that Sorren had struck a nerve. He had asked the one question Jason could not answer, not without unraveling the very foundation of the faith they all stood on.

"I follow Heir's path," Sorren said softly. "But I will not follow blindly. Not anymore." He turned to leave, not storming out like Arlo had, but with slow, deliberate steps of a man wrestling with something too large for him to grasp.

Jason watched him go, his heart heavy. He had no words of comfort to offer, no scripture that could soothe the storm brewing inside Sorren. All he could do was watch his student, his friend, walk out of the room, leaving behind a question that gave him no answers.

As the door closed behind Sorren, the others all shifted uncomfortably. Even the King, usually composed, seemed lost for words.

Illana broke the silence with a dry laugh, though no humor was behind it. "Well, that was unexpected."

Felix ran a hand through his hair, visibly flustered. "What in the hell just happened?"

Jason traced the grain of the wood before him. "He is questioning the nature of our faith, Felix."

"And can you blame him?" Illana's voice was sharp but not unkind. "We have all twisted faith to our ends at one point or another. Sorren just had the courage to say it."

Jason sighed deeply, his shoulders sagging as if the weight of the world had finally settled on him. "It is not a matter of courage, Illana. It is a matter of truth. And Sorren may have seen more truth today than the rest of us."

INTERMISSION THREE: THREADS OF TOMORROW

I paused and lifted my trusty spoon, weaving it through the air while the last embers of purple mana faded from its reflective surface. I looked over the gathered patrons, taking in their mix of tension and anticipation.

"It is not only about the choices we make," I said quieter than usual, drawing them in. "It is the echoes, the ripples of consequence, and sometimes the moments we wish we could take back. Arlo, stubborn lad, found himself caught in a storm not of his own making. A storm he had no way to understand."

Before I could continue, Apple's voice cut through the growing hush of the room.

"Oh, Spoony, stop acting like this place is a funeral," she teased as she sauntered toward the center of the inn. Her deep red hair caught the firelight and framed her in a warm glow. She set her hands on her hips, letting her endlessly long legs shine in the flicker of the hearth. "Let these people have some joy. They did not come here to brood. They came to feel alive. Am I right?"

She turned to the crowd with a smile that could start a small revolution. With a bright clap of her hands she declared, "Now you folks came for a story, so the least our Master of the House can do is help you relax. A round on the house."

Her voice was clear and bold. Cheers rose at once as Candy arrived with several drinks balanced effortlessly in her arms. The sound of the crowd mixing with Apple's laughter warmed even the gloomiest corners of the inn.

I leaned back and let her have the spotlight. Apple always had a way of commanding the room without effort, her energy pulling people in like moths to a flame. Something I have always appreciated about her, and something that never fails to be useful in our work.

"You have always had a knack for stealing the show, have you not?" I asked, no malice in the words, only amusement.

She twirled in place, her dark red hair fanning out as she struck a playful pose beside a table. "Stealing?" she asked in a mock wounded tone. "Oh my dear Spoon, I prefer to think of it as borrowing with style. Besides, this room needed a bit of color."

The crowd chuckled as Apple leaned against the bar and gave me a wink. She moved back through the tables with Candy, placing drinks into eager hands. I watched her lift the room with nothing more than her presence. She set one drink down beside me without a word. My favorite of course, a liquor we import from off continent that blends perfectly with fruit juices.

I took a long sip and felt the cool spirit hit my lips. My eyes nearly rolled back as the flavor settled. The perfect companion for the rest of the tale. For a moment I watched the crowd, then lifted my spoon and tapped it against the glass. The soft ring pulled every eye back to me.

"So we have spoken of Arlo," I said as the spoon hovered in the air again. "But what of the others. What of our other heroes, or heroines, such as Lucy."

The spoon's reflective surface shimmered as it moved. Shadows and memories fluttered across it like pages turning.

"She is strength wrapped in uncertainty. A woman navigating a world that gives her more questions than answers. Lucy does not demand attention like Apple, but her presence is undeniable. There is a fire in her too. She sees it. She fears it. She struggles to trust herself."

"And what of Sorren," I said, straightening my posture to mimic his broad shoulders. "A man whose duty has always guided him. Raised by the church. Sworn to a god of justice, lightning, and war. Yet burdened by doubts that claw at the edges of his belief. What does a man like that do when the ground he stands on begins to crack. He is a warrior. But he is also a man. And men often face battles that no blade can win."

I tapped the spoon lightly against the bar once more. The chime echoed across the room and pulled drifting whispers back into silence.

"Each of them carries a fire of their own. A light they do not yet know how to wield. These threads pull and twist and tangle with one another. It is the way of stories. It is the way of life."

A few murmurs of agreement passed through the crowd before quiet returned. I let the silence settle.

"My friends, here we are. The last intermission. The final pause before we step into what waits ahead. What comes next will test them. It may even test us. The watchers. The listeners. The readers. Tomorrow is already being woven, whether we are ready or not. The end is uncertain, but it is the journey that stays with us. Always."

The inn seemed to exhale with me. Warmth drifted through the room. The patrons leaned closer, eager for what was to come.

I lowered my gaze to the spoon once again. The surface shimmered with the faintest swirl of memory and old stories. From somewhere behind the bar I heard a soft clatter, something small and curious moving where nothing should be moving at all. Apple's eyes flicked that direction, wide for a moment, before she forced a smile to hide whatever she saw.

I pretended not to notice. Some secrets are best left sleeping until the right chapter turns.

With a breath I continued the tale.

CHAPTER 31

The day was bright. The sun hung high in the sky and cast a golden glow over the assembled masses. The feast that the king had prepared for the citizens was soon to begin. Banners bearing the sigils of the kingdom, of Heir, and of Grace adorned the grand platform where the king sat. A sea of people stretched out before him, while the ocean rested at his back. Nobles, warriors, citizens, clerics, and the adventurers who had aided in the city's development gathered to witness the momentous event.

The king rose. His flowing robes were embroidered with intricate patterns of the lion that marked his family's line. He stepped forward. His voice boomed across the gathered visitors and revelers, clearly enhanced by the magic of the mages stationed nearby.

"People of Davenport," he began warmly, "today marks not only the setting forth of a vessel, but the launching of new hopes, new dreams, and the courage to face the unknown. Before you stands the ship that will carry our finest into the horizon, a beacon of our strength and unity."

He paused, letting the cheers swell and then soften again.

"And now, we look to the future, to the brave soul who will guide us forward and lead this ship and its crew into uncharted waters. A man of honor, strength, and dedication. As Protector within the Porters ranks and captain of this new ship. Ladies and gentlemen of Davenport, I give you Sorren Blaze."

The crowd erupted, cheering Sorren's name as he stepped forward, standing tall over the sea of people. Paladin Danladin and Archbishop Dolph moved toward him. Danladin held a mantle, the symbol of Sorren's new title. Sorren basked in the presence of his leaders as they presented him with his new duties. Arlo and Lucy clapped proudly and cheered for their friend and ally, but something far off in the crowd pulled Arlo's attention away.

Deliberate in its stillness, far beyond the front rows of cheering citizens, a flash of gold caught his eye. It was subtle at first, like sunlight glinting off metal, but Arlo knew better. This presence had become unpleasantly familiar. His heart skipped a beat as he searched the crowd more intently, scanning faces until he saw it again. The golden figure. Malik. It stood impossibly still amidst the sea of motion. Its presence sent a shiver down his spine, and his hand moved at once to his hammer. They had fought this thing before and it had outmatched them completely.

Why now?

His eyes flickered to Sorren, who was now bowing slightly as Danladin draped the mantle over his shoulders.

Unable to shake the feeling of unease, Arlo leaned toward Lucy. She had already noticed the shift in his demeanor. His body ached, the lingering wounds from Fall Lake flaring within him again. Voices pressed at his ears. Faces bled together with visions of blood and fire.

Was this being causing it.

"I see it again. Malik," he whispered, keeping his eyes locked on the figure. The flow of bodies moved it in and out of view. "It is out there. Watching."

Lucy followed Arlo's gaze, trying to find what he felt. She did not see anything in the crowd. Only a strange golden shape drifting away high in the sky. Her fingers wrapped around his. Her voice dropped low and gentle.

"Arlo, it is not here anymore. It is all right. It would be stupid for it to attack with all these followers of Heir in attendance. Would Heir's deva do that." She placed her other hand over his. The spark of red and blue flared between their fingers once again, easing his vision, his hearing, and his pain. It came slower this time, as if what ached him now was heavier than before, but it still helped steady his heart and draw his focus away from the specter and back to her.

"Relax. Let us enjoy this moment. You said you had something exciting to show me later. I am still looking forward to that."

Arlo managed a brief smile and tried to steady himself. He forced his attention back to the ceremony, back to the king and Sorren, though he had already missed parts of the speech and the promotion itself.

"And with Sorren at the helm, I know this ship will carry not only our banners but the hopes of our people. May the gods bless this journey, and may the light of Heir guide them through the darkest sea."

Sorren took a bow and raised his fist to the crowd. Voices rose in response. Many in the crowd lifted their hands and cheered as he gave his own closing words.

"This ship, the Sea Sentinel, will serve as a guardian of the seas, a protector of Zenaria, and a champion of Shularix. Just as I have trusted my life to my comrades, I trust this ship to the sea and to the people who sail with me."

A wide grin spread across Sorren's face as he took in the honor that had been bestowed upon him. Only a month before he had been making slow progress on the ship of his dreams. Now it was complete, finished by dear friends and funded by the state and the church. He felt honored and trusted. Yet some part of him knew it was not only his work that had carried him here. There was another whom the crowd would love, someone who had helped bring him to this moment.

"And now, it is my pleasure to present a dear friend of mine. The Hero of Fall Lake himself. I call upon Arlo Devine."

Arlo stiffened. The Hero of Fall Lake. The title still felt foreign, heavy with the lives that had been lost that day. The memory of the golden figure tugged at him, and with it the pain returned like a wave that might break his ribs.

He stood upon the wooden stage. Faces stared up at him. He had never cared for an audience and never wanted to be the center of attention. The idea of everyone looking at him as if he knew what to do made his stomach twist. As if he held all the answers and every person needed him to guide them. Which way to go. How to get there.

A flash of fire roared past. Children screamed. Women cried. Men died.

The vision swallowed him.

A monstrous scaled creature thundered through the streets of Fall Lake. It belonged in myth, not reality. Swords clanged off its hardened scales. Spells fizzled and broke against its hide. Screams turned to pleas. Cries turned to prayers. Hopes burned away before they could take root.

The face of a woman and her children. Her hands pushed them toward the last safe doorway she could find. The final glimpse of a city where so many days of blood and sweat and tears had built a new future. Gone. Burned. Trampled.

Arlo's eyes were filled with blue. He stood at the window of the tower once more. Hundreds, thousands of people filled the streets below and looked up at him. Their voices crashed together in a deafening chorus that tore at his mind. One by one they fell. Trampled. Eaten. Burned.

The monster pushed straight toward him. At his feet, a foxlike creature brushed against his leg and then vanished. The beast drew closer. His heart hammered in his chest while his lungs refused to work. He was no hero. He had never wanted to be one. Yet he had never turned away from what was right, even when the world refused to make sense.

As the creature closed the distance, the cries of the people grew clearer.

"Help us."

"Save my children."

"Please."

Perhaps it was foolish. Perhaps it was exactly what he was meant to do. By the time the blue haze faded from his vision and the tower melted away, he was already moving. Breath rushed back into his lungs and drove him forward. His voice rose with the strength and determination of thousands who could no longer speak.

"I have been called a hero," Arlo began quietly. His voice carried across the crowd with the help of the king's mages. A hush rolled outward as people stilled and leaned in closer. "But being a hero is not about titles. It is not about fame or glory. It is not about standing here and hearing you cheer for me."

He paused. The images of Fall Lake rushed up again, pressing against the edges of his thoughts.

"Being a hero is standing up when you are afraid. It is fighting for what is right, even when it feels like the whole world is crashing down around you."

The words came without planning. He barely knew what he would say next. The voices of the lost pressed forward in his mind, not as ghosts that wanted to drag him down, but as something else. A push. A weight that lifted him rather than buried him.

"I have stood in the face of horrors," he continued. "I have seen what happens when hope dies and when darkness takes hold. I have seen what happens when people are left with nothing but fear. But in those darkest moments I have also seen something else. I have seen the way we rise. The way we keep fighting. Not because we want to. Because we have to. For those we love. For the future we believe in. For the people who no longer have a voice and whose dreams now rest in our hands."

Arlo drew in a slow breath and let his eyes move across the crowd. He could not read every face, but he could feel the shift in the air. Heads nodded. People leaned forward as if they were reaching toward him. For the first time he understood that the voices of the past were not there to tear him apart.

They were there to carry him forward.

His voice grew stronger. Bolder. Filled with a passion he had never felt before. Perhaps this was what he was meant to do. Not simply to fight monsters in the dark, but to help others stand with him.

"So I ask you now, not as a hero, but as a fellow man. Stand together with us. Not only today, but every day. Stand against the darkness of despair. Stand against the fear of the unknown. Stand against the forces that would tear us apart. Together, we are stronger than anything evil can throw at us."

Arlo's hands moved as he spoke. He tried to meet as many eyes as he could. He poured his belief into every word, hoping it would awaken belief in them as well. The feeling that rushed through him was unlike anything he had known. A living current of blue mana stirred within him and grew with every heartbeat. The people loved their displays, and he could feel his words pushing toward a peak. He wanted to give them something they would never forget. Something they could hold on to when the night grew long and cold.

"Together, we are the light in the darkness. Together, we are hope."

The crowd erupted. A sea of faces cheered and shouted, their voices merging into a single triumphant roar that seemed to echo from the heart of Zenaria itself. Arlo felt the weight of their belief crash over him. It was heavy. It was also strangely lifting. His chest rose and fell with ragged breaths as the power inside him grew more tangible. Blue mana pulsed beneath his skin.

He glanced down at the hammer. The weapon that had become part of him. Blue sparks of lightning trickled along the metal, crackling in the air around his hands. The energy grew. It was impossible to ignore and impossible to fully contain, yet it was his.

It listened to him.

A sudden fierce jolt of energy rippled through his body as he leapt from the stage. Lightning roared from the hammer and raced up into the sky, splitting the clouds with a single deafening crack. The crowd gasped. There was no fear in the sound. Only awe.

Arlo landed on the sand and grass at the edge of the stage. Sparks danced outward from him and streaked toward the crowd. Each arc faded into soft light that fizzled out in the hands of men, women, and children alike. The power surged around him and slowly faded as the people rushed in to rally around him.

In that moment he was not only Arlo Devine, the Hero of Fall Lake. He was the form their hope had taken. Their will to survive. Their defiance against the coming war. He stood there, surrounded by the storm he had unknowingly summoned. The weight of the world still rested on his shoulders, yet somehow it felt lighter.

He would carry their burdens. They were heavy and daunting, but he did not carry them alone. Those who believed in hope believed in him, and in doing so they helped lift the weight.

As the day settled into afternoon, the celebration carried on along the edge of the beach. People feasted, laughed, and danced beneath tents and along the sand as the sky slowly shifted toward evening. For a little while, the threat of war felt far away. Today they basked in the revelry of hope.

Sorren moved among the people. Ale and wine warmed his blood, though only a soft buzz tugged at his thoughts. Brother Jason called him over with a gesture, and Sorren made his way back toward the stage where they had given their speeches only hours before. A long decorated chest rested on a stand beside Jason.

"Seems you are enjoying the festivities, Captain Sorren," Jason said. There was a small smile in the way he spoke the title.

"Captain," Sorren repeated with a laugh. "I think I can get used to that."

His grin stretched across his face and his laughter rang out over the nearby music. Yet there was a careful look in Jason's eyes that did not match the light tone.

"Sorren, I have been with you since you were a boy," Jason said. "You squired with me when you lost your family. I have watched you grow into a remarkable man and a Porter who has made everyone proud."

Jason reached into the pocket of his surcoat and drew out a key. He placed it in Sorren's hand. The key was golden and bore a carved W along its front.

"You are a brother to me, Sorren. There is no one more deserving of this."

"You must be shitting me," Sorren blurted. "This is not what I think it is."

Jason's smile widened.

"You recently lost your sword, and with the remarkable efforts you have made this past month, I can think of no one more worthy. Sorren Blaze, I hereby pass on the Wood family sword. Justice."

Sorren's heart seemed to stop, then rushed back to life. His breath came faster as he turned to the chest and unlocked it. The box was massive, and if it had stood upright it might have matched Sorren's own height.

The wood creaked as he lifted the lid. Inside lay a finely crafted cloth wrapped around a long shape. Sorren could not help himself. He reached in at once. His fingers trembled as he unwrapped the cloth and revealed the steel beneath.

Justice.

He had known it from the shape alone. He had admired this sword years ago and had often told Jason that one day he would claim it for himself.

The blade shone with a mirror like gleam and stretched more than five feet in length. Its wide base flared near the hilt before narrowing to a razor sharp point. Along the edges ran intricate runes of an ancient prayer to Heir. They glowed faintly with a soft silver light.

From the cross guard, a pair of golden wings swept outward. Each feather was carved with careful detail. At the center of the cross guard, set within a circular golden frame, rested a clear diamond that caught the light of the setting sky. The hilt was wrapped in dark leather, worn and shaped by years of use.

Sorren traced his fingers along the blade, memorizing every line and etching each detail into his mind. Justice was a known legendary artifact among the Monastery of Heir's Reign. Now, as he stood on the shore with the ship he had dreamed of behind him, the sword that had once belonged to his mentor's family lay in his hands.

Honored. Proud. None of the words he knew seemed enough. He looked back up at Jason, his smile so wide it hurt. He wrapped his hand around the hilt and felt the blade answer his touch. It lifted easily, the balance settling into his grip as if it had been waiting for him.

He raised Justice high. The weight of its history settled around him and, for a breath, he felt it adjust to him as well. This was more than a weapon. It was Jason's family legacy and a symbol of faith, honor, and duty. The hum of power within the metal seemed to vibrate through his bones as the runes flickered. He stared at the blade for another long moment, his chest swelling, then lowered it and rested it across his shoulder with familiar ease.

"Jason, I do not know what to say," Sorren admitted. "I always imagined holding this weapon. I never expected you to give it to me."

Jason smiled at him with the quiet pride of a father who knows his son is ready to step into a world that might no longer need his guidance.

"You do not need to say anything, Sorren. The blade chose you, just as I have. The Wood family sword belongs to you now. Use it well and continue to honor Heir with it."

The sky above deepened into dusk as the last gold faded and the light of the red and blue moons began to spread. Celebratory cheers and chants continued behind them. Laughter and music blended with the roll of the waves on the shore. Yet for Sorren, the world had narrowed to the weight of the sword in his hand and the man who had placed it there.

"It will be wielded only by the just and the righteous," Sorren said in a clear tone.

"Good," Jason replied. "War is coming, and a new young leader needs a weapon that can withstand the legacy he will leave behind. Today you are a captain and a Protector of Heir. Tomorrow, who knows what legends they will tell of Captain Sorren Blaze."

Jason punched Sorren's arm. Sorren answered the gesture in kind, as he always had, but now the simple motion carried something new between them.

A promise.

CHAPTER 32

Revelry in the air continued, many of the children and their parents had left the feast for the night. Stories were shared of other travels by sea, local hunts, and futures of what this new vessel would tell. For now, in this blissful moment, the people of Davenport were at peace, their minds not lingering on the potential threats. Filled with hope and the promise of a safe future, they were able to enjoy a night without worry.

Arlo and Lucy walked aboard the newly christened ship that they would soon venture on. The sounds of the waves knocking against the hull, rhythmically in tune with the music from the seasoned minstrels on the land. A warm breeze carried the scene of salt water.

"So, mister Devine, what kind of trouble are you getting me into tonight?" Lucy said with a curled lips over a mischievous smile.

Arlo grinned, "Trouble? I didn't think you were one to shy away from a little adventure."

"Oh, I'm not," Lucy's emerald eyes sparkled playfully. "Just wondering what sort of 'adventure' you are taking me on. I hope this is where we find some grand treasure hidden amongst the ship."

"Not exactly that, you will just have to wait and see."

Lucy let out a dramatic sigh, as Arlo reached the stairs leading below deck. He had turned to face her just as she waved her hand across her face mockingly. "Well, I'm disappointed already."

The corridors were dimly lit by lanterns, of the remaining crew members performing their finishing touches and preparations. Arlo and Lucy passed the larger cabins, each one adorned with a locally crafted sign.

Captain's Quarters

First Mate

Honored Guest

"Let me guess, you came here to gloat about your new quarters, and to tell me that I get to sleep in the hammocks next to Willy and Wicket?"

"Next to Willy and Wicket? Absolutely not," Arlo laughed, opening the door to the 'Honored Guest' room. "I did want to show you *my* new room, though."

The room itself was decorated in fine linen, inscribed with the regalia of the Zenarian Kingdom and Heir. A larger bed sat central to the room, with a credenza just inside the room. The room was spacious, and had the intentions for this room to be potentially occupied by the King or any other important figure, Arlo, in the current case.

"Here we are, the room that I'll be staying in alone," he said with a smirk, walking into the room with his arms proudly spread wide. "I just thought you would like to see where I will be staying."

Lucy's face dropped, as she looked at him with a cocked face of her biting her tongue. "Your room, I think you meant my room," Lucy whimsically moved over the room and leapt onto the bed, sinking into the soft cool bedding. She began to sway her hips back and forth, her crimson hair spread across the bed like a painting of silken display. A red fitted dress that slit along her hip exposing her bare legs.

Arlo fought through many things in his life, but not taking a glance at the beautiful woman that taunted and teased him was too much. He knew she was putting this display on for him, he had felt the bond between them growing ever day. Yet neither of them made the plunge, every moment ruined by someone or something else.

Her head rolled downward, catching him looking her up and down, her face almost turning the same color as her hair. She sat up, batting her eyes almost beggingly for him to come closer. They could feel the desire, the magnetism an unseen force pulling them closer and closer. He walked slowly, never losing eye contact with the shimmering emerald eyes.

A fire grew inside them, warmth that sought each other out as fuel. Her leg rest against his, slowly sliding up his. She let out a small moaning gasp for air as his palm met her cheek sending a spark throughout her entire body. The arching of her back lifting her head to look up at him, her lips pouting beneath her teeth. Their body's quivered at the touch of the other. The room was charged. Electricity sparked through burning embers.

Hearts beat rapidly, ready to burst out of each of their chests to find the other.

His head lowered, his palm raising hers.

Tilting of the heads in anticipation.

Inches away from what was a long time coming.

Their breaths met each other.

Their sent filled each other with a moment of hesitation.

As their lips barely caressed each others.

The sound of thudding footsteps above deck stirred their moment as the brutish buffoon they called Captain began to speak. His voice echoing throughout the entirety of the ship.

Just as quickly as the moment had come, so too had it fallen.

Yet still upon their lips, lingered a taste of the other. Arlo's face reddened as he shuffled around the room.

For a moment she hated how easily the world barged into their lives. Monsters, kings, gods, even overexcited captains. Never just them.

Lucy fell backwards onto the bed, releasing a heavy sigh. Her heart still beat rapidly as she tried to even her breaths.

The call of the captain rang out faintly, his voice distinguishable enough through the muffled wooden planks.

"My first order as your Captain, take the boats, all of ya. Go back to land, enjoy your night! Every single one of ya will make history tomorrow as we set sail on this beaut. We have struggled hard to put this majestic prize together and you have earned a single night of good rest before we take off. There will be no speech in the morning, No fabulous send off, we will get right to our mission and let this girl ride the waves of the unknown." Sorren's pride sang through the entirety of those in attendance, each of them who were involved in the vessel's construction stood tall and proud.

Many of the crew members had joined the festivities, but came back to the ship to finish last minute preparations. And Sorren wanted to make sure each of them got to spend this day in celebration and not work.

"But, Cap'n, some of us would rather stay. We worked hard for this, this is our contribution for those lives lost in Fall Lake." One of the crew said.

Sorren had paused, he respected what they were doing and let them all get their rallying cheers and agreements in. He understood how they felt, some of them were survivors, people whom lost their livelihoods and families in the destruction that day.

"Aye, I understand. But that is why you must take tonight on shore, not for yourselves. But for those we lost, drink, eat, and celebrate what time we had with those we loved, brothers and sisters we didn't know. This celebration isn't an insult to their lives, but in celebration. The ship can wait, all of ya earned this."

The crowd took persuasion, but they all eventually agreed and met their ways back to shore, where they would spend the remainder of the night enjoying themselves. There were plenty of time for work later, for now he wanted to find the two friends of his he saw sneaking up here earlier. The ship would get loud again, and tonight he wanted to celebrate with the two people he had become remarkably close with during the ships construction.

He walked the deck, nodding to the crew members whom he would trust his life and this vessel to as he made his way through the double doors that would lead to the belly hold where he would find the main quarters, he stopped to admire the decorated door labeled as Captain's quarters and with a large shit eating grin he continued down the hall.

He stopped when he noticed that the "First Mate's" door was left ajar, he poked his head in and noticed the chaos of Alf's belonging's and tools scattered throughout the room. He remembered Alf and his brothers being amongst the crew and leading the rest of the crew off the boat. He closed the door and continued on towards the "Honorary Guest" door.

He heard nothing from inside but assumed they would have came here anyway, with a bellowing announcement to his arrival in both voice and knock to the door he slid the door open. "Arlo, Lucy! Ya decent?"

The room was empty, although the presence that someone had been in the room lingered. Fine linens dropped the bed, untouched save for the slight wrinkles curved to fit the shape of a body. A white coat was hung on a hook across the room, Arlo's. Sorren walked further into the room, there was something here that most others would overlook, hidden around the decorations. The paneling in the far corner was different, the slightest difference in tone and pattern that was hidden to the naked eye. His hand traced a slight symbol carved into the frame, barely visible sigil of a bird with wings spread, a crest used by older Zenarian scouts, often used by military and noble families to denote hidden passages or safe areas.

He pressed the sigil firmly, at first nothing happened. But as his fingers tracked the edge of the paneling, he found a hidden seam. A click followed and the panel slid away, revealing a narrow pathway he had secretly built into the ship. Hidden paths meant choices, and Sorren had learned the hard way that sometimes a single hidden path was the difference between a rescue and a grave.

"Sly dog, wanted some privacy did ya?" Sorren whispered with a grin before moving down the passage.

The passage itself was narrow, barely able to fit Sorren's larger frame inside of it. But he managed to move his way through when he noticed the flicker of a candle around the corner, and the sounds of the waves pressing against the hull of the ship. It was quiet and no other voices filled the room save for the distinct but far off revelry on land. Sorren passed the corner to a small secluded room. Just enough space for one to sleep and store some things along with it. The passage would have continued on to the "Captain's Quarters" as well, linking the two larger rooms with this smaller one.

On the opposite side of the room was a small doorframe that barely opened to a small balcony. Their backs turned, and standing side by side, Arlo and Lucy took in the sight of the sea in the distance, the twin moons' glow sending a shimmering glow of red and blue past them. They looked at peace, and Sorren thought about disturbing them, but remembered what he had said to the rest of the crew, this was your knight, maybe this was how they wanted to spend their evening.

He quietly made his way back down the hall, retracing his steps to close and adjust his steps as if he wasn't there. Arlo had shown Lucy to the room they had made for her, in case she wanted her own privacy or place to call her own. Sorren decided he would take to his own place of serenity.

He moved back through the room, and into the main hall, taking a stairwell that led him to a lower level within the ship and found a door with the engravings "War Room".

Customary for all Zenarian's to have a war room, one where they would store their armaments and battle supplies. Heir was known as the God of War after all, and anyone in his order was trained in combat, and expected to always have a room dedicated to Heir of their own.

The room was lined with bookcases that held several books, trinkets, and artifacts that were donated to the cause. In the center of the room was a large table made from the same wood as the rest of the ship, framed in its center was a finely crafted and heavily detailed map of Shularix. To the south just a few clicks below the marking for Davenport was an area unmarked, untraveled, and undocumented. This was their destination, they only had some understanding of the size of what many now know as "The Gauntlet". Few have every stepped foot there, and even fewer have lived to talk about it.

He traced along the map, the path they would take, his thoughts wandering in his solitude. The was the first time anyone had attempted to take such a large vessel through the cursed waters. The Sea Sentinel was built for this, reinforced to handle the rough waves, and hidden rocky spires that scattered its seascape. Many other ships had already been lost to the Gauntlet's storms. Somewhere beneath that empty stretch of sea lay the bones of the Dawnspear and the souls who thought they could outrun the storms.

Was he truly going to be the first to conquer it, or would this be another devastation for the people of Shularix when they needed hope. Their legacy to be another sunken wreckage amongst the graveyard.

Sorren leaned back in the chair he had labeled just for him, finger's tapping idly. The thoughts lingered longer than he would have liked, eating away at his confidence, but with a heavy breath he pushed it aside. This ship was stronger, more prepared than any others. He glanced once more at the map, letting the uncertainty drift away.

'No time for doubts now,' he thought to himself. They had already set everything in motion, and in just a few short hours the Sentinel would be pressing forward. And Sorren was determined to leave a larger legacy behind than just another sunken ship.

Time passed before the subtle creak of the door broke the silence of the room. Sorren looked up and gave a welcoming nod to Arlo and Lucy, "Glad you could join me," he said with his usual grin.

"I was just showing Lucy the extra room we had built," Arlo responded, pulling a seat out for Lucy.

"We kind of lost track of time looking out of the sea," Lucy added, "what are you up to?"

Arlo took several glasses and placed them on the war room table, pouring a reddened wine for each of them.

"I was just going over the route again, thinking about what awaits us in the Gauntlet."

"It's hard not to wonder what we're walking into. The Gauntlet, everything I've heard about it sounds like it's a death sentence," Lucy said solemnly.

Arlo stood at the edge of the table, taking a sip of the drink Mama Gretta had graciously donated for their trip. Arlo felt the weight of what was to come as well, as he absentmindedly touched the amulet around his neck. He didn't speak right away, not only on the dangers of the Gauntlet but also to the silence that had fallen over Eckerd. It has been many days since Eckerd has reached out to him through the amulet, and it worried him more as they were merely a few days travel from their destination.

Sorren nodded, swirling the contents of his glass. "Aye, and it's not just the Gauntlet either. The Draconis Legion, the peace we have currently is fragile, at best. I worry what secrets we uncover, and what dangers show themselves as we move forward."

Lucy crossed her legs, sinking into the seat. "Right, but that is why all of us uniting is very important. If the evil forces make their move, then whatever alliance Eckerd can aid us with will be…"

Lucy's words were interrupted by the faint amber glow from the amulet around Arlo's neck. Startling all three of them as Eckerd's voice quickly rang out in the room.

"You must hurry," Eckerd's familiar voice urged.

"Eckerd, your silence has had us worried," Sorren said from across the room.

"Sorren is right, are you okay?" Arlo asked.

"Something is here, we're running out of time. When you get to the island, follow the path to the highest point, there you will find a gate."

"What do we do?" Lucy tried asking.

"It will…away… you… It… Here… Hurry."

The voice had been lost to what sounds like waves piercing through Eckerd's voice. A shifting wind whisking pieces of his words away.

"Eckerd?" Arlo repeated over and over tapping the amulet.

Sorren had already rose from his seat, leaning forward over the table. "Dammit, what did he mean?" His fist drove down onto the table, vibrating the entirety of the room.

He hated how helpless the amulet made him feel. A man on the other side of the sea was begging for help, and all Sorren could do was listen to the ocean drown him out.

Lucy went to speak, interrupted by the sound of glass shattering in another room.

The three of them looked at each other, the weight of Eckerd's words heavy on them. Was he not the only one with an unwanted guest?

"Sorren, didn't you send everyone home?"

"Aye, watched 'em all head off." Sorren's jaw clenched, pushing the chair away and immediately heading towards the door. Drawing the newly gifted blade of Justice from his back.

As they searched throughout the ship, they found nothing out of the ordinary. They searched through and through until they reached the apothecary. The door opened quickly and revealed a shattered vial on the floor and open cabinets. There, standing amidst the mess, was a tall figure, a woman cloaked from head to toe, only her face and the white-blue strands of her hair visible.

Sorren's eyes narrowed as he stepped forward, his greatsword leveled at her neck and his voice booming, they were certain the party on shore would have heard him. "You've got exactly three seconds to tell me why you're here before I remove you myself," Sorren growled.

The woman froze, her radiant blue-specked purple eyes were widened as she realized she had been caught. She took in the massive frame of the man in the doorway, she tried to back away but realized she was cornered and against the wall. She wasn't prepared for this, for everything to end here.

Behind Sorren, Lucy stepped into the room. Her face held a tight glare, her body radiating something deeper, darker than the beautiful appearance she first gave. Lucy's fingers twitched towards her leg to release the dagger Arlo had assured her she should keep on her for protection.

Sorren followed in with a step forward, his body leaving no room through the door for escape, the girls hands raised in submission. "I, I meant no harm. I swear."

Lucy moved closer, the blade twirling in her hand in a theatrical display with touches of flame emerging off the blade. The storm behind her eyes locked onto the girl, searching her eyes for something deeper.

"You don't look innocent," Lucy said, her voice quieter, but filled dark enough that it sent a shiver through the entire room. The air around her seemed to grow heavier, the candlelight bending for a breath as if it did not want to be near her.

Arlo's hand met Lucy's shoulder as she moved further in towards the girl. He had noticed her shift in demeanor, he wanted to know what the girl was doing here just as much as the others. But he had seen the same darkness begin to wash over her before, and concern took over him. "Lucy! Back off."

Lucy stopped moving forward but never let her gaze leave the girl. "Something is different about you," she said, her tone almost alien. She started into the hooded figure's eyes, seeking beyond the surface. The woman shrunk back, terror painted on her face.

"Lucy!" Arlo repeated again, a slight jolt of blue mana twisting up her arm.

The jolt brought awareness to Lucy, whose eyes flickered leaving behind the darkened glare to a shift of recognition. Her emerald eyes now filled with fear, not of the girl, but of what she was about to do to her. She gasped, blinking rapidly, and took a step back, stopping briefly against Arlo's chest.

"I… I need to leave," her voice trembled as she spun past Arlo down the hall.

Arlo started to take a step towards Lucy, before recognizing the need to also check on the innocent girl staring down the blade of Sorren.

Sorren's instincts screamed that something was off, unnerved by Lucy's actions that kept him in hesitation.

Arlo stepped forward through the doorway. His warhammer was still in hand, but hung loosely in his hand to be more authoritative than threatening.

"Sorren, let's hear her out."

Sorren grunted, "Hear her out? We don't even know who she is. She sneaks about MY ship, starts rummaging through supplies, and you want me to believe she's not here to cause harm? Heir be damned if I let this ship sink before we even set sail."

Arlo gave a shrug, a contrast to Sorren's frustration he maintained a calm composure. "I never said she was harmless. She must be here for a reason, you won't know what that is if you kill her before she speaks. Besides, she doesn't look like a soldier of any kind, she's scared Sorren."

Sorren Glared at Arlo, his jaw clenched tightly. "She could be an Elfar spy for all we know."

The girl flinched at Sorren's words, Arlo noticed the subtlety in her movement. He took in her hood, nervous glances, and tight posture, she was hiding something, that much was clear. But whether it was dangerous, Arlo wasn't sure.

"Maybe," Arlo admitted, "But we won't know unless we let her speak."

Arlo inserted himself between Sorren and the girl, he stood relaxed and calm in an effort that the girl wasn't threatening she may herself ease up. "What's your name?"

The girl hesitated, barely more than a whisper she managed. "Nyla," she finally released a moment later, her gaze stuck to the broken potions on the floor.

"Nyla, you've put yourself in a dangerous spot. You snuck aboard our ship, you best have a good reason for doing that."

Nyla's eyes flicked up toward him briefly before she swallowed hard. "I…I was… I was looking for something…. Medicine."

Sorren huffed, very clearly unconvinced. "Medicine? You risk your life for herbs and potions?"

Arlo raised a hand, signaling Sorren to ease himself. "You're going to need to be more specific than that, Nyla." Arlo continued with a steady voice, easing himself to stay calm and ideally bring Sorren with him. "Who is the medicine for? Why do you think we have the supplies you need?"

Nyla's shaken breath continued, tears poured from her eyes, falling to the floor with audible droplets. "My mother. She's… very sick. Nothing I've found has helped her. I heard rumors, about medicine, and books that might save her. I… I had to try… I couldn't let her die."

Arlo glanced back at Sorren, who wore his battle on his face. "She's desperate. Not any different than we are."

"Fine," Sorren sighed, rubbing the bridge of his nose. Memories of his own journey raced in front of him, the moment his mother died during a raid, he was desperate then too. Desperate to keep her alive, he would have done anything, and he was just a boy. "But if she steps out of line again…" Sorren trailed.

"She won't," Arlo interrupted, giving Nyla a reassuring look before turning back to Sorren. "We're all looking for something, right?"

Sorren grumbled, but nodded. "Alright, but I'm keeping my eye on her."

For years he had taken comfort in the belief that Heir watched every step. Lately, as the storms grew louder and the orders from the church grew stranger, that comfort felt more like a story he told himself.

CHAPTER 33

The heavy door to the war room creaked as Arlo, Sorren, and the newfound passenger Nyla stepped inside. Sorren led the way. His heavy footsteps spoke not only of his strength and presence, but of the sense of ownership he held over the ship itself. Arlo ushered Nyla to a seat at the table. Lucy, who had been sitting quietly while they entered, had already refilled drinks for everyone.

Lucy glanced around the room and noticed Nyla joining them. She was on her feet in an instant.

"I am so sorry," she began, her voice full of sincerity. "If I frightened you back there. That was not my intention."

Lucy looked Nyla in the eyes, using everything within her to share her compassion.

The girl seemed reluctant at first, but after a small, comforting look from Arlo she let her guard down a little.

"It is okay. I am Nyla," she whispered so softly that Sorren might not have heard her.

Sorren sat at the head of the table, arms crossed and jaw tight. His eyes had not left Nyla since the moment he had seen her in the apothecary. He said nothing. His glare alone was a reminder that trust was earned, not given.

Arlo took a seat between Nyla and Lucy and took a drink from the glass waiting for him. He looked around the table, then settled his gaze on Nyla.

"You mentioned your mother. Tell us more about what is wrong with her. Maybe we can help."

The hooded girl hesitated. Her hands were clasped tightly together, only moving so she could push strands of blue tinted white hair out of her face. She clung to a secret she was afraid to let go. If she told them everything, would these strangers help her, or would they reach her mother first and take her away. Her heart raced faster now than when she had run from the beast in the woods.

After a long moment of gathering her courage, she drew in a steadying breath and spoke.

"My mother has been sick for some time. It started small. Just fatigue. We thought it was something common, but nothing helped. Over time she grew weaker and weaker. Her body is wasting away."

Her hands trembled as she spoke, the memory of helplessness washing over her again.

"She barely moves now. We have tried everything. Potions, remedies. Sunny even brought a magic user. Nothing helped. I did not have a choice but to leave her and look for answers. Sunny used to tell me stories about royal ships with special magical potions that could cure any illness, and mages across the waters with unbelievable power. I did not mean to steal. I just… I…"

She trailed off as tears filled her eyes. Her head dropped into her palms.

"She is running out of time."

Lucy frowned and moved closer to offer comfort. She leaned against the arm of Nyla's chair and placed a hand on her arm.

"That must be so hard. I cannot imagine what you have been through."

Arlo leaned forward and studied Nyla's face for any sign of a lie. The girl had conveniently appeared the night before they set sail. Was this fate. Destiny. He pushed that thought aside. He had spoken so much about hope and unity. Maybe this was his chance to make up for some of the lives he could not save in Fall Lake.

"So you are hoping to find something on this boat. Some kind of cure?" he asked.

He glanced at Sorren, who let out a low grunt. Sorren's arms loosened slightly as he listened. It seemed he could see the truth in the girl's words and feel his own sense of compassion stirring.

"Yes," Nyla said. Desperation filled her purple eyes. "I have to be honest. I do not know what I am looking for. Mother rarely let me out to see things. It was even more rare that I was allowed to leave the woods near our home. But I have to find something. I have no options left. Magic, a relic, a person. I do not know what I need."

Sorren finally broke his silence. His deep voice cut through her quiet sobs.

"You are risking a lot on rumors, girl. Instead of spending more time with your mother, you are off on a fool's errand. You are looking for something you do not even know exists."

Tears pooled in Nyla's hands as more fell. She managed to choke out an answer while the others waited.

"I have to try," she said. "She is all I have."

Lucy shared a glance with Arlo as he rose from his seat and walked over to Nyla. He held out a cloth for her to wipe her eyes. He leaned over the chair, close enough to offer comfort but leaving her room to breathe.

"It is not that we do not understand," he said softly. "But we need to know who we are bringing with us. There are dangerous things out there. We do not want you to be hurt either."

The room grew quiet. Nyla's sobs faded as she stared at the cloth in his hand, then at the others gathered around the table, and finally back into Arlo's eyes. Sorren's hardened gaze had softened. He was a brute, but he knew when compassion had its place. As much as he wanted to trust the girl, something still made him hesitate.

Lucy gave Nyla's arm a gentle rub.

"We will do what we can to help," she said. "But you will need to trust us. In return, we will try to trust you."

Nyla nodded slowly. She looked at Arlo and whispered a soft thank you as she took the cloth from his hand.

As their hands met, a jolt of blue energy pulsed out from Arlo's palm and rolled over Nyla's skin.

A woman rose from a makeshift bed, her body weakened by an unseen illness. She had no muscle left, no fullness. Her body had become little more than skin and bone. The lines of her face still held faint traces of the beauty she once carried in her youth, before her health was stolen away.

She pushed herself to her feet and reached for a simple canister to pour a drink.

Her hands trembled from the small weight. Before she could spill it, someone rushed to her side.

The girl who stepped in was tall, her face a younger mirror of the sickly woman's, only with the fullness of proper food and years still ahead of her. Pale hair glistened with a hint of blue in the dim candlelight.

The older woman's robes shifted and revealed strange markings along her back. The younger girl steadied her, holding her upright and taking the canister from her hands.

"Let me help you, Mother," the girl said, stubbornness in her voice.

"Nee, you must learn to take care of yourself instead of an old woman like me," the older woman answered.

"I can take care of myself. But who will take care of you."

"Oh, I have been through worse, girl. You should stop worrying about me and focus on yourself."

She barely finished before a coughing fit took her. Small droplets of blood flecked the cloth at her lips.

"Here, Mother. You do not have to be so hopeless."

The girl held out a cloth and helped her mother clean the bits of mucus and blood that escaped.

"It is not hopelessness, Nee," the older woman said weakly. "I am stubborn because I have hope in you. That you will become a wonderful woman. That you will make a difference in the world. You are more than you know. Promise me, Nee. When I am gone, you will carry on and make me proud."

The air in the war room shifted as blue light washed through both Arlo and Nyla's eyes. The vision faded. Nyla took the cloth from his hand and wiped her tears away, unsure how such a vivid scene had stormed through her mind. She set a hand on Lucy's arm and whispered a heartfelt thank you.

Arlo took a few steps back and stumbled. The familiar ache of his wounds surged through him again. Bruises bloomed across his body, making themselves known. The change in his steps was subtle, but not subtle enough to slip past Sorren or Lucy. Both of them had seen the strange way Arlo and Nyla had stared at one another in the moment before the light faded.

Was that the past. Was it the future. The feeling was strange, almost like he had stepped into one of Nyla's own memories. The weight of her promise to her mother now seemed to rest on his shoulders as well.

"Everything all right?" Lucy asked, watching the way he moved.

"I am fine," he lied, as he did every time the wounds returned. The pain was not enough to stop him, but it made every breath uncomfortable. If it came back at the wrong moment during the voyage, they could all be in trouble.

"Nyla, I believe you," Arlo said as he sank back into his chair. "Sorren is the captain of the Sea Sentinel, but you have my approval. If you are willing to face the danger."

Nyla's eyes lit up, fresh tears gathering.

"I will not slow you down. Or interfere. I can keep up." She turned to Sorren with hopeful eyes. "Please, Captain Sorren."

Sorren felt a twist in his gut. The girl was young and naive. She had admitted herself that she had never truly been out in the world.

He rose to his feet, his face set and unreadable. A man like a boulder who could terrify anyone who found themselves on his bad side. He had been lied to before by people who tried to use him. Part of him wanted to follow Arlo's lead and trust her. Another part recognized there was something different about this girl. Her white hair was unusual. She was taller than most young women he knew. Her eyes were a color he had never seen.

"Fine," Sorren said gruffly.

He drained the rest of his drink in one long swallow. A bit of wine spilled as he slammed the mug down onto the table.

"You can come with us. But you will not hold us back. Keep up or get left behind. And if we see any trouble or tricks, your neck will meet the blade of Justice."

Arlo glanced at Sorren, but held his tongue. Sorren's heavy boots echoed across the floor as he moved away to pour another drink. On his way back he set a hand on Arlo's shoulder and lowered his voice so only Arlo could hear.

"Dragging her into our mess will not solve her problems."

Arlo nodded and grimaced through the pain. He understood why Sorren was on edge. Something was different about this girl, and they knew nothing real about her yet. For all they knew, she could be lying through her teeth and waiting to sabotage the ship in the middle of the night.

"We should get some rest," Arlo said.

"You are right. We have a long trip ahead of us," Sorren agreed, knocking back his next drink without effort.

Lucy stood as well and took Nyla by the hand. She offered her a warm, welcoming smile.

"I will show you to your room, Nyla. We have an extra one. It was meant for me, but I am sure you will be more comfortable there."

Nyla looked up, surprised, and rose to her feet.

"Oh, I do not want to take someone's room."

Lucy waved her free hand, dismissing the concern.

"Do not worry about it. Arlo and I have been sharing anyway." She shot a teasing glance at Arlo over her shoulder as she led Nyla to the door. "We will just keep sharing. Right."

Arlo rubbed the back of his neck, his cheeks as red as Lucy's hair. Sorren did not even need to look to know the embarrassment was painted across his face. A devilish smirk tugged at Sorren's lips.

"Oh yes. Just keep your cold feet on your side," Arlo managed.

Nyla hesitated at first and lagged a step behind Lucy, but a small smile crept across her face as she watched their playful exchange. She still felt the weight of tension in the room, but she had little choice if she wanted to save her mother.

"Thank you," she said. She moved closer to Lucy and murmured, just loud enough for her to hear. "For everything."

Lucy led Nyla down the narrow hallway, her voice lingering as they disappeared from the war room.

"Do not mention it. We will get you settled. Tomorrow we set off. Big adventure awaits us all."

Arlo remained seated for a moment, listening to their voices fade into the distance. Sorren had started toward the door when Arlo spoke again.

"Give her a chance, Sorren."

"Ah, fuck, Arlo," Sorren said, pressing his fist against the doorframe. Frustration poured out of him. "We have not even set sail yet and now we are babysitting."

Arlo's footsteps were quieter as he crossed the floor and joined Sorren in the doorway.

"I get it. I really do. But she is just a young woman trying to do the right thing. She is not doing anything different from us. You took me in. We took Lucy in. Everything has turned out well enough so far."

"Yes, but back then we did not have anything to lose."

"And now?" Arlo asked.

Sorren shook his head and waved his hands at the room and the ship around them.

"Now I have everything to lose. This is my dream, Arlo. This is all I ever wanted. To live on the water. To be free at sea, same as my da. We worked our asses off for this, and I will not lose it because of a pair of pretty legs."

Arlo could not help it. Laughter escaped him and cracked the tension hanging in the air.

"What are you laughing at?" Sorren asked, one brow raised.

"You. Trying to act the serious captain and still taking time to appreciate a woman's body."

"Listen. Great power, great responsibility and all that," Sorren replied with a mocking tone. "As captain, I have to make sure my lady the Sea Sentinel is taken care of. But I would be lying if I said I did not enjoy a bit of flesh too. Did you see her. She fills out those pants well enough. But I do not need distractions. Not tonight."

"Sure, Captain," Arlo said, giving him a playful salute.

Sorren rolled his eyes and let out a booming laugh.

"I do not think I will be the one distracted tonight. Looks like you are the one who will not have an empty bed."

"Shut up, or we will have a mutiny before the ship has even left port."

"Over my dead body. I will throw you overboard first."

The two men laughed together as they made their way down the hall to their rooms. For a little while, the weight of what lay ahead felt lighter on their shoulders.

CHAPTER 34

The evening had settled into a calm quiet. The fires from the festivities on land had died down, left only as a low simmer where a few stubborn revelers refused to let the night end. The hours wore on, and soon the sun would rise and signal the launch of the Sea Sentinel. Inside the small shared room, the air was warm and still, carrying the familiar salty scent of the sea around them.

Arlo sat on the edge of the bed, running a hand through the beard he had recently allowed to grow out, weighing the events of the day and what was soon to come. Lucy had just returned after guiding Nyla to what would be her own room. Her dress clung with sand, dust, and grime from the day. She teased Arlo with a quick warning not to peek as she shook the fabric free, then folded it neatly on the chest of drawers. A slight tremble lingered in her fingers as she reached for her nightgown, a simple pale garment that draped loosely over her slim figure. It was modest and soft, yet the dim light of the oil lamp beside the bed wrapped her in a gentle glow that made her beauty difficult to ignore.

"You seem quiet," Arlo said softly, breaking the silence that had hung between them since she came back. He reached for his shoulder and rolled it, trying to work out the last of the pain that still lingered there.

Lucy paused and let out a small breath as she drew her hair over one shoulder. She sat on the opposite side of the bed and turned toward him with a small, forced smile.

"I have been thinking," she said, her voice quieter and more direct than usual. "About everything. About whatever power is inside me."

Her hands gripped the edges of the nightgown as if hanging on to the fabric might help keep her steady.

Arlo nodded. He understood what she did not say out loud. They had not known each other long, yet the connection between them felt as though it had been shaped over years rather than weeks. So much had happened in the month leading up to the launch of the ship they had poured their hearts into. For Arlo, the strange power in him had come almost naturally, answering when he called. For Lucy, it was wild and unpredictable, bursting forth in moments of fear or anger. It scared her more than any danger that waited out on the water.

"I do not know if I can control myself," she whispered. Her voice faltered and her eyes shimmered. "I am scared, Arlo. What if I hurt someone. What if I hurt someone innocent. What if I hurt you."

Arlo rose and stepped around the bed to close the distance between them. He took her hands in his and gently pulled her closer.

"You will not," he said firmly. His thumb brushed over her knuckles. "You are stronger than you think, Lucy. But you have to face it. We cannot keep running from it."

She looked up at him, her emerald eyes wide and uncertain, the corners tight as they tried to hold back tears. For a moment she said nothing, weighing his words and searching for strength inside herself. Then, slowly, she nodded.

"All right," she whispered. "But promise me something. Promise me you will stop me if things go wrong."

"I promise," Arlo said without hesitation, though the weight of that promise pressed harder on his chest than he let her see.

He guided her toward the center of the room where the lantern cast a faint, steady circle of light. He watched her stand there, every line of her form softened by the glow, as if she belonged to some other, more magical world. Yet Arlo knew this was not about beauty or wonder. This moment was about control, and as much as he wished he could carry it for her, it rested in her hands.

Lucy closed her eyes and raised her arms, palms facing upward. The air shifted into a warm crackle. The room seemed to hold its breath with her. Arlo felt the heat begin to rise as a crimson aura gathered around her hands, trickling outward like the first spark catching on dry wood.

At first it stayed small and steady. Flickering strands of mana danced between her fingers. Her face tightened with effort as she tried to shape it, each breath a careful step forward along a fraying edge.

"You are doing great," Arlo said, his voice low and calm.

The flames, once small and obedient, suddenly swelled. Lucy gasped as they burst higher, surging beyond her grip. Heat slammed into the room. Fire roared into a scorching blaze and raced along the walls. Shadows leapt and twisted, shifting into shapes that moved like living things.

"No. No, this is not right," Lucy cried, panic rising in her voice.

The world around them changed.

The wooden walls of the room warped and vanished, swallowed by a vision more sinister. Arlo blinked against the shock as the cabin was replaced by a barren wasteland. A once green field lay burned to blackened earth. Jagged stone spires rose around them, forming a cage that seemed to close in tighter with each breath. Blood seeped upward through the cracked ground, thick and dark, pooling around their legs. The sky above turned a deep, choking red, ash drifting down in slow, painful breaths that stung their lungs.

Lucy stumbled back, her eyes wide with horror as fire and blood wrapped the world. She reached for Arlo, but he was already sinking into the rising pool. Bodies fell from the red sky and crashed into the seething surface around him. The sight dragged at her mind, pulling her deeper into the storm of her own power.

Arlo pushed forward through the burning water, ignoring the fire that clawed at his skin. His hands burned the moment he reached for her, but he did not let go. He locked his fingers around hers and pulled her close.

"Lucy," he shouted above the roar. "You have to control it. You are stronger than this. Lucy, look at me."

For a heartbeat she did not answer. Her eyes were wild, glowing with a fierce, untamed green that threatened to swallow her. He held on tighter, his voice forcing its way through the chaos until something in her gaze shifted. She gasped, fighting for breath, fighting for herself.

"I cannot," she choked out. Tears poured from her eyes, her whole body shaking.

"Yes, you can," Arlo insisted. "Focus on me. Breathe. You are in control."

The flames wavered. The heat pulsed like a living heartbeat that stuttered and faltered. Arlo saw the war in her eyes. Fear and doubt clawed at her, but beneath it all he saw what he had seen from the first day they met. A strength that refused to die.

Slowly, painfully, the fire began to fade. The blood red sky softened into darkness. The jagged spires and churning ichor broke apart into smoke and drifted away. The air cooled, easing back into the familiar salt scented quiet of their small room.

Lucy collapsed to her knees as the last of the flames vanished as if they had never been there. She trembled, gasping for breath. Arlo dropped beside her, his hands raw and blistered, but he did not seem to notice. He wrapped his arms around her and held her against his chest.

"It is all right," he whispered. "It is over."

His hand moved gently through her hair as she sobbed, streaks of blood tinted tears marking her cheeks.

"You are all right. We are all right."

For a long while, neither of them spoke. Only her ragged breathing and the faint crackle of the lamp filled the silence.

"I lost control," she said at last, her voice unsteady. "I could have burned everything."

"But you did not," Arlo said, brushing a strand of hair from her face. "You stopped it. You took control."

"But I nearly killed you," she replied. Her breath came fast as she took in the sight of his burned hands and the faint blood on his chest. "Arlo, you were burning. Your hands."

"It is all right. I have been through worse," he said, forcing a small smile, even though the pain throbbed through every finger.

"No. No, I cannot do this. I cannot control it. If you had not been here I would have. I would have hurt you," she insisted. Her voice cracked as she lifted her hands and pressed them over her eyes, as if she could hide the memory from herself.

Arlo reached for her again and rested his hands on her shoulders.

"Lucy, listen to me," he began.

"No," she cut in, pushing his hands away as she rose unsteadily to her feet. "You need to go. Please."

"Lucy, do not," he tried again.

"Arlo, go," she shouted, taking a step back as the air around her stirred with a faint heat. Her eyes flashed with a darkened red. "I cannot be around anyone right now. I almost killed you. I need to be alone."

Arlo stared at her in disbelief. He saw the terror in her eyes and the way her whole body recoiled from him. She was not afraid of him.

334

She was afraid of herself. Afraid of what might happen if she lost control again.

Every part of him wanted to stay. To pull her back into his arms and refuse to leave. But he knew this was a battle she needed to face inside herself, at least for now.

"All right," he said after a long pause. His voice was quiet and thick with sadness.

Lucy did not answer. Her shoulders sagged as if some invisible weight had settled on her back. She turned away and stared out the small window of their room.

Arlo lingered a moment longer, wanting to say more, then slipped out and closed the door behind him without another word.

A sharp stab of guilt pierced him as the latch clicked. He hated leaving her alone, especially like this, but he understood why she had pushed him away. The fear of losing control. The fear of hurting the people she cared about. The burden of power she never asked for, and the hollow ache of not knowing who she used to be.

They had asked around in every place they passed, hoping someone might recognize her, or know something about the woman with crimson hair and emerald eyes. Night after night she lay awake with the feeling that something important was missing, just out of reach. Every time she tried to force her memory to return, all she saw was the field. The hammer poised above her. Fire. Blood. Death.

Arlo made his way to the deck and spent the next aching hour in silence, staring at the light of the twin moons as it shimmered across the open sea. A few voices still drifted from the shore and faint orange embers showed that the party on land had not fully ended. His mind never left Lucy. He replayed what had happened again and again, wondering if he should have stayed, if he should have pushed harder to help her fight it.

Each time the thought rose, he reminded himself that this was what she had asked for. Space to find her footing.

He leaned on the railing and let the cool breeze wash over his burned hands. He had not bothered to bandage them. The pain did not matter. That was something he could bear. The only thing that mattered was the woman just below deck, drowning in fears she did not deserve.

Time dragged. Every passing moment felt heavier, crowded with the worry that she would decide she was a danger to everyone and shut him out for good.

"I am sorry."

Lost in his thoughts, he had not heard the soft steps behind him. He turned, and there she was. Lucy stood only a few feet away, bathed in the pale glow of the moons. Her face was pale and tired. Her eyes were red and her cheeks streaked with dried blood and tears, but she no longer shook. Time and solitude had given her space to breathe.

"I am sorry," she whispered again. "I should not have pushed you away."

Arlo straightened and stepped toward her slowly, careful not to crowd her. This time she did not pull back. She took a small step closer, and his heart began to race.

"You went through something intense," he said, offering her a gentle smile. "I understand."

"I was afraid," she said, her gaze dropping to the planks under their feet. "I still am. But I do not want to be alone. I do not want to be without you."

Arlo reached out and took her hand. A soft spark of red and blue flickered where their fingers met.

"You are not alone, Lucy," he said. "Not now. Not ever."

Her fingers curled tighter around his. The quiet energy tingled between their hands. They stood like that for a while, letting the silence settle until she finally looked up into his sapphire eyes. The storm that had raged in her earlier had eased, but a faint shadow of fear and doubt still lived there.

"Come on," he said softly, giving her hand a gentle tug. "Let us go back inside."

Lucy hesitated, then nodded and let him lead her. He guided her back into the room and closed the door behind them, shutting out the rest of the world. No one would have guessed what had taken place in their minds not long ago. The cabin looked as it had before. Clothes rested on the drawers and faint impressions marked the bedding. The room itself seemed untouched by her outburst.

Lucy drew in a deep breath and crossed to the small washbasin in the corner. She poured cool water into it and watched it swirl before dipping a cloth and wringing it out. She began wiping away the more obvious marks of ash and dried blood on her arms. Thin stained lines still traced across her face and down her neck and shoulders. The more she wiped, the more she discovered.

As she worked, she glanced over her shoulder at Arlo watching her.

"I am sorry I am such a mess tonight," she said with a small laugh, trying to lighten the air. "I think I need a full cleansing ritual after that."

"Do you want help?" he asked. "If it helps, I am a great scrubber."

Lucy let out a soft giggle and smiled, then handed him the cloth with a small nod.

Arlo stepped closer and began to wipe away the remnants of her power from her arms. One hand cradled her forearm, steady and gentle, while the other guided the cloth over her skin. The moment their skin touched, the spark between them rose again. Arlo felt the ache in his burned hands ease with each pass of the cloth.

He did not question it. He simply focused on Lucy. On the woman standing in front of him, not the flames and visions that had tried to swallow her.

He rinsed the cloth and moved to her other arm. Lucy looked away, color blooming in her cheeks, her heart pounding hard enough that she felt it in her throat.

"You know," she said, her voice soft. She tilted her head slightly and glanced up at him from the corner of her eye. "I do not like feeling vulnerable like this. But with you, it feels different."

He drew the cloth slowly along her arm, leaving her skin clean and unmarked. He folded the damp cloth neatly, then took a fresh one and dabbed away the lingering dampness.

"Safe," she added in a whisper.

Arlo lifted his hand and studied it, searching for any hint of the burns that had marred his skin only moments ago.

Gone.

Instead, fresh skin untouched and clean to the world. He used the same hand to place a finger under her chin, lifting her face to look at his. The warmth in his voice wrapped around her like a comforting blanket. "That's what I want for you, Lucy. To feel safe and free to be yourself."

Lucy's breath caught as the words settled into her. No one had ever spoken to her that way, not with that kind of steadiness, not with that kind of faith. Something inside her loosened, something tied tight since the day she woke with nothing but terror and fire clinging to her memories. The idea of safety felt distant to her, fragile even, but in his voice she felt it for the first time like it was something she could reach.

Lucy's heart raced as the intimacy between them deepened. A warm flutter rose in her chest, tightening her throat with a mix of longing and fear. The room felt smaller now, not confining but protective, as if the world had stepped back to give them this one moment. Even the hum of her power seemed to quiet, settling under her skin like it, too, was waiting for her next move.

She looked up at him, meeting his gaze, everything else around them lost and faded away. She could feel the warmth in his eyes, understanding tenderness that had drawn her to him since she met him.

Arlo took the cloth and started wiping away the tears and blood stained across her face. A brief touch of his finger against her skin made her let out a soft moan as her head tilted slightly and her eyes closed. The sensation of warmth, excitement, and safety wrapped itself around her.

"Just a little bit more," he whispered into her ear, his hand now cupping her face and leaning her head to the side. Tracing every detail of her face into his memory. He brushed his fingers from the base of her ear down, sending a warm jolt along her spine, forcing another moan to unintentionally escape her lips.

A different form of tension filled the room, this one more sensual, electric, warming, and one that sent both of their hearts into a hastened sprint.

Her lips pressed inward against her teeth. An unspoken desperation clawing to release. His own eyes lingered over her lips before meeting hers, together they could feel the heat between them.

Both held a declaration buried within themselves. Both on the verge to lay claim to what they wanted from the other. He wiped the last bit of dirt from her cheek as his thumb gently flicked her plump and waiting lips.

He eyed her entire body from head to toe. Her skin had been cleansed, yet some more remained. Hidden beneath the thin white fabric of a nightgown she had put on only a short while ago. Courage took hold, as she let her hands grace the edges of the nightgown, and slowly slid it off.

For a heartbeat she hesitated, her fingers trembling against the thin fabric. So much of what she knew of her life had been fear and uncertainty, shadows of memories she could not reach and flashes of power she could not control. For once she wanted something simple and human. She let the hesitation leave her with the garment, choosing him, choosing this, choosing herself.

"Just a little more," she whispered with a low sensual moan as the fabric fell to the floor at their feet.

Arlo hesitated for a moment, his breath taken, the sight more intoxicating than any drink could ever give him.

Their hearts raced separately, both of them urging to break free and be together.

"Lucy…" He began.

"Help me Arlo, take it all away." Her voice shook, not with weakness but with all the things she carried. The fire she feared. The blood she saw when she closed her eyes. The emptiness of not knowing who she was. The weight of wanting him despite it all. Every word she spoke trembled with the plea to be more than her fear, to be held as something other than a danger waiting to happen.

"Will you?"

He met her step, entranced by her beauty and bold passion. He took the cloth and pressed it against her collarbone, slowly pressing it more firmly and washing away the scars of earlier. The cloth, and with it his hands, drifted slowly down her body, raising over the hills of her bare breasts where dried droplets had scattered.

A powerful moan escaped her once again as he wiped away at her intimate areas. Dabbing away around her soft, perky nipples. He had briefly become hesitant, but her reassuring words and seeking gaze welcomed him to continue. A sensation of heat igniting something stronger than her own flames within her.

"I want this, Arlo," she breathed into him, her voice trembling again, this time not with fear, but with desire. She pressed herself closer to him, an offering of herself and her own vulnerability, her head tilted upward and leaning closer to his.

Their eyes met again as a primal hunger snapped between them. Arlo dropped the cloth to the floor, his hands finding her waist as he brought himself to meet her the rest of the way. Their lips met in a heated clash, fully igniting the spark of passion that had been simmering just out of reach. Lucy's arms wrapped around his neck, pulling him closer into a more deepened kiss as their hearts raced in synchronization.

The kiss broke, and Arlo looked into her emerald eyes with a deep blue that burned with its own quiet passion. They were the brightest he had ever seen, and within them was everything he felt he had wanted.

"Are you sure?" he asked, searching for any hesitation.

Lucy nodded subtly and pressed her body closer to his, her lips just hovering over his. "More than anything."

Arlo lifted her effortlessly, their lips meeting once again as he carried her to the bed. He laid her down gently, ripping away at his shirt to expose the chiseled physique beneath. He stood over her briefly, taking in her beauty before he crawled over her, providing a weight from his body that was both comforting and electrifying.

Their kisses grew heavier and less controlled, hands explored the curves and lines of each other's bodies, every touch met with red and blue spark that only heightened their desire for one another. The room disappeared, their mission, their goals, nothing else mattered in this moment beside the magnetism of intimacy between the two of them.

For Arlo it felt like the first moment since Fall Lake where he was allowed to want something only for himself. All his guilt and responsibility eased under the warmth of her touch. For Lucy, the world narrowed to the feeling of being seen, not as a mystery or a threat, but as a woman who deserved to be held. For the first time since she had opened her eyes in this world, the fire inside her did not frighten her. It softened, steady and warm.

Time blurred as their passion grew to be uncontrollable. Slowly the remnants of clothes were no longer an issue, instead they lay bare and vulnerable to each other. A rising form of ecstasy gripping them as they became one. A union of bodies and souls that transcended everything around them. Each of them feeling as if a piece of them had become complete as their shared breath and heartbeats moved together in unison. Their bodies in a rhythm that sang with their desire for each other.

Lucy had surrendered herself completely, swept away by the tide of passion that enveloped them as they reached their peak.

Time stood still, the intensity of the moment carrying them to heights they had never known. With a final thrust of passion, they let go of everything.

The red and blue sparks that always danced between them rose and swirled in a quiet pulse, not wild or dangerous, but gentle as the tide brushing the shore. Their magic mingled in soft waves that glowed along their skin, folding into each other like it had been waiting for this moment too. For a breathless instant, she felt whole, and he felt the ache inside himself quiet to peace.

Outside, the Sea Sentinel drifted on the slow roll of the tide, the last embers of celebration on shore fading into the dark. Inside their small cabin, the world beyond the thin wooden walls washed away like a receding wave, leaving only the warmth of their joined bodies and the soft hush of shared breath. Wrapped in one another, with red and blue light dimming to a gentle glow beneath their skin, they let sleep take them at last, holding on to the fragile, impossible feeling that for this one night, they were safe.

Whatever waited in the Gauntlet and beyond, it could wait until morning.

CHAPTER 35

The sun had just risen over the horizon while the Sea Sentinel cut through the perfect morning waves. Sorren Blaze gripped the wheel with steady hands and watched with quiet pride as his ship rode the swell of the sea. The deck hummed with movement and low chatter, a shared current of excitement and confidence that ran through the crew who had helped bring her to life.

Alfonze stalked the deck nearby, pointing and barking orders, his voice carrying easily over the creak of wood and the slap of rope.

"Rig those sails tighter, Mern. Willy, keep that leg of yours in check, we do not need you rolling overboard."

Momentarily satisfied, he strode up behind Sorren and gave him a sharp slap on the backside.

"Good winds for a start, huh, Captain?"

Sorren nodded and turned the wheel a touch, adjusting to a subtle shift in the breeze. "Aye. Good winds and good hands to meet them."

This was not his first time at a helm. Porters began their sea training early, and Sorren had spent enough years on the water to know how a ship should feel under him. The Sea Sentinel was larger than anything he had captained before, heavy and solid. Instead of daunting him, the size rooted his confidence even deeper. She had weight, presence, and his hands belonged on her wheel.

His gaze drifted to the horizon, to the endless glitter where sky and water met. For a moment he saw not the new ship, but a younger version of himself standing beside his Da on an older, smaller vessel. His father would have been proud to see him here, guiding a ship of his own on her first true journey.

"You do not think she is all looks, do you?" Alfonze asked, grinning up at him while he twisted the thick ends of his moustache.

"She is built like an ox, Alf. She will make it there and back for many years yet. Besides, the captain always goes down with his ship, and I am far too young and ruggedly handsome for that."

He stroked his chin, letting his gaze slide briefly over one of the heartier women on deck, a crew mate who had caught his eye in recent days. His grin lingered a beat too long before he pulled himself back to the task and tightened his grip on the wheel.

"You got that right, you big oaf. Do not let your willy get in the way of your duty," Alfonze muttered, already turning to redirect a younger sailor who seemed lost in the maze of rigging.

The day stretched into a steady rhythm. It felt as if the crew had been born for this moment. Once everyone fell into their tasks, they moved with an easy flow that only needed the occasional correction barked from Alf. The sky stayed clear and bright. The water rolled smooth beneath the hull. Behind them, the land they had left that morning had long since faded from view.

The sun carved a golden path over the waves. The ship matched its pace as if the two were in simple agreement. For hours, Sorren stood at the helm with a calm that settled deep into his bones. His smile was small but steady, an easy contentment that felt almost like freedom.

When uncertain footsteps approached the helm, he did not tense. The calm only shifted when he noticed the figure draw near and lean over the railing beside him. Nyla stood there, hood still up, her pale face drawn tight with discomfort.

A grin tugged at Sorren's mouth. He recognized that expression well enough.

"First time at sea?" he called, amusement softening his voice.

Nyla swallowed and nodded. "It moves a lot more than I expected."

"The sea has her own way of greeting new faces. Bit of unease comes with the welcome." He studied her a moment, noting the greenish cast to her cheeks.

"Come here." He motioned to the railing directly in front of the wheel. "Look out over the horizon. Keeping your eyes there can help steady your stomach."

She moved carefully, each step measured, as if she expected the floor to tilt out from under her at any moment.

"The sea is a shock to the untested," Sorren went on. "She will roughen you up, then toughen you once you settle in. Do not stare at the way the ship bobs or at the water under your feet. Fix your sights out there and breathe. You will make it through."

Nyla nodded and tried to slow her breathing, but the twist in her stomach did not let go. She lifted a fist to her mouth and pressed against it as a small gag escaped. To her relief, that was all.

"If that still does not agree with you, we have ginger root down below. Chewing it can help keep things settled."

"Ginger root" she repeated and turned her head carefully to look at him.

"Aye. We keep it to help rations stay fresh, but it works for nausea as well. Take a sliver, chew it, and you will be less likely to feed the fish your lunch."

"Thank you, Captain." Nyla managed a small laugh. She gave him a shy smile that stirred something in Sorren that he tried not to show. Her height, her strange beauty, those long legs. It all sent a small pulse of heat through him that made his smile turn a shade more roguish.

Against his better judgement, he leaned into the habit that had served him well in every port.

"And if it gets too lonely down in your quarters," he added, voice dropping to something more playful, "there is always space in my bed."

Nyla blinked and turned away slightly, cheeks flushing pink. She looked more confused than embarrassed.

"Your bed" she echoed.

"Aye. I have the largest and softest one." He gave her a clear wink when she risked another glance his way. Her empty stare made him falter. It was rare for anyone to miss his meaning. Rarer still for them to pass it by.

"You know. In case the sea gets to you, and you would prefer some company."

Her lips parted as she tried to follow the line of his words. It took her several long heartbeats before her eyes widened in sudden understanding.

"Oh. Thank you, but I think I will stick to the ginger root," she said quickly. Her blush deepened to a color that might have rivaled Lucy's hair.

Sorren cleared his throat and let out a short laugh. Her innocence caught him off guard. The way it disarmed him felt almost refreshing.

"Right. The ginger root. Good choice," he said, smoothing his surprise with a grin.

Nyla nodded, still not entirely certain what part of the exchange she had missed. Her mother had given her that talk, but theory was a poor match for practice. No one had ever flirted with her before.

"I should get back to my room and sleep this off," she added. "Thank you, Sorren."

346

He waved her off and shook his head as she made her careful way back across the deck. When she disappeared below, he let out a fuller laugh. A few nearby sailors glanced at him, puzzled.

"There is something else about that girl," he murmured under his breath. "She is not meant for this life. I hope she knows what she is walking into."

He lifted his face to the sky. The air tasted clean and sharp. Several birds wheeled above, one darker than the others, circling back once before soaring away. This was life to him. The creak of the ship, the endless water, the simple rules. No court politics, no whispered orders from men in gold robes. Out here, everyone was equal in the face of the sea, and the only thing anyone truly answered to was the vessel beneath their feet.

Nyla settled into her small room and curled up on the narrow bed, arms wrapped tight around her shins. The boards beneath her seemed to sway even more now that she was alone. She had found the ginger root with the help of the provisioner, though not without enduring his laughter about her turning green at first light.

She stared at the space between her knees, watching the subtle listing of the Sea Sentinel and feeling it deepen her sense of distance. For a quiet, aching moment she wished she were back in her mother's cottage, cramped as it was. She could almost smell the herbs hanging from the rafters, hear Sonny's uneven humming from the other room.

She did not regret leaving. She had left her sick mother in Sonny's hands because she had to. Because the world she came from was not safer than this one. But everything here was louder, faster, full of faces she did not know and expectations she did not understand.

She had promised herself she would stand on her own. That she would prove to her mother that she was ready. That she could do something to change what awaited them back home.

A soft knock broke her thoughts apart.

Nyla straightened and brushed a hand across her face.

"Come in," she called.

The door creaked open and Lucy stepped inside with a tin bowl in her hands. Steam curled from the top and carried the smell of broth and herbs into the room.

"I brought you some stew," Lucy said. "It is not much, but I wanted to make sure you were eating."

Nyla took the bowl in both hands, comforted by the warmth in Lucy's gesture as much as by the heat bleeding through the metal. She had seen the terrible side of Lucy's power already, but she had also seen the way the other woman carried herself afterward. There was something steady in her now that Nyla clung to.

"Thank you, Lucy." She set the bowl on the small table beside her bed. The smell reminded her of something Sunny had made not long before she left. For a moment she saw his hands moving over a pot, his easy smile when he caught her watching.

"Are you doing alright?" Lucy asked. "I saw you asking for the ginger and wanted to see if there was anything else I could do. Arlo told me sea travel tends to make a good number of people sick at first."

Nyla shook her head and lifted the bowl again to breathe in the steam. It eased her stomach a little.

"I am fine. Or I will be. It is not just the sea. It is everything. This whole life is unfamiliar to me."

She lowered her voice and glanced around the small room as if the boards could grow ears.

"I do not fit here," she whispered.

348

Lucy's eyes softened. She crossed the few steps to the bed and sat on the edge, reaching out a hand for Nyla's arm in a quiet offer of comfort.

"What do you mean?" she asked gently.

"I mean" Nyla began. She swallowed and tightened her grip on the bowl, the metal biting lightly into her palms. She drew a deeper breath, trying to find words that would not get her killed.

Her mother's warnings rose up in her mind. Never let them see your ears. Never let them know what you are. Not if you want to stay safe.

"It is just that I am not like everyone else here." The words tumbled out now that she had let them loose. She had held them back for so long. She needed to say them to someone, anyone, or they would tear her in half.

"I am part Elfar," she added, so quietly that Lucy almost missed it.

Her heart lurched. Her stomach flipped in a very different way than the ship had done. Her thoughts scattered into skittering images.

Lucy stepping forward and pulling her into a hug, telling her none of it mattered and everything would be all right.

Lucy standing up and leaving the room to tell the others, and a dozen heavy boots coming back to drag Nyla to the rail and throw her overboard.

Lucy's eyes turning that burning red, the fire she had seen the night before roaring to life in this tiny room with nowhere to run.

A thousand other possibilities flashed through her mind. She felt lighter for having finally spoken the truth. She also felt stripped bare. This was the thing her mother had warned her about. Trusting someone when you did not know what they honestly believed. Telling them anyway. Hoping they did not break you with it.

The room went still. Lucy's eyes widened, but there was no disgust there. No fear. Only a startled kind of empathy.

She scooted a little closer and set her hand more firmly on Nyla's leg, giving it a reassuring squeeze.

"You do not need to worry about that with me," Lucy said. Her voice stayed kind and steady, her gaze never leaving Nyla's face.

Of course Lucy had suspected something. Nyla's eyes were unlike anyone else's on board, purple with flecks of bright blue. Her white hair carried cooling streaks of blue beneath. There was something otherworldly about her that you could not quite explain away. Lucy had spent enough time staring at Arlo's pure white hair to accept that some people were simply born with marks the world did not understand.

Nyla stared down into her stew, unsure what to say. Her shoulders loosened as if a weight had slipped from them, even while her heart continued to pound against her ribs.

"There is a lot happening in the world right now," Lucy went on. "Many people place blame on whoever looks different. It is easier than facing their own fears. But not everyone deserves to be punished for what others with the same blood have done. You did not ask to be born the way you are."

"But I heard some of the crew talking," Nyla said. Her fingers trembled as she lifted a hand to her hood. "They were talking about what they would do if they ever caught a pointed ear. Especially an Elfar spy."

She pushed her hood back and let her hair fall away. The long white and blue strands slipped aside to reveal the pointed ears beneath.

"How am I supposed to forget that?" she whispered. "They do not even know who I am, and they already want to cast me out. Or worse."

Lucy looked at the sharp tips of Nyla's ears, then back to her face. She smiled, small and bright.

"People are often driven by fear more than hatred," she said. "The attack on Fall Lake involved Elfar and Draconis, or at least that is

350

what people say. So fear took root and spread. But that does not mean every Elfar or Draconis shares the same beliefs. Many follow leaders who are afraid of losing their power. But many more would give you a chance if they saw who you are, not just where you come from."

Nyla lifted a spoonful of stew and brought it to her lips. She tried to blink away the tears rising in her eyes. She appreciated every word Lucy offered, but the memory of those ugly voices below deck still scraped at her.

"Thank you, Lucy," she said. "It is just that it seems easier for everyone else to belong. I want to be brave. I want to prove I am strong enough to be here for my mother's sake. But that fear is hard to ignore."

"To be honest," Lucy said quietly, "I understand that more than you think. I do not feel like I belong here either."

Nyla looked up, surprised.

"I feel like my missing memories hold every answer to why I am different," Lucy said. "If I had them, maybe everything would click into place. But I do not have them, and I cannot wait for them to return before I keep moving."

"Do you not feel like you are missing something all the time?" Nyla asked. She had leaned forward without realizing it, sitting like a child waiting to hear the next part of a story.

"All the time," Lucy admitted. "But that does not mean I stop living. Maybe you and I can be brave together. You are already braver than you think. You came here. You trusted us enough to tell us who you are. That proves more than you know."

Nyla met Lucy's gaze and found warmth there. It was the look of someone who saw more than the frightened girl curled in on herself. Someone who saw the courage beneath the fear.

"Thank you," Nyla whispered, returning to her stew.

"Anytime," Lucy said as she rose to her feet. She moved toward the door with an easy, almost playful step. "I would keep the hood up for now, though. At least until we know the right time to let others see. Especially the captain. He is a big soft thing under it all, but he is loyal to his church and king. It will be simpler if he does not have to choose between what he sees and what he has been taught."

"He actually told me about the ginger root," Nyla said. A small smile touched her lips. "He was kinder about it than I expected. A lot kinder than last night."

Lucy smiled back and lifted her brows in a knowing way. The connection between them settled a little deeper.

"Do you know why Sorren would offer to share his bed with me?" Nyla asked as the other woman reached for the door.

Lucy's cheeks warmed at once. She debated how much to explain and how.

Nyla saw the answer in the color on Lucy's face before she heard it in words. Her own ears grew hotter as understanding slid into place in a different way than it had on the deck. Here, in the small quiet room, it felt less like a joke she had missed and more like a world of things she had never had time to learn.

"Oh," Lucy said. "He meant that."

Nyla stared at her, heart thudding. For a moment she did not know whether to laugh, hide, or ask a dozen more questions. The ship rolled gently beneath them, carrying her farther from the life she had known and deeper into one where people offered beds for reasons that had nothing to do with sleep.

She swallowed, and for the first time since stepping on board, the strangeness of this new life stirred something else under the fear. Curiosity. Possibility.

Lucy gave her a softer smile and slipped out, leaving Nyla with her stew, her secrets, and the first fragile sense that maybe there was a place for her here after all.

CHAPTER 36

The smell of stew filled the galley that evening as the crew of the Sea Sentinel gathered for their meal. Lanterns swung from the beams overhead and cast an amber glow across rough tables and tired faces. The sea rolled beneath them in an easy lull that set bowls and mugs to a gentle clink.

Sorren had rolled in a barrel of ale to mark the first day of their journey. He poured drinks with a wicked grin for anyone who brought a cup to him.

He started humming a familiar sea song under his breath. A few nearby sailors picked up the tune, then a few more, until the entire room thrummed with voices. The song rolled along the walls like the tide.

Some of the younger sailors lost their place in the lyrics and broke into laughter. The older ones laughed with them and pounded their fists on the tables to keep the beat. The tempo climbed along with their spirits.

At the center of it all stood Sorren, cheeks flushed from ale and sun, his laughter louder than anyone else's. He moved from table to table, clapping shoulders, trading toasts, and throwing out stories from earlier voyages. Most were wrapped in such exaggeration that they felt more like legends than memories.

"And there I was," he shouted, planting a hand on one of the tables. "Clinging to the rig while the waves crashed around me like an angry sea titan. Wearing nothing but what my mama gave me."

The crew howled. Some shook their heads at the ridiculousness of it. Others beat their fists on the wood and raised their mugs in salute.

Sorren lifted his own mug high above his head.

"To the Sea Sentinel," he cried. "May her sails be brave and her crew never empty."

Every voice in the room joined the cheer. The words tangled and fell apart in the end, but no one seemed to mind.

The night stretched on in good humor. Someone suggested a show of talents, and the idea caught fire at once. One after another, sailors stepped forward to offer what they called talents and what the others called disasters.

One man tried impressions of different officers. His voice cracked halfway through Sorren's growl and sent the room into a fit of laughter. Another claimed to be a magician and dropped more cards than he managed to produce.

The tone shifted when one of the largest men in the crew lumbered forward and squinted at the hammer resting beside Arlo's seat. He was broad enough to rival Sorren in size, his shoulders filling the space between benches as he moved.

"Let me use that as my talent," he said, pointing at the hammer. "Test of strength. I can give them a proper show."

Arlo, his mind softened by ale and the ease of the night, lifted the hammer without effort and carried it to the cleared space at the center of the galley. He flipped it in his hand once to the delight of the crew, then set it down with deliberate care.

354

A circle formed around it. Lucy watched from near the wall, Sorren just behind her, his arms crossed and his eyes amused. He did not call out a warning. He was curious how far they would push themselves before they accepted the truth.

One by one the sailors tried. One man strained until his face turned nearly purple. Two men tried together. Then three. Then five. None managed so much as a twitch from the hammer.

"Drop the witchcraft, Arlo," one of them groaned, rubbing his aching back. "Let us have some real fun."

Wicket stepped in next, rubbing oil over his hands.

"The key is handling her right," he announced. He slid his slick palms up and down the handle, searching for some perfect grip only he could sense. When he was satisfied, he planted his feet and pulled.

His face twisted with effort as the veins in his neck bulged. The hammer did not move.

He stepped back, panting, and gave it a quick, frustrated kick as if a sudden jolt might dislodge it.

Instead, his foot bounced off solid metal. His small body pinwheeled backward into a table, leaving a Nogmi sized dent in the wood.

Sorren winced and shouted at the crew to mind the furniture if they wanted to stay in one piece.

Willy tried next. He tied the hammer to his chair and rolled forward with all his strength, hoping his own wheels might win where muscle had failed. The hammer stayed exactly where it was. His chair jerked instead. One of his wheels broke loose and went wobbling across the room.

Alfonze took his turn, climbing onto the hammer and tugging at it with both hands, muttering curses under his breath when it did not give.

"Captain Sorren," one of the younger sailors called. "We need you to take your test of strength."

Sorren snapped his head up, caught off guard by the sudden challenge.

"Nah," he boomed with a laugh. "I would hate to make the rest of you fools look bad."

He had not thought much about lifting the hammer before that moment. The question planted itself in him now, stubborn and unwelcome. Would it rise for him, or was it truly bonded to Arlo alone

His faith in Heir had never faltered. His life belonged to the god of war and justice as much as it belonged to the sea. Yet the hammer had chosen Arlo, a man who did not belong to the church at all, before it ever came to a Porter's hand.

Was it Heir's will that guided the hammer, or something else entirely

The crew began to chant his name.

"Sorren. Sorren. Sorren."

They clapped and stomped, calling their captain into the circle.

Sorren rolled his shoulders and stretched in comical fashion, playing to the crowd as he stepped away from the wall.

Before he reached the hammer, a heavy pounding shook the galley door. The sound cut sharply through the laughter and song.

A young sailor burst in, face flushed, eyes wide.

"Captain. You are needed on deck."

The room fell quiet at once. Sorren straightened, the shift from revelry to duty as natural as breath.

"All right," he called. "Finish your meals and get back to your posts."

He shot Arlo a smirk as he passed.

"We will leave the tricks to you for now," he said.

Arlo chuckled and pulled the hammer back to his side. The circle dissolved. Sailors carried their bowls and mugs away. Others drifted toward the stairs.

Lucy had already started cleaning, gathering stray cups and stacking bowls. Most had cleared their places out of respect, but a handful had bolted the moment the captain gave the order. Lucy made a mental note to remember which ones.

"Do you want your turn?" Arlo asked from behind her. He held the hammer handle out in her direction with a teasing tilt.

She turned her head and flicked the back of her hand against the hammer.

"As if," she said. "If I lift it, they will start calling me hero again. I am too tired for all that."

She brushed past him with a grin and a small bump of her shoulder.

"Now stop showing off and help clean this mess. I am going to check on Nyla and call it an early night. Someone did not let me get much sleep."

She did not look back to see the color that rose in his cheeks.

The air on deck had cooled. The twin moons washed the sea in pale blue light. Luna, the smaller moon, hung low, painting a shimmering road across the water. Arlo leaned against the railing with his eyes closed, focusing on the feel of his own breath, the gentle shift of the ship, and the pulse of mana that lived somewhere in the center of his chest.

He did not have a private space to practice. The deck would have to do.

Heavy footsteps approached. He opened his eyes as Sorren came to stand beside him.

"Smooth ride today," Arlo said.

"Indeed," Sorren replied. "The crew held tight. The green ones will catch up with time."

He took his place at the rail, arms crossed, Justice resting across his back. For all the ease in his posture, there was a weight hanging on him that had nothing to do with the sword.

"What brings you over?" Arlo asked.

"There is a shift in the air. Likely means a storm is brewing," Sorren said. "We are getting close. We will need every head steady and the ship tighter than a fortress if we want to make it through the Gauntlet."

"It has been on my mind too," Arlo admitted. "Everyone talks about it like it is a death sentence. What is the plan to get us there alive"

Sorren stared at the line where sky met water.

"We will likely see rough weather tomorrow. I can feel it in the wind. It will be the day after when we hit the worst of it. We need only the strongest and surest on deck then. Everyone else stays below. Those jagged spires will not forgive mistakes. We reinforced her hull, but that does not make the job easy."

He glanced at Arlo.

"We agreed I lead at sea. Once we touch land, command is yours."

"Then we keep it lean," Arlo said. "We only bring who we must. We do not know what waits for us there. You. Me. Lucy. Maybe one or two more."

"Aye. Lean and sharp," Sorren answered. "No room for anyone with a loose grip or slow wits."

He paused.

"Have you spoken to Lucy about what happened when we found Nyla?"

Arlo let out a long breath and finally opened his eyes fully, looking out over the water rather than the place in his mind.

"She is struggling," he said. "I think everything is harder for her than she lets on."

"Aye," Sorren said. "I have seen her try to carry it alone. Strong as she is, even steel bends if you press it long enough. She should be careful about how much she keeps inside."

"We talk," Arlo said. "She will get there. She just needs time."

Sorren's mouth curled in a knowing smirk.

"Sounds like you did more than talking from those thin walls."

Arlo flushed and shifted his stance.

"I have been wanting to ask you something," he said quickly.

"If you need advice on women, you came to the right captain," Sorren replied with a booming laugh that startled a passing sailor.

"It is not about that," Arlo said, though he could not help a small smile. "I meant what happens after."

Sorren raised a brow. Silence stretched for a breath.

"After what?" he asked.

"After the Gauntlet," Arlo said. "After we return Eckerd. I do not know that I can go back to being just a mason."

"You always have a place on my ship," Sorren offered without hesitation.

Arlo shook his head.

"The sea is not my calling the way it is yours," he said. "I want to make an impact."

He lifted the hammer a little, feeling its familiar weight in his hand.

"This makes a certain kind of impact," Sorren said. "You sure you do not want to ask the king for a command of your own?"

"Absolutely not. I am not that man. I do not want to follow selfish orders. I would rather help everyone I can, no matter who they are or what blood runs in them."

He hesitated, then let the thought fall out as it had been forming in him.

"Maybe I start my own group. Not mercenaries. Something better than that. Knights of a sort. A company of people who only want to do the right thing together."

The idea hung in the air between them. It did not feel foolish spoken aloud. It felt possible. Heavy, but possible.

Sorren nodded slowly, his expression unreadable.

"You have a rare kind of ambition, Arlo," he said. "You are not chasing gold or glory. It feels like something more honest."

"I want to be a force for change," Arlo said. "Not a king's pawn or a church puppet. Something different. Maybe this hammer is not meant only to destroy. Maybe it is meant to protect. To carry hope with it."

Sorren kept his gaze fixed on the horizon, but a darker note passed through his eyes.

The church had always spoken of change, of unity, of fighting for the good of the people. Yet his studies and the book from the librarian had shaken the simple trust he once had. The pages had been full of battles dressed as holy work. Wars used to gather power. Entire campaigns framed as necessary sacrifice.

Heir was the god of war and justice, yet these stories had begun to sound less like justice and more like control. The church's hand was often not far from the spark of conflict.

Arlo did not resemble those stories at all.

"You would be stepping into something big," Sorren said at last. "A man could lose himself trying to save everyone. You cannot fight every battle. Not alone. You need to choose what you are fighting for and why."

He glanced at the hammer.

"But with that in your hands, you could build a legend of your own."

"I do not care about legends," Arlo said. "I care about doing what is right."

His eyes drifted down to the hammer again. It remained a mystery. He had not asked for it. He had not wanted the responsibility it brought. Yet it had answered when he called. It had found him when he leaped from a tower ready to die. The blue light that led him

360

through Fall Lake. The tiny creature that had guided him upward. All of it had led here.

Silence settled over them as they each sank into their own thoughts. Sorren weighed his childhood, his faith, the years he had given to a god whose servants wore crowns as much as armor.

On land, he was bound to the church and the crown by oath and duty.

Out here, beneath the moon and with salt on his skin, he was simply Sorren. A man and a captain.

"A group like that would have to face the best and worst of every corner of Shularix," Sorren said. "You would walk into fights others only whisper about. You might even force those same cowards to act when they would rather look away."

Arlo pushed away from the rail and turned toward him. There was a light in his eyes Sorren had seen only a few times. It made him think of the day at Fall Lake. Of a man standing between a monster and people who had no way to defend themselves.

"That is the point," Arlo said. "Someone has to pick up the battles everyone else drops. And I would not be alone. With people like you. Like Lucy. I am sure there are others out there who are strong enough and kind enough and hopeful enough. They just need to see that they can matter."

Sorren let out a quiet huff that passed for a laugh.

"It is a noble idea," he said. "The sort that grows thorns when you are not watching it. But if anyone is stubborn enough to drag it into the world, it is you. I do not know if that life is meant for me, but when you are ready to start it, I will stand beside you and give what I can."

Gratitude brightened Arlo's face. He reached out his hand.

"I will hold you to that, Captain."

Sorren's smile turned genuine.

"You had better," he said.

361

He clasped Arlo's hand and pulled him into a strong, brotherly embrace. They did not need more words. The promise between them settled into place, solid as the ship beneath their feet.

Nyla sat on her bed again, her knees drawn to her chest, arms wrapped tight. Her thoughts had drifted back to the small cottage and the last time she had seen her mother. The ship groaned and the crew shouted somewhere beyond her walls. The sea rolled and bumped beneath her. She had kept down her meals this evening, but the strain of the morning still clung to her.

She had Lucy now. Arlo. Even the loud captain who did not quite understand what to do with her. None of that stopped the ache of missing home.

A faint flutter of air brushed across her bare ankles.

She looked toward the doorway.

A small, familiar shape slipped through the open space and into the cabin.

"Oh, Akira," Nyla whispered.

She reached out as the tiny creature glided to her and perched beside her on the mattress.

He was no larger than a raven. Blue black scales shimmered along his little body, reflecting the lantern light with an oily sheen. His narrow wings beat once before tucking in close. Cold blue eyes watched her with keen, knowing attention.

The small Draconis nuzzled his snout against her fingers and gave a soft squeak that sounded almost like a greeting.

Some of the tightness in her chest eased as his small weight settled against her side. Akira had been with her for a year, a gift from a friend of her mother's. A guardian who was more partner than pet.

"You should not have come," she murmured. "You are supposed to be with Mama. It is too dangerous here. I can barely keep myself safe. How am I supposed to protect you too?"

Akira tilted his head and chirped again, eyes bright with that same stubborn look she knew too well. The one that seemed to say he was the one protecting her.

She had left him behind on purpose. Her mother was safer with him near. He could warn her of trouble, fetch help if needed. If he had followed Nyla here, who was watching over her mother now

She stroked his head with gentle fingers, worry settling over her like a second skin.

A knock sounded at the door.

Nyla froze. She scooped Akira up against her chest and tucked him beneath her cloak, pressing a finger to her lips as if he could understand the gesture as well as the words.

"Nyla. It is me. Are you awake" Lucy's voice drifted through the wood.

Nyla smoothed her face as best she could and called, "Come in."

The door opened and Lucy stepped inside holding a steaming cup.

"Couldn't sleep?" she asked.

Nyla accepted the cup and took a careful sip.

"Thank you," she said. "I was just thinking. Again. Everything is a lot to take in."

Lucy sat beside her on the narrow bunk, hands resting loosely in her lap.

"Leaving home for something you believe in is not a small thing," she said.

Nyla managed a faint smile. Akira shifted beneath her cloak, a small, living heat pressed against her ribs. She hoped Lucy would not notice.

"I just do not know if I am strong enough to keep it all together," Nyla confessed.

Lucy laid a hand on Nyla's shoulder.

"You are stronger than you think," she said. "Most people here only look like they have it all together. Everyone is carrying something. We are all trying to hold our pieces in place. You have a purpose, Nyla. A real one. That is more than many can say."

She smiled softly.

"Like Arlo always says, hope is how we stay connected."

Nyla bit her lip and held Lucy's words close. She was not alone, not really. She had chosen this path for her mother's sake and for her own. She had people now who cared whether she stumbled.

"I will let you rest," Lucy said. "If you need anything, I am here. Just a knock away."

Nyla nodded. She watched Lucy leave and wondered how she would have survived that first night on the ship without her. She barely knew this woman, yet already Lucy felt like an older sister she had never had the chance to grow up with.

When the door closed, Nyla let out a long breath and opened her cloak. Akira peered up at her, unbothered by the brief hiding.

"Maybe she is right, Akira," Nyla whispered. "Maybe we can really do this. Both of us."

Akira gave a firm, bright squeak, as if he agreed.

She wished her mother could see her like this, and not be afraid. To see there is a life that could trust her.

Nyla smiled, a small and fragile thing, but real. She was far from home and surrounded by strangers. The sea was vast and the storm ahead would be worse. Her blood marked her as something many would hate on sight.

But she had Lucy. She had Arlo. She had a captain who did not yet know how much he would care. And she had Akira, stubborn and loyal and unwilling to leave her.

For the first time since stepping on the Sea Sentinel, Nyla let herself believe that maybe she was not as alone as she felt.

CHAPTER 37

The Sea Sentinel bucked against the ruthless waves, every impact shuddering up through her ribs and into the bones of the crew. Darkness had swallowed the horizon whole. There was no line between sea and sky anymore, only a heaving wall of black water and clouds that churned like a living thing. Lightning tore the sky open in white streaks that froze the world for a heartbeat at a time and showed the strain carved into every face on deck.

Rain came down in sheets. It stung exposed skin and hammered the planks until the whole ship felt like a drum.

Sorren Blaze had both hands locked around the wheel. His knuckles were white. Water streamed down his hair, his beard, the ridge of his nose, and dripped from his jaw. Wind roared past his ears, wild and high and sharp, like some great wounded beast.

Every lurch of the Sea Sentinel punched fear through his chest, but he refused to loosen his grip. This ship was more than timber and canvas. She was his pride. His answer to every order that had ever tried to box him in. His proof that he was meant for more than marching in lines and bowing before altars.

He would not let a storm sink her before she had even carved her name onto the sea.

"Brace the sails. All hands steady." His voice ripped out of him, deep and booming, riding the wind instead of fighting it. No doubt. No hesitation.

The words cut through the chaos and gave the crew something to cling to. Some of them were new to weather like this. Fear flickered behind their eyes whenever lightning lit their faces. Their gazes jumped to Sorren, to Alfonze, to any of the veterans who looked like they knew what to do.

The older hands moved with purpose. They dug their boots in. They wrapped lines around posts. They grabbed the green ones by collars or belts and shoved them where they needed to be.

Alfonze barreled across the rain slicked deck, a squat force of nature in his own right. He moved through crew and flying spray as if the storm had no say in where he went.

"Keep steady, lads. She will not give if you do not." His words boomed just as loud as Sorren's, somehow cutting through the wind.

A wave smashed against the hull and the ship groaned, tilting hard. Water spilled across the deck in a cold rush that soaked boots and sent one of the younger sailors skidding. Alfonze snatched the boy by the scruff and flung him back toward the rail with a sharp smack between the shoulders.

"Quit kissing the boards and get that line secured."

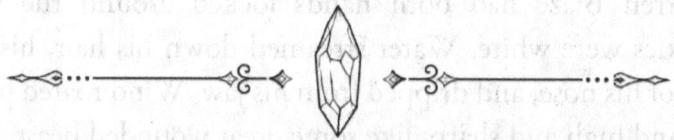

Arlo and Lucy fought their own battle along the starboard side. They had wedged themselves against the railing, bracing their backs and legs while they wrestled with a crate that had snapped free and was battering itself against the rail like it was trying to leap into the sea.

"Lift." Arlo grunted as another roll of the ship drove the crate into his ribs. The impact knocked the air out of his lungs, but he wrapped both arms around the slick wood and heaved.

Lucy jammed her shoulder under one corner and pushed as hard as she could. Rain plastered her crimson hair across her face. Strands clung to her cheeks and jaw, but her eyes burned clear and focused.

"We have got this," Arlo shouted over the storm, catching her gaze for a brief second.

Her answering nod was tight and fierce. Her hands were already raw. Rope fibers had chewed lines into her palms. She welcomed the sting. It reminded her she still had a body to fight with. It reminded her that the world was real and solid around her, not just broken memories and ghosts.

They shoved the crate back into place. Lucy slapped a line over it, fingers fumbling only once before she yanked the knot tight. Arlo secured another rope through an iron loop and hauled until his shoulders screamed.

A spray of water slammed into them, drenching them again as if they had not been soaked for the last hour. Lucy spat salt from her mouth and blinked hard.

"Move. Next one." Arlo jerked his head, already pushing off the rail.

Below deck, the storm was a different kind of monster.

The Sea Sentinel creaked and groaned. Her timbers complained with every twist of the hull. Lanterns swung wildly on their hooks. Light jumped and stretched across the cramped passageways, throwing long shadows that swung like reaching hands.

Nyla clung to her bunk. Her fingers dug into the thin mattress until her knuckles ached. Every time the ship lurched, her stomach lurched with it. Every thunderous crash of wave against hull tore a small scream from her throat before she could swallow it down.

She had known storms on land. She had seen the sky darken and heard wind howl through trees, watched rain pour off thatched roofs. None of it had been like this. This felt personal. The sea was not just angry. It felt offended that they were even here.

One wrong move and the whole ship might roll, might fill, might drag all of them down into black water with no bottom.

Nyla squeezed her eyes shut and breathed a small, shaking plea.

"Please. Please. Just let us make it. Let me get to the Gauntlet. Let me help her."

A soft, familiar weight pressed closer against her side. Tiny claws pricked through the blanket in a careful way that never broke skin. Warm breath puffed against her ear, followed by a quiet, rumbling sound that was nearly a purr.

She slid a hand down and found smooth scales beneath her fingers.

"Akira." Her voice came out thin. She stroked the small Draconis, feeling him tuck himself tighter into the curve of her stomach as if to shield her from the way the world tilted.

"We will be all right. Will we not" she whispered. The question was for herself as much as for him.

Akira answered with another low sound and a bump of his nose to her wrist. The ship groaned again. The floor under her felt like it dropped, then surged up, then twisted sideways.

She swallowed bile and clung a little harder.

<hr>

On deck, the storm found a new rhythm.

Rain became a steady wall. Wind punched hard enough to yank ropes from wet fingers. Waves climbed higher, slamming against the hull with a weight that felt like the whole ocean was trying to roll the Sea Sentinel over and hold her there.

Sorren's muscles burned. Every joint in his hands protested, but he did not relax his grip on the wheel. Every time the ship started to veer, he hauled her back in line.

His beard dripped. Water stung his eyes. It did not matter. The map lived in his head now. The spires of jagged rock that ringed the Gauntlet waited somewhere ahead in the dark, not yet visible but very real.

We either ride through this, he thought, or we die before we even see it.

Lightning tore the sky open again.

For an instant, he saw Alfonze at the main mast, three men on a single line, heels skidding as the wind tried to yank the sail right off the yardarm. He saw Arlo and Lucy moving from lash down to lash down, two streaks of stubborn will in a blur of water.

He felt something sharp and cold twist in his chest. A flash of worry cracked across his face before he scrubbed it away.

He shouted again, throat raw.

"Hold your lines. She will ride it. She is built for worse."

He did not know if she truly was, but he believed it, and sometimes belief was all a crew had to keep their hands on the rope.

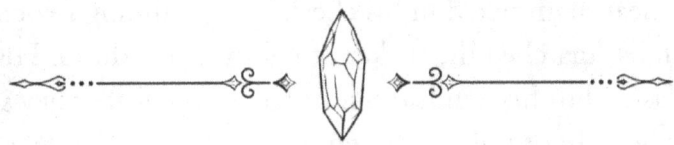

Arlo stumbled as another wave rolled under the hull. The deck pitched and he slammed a hand out, grabbing a length of rigging to stay upright. His lungs burned. His arms shook from effort. His clothes clung to him like a second soaked skin.

He became aware of something else under the cold and strain. The air around him tingled. Tiny pricks of sensation crawled along his forearms, raised the hair on the back of his neck.

He looked up.

The clouds churned above them, heavy and swollen. Lightning forked between them and the sea in jagged paths. Every flash painted the deck in ghostly blue for a heartbeat.

His own heartbeat began to fall into step with it.

Thump.

Flash.

Thump.

Another.

The world seemed to narrow. The roar of the storm drew back at the edges. The slap of water and the screams and the shouts blurred into a distant hum.

His feet moved without asking his permission. He drifted away from Lucy, away from the crate they had just secured, toward the open center of the deck.

His boots slipped on the wet planks, but he did not fall. It was as if something unseen nudged him when he needed it, steadied his path.

Blue threads of light began to flicker at the edge of his vision. They curled at the corners of his sight, then winked out, then came back stronger. Little veins of color that did not belong to the storm alone.

His heart hammered in his chest. The pounding matched the roll of thunder, matched the flicker of lightning overhead. His breathing came faster, but his hands did not shake from fear. They shook from a force he did not fully understand.

Lucy had just finished knotting another line when she noticed the shift. The hair on her arms stood up. The air tasted different, sharpened, as if every breath carried metal and ice.

She turned and spotted Arlo in the middle of the deck.

He should have been at the rail. He should have been with her, wrapping rope, shouting orders, fighting the sea the way everyone else was.

Instead, he stood alone. Rain pounded down on him and then seemed to slide away, veering around him in strange lines. His shoulders were squared. His head tilted back slightly. His eyes glowed.

The blue she had seen before, that strange, piercing light that did not belong to any human she had known, burned brighter now.

"Arlo," she shouted his name, voice snapping in the wind. She took a few steps toward him.

Something in the way he held himself stopped her. His posture was not loose, not swaying like a fool who had lost his footing. He looked braced, anchored in a way that had nothing to do with the planks beneath his boots.

Lightning flashed again, and for an instant she could have sworn it answered him, curving, angling, bending as if drawn to the man on the deck.

Her throat went dry.

Alfonze dug his heels into the decking and yelled up at a pair of sailors who were clinging to the mast and fighting to haul a line down to a lower cleat.

"Put your backs into it. I am not fishing you out of the drink if you get clever with that knot."

A hard gust hit. The sail snapped like a slapped hand. The line jerked and nearly tore free of their grip.

Alfonze grabbed on with them, adding his strength. The three of them grunted together, muscles straining as they dragged the line down and wrapped it.

He glanced toward the middle of the ship and caught sight of Arlo standing there as if he had not a care in the world.

"What in all the hells is he doing?" Alfonze roared, spitting rain from his mouth. "Arlo. Get down. Take cover, you daft bastard."

A wave slammed over the rail and washed across the deck. It hit Alfonze waist high, cold and heavy enough to stagger him a step. It rolled around Arlo and broke on either side of him like it had hit a rock still rooted in the earth.

Alfonze stared, water streaming from his moustache, fingers still wrapped around the rope.

"That is not right," he muttered. "That is not right at all."

CHAPTER 38

Arlo lifted his arms.

The weight of the storm pressed down on him. He felt it in his bones. The sky pushed. The sea reached. The air between them shook with raw force.

He sucked in a breath and held it.

Every crackle of lightning ran through him. It crawled along his nerves like fire and ice wrestling inside his veins. His muscles tightened with the strain. His skin buzzed. Shadows jumped and pulled at the edges of his vision.

Focus.

He tried to gather the power the way he had gathered a handful of blue sparks in Fall Lake. The way he had drawn light to his hand and into the hammer. This was different.

This was not a handful. This was a flood.

His thoughts raced, fighting for a sense of control. He tried to push the energy into a single line, to shape it, to make it listen. The storm did not want to be tamed.

Tendrils of lightning snapped from his fingertips. They ran in bright threads through the air, searching for a path. Some arced up, some down, some sideways, curling through the rain like they were alive.

Pain lanced through him as if someone had driven hot metal through his arms and spine. His back bowed. A scream ripped out of his throat, torn straight from the center of his chest.

The sound clawed up into the storm and vanished into the thunder.

On deck, men froze. One by one their hands slipped from rope and rail as they turned to stare. It was not just a scream of pain. It carried something else, something bigger, a note of furious refusal that sent shivers through hardened sailors.

Blue light crawled over Arlo's skin. It built and built, lighting his veins from the inside.

For a heartbeat, the storm answered.

Everything stopped.

Wind died in a hard, unnatural cut. Rain halted mid fall in a ring around the Sea Sentinel. Thunder fell silent as if someone had closed a door on the sound.

The only thing that moved was the flicker of blue around Arlo and the ragged rise and fall of his chest.

Below deck, Nyla felt the change.

The constant pitch and roll staggered. The relentless roar quieted. There was an awful, almost worse stillness that settled over the hull.

Her eyes opened wide in the dimness.

"Akira"

The little Draconis lifted his head. The crest along his neck flared slightly. He tasted the air with a flick of his tongue and let out a questioning chirp.

For one breath, Nyla hoped it meant the storm was over.

Then the ship lurched a new way, not with wind, but with a strange jump in the water under it. Her stomach turned with it.

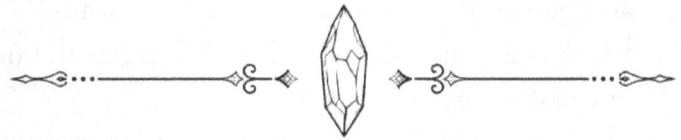

On deck, the world crashed back in.

The storm surged, as if it had pulled in breath for a single moment and now exhaled all of its fury at once. Wind slammed into the sails. Rain came down in a hard slap. Thunder cracked so close overhead it felt like the sky had split.

Arlo's scream rose higher, tearing through his throat until his voice broke. His body shook with the effort. Every heartbeat slammed another wave of energy through him.

His vision blurred. The edges darkened. Within the blur, flashes of color and shape punched through.

He saw a room, grand and cold. Stone pillars. Tall windows. A throne at the far end. He looked down and saw his own hands encased in white armor, polished so clean it shone even in the dim light. The armor belonged to someone who never lifted stone or mortar. Someone who commanded from a height.

He lifted his head and saw a figure standing in front of the throne. Black and purple, humanoid and not, eyes like polished stone. A smile cut across the face, slow and knowing.

The vision snapped, replaced by the beast from Fall Lake, maw wide, eyes blazing, the spray of blood and water as his hammer met its body.

Then the storm roared back into focus around him.

The weight did not lessen. It crushed down harder.

He could have let go. Every instinct in his body screamed at him to let go. To drop his arms. To fall flat. To let the storm do whatever it had planned.

He did not.

There is too much at stake.

The thought was simple. It came without words at first, only feeling. Faces flashed through his mind. Gretta. Sonny. The children of Fall Lake. His crew mates. Nyla pale and frightened. Lucy with her hands on fire and terror in her eyes.

His scream rose one last time. It tore his throat raw and came out rough and broken, but it carried that defiance with it.

The blue light surged.

It exploded outward in a shockwave that kicked water away from the ship in a great ring. Rain turned aside, whipping around the path he had chosen rather than straight through it. Thunder rolled away, redirected, its heart pounding somewhere to the left and behind them instead of straight ahead.

For a narrow line of sea, the way cleared.

The Sea Sentinel lunged forward into that path. Sorren felt the change through the wheel. He did not know what Arlo had done. He did not need to. The air opened in front of them and he drove his ship straight through it.

"Hold fast," he shouted. "Ride it. Ride it."

The crew stared.

For a few heartbeats, no one moved. All eyes locked on Arlo.

The blue light in his eyes faded. His knees buckled. He dropped, hands slapping the wet deck as he caught himself just before his face hit the boards.

His whole body trembled. Every breath sounded like it had to fight its way back into his lungs.

Lucy reached him first. She slid across the slick deck and dropped to her knees at his side, wrapping an arm around his shoulders to keep him from pitching forward.

"Arlo. Arlo, look at me."

His head lolled toward her. The glow was gone from his eyes. They were back to that familiar blue, only now they were hazy and lined with pain.

Behind her, men were only starting to pick up ropes again. Sorren's shout carried from the helm, shaken but firm.

"Back to it. The sea does not care what tricks you have just watched. Move."

Lucy held Arlo as long as she could while the others stumbled back to motion. Rain poured down on them both. Her hair stuck to his cheek.

He swallowed and tried to push himself higher.

"Behind you," he rasped.

She frowned, confused.

Then she heard the scrape.

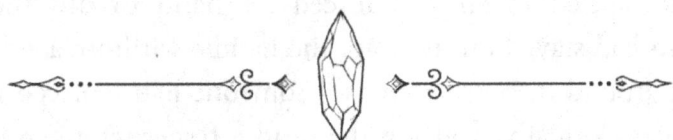

Something dragged wet claws across the deck with a slow, heavy sound that did not belong to boots or wood. A smell rose, thick and rotten, cutting through the salt and rain. It was like fish left out for days, like swamp water and old blood.

Lucy turned her head.

From the black water that churned along the port side, a shape hauled itself up and over the rail. It moved with a horrible, boneless grace, as if its limbs were never meant to walk on a solid surface.

Long arms ended in webbed claws that hooked into the planks. Its body was a stretched, slick length of scales in sickly shades of green and brown. Barnacles clung to its skin in rough patches. Strands of algae trailed behind it like wet hair.

Its head was wrong.

Too wide. Too flat. Amphibian more than anything else. It had no lids. Its bulging eyes stared without blinking, film covering the milky surface. When its mouth opened, it unhinged slightly, revealing rows of narrow, needle teeth that gleamed even in the storm dark.

It hissed.

Lucy's body moved before her mind caught up. She let go of Arlo and pushed herself to her feet, dragging a dagger from her belt in one smooth motion.

Her heart pounded in her throat, but the familiar weight of the blade in her hand steadied her.

⬥⬥⬥

Arlo sucked in air and forced his hand toward the hammer. Elduun had stayed on its strap, the handle within reach. His fingers closed around it, but he felt as if someone had replaced his muscles with wet cloth. Even lifting the head a finger width from the deck made his arms burn.

He grit his teeth and dragged the hammer closer.

He could not sit this out. Whatever these things were, they had chosen the worst moment to climb aboard.

⬥⬥⬥

The creature lunged at Lucy.

Webbed claws swiped. She stepped inside the reach of one arm and drove her dagger up. The blade bit into the soft flesh of its palm. A dark, thick blood seeped out, almost tar like. The creature shrieked, a sound that cut straight through her skull.

She staggered back a step as pain flared in her own palms. Heat gathered there, crawling up her wrists, licking at her fingers. She felt that dangerous friction again, that edge where her control could slip and fire could come roaring out without aim.

Not here. Not on a wooden ship. Not in the middle of a storm.

She bit down on the urge and focused on her breathing, on the cold rain pouring over her hands. The heat remained, waiting, but did not break free.

More shapes hauled themselves over the rails. Three. Five. Eight. They came from both sides, claws hooking into the wood, bodies slopping onto the deck with wet thuds.

Crew members stumbled back, then surged forward again with a chorus of curses and shouted warnings. Steel scraped free of sheaths. Axes came up. One man swung a boat hook at the nearest monster and caught it across the jaw.

The creature barely flinched.

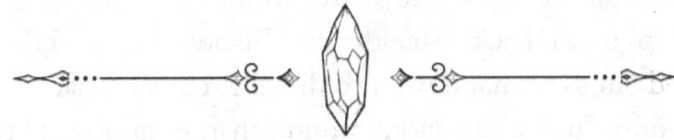

Lucy ducked another swipe and slashed across the creature's thigh. Her blade cut skin, but not deep. The creature hissed, then snapped at her. Its teeth clamped on the air inches from her shoulder.

She planted a boot against its chest and kicked hard, shoving it back.

Somewhere to her right, a deafening crack split the air. Not thunder. Not lightning.

Elduun.

Arlo had managed to haul himself to his feet long enough to swing the hammer once. The head collided with the chest of a creature that had been crawling toward one of the fallen sailors. The impact detonated like a small storm of its own. A shockwave of sound and pressure rippled outward.

The creature flew backward, body lifted from the deck and flung over the rail into the dark water.

Arlo sagged, breath tearing at his lungs. His arms felt like they were full of lead. Still, he dragged the hammer back into position, refusing to drop it.

Sorren took it in with a single sweep of his gaze.

Monsters on his deck. Arlo barely standing. Lucy with a knife and that tight look on her face that told him she was fighting more than just what was in front of her.

Rage swept through him, quick and hot. It pushed aside the leftover fear of the storm. Something had dared to climb onto his ship during a fight he had already barely won.

"Keep them back. Shields up. Blades ready." His command snapped out as his hand went to the hilt across his back.

He drew Justice in a clean motion that, even now, felt right. The sword was massive, almost as tall as some of the shorter men on board, but in his hands it moved like something half its size. Its weight balanced perfectly as it came free.

One of the creatures leaped toward him, mouth open. Sorren stepped into the swing, planted his feet, and brought Justice across in a heavy arc.

The blade cut clean through scaled flesh and bone. The creature's body split from shoulder to hip. Dark blood splashed the deck, hot against the rain.

Another creature scrambled over the fallen one and lunged. Sorren did not have time for a full swing. He snapped the blade up and forward instead, driving the tip straight through its throat.

"You picked the wrong ship," he growled under his breath.

A cabin boy flew past him, eyes wide with terror and feet sliding on the wet deck. Sorren reached out, grabbed the boy by the back of his shirt, and hauled him close.

"You. Here. Hold Justice's sheath and keep your head low."

The boy nodded frantically and clung to the scabbard, grateful for any task that kept him behind the man with the enormous sword.

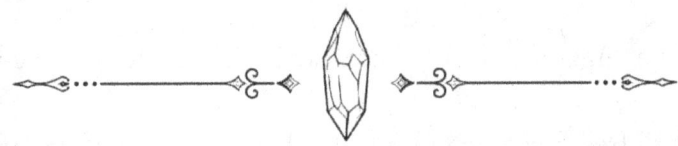

Lucy moved like a dance she had never been taught but somehow knew.

Her knives flashed in the dim light, stuttering bright each time lightning cracked overhead. She slashed at reaching claws, ducked under grasping arms, and drove steel into soft joints where limb met shoulder or leg met hip.

Her focus narrowed to moments. A claw here. Teeth there. Arlo fighting to stay upright in the corner of her eye. She angled herself so that anyone reaching for him met her first.

"Arlo. It is all right. Let us take it from here," she shouted as she gutted another creature with a quick, hard thrust.

He shook his head, sweat and rain running together down his face.

"Cannot. I will not let them overrun us," he ground out.

He lifted the hammer again as two more of the creatures skittered toward him, claws scraping grooves into the wood.

A sound broke across the fight.

A shrill screech, sharp and fierce, cut through the deeper growls and hisses. It was followed by a sudden streak of silver that dove straight down from the upper deck rail.

Lucy whipped her head toward it.

A small, winged shape, no bigger than a raven, plummeted toward the two creatures that were climbing for Arlo. It was all scales and motion, a compact body coated in blue black plates that gleamed even in the storm dark.

It hit the first creature's face, jaws snapping. Tiny teeth sank into the milky surface of one bulging eye. The creature shrieked, flailing backward as blood burst from the ruined socket.

The small Draconis tore free and spun midair, beating narrow wings. It darted past the second creature, claws raking across its throat.

"Akira. Again." Nyla's voice carried from the stairwell, thin but clear.

Lucy lifted her gaze and saw Nyla at the edge of the upper deck, soaked and pale, one hand gripping the rail, the other held out as if she could catch the little dragon out of the air.

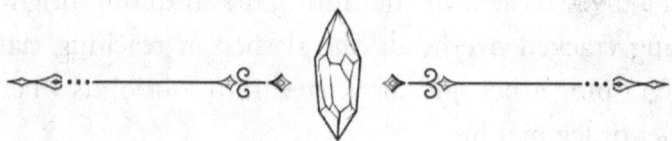

Nyla had felt the change from below.

First the unnatural stillness that had made her breath catch. Then the heavy crash of something against the hull. Then the new sounds. Screams that did not sound like men. Thuds and scrapes and shouts for blades.

She could not stay in her bunk.

She had stumbled into the narrow passage, clutching Akira to her chest while the ship lurched under her. A shape had appeared at the end of the corridor, clawed hands and milky eyes and teeth gleaming.

Akira had ripped free from her arms before she could stop him. He had launched himself at the thing, jaw opening to reveal a crystal bright shard forming between his teeth. Cold breath swirled around it.

He fired the icicle straight into the creature's neck. The shard punched through scaled flesh and out the other side in a spray of black blood. The monster toppled backward down the narrow stair and vanished into the dark.

Nyla had stood shaking, fingers pressed to her lips.

Akira had turned to her, eyes bright, waiting. He had always listened when she asked him to hide. He had always kept himself small and out of sight for her sake. Now his gaze held a question. Stay or go.

Nyla had looked toward the sounds of fighting above. The screams. The shouts. The hiss of more of those creatures.

Her fear and her guilt twisted together.

"Go, Akira. Help them. I will follow," she had said.

Now she watched him streak through the rain and blood and chaos and felt something inside her chest break open. Pride and terror and relief all at once.

Arlo stared as Akira flew.

He had seen depictions of Draconis before. In books. On tapestries. In carved reliefs above old doors. Great scaled beasts with wings like sails and jaws that could swallow a man whole.

This was different.

Akira was small, quick, all sharp corners and bright eyes and precise rage. Frost gathered around his mouth as he drew another breath, the air crackling with cold. He spat another icicle into the open maw of a creature that had lunged for one of the younger sailors. The shard burst from the back of its skull.

The sailor stumbled away, eyes wide.

"By the gods," he whispered.

Sorren saw it too.

Mid swing, Justice splitting another sea creature from shoulder to hip, his gaze snagged on the darting shape of the tiny dragon. The ice. The scales. The way it moved.

His jaw clenched. His eyes went hard.

Draconis.

Not a legend carved in temple stone. Not an enemy banner to the far north. A living, breathing one on his deck, commanded by a girl he barely knew.

"What in all the hells?" he breathed.

He watched as Akira circled back toward Nyla, who had now made it down to the main deck, one hand on the rail, the other held out as if to guide him. The little dragon answered her voice and her gestures, not the creatures' calls.

It was fighting for them.

That did not erase the knot twisting in Sorren's gut.

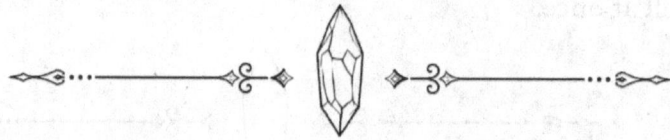

The fight did not last much longer.

Between Sorren's blade, Arlo's hammer when he could manage it, Lucy's knives, the crew's renewed fury, and Akira's icy assaults, the numbers of the creatures dwindled.

One by one they fell. Their bodies hit the deck with heavy, wet sounds. Dark blood mixed with rain and sea water, turning the planks slick and stained.

The last few monsters hesitated, milky eyes darting between the dead and the living. Some hissed, some clicked their teeth. Then, almost together, they turned and hurled themselves back over the rail, vanishing into the churning black water from which they had come.

Silence did not fall. The storm still raged around them, but the sounds of battle faded, leaving only panting, groaning, and the creak of a ship that had survived more than it should.

Men leaned on their weapons. Some laughed in short, startled bursts. Others bent double, hands on their knees, dragging breath into their lungs.

The deck looked like a slaughter yard. Scales. Splintered wood. Broken netting. Blood smeared in long arcs.

Nyla stood amid it all with Akira clutched to her chest. He had shrunk himself down as small as he could manage, but his scales still shimmered and his eyes still burned.

She could feel stares crawling over her skin.

Arlo and Lucy stood a short distance away, both breathing hard, both streaked with grime and blood and rain. Their eyes were on her and on Akira, full of shock and something like wonder.

Those looks did not scare her.

Sorren's did.

His gaze found her and locked in place. It was not the quick, assessing look of a captain checking the condition of a crew member. It was a slow, hard stare that pinned her where she stood.

He stepped forward.

"Who in all the hells are you?" he asked.

His voice was low, but it carried across the deck. Every nearby conversation or nervous laugh died at once.

He stopped a few paces from her. Justice still hung in his hand. His grip on the hilt had not relaxed. Rain ran down his face, carving paths through the grime and the flecks of blood.

"That thing." He jabbed a finger toward Akira. Fury leaked into his tone now, too strong to hide. "Why is it on my ship?"

Nyla's first instinct was to back away. Her heel slid a little on the wet deck. She caught herself and forced her feet to stay planted.

She shifted Akira slightly behind her elbow, not to hide him, but to keep him from jumping forward if Sorren made a sudden move.

"Akira is a friend," she said. Her voice shook, but she got the words out. "He protects me. He protected all of us tonight. We needed him. He saved lives."

385

Sorren's jaw flexed. His knuckles whitened around the sword hilt. The tendons in his free hand stood out as he clenched it so hard he might have broken his own fingers.

"Where does a friend like that come from, Nyla?" he asked. "And do not tell me you are only a frightened girl seeking medicine for her mother."

He took a step closer. The difference in their size was stark. He could have wrapped one hand around her upper arm and lifted her off the deck without effort.

"Who are you really?"

Nyla opened her mouth. Nothing came.

Every warning her mother had ever given her screamed through her mind. Hide your ears. Hide what you are. Hide what walks beside you. Humans do not understand. Humans are dangerous.

She looked up at Sorren and saw that danger written plainly in his eyes now. Not mindless hatred. Not yet. But suspicion edged with decades of training and a lifetime of loyalty to a church that treated Draconis and Elfar like stories of distant threats.

Her throat closed.

Arlo stepped into the space between them.

He practically folded himself into that space. His body wanted to crumple. His legs shook. Every bruise from the storm burned, and a deeper ache gnawed at his bones from the lightning he had dragged through them.

He still planted his boots shoulder width apart and set the hammer's head down at his side, using it to steady himself as he straightened.

"She was protecting the ship and the crew," Arlo said.

His voice was not loud, but it did not waver.

"They both were. Whatever Akira is, he is on our side. You saw it. He fought those creatures off. Saved your men. Saved me. That is not what an enemy does."

Sorren's teeth bared in something that was not quite a snarl, but close. His gaze flicked from Arlo to Nyla to the small dragon and back.

Sending them both overboard would end the risk. One clean strike, one shove, and the sea could decide what to do with them. It would protect his crew. It would keep his oath to the church simpler.

The thought coiled in his mind, ugly and easy.

His hand twitched on Justice's hilt.

He saw again, in his mind's eye, the way Akira had sunk icy teeth into a creature's throat. The way Nyla had shouted for him to help others, not just her. The way Arlo had stood in the center of a storm to carve a path for them all.

He thought of the book tucked in his coat. The passages he had been reading in secret. The stories of gods and power and the way the church had shaped those tales into something that suited them.

He let out a harsh breath and lifted his hand from his sword entirely. He threw it up in the air in a rough gesture.

"Fine," he spat. "Keep that thing out of sight when you can. When we go on land, you are at the front, Nyla. You will be the first out on the stone. You make one wrong move, and I will not hesitate again."

His tone left no doubt that he meant it.

He turned sharply and stalked back toward the helm.

"Get these bodies overboard," he called to the crew. "Check for damage. Back to your posts. We are not at the Gauntlet yet."

Men scrambled into motion. They dragged the strange corpses toward the rails and heaved them into the sea. They checked lines, patched splintered boards, wiped weapons clean.

Nyla clutched Akira to her chest. Her heart thudded against his scales.

She had done what she feared most. She had revealed him. She had helped. And still they were treated like a threat.

She blinked hard against the sting in her eyes and turned away, making her way back toward the hatch and the narrow stairs below.

CHAPTER 39

Arlo sat on the edge of the bed later, stripped down to his trousers. His shirt hung over a peg, still damp.

Bruises bloomed along his ribs and shoulders, dark and angry against his skin. Some came from the storm, from rope and crate and rail. Others were deeper, aches that did not show on the surface. Those came from the lightning. From asking his body to carry something that had not been meant for it.

The room swayed gently with the sea. After the violence of the storm, the motion felt almost soft.

He rolled his shoulders and winced. A sharp pain shot down his back.

Manipulating his own mana had become something he could practice. Calling sparks, shaping small arcs, turning that power into focused blows with Elduun. This had been different.

This had been the sky.

He had felt every raindrop like it was tracing a path along his skin. Every gust of wind had felt like it moved through his lungs. The lightning had surged through him and left something behind. He felt hollowed out and heavy all at once.

He thought of Fall Lake. Of the faces he would never see again. Of the beast falling under his hammer. Of the way the blue light had led him upward that night, like something guiding a tool toward its task.

He wondered where his limits were. How many times he could pull on that kind of power before something important inside him simply snapped. What would be lost if it did. Who would pay for it.

He knew one thing. The Gauntlet was always surrounded by a storm like this one. Maybe worse. If he had to do what he had just done again, he would.

He only hoped there would be enough of him left after.

A heavy knock rattled the door.

"Enter," Arlo called, voice rough.

Sorren stepped inside without waiting for further invitation. His stride was as solid as ever, boots beating a steady rhythm on the planks.

"I was not sure if you would be up," he said. "Figured you would be close to dead. Someone could have been."

Arlo let out a breath that might have been a laugh if it had not hurt.

"Closer than I would like to be," he admitted.

Sorren lingered just inside the room for a moment, eyes taking in the bruises, the way Arlo's shoulders sagged despite his efforts to sit straight.

"I wanted to talk about what happened out there," Sorren said. "That power you used. I have never seen anything like it. Not from anyone in the church. Not from anyone outside it either."

Arlo's hands curled loosely on his knees. His gaze dropped.

"Neither have I," he said. "I do not even know where it came from. Not really."

Sorren hesitated, then reached into his coat and pulled out a small, worn book. The leather was scuffed at the corners. The pages had been thumbed through many times. He held it with care, as if it mattered more than the battered binding suggested.

"I might," he said.

He flipped the book open with a practiced motion, thumb stopping at a marked page. He did not look down at the words yet. His eyes stayed on Arlo.

"There is a passage here I found a while back," Sorren said. "Talks about the gods walking among men. Taking mortal forms. Carrying with them power that can change the fate of kingdoms."

He shifted his grip, his finger holding his place.

"Speaks of people manifesting that power when it is most needed. To protect. To heal. To destroy if they must."

Arlo's head lifted a little. His eyes went to the book, then to Sorren's face.

"You think that is what I did out there?" he asked quietly. "Manifested the gods"

"I do not know what to think," Sorren answered.

For once, there was no easy certainty in his voice. No pat answer from a catechism. Only honest confusion and a thin thread of hope.

"But if these stories are even halfway true," Sorren went on, "you might be something more than you realize. And I would be lying if I said it did not put a fire of hope in my chest, knowing we have you with us while we are headed into the Gauntlet."

The room felt smaller.

Arlo's thoughts spun. The throne room. The armor. The black and purple figure with the knowing smile. The hammer leaping into his hand. The way the storm had bent.

He did not want to be a god. He did not want to be anyone's weapon either. He only wanted to keep people safe. To stop things like Fall Lake from happening again.

Whatever label Sorren put on it, the power was there now. Ignoring it would not make it leave.

He drew in a slow breath.

"Whatever I am," he said, "I cannot afford to hold back. Not if it means losing everyone else."

Sorren nodded once. A heavy, deliberate motion.

"Good," he said. "Because I do not think the Gauntlet will let any of us leave if we do."

He stepped forward and clapped a hand on Arlo's shoulder. His palm landed right on a fresh bruise. Arlo grimaced in spite of himself.

Sorren's mouth twitched.

"Rest up," he said. "We will need whatever that was again soon."

He turned and left, his footsteps fading into the hum of the ship. Shouted orders drifted up from the deck as he returned to the work of keeping the Sea Sentinel alive.

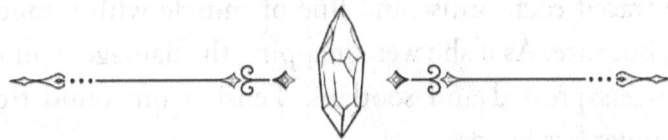

The secret door in the wall panel eased open a few breaths later. The movement was soft, familiar now.

Lucy slipped inside, closing it behind her with care.

Her hair was damp but no longer plastered to her head. Someone had found enough spare cloth for her to towel off. She had changed into dry clothes, though the sleeves were pushed up and already smudged with faint traces of soot and herb from whatever she had been doing to help patch up the wounded.

391

Her shoulders dropped a fraction when she saw him sitting upright and breathing.

"You look worse than I thought," she said.

There was no joke in it. Only concern.

She crossed the small space and knelt between his knees, reaching for his hands.

"The storm is over for now," she said. "You should be resting."

"Could be worse," he said. "I will be fine."

She tightened her fingers around his.

"Do not give me a could be worse," she said. "You went toe to toe with a storm and sea monsters in one night. You should be in this bed, letting your stubborn bones remember how to heal."

He opened his mouth to argue. The look in her eyes stopped him.

Heat burned in her emerald gaze, but it was not anger. It was a fierce protectiveness that he had seen in her on the field. The same look she had when she stepped between someone and danger. Only now, the someone was him.

She lifted his hands and placed them on her shoulders.

"You always take it on yourself," she said. "Every burden. Every fight. You do not have to. Let someone help you for once."

Her hands slid up his forearms.

She traced each bruise and line of muscle with a touch that was gentle, but sure. As if she were mapping the damage to understand it. Her fingers pressed and soothed. Tension unwound from him in layers under her hands.

He felt that faint red warmth rise from her, visible at the edges when he half closed his eyes. It flickered, a soft glow that met the last threads of blue that still lurked under his skin. They twined together for a moment, red and blue humming in a way that felt less like fire and lightning and more like a shared breath.

Her fingers reached his shoulders and pressed into the tight muscles there. He groaned quietly as knots loosened.

"Nyla asked me to thank you," Lucy said.

392

Her voice had gone softer.

"For standing up to Sorren. For her. For Akira."

"She does not need to thank me," Arlo said. A small smile touched his mouth. His eyes slipped closed again under her touch. "I did what felt right."

Lucy worked her fingers up along his neck, kneading away the tightness there.

"I asked her how she became friends with Akira," Lucy said. "She told me he was a gift from her mother's friend."

Arlo's brow creased.

"Her mother's friend," he repeated. "Did she say who?"

Lucy shook her head slightly.

"No," she said. "I did not push. She is holding some things close for now."

"It probably does not matter yet," Arlo said. "Although it does not make Sorren sleep easier. She will likely be heading into the Gauntlet with us."

Lucy hummed in quiet agreement, but she did not follow the thought further. Her attention had shifted entirely to him.

Her hands slipped from his neck down across his chest. Her fingertips brushed over bruises there as if apologizing for the hurt, then traced lower. His head tipped back a little under the slow, steady pressure of her palms and the warm energy she was sharing without thinking about it.

Every knot unwound.

Every pulled muscle eased.

His hands, which had been resting lightly on her shoulders, slid down to her upper arms, then her sides. He wanted to anchor himself to something that was not pain or storm or questions about gods.

He chose her.

She stepped closer, knees pressed to the edge of the bed. Her hands trailed down his back, fingers kneading along his spine. She leaned into him until her body met his chest fully. The contact stole a breath from him.

The red flicker around her hands deepened for a heartbeat, not hot enough to burn, only warm. Comforting. Thrilling.

His hands traveled to her waist and settled there, thumbs brushing small circles through the fabric. He opened his eyes and found hers inches away, green and bright and steady on him.

Her lips curved into a smile that held a whole world in it. Relief. Want. A quiet promise that whatever he faced, she had no intention of leaving him to face it alone.

Their breaths mingled in the small space between them.

She shifted, climbing onto the bed to straddle his lap. Her legs wrapped around his hips with easy familiarity, drawing him closer. The movement pressed them together, chest to chest, heartbeat to heartbeat.

He slid his hands from her waist up under the hem of her top. His palms met warm skin. He traced along her sides, over the curve of her ribs, slow and reverent.

His fingers brushed over the faint raised lines of the scarred markings that crossed just over her shoulder blade. He paused there, thumb resting lightly on one of the strange, old marks that did not match any wound he knew.

Images flashed through his mind.

The passage Sorren had just read from the book. Gods walking the land. Power manifesting when needed. The shared visions he and Lucy had touched, wings and light and something ancient looking back at them from behind a veil.

He could have followed those thoughts. He could have tried to tug at them, to name them.

He did not.

Whatever she was. Whatever he was. Those answers would come in their own time. Right now, in this small space, with the sea still muttering outside the walls and the taste of lightning still faint on his tongue, he knew one thing with absolute clarity.

He did not want a world that did not have her in it.

He let the questions drift away.

Her hands slid up his neck and into his hair. She drew him forward. Their foreheads touched for a brief, quiet moment, one last breath held between them.

Then they closed the distance.

Their mouths met, slow at first, then deeper as the last of his resistance melted under the combined warmth of her touch and the relief of still being alive.

The ship groaned around them. The sea rolled. Somewhere above, a shout rang out as someone finished tying down a line.

In the small, dim cabin, two people who had seen gods and monsters and storms found something human to hold on to. Lucy's legs tightened around his waist. His hands traced the path of her back under her shirt, memorizing every line.

The rest of the world fell away for a while.

CHAPTER 40

Tension hung in the air, the sort of quiet that whispered of things unseen and dangers waiting just beyond sight. Arlo stood at the bow, fingers curled around the rail, eyes narrowed as he scanned the distant line where water met sky. On any other day, the view would have been peaceful. A soft and pleasing moment of open sea and steady wind.

Today, it felt like standing on the lip of a cliff.

Clouds built on the horizon, dark and layered, drawing closer with a slow and inevitable crawl. The wind picked up, sharp with salt and a deep chill that pierced straight through wet clothes and tired muscles. Every crew member seemed to feel it at once. Voices dropped. Movements grew tighter, more measured.

Arlo's bruises throbbed. Not from the actual pain alone, but from the knowledge of what it had cost him yesterday and what it might cost him again. Lucy had eased the worst of it with her strange,

396

warming touch, but he was far from clear. The ache in his bones felt older than he was.

Behind him, Sorren took his place at the wheel. He squinted against the growing storm, jaw set, eyes tracking the shape of the approaching clouds and the swell of the waves.

He leaned slightly toward Alfonze, speaking low. The shorter man nodded at once and moved off, his voice rising to carry over the deck.

"Prepare for rough waters ahead. Sails up and keep her steady. I want all lines checked and ready."

Men scrambled. Some climbed, some ran, some braced already, hands on rails and ropes, waiting for the first real hit.

Lucy stepped up beside Arlo. The boards creaked faintly under her weight. She followed his gaze outward, eyes narrowing as she traced the dark line where the storm began to swallow the horizon.

Her usually vibrant green eyes held a touch of apprehension. She reached out and rested a hand on his shoulder, fingers warm through the fabric.

"We are almost there," she said quietly. She leaned in to speak closer to his arm, so the wind did not steal the words. "I think that is land in the distance."

She pointed.

Far ahead, barely more than a shadow at first, a darker shape rose where sea met sky. As the ship rose and fell on the swells, the outline shifted. Low cliffs. Jagged peaks. Something else as well, a faint shimmer that caught light in places the sun should not have reached.

Arlo nodded, a small flicker of relief touching his chest. No matter what waited for them, the crossing itself would not stretch on much longer.

He focused on that distant coastline. The weight inside him grew heavier, pressing down with every wave. Each swell prickled something deep in his core, the same place that had lit with blue the day before. Every ache from yesterday began to wake again with a vengeance.

"There is something wrong," he murmured.

"You feel it too?" Lucy asked. A frown formed at her lips. "It is like my energy is fading. Like something is pulling it right out of me."

The first low rumble of thunder rolled across the waves. It did not sound like the random growl of a passing cloud. It sounded deliberate. The sky flashed, lightning striking the surface of the water far ahead. The bolts crawled along the waves in strange, branching lines before vanishing.

The approaching storm felt less like weather and more like a curtain lowering to hide whatever lay beyond.

Sorren's voice rose from the helm. Steady. Bound and determined.

"We are heading into unknown waters," he called. "And this storm is not like the others. Eyes sharp. Hands ready."

The crew steadied themselves, each man and woman finding a place, a rope, a task. Even the newer sailors seemed to understand they were crossing some invisible threshold.

Sorren's eyes found Arlo. For a heartbeat they held there. Something grim and respectful passed between them.

"Arlo." He raised his voice just enough to be heard. "Whatever you did yesterday. If you can find even a hint of that power, now is the time to think on it. There is no telling what we are facing. If you can calm the storm enough to steady her, we might make it through."

Arlo nodded once. His heart sank a little, but there was no surprise there. He had known the request was coming.

He was not sure he could pull that much again. Not so soon. Not with this invisible pressure already chewing away at what energy he had. It felt as if the very air ahead of them reached back, biting at his mana and Lucy's both.

Rain began as a whisper, then grew into a steady sheet. The wind climbed, pulling at hair and clothes and the edges of loose canvas. The storm's fury mounted with each passing breath. Arlo drew in slow, deliberate air, trying to settle his pulse, to brace himself for what he knew he had to attempt.

The sea around them did not welcome them. It heaved and shifted as if trying to roll them away from the narrowing passage ahead. Through the sheets of rain, he caught glimpses of what waited.

Crystal.

Pale blue and white formations jutted from the water at strange angles. Some thin as spears. Some thick as pillars. They glowed faintly from within, a cold, eerie light that pulsed like a heartbeat. The Gauntlet's teeth.

An echo of that same light prickled under his skin.

He moved away from the bow and toward the center of the ship. The boards shuddered under his boots. For a moment, just from the storm itself, his legs wavered. He caught the rail and held it, fingers tightening until his knuckles whitened.

His eyes stayed fixed forward. His feet planted. He reached inward for what little energy he felt he had left.

The storm rolled around him. Thunder beat like a drum. Wind screamed past his ears. Rain lashed his face. He closed his eyes and tried to find that same rhythm he had touched yesterday.

Slowly, he began to pulse alongside the storm. His breathing. His heartbeat. The faint stir of blue inside him. Sparks scattered out in response to every crackle and roar. Tiny arcs of light flickered across his arms, too small yet to matter, but there.

Lucy clung to a set of ropes nearby. The wind whipped at her hair and clothes. Her face twisted with a mix of determination and fear.

Her gaze never left Arlo.

To say she was worried was too small. Hope clawed at her chest, bright and desperate. She believed he would be fine. That they would survive the storm and the Gauntlet. She had to believe that.

But what came after.

Two days now, his body had become a canvas for bruises, aches, and burns. Every time he used that strange power, it tore something away from him. At what point would there be nothing left to give.

The blue energy around him wavered as another heavy gust slammed into the ship. Arlo staggered, catching himself at the last moment. The storm challenged him from the first breath of this new fight and he was already losing ground.

He knew he had used a great deal yesterday. More than any sane man should. But this felt worse than simple exhaustion. There was something else at play, a dragging weight that did not belong only to him.

He shut his eyes tighter, shutting out the blur of movement around him. He reached down past the pain, past the fresh bruises, toward the place where the hammer had answered him that first night in Fall Lake.

He thought of the people who had fallen there. Faces, names, voices. Gretta's husband. The fisher who had tried to drag children from the water. Lives snuffed out with no warning.

If he was to carry their burdens, then perhaps they would help carry his.

The flicker at his core steadied. A dim, dwindling light pulled itself into a thin, consistent thread that circled him. He slowed his heart as best he could, feeling each beat deliberately, forcing the rhythm into something he could control.

He tried to align it with the storm's pounding.

Somewhere within, half imagined but no less real to him, he heard whispers. Not words he could repeat. Just a sense of encouragement. A push to keep going.

He thrust his arms forward.

His body trembled as he reached for every last scrap of mana he could find inside himself. Blue light flickered, almost failed, then returned with a renewed but ragged vigor. It crawled up his arms in faint streaks, tracing the edges of his bruises and illuminating them in sharp relief.

Lightning tore the sky in jagged lines. It crashed around the ship in pulses that began to mirror his own heartbeat. He could feel those strikes now, each one feeding something that wanted to answer.

The invisible presence pushed back.

It felt like a hand made of stone pressing against his chest. Heavy and cold. It tried to drag the light out of him and down into the dark water, the same way it tried to drain Lucy's warmth.

The very land resisted. The air above the Gauntlet, the rocks below, the crystals themselves. None of it wanted them here. None of it wanted him to touch it.

His knees buckled. He dropped to one, the boards jarring his bruised leg. He grit his teeth and forced the power outward, desperate to keep some kind of shield between the storm and the ship.

"Arlo."

Lucy's voice cut through the chaos. Sharp. Clear. It found him when other sounds vanished into the roar.

He glanced her way, eyes strained, vision already blurring at the edges. Her face was tight with effort and fear as she clung to the rope. Her knuckles were as white as his.

He could not hear the rest of whatever she shouted, but he felt her. The line between them had grown too strong to ignore. Her presence steadied something that had begun to slip.

The blue flared. He pushed his will out across the waves. He pictured water parting, winds breaking, a tunnel carved through the worst of it.

His vision washed white for a heartbeat.

Every muscle in his body screamed. Each breath felt like it scraped his ribs raw. Every bolt of lightning that snapped around them felt like it had passed through his own bones first.

401

"Come on," he whispered. His voice trembled. "Just a little more."

Another wave slammed into the hull. The ship lurched. The impact threw him sideways. He hit the deck hard, palms skidding across wet boards. The blue light sputtered. He clung to it with everything he had left.

He tried to push to his feet again. His arms shook. His legs wobbled. His body wanted to give up, but his soul refused. The split between them grew wider. His will continued forward, his body stayed behind.

"Steady, Arlo. Just a bit more."

Sorren's shout carried from the wheel, strained but full of a rough admiration he could not hide. He had seen men dedicated to their god. He had seen soldiers give their lives on command. He had never seen anyone tear themselves apart like this when they could have stayed out of the way.

Even Heir's most loyal would have balked at giving this much.

Arlo could barely hear him. The world had narrowed to a thin thread of sound and light. His consciousness hung by that same thread. His body convulsed with effort as he screamed into the teeth of the storm.

The storm did not break.

It grew worse.

Wind clawed at the sails. Rain hit hard enough to sting. The Sea Sentinel juddered as hidden spires scraped along her side, turning the proud ship into a battered leaf caught in the ocean's fist.

Lucy watched all of it.

Every flinch of pain that crossed Arlo's face. Every time he tried to rise and nearly fell. Each movement became its own small battle.

She felt her own power draining. She could taste it. Heat that normally bloomed easily under her skin felt sluggish, as if something in the air was drinking it away.

If he was spending this much, how much did he actually have left. How much of him would be left if he tried this one more time.

Another wave crashed against the hull. The impact rattled the entire ship and sent Arlo sliding. He hit the boards again. He let out a roar as he forced himself back onto hands and knees, refusing to stay down.

The bruises across his body throbbed at once. His teeth ground together as he fought to keep his eyes open. He could not let the storm slip free of his grip.

"Lucy." She saw his mouth shape her name.

The sound did not reach her over the wind, but she did not need the sound.

She took a step toward him. It felt like stepping off a ledge.

Her heart tore between fear and a rising, undeniable urge to help him. The storm cracked around them. Lightning crawled across the sky. Fire tingled at her fingertips, eager and anxious and dangerous.

She remembered the last time she had lost command of it. The dream. The way it had rolled out of her and burned the man she cared most about. That had been in a controlled space, half real, half not.

Out here, if she slipped, she could burn the ship. She could kill them all.

Her fingers clenched around the rope, knuckles aching. Doubt rushed through her.

What if she could not control it now. What if her flames reached for Arlo instead of the storm. What if she ended him before the sea did.

The ship jerked again as a submerged spire scraped along the hull. Wood screamed. Men stumbled. Arlo was flung sideways once more, barely catching himself before he rolled.

She saw his face.

Not just pain. Not just strain. Fear.

Not of death. Not of the storm. Fear that he was not enough. That he would fail them.

He was wrong. He had been wrong from the start. None of this had ever been his alone to bear.

403

Her fear cracked.

"Arlo," she called. Her voice shook, but it did not break.

His head turned toward her. His gaze locked on hers, blue eyes rimmed in red from the strain, pupils thin from lightning and pain.

She stepped forward. Then another. Each step felt like it might be the one that tipped the balance. But the trust she saw in his eyes burned hotter than the fear in her chest.

Without another word, she reached out and took his hands in hers.

Her grip was cautious at first. Her touch light, as if afraid she might set him alight by accident. Heat sparked from her palms, small sparks that danced along his skin and met the faint remnants of his own power.

She swallowed hard.

If she could mend bruises and ease his body with her fire, then perhaps she could lend that same fire to the storm.

"Together," she whispered.

She tightened her fingers around his. The word settled something inside him.

He nodded, jaw clenched. His own grip strengthened, welcoming her power into his. The blue threading through his veins stirred, reaching toward the red that flared from her.

At first, the two forces collided.

Her flame jumped. His lightning snapped. Sparks flared wild and scattered, crackling in the air around them and fizzling into the dark. It felt like two storms smashing into each other.

Then the line between them steadied.

Her fire softened, no longer a roaring blaze, but a steady, focused heat. It melded with the blue arcs that crawled across his arms. The energies began to twist together instead of fight. Red flowed around blue. Blue threaded through red.

Lucy closed her eyes.

She felt it. The surge through both of them. No longer wild. Guided now. Shaped by two wills instead of one desperate man forcing his body past its limits.

She felt his heartbeat. Strong, battered, still stubborn. She matched her own breathing to it, letting their rhythms fall into the same pattern.

Together, they pushed.

Their hands glowed, bright enough that even in the storm dark the light stood out. Red and blue mingled like the twin moons when they rose together over a clear sea. The glow spilled outward, casting strange colors across the wet deck and the frightened faces of the crew.

Sorren risked a glance their way.

For a moment, he saw not just a man and woman kneeling in the storm. He saw something more. A shape of hope and fury and stubborn life that refused to be pushed aside.

"Hold her steady," he barked to the men nearby, voice rougher now. "They are buying us our path. Do not waste it."

The wind shifted. Not much. Enough.

Waves faltered, losing some of their wild aimless rage. Lightning no longer struck wherever it pleased. It coiled instead into a loose ring around the Sea Sentinel, crackling and flashing, but bending away at the last moment, like a barrier made of storm itself.

The spires loomed closer, rising up on either side. Some were bare stone. Others were crystal, glowing with that inner light. The combined energy from Arlo and Lucy brushed against them. The crystals pulsed in answer, humming deep in the bones of the ship.

The path between the spires remained narrow and treacherous, but the worst of the chaos relented. Enough for a skilled captain to thread a needle.

Arlo's breath sawed in and out of his chest. Each inhale hurt. Each exhale felt like it might be his last.

Lucy's touch did not let him slide away. Her fire held him up when his strength dipped. It soothed some of the ripping feeling inside him, knitting his fraying focus together for a few precious moments longer.

Some spires still rose ahead, jagged and unforgiving, but with the storm softened, they were visible and avoidable instead of hidden knives.

The furious clouds thinned overhead as they passed the outer edges of the Gauntlet and moved into the sheltered bay, the inner sanctum that so few ships had ever reached and lived to speak of.

Their grip loosened, but neither let go yet. Their faces were flushed, hair plastered to their skin, eyes wide. When Lucy opened hers, she found his already looking back.

Relief and pride shone there. In both of them.

As the storm finally eased, the energy that had poured through them drained away. The glow faded from their hands. His bruises throbbed with renewed intensity. Pain rose in a full wave now that nothing held it back.

His body buckled forward.

He fell into her.

"Thank you," he whispered, voice ragged, barely more than breath.

She curled an arm around his shoulders, holding him there.

"I told you," she murmured into his hair. "You do not have to do this alone."

Around them, the crew cheered. Some shouted Arlo's name. Others shouted Lucy's. Some cried out for the Sea Sentinel herself. All of it bled together into one raw sound of victory and exhausted disbelief.

They had crossed what others would not even attempt.

Sorren held the wheel until the last dangerous spire slid past. His eyes swept the shoreline where cliffs rose and strange formations clung to the rock. The bay was not calm, not truly, but it was a different kind of stillness now. Watchful instead of furious.

He guided the Sea Sentinel to a place where the water was deep enough to anchor, but close enough that a rowboat could carry them to the stony shore.

"Drop anchor," he called.

Chains rattled. The ship settled with a low groan. The rest of the way would be on oars and nerve.

"Captain," Arlo whispered.

Sorren approached with Lucy still sitting on the deck, Arlo's head resting in her lap. Both were drenched and streaked with grime, but grinning in spite of it.

"How is the crew?" Arlo asked.

He had taken what little rest he could right there on the planks, Lucy's hand in his hair, her presence a thin shield against the exhaustion trying to drag him under. She hoped it would be enough to get him through whatever waited on the island.

Sorren's expression shifted. Some of the glow of victory dimmed. Sadness flickered, quick and sharp.

He exchanged a brief look with Lucy. She saw the answer in his eyes before he spoke.

"Most of us made it through," he said. "Thanks to you and Lucy."

A hollow feeling opened in Arlo's chest. The word most lodged there like a stone.

"Most of us" he repeated.

Alfonze stepped forward from just behind Sorren's shoulder. For once, his usual bluster was gone. His voice was low. His eyes shone with wet that had nothing to do with the sea.

"One of the younger lads," he said. "Finn. He did not make it."

Air left Arlo's lungs in a slow, painful leak.

"Finn," he said. "The boy who had barely come of age. The one who kept asking about seeing real storms."

"Aye," Sorren replied. "He was a good lad. Brave. He held his post as best he could until the last wave hit and we crashed against the spire."

Arlo clenched his jaw. His fingers tightened on the wet boards.

"I should not have wavered," he said. "I should have held the storm longer."

Guilt dropped over him like a fresh weight. Another face in the growing line of those he had not been able to save. Another dream cut short.

Sorren's hand came down heavy on his shoulder.

"Arlo. Listen," he said. "You did everything you could. Without you and Lucy, none of us would have made it through that stretch. Not one."

His voice softened a fraction.

"The boy saved a lass in the process," Sorren added. "Fara. She almost went over when the deck jumped. He grabbed her and got her back where she needed to be. That was his choice. His courage."

Arlo swallowed hard. The words did not ease the knife in his chest.

"That does not make it right," he said. "It does not make it fair that he is gone. I should have been stronger. More capable."

He looked away, teeth grinding, fighting the rise of anger that had nowhere to go but back into himself.

Alfonze spoke then, voice steadier than Arlo had ever heard it.

"We are here because of what you did," he said. "I know that does not change anything for the boy. It should not. But you gave us a chance. He gave Fara a chance. That is more than anyone else who has ever been trapped in the Gauntlet."

Arlo nodded slowly. The guilt did not vanish. It never did. But the words found a place beside it.

"It does not get easier, does it?" he asked.

Sorren met his gaze, the lines around his eyes deeper than usual.

"No," he said. "And it is not supposed to. If it did, you would not be the man you are."

He squeezed Arlo's shoulder once.

"Carrying that weight is what makes you who you are. A protector."

Arlo waved off the word hero with a small, tired flick of his hand and pushed himself up. His legs wobbled, but he found his feet with Lucy's help.

"All right," he said. He braced one hand on his knee for a moment, catching his balance. "Let us get ready."

Sorren nodded. His gaze slid to the shoreline, then back to Lucy, then to the crew busy checking damage and tending the wounded.

"We are as close as we can get with the Sentinel," he said. "Alfonze. Prepare the rowboat. The four of us will go ashore. If we do not return, you do what you must to get them home."

Alfonze's throat bobbed. He gave a sharp nod and moved to follow the order, barking for a couple of hands to help lower the small boat and check the oars.

Lucy stayed by Arlo's side, giving him a shoulder to lean on until his legs stopped feeling like soaked cloth. Her eyes met Sorren's for a brief moment. There was no need for words between them. They both understood what they were about to walk into. None of them would come back the same, if they came back at all.

"Are you sure you want to go on?" Sorren asked Arlo. "You do not have to."

Arlo shook his head. A faint, grim smile tugged at the corner of his mouth.

"I appreciate it," he said. "But I will be damned if I came this far not to go all the way."

Silence held for a breath. Then Sorren nodded once.

"Then we go," he said. "And we do not stop until we have what we came for."

Arlo drew in a steadying breath. Lucy slid her arm more firmly around his waist.

"All right," she said. Her gaze drifted toward the fog that clung to the rocky shore ahead. Strange shapes whispered in that mist. "Let us get Nyla and head out."

CHAPTER 41

"What... are those?" she asked, eyes fixed on the strange crystalline formations ahead.

Sorren squinted into the mist, shoulders rolling with each pull of the oars. "Not like anything I've seen before. Almost looks like a fortress."

Jagged rocks and peculiar crystals jutted from the earth like broken bones. The shoreline was littered with clusters of faintly glowing crystals that cast an eerie light across the water, pale colors rippling over the waves.

Nyla's eyes darted between the towering spires. When she spoke, it was almost to herself. "It's like the land itself grew these shapes. Not built. Twisted into place."

Sorren's hand tightened on the oars. His gaze stayed locked on the spires ahead. "Almost looks like they're guarding something. Defensive. But who, or what, built something like this?"

They each took in the shapes rising over the shoreline. Dark stone spires veined with crystal, growing at odd angles. Some were broken and jagged, splintered as if something had snapped them off. Others rose straight and tall, like watchtowers planted by the earth itself.

Lucy leaned over the side of the boat. Down in the shallows, clusters of crystal jutted from the seabed, throbbing with a slow, steady light. Awe and unease tangled in her chest.

"These crystals…" Her voice dropped. "They're pulsing with light. Almost like they're alive."

Arlo felt a strange answering pulse in his chest. The amber amulet at his throat warmed and began to thrum, the jewel at its center vibrating in the same rhythm as the crystals. Reactive. Aware.

"I've heard of powerful magic warping the land," he said, forcing his voice steady as he watched the shoreline. "But this feels… designed."

Sorren watched the mist swirl around the formations, clinging to shattered ribs of wood and stone. Old shipwrecks littered the shallows, broken hulls caught on teeth of rock and crystal. Beyond that, sand and scrub grass, stalagmite like spikes, and more crystals stabbing out of everything in sight.

The whole scene felt like something out of a story meant to scare children away. A place you warned people about but never truly expected to see.

A chill crept down his spine. His jaw stayed tight. "The whole place looks like it was meant to keep people out."

Arlo nodded, though his mind ran in circles. His whole body ached. The pool of blue energy he had learned to pull from was dry, leaving him hollow and spent. "Let's just hope it's as empty as it looks."

The rowboat scraped the sand-covered rocks as they reached the shore. Together they dragged it above the surf, securing it where the tide would not steal it back.

As they took their first steps onto the island, an eerie wind slipped past them. It curled through the crystals with a sound that almost resembled words.

The five of them stood in a hesitant line, staring at the forest of stone and crystal waiting ahead.

"Welcome to the Gauntlet," Sorren said.

Akira spread its wings and lifted off, circling them. The Draconis drew a few narrow looks from Sorren as it wheeled overhead, but he said nothing. Akira landed on a nearby rock where a thick band of crystal wrapped from base to tip.

The moment Akira's talons pressed into the crystal, it hummed. A soft, resonant tone rippled out, and one by one the other crystals in sight trembled in response. Color flared along their faces. Some shone in pale blue, others in green, amber, or violet.

Lucy stepped closer, running her fingers along Akira's dark scales, then over the crystal itself. The surface was cool and smooth. A flicker of red heat trembled at her fingertips. It slipped from her skin before she could stop it. The ember sank into the crystal.

A thin ribbon of crimson light swirled inside, winding around its center before bursting outward.

Lucy and Nyla both gasped as the crystal ignited with a deep red glow. The hum grew louder. Other formations along the rocks and shore caught the color, one after another. Within seconds, dozens of crystals burned with the same crimson hue, all beating in time with Lucy's mana.

"Lucy, what did you just do?" Sorren asked. His hand was already on Justice, knuckles white on the hilt.

She snatched her hand back, staring as the red washed over the shoreline. Fear and fascination twisted together in her face. "I... I don't know. I didn't do anything. Not on purpose. It felt like it was calling to me, and then it pulled something out of me."

Arlo took a slow, weighted step forward. His legs shook under him. He leaned closer to the same crystal and let his hand hover above it.

A thread of blue mana peeled away from his fingertip.

The crimson inside the crystal deepened, touched with a flicker of blue that sank into the glow. The hum dropped into a low, constant resonance that buzzed in his teeth. It almost felt like speech, right at the edge of understanding.

"It reacts to mana," he said. "But it's more than that. It is trying to draw it in. It takes what it can, then pushes it out to the others. Like they are linked. Feeding each other."

Sorren's eyes narrowed. He strode over to another cluster, itching to drive Justice straight through it. The closer he stepped, the weaker his limbs felt, like something was peeling strength out of his bones.

"If they are feeding on energy, that explains why the whole place feels drained," he said. "It is siphoning from us the more we move in."

"We are not even inside," Arlo muttered. His face was tight. His posture sagged as if the weight of his own body and armor was too much. He swayed.

Lucy reached him first, slipping his arm around her shoulders and bracing her weight under his. "Arlo, it is alright to stay. We can find our way in and come back for you."

He tried to shrug her off and forced his feet to move. He stepped up beside Sorren and planted Elduun like a walking staff.

"No. I have come this far. I am going to see this through."

Sorren glanced back at him, then at Lucy, reading the tension in her face. "There is no point fighting him, Lucy. He is too stubborn to listen."

A strained smile tugged at Arlo's mouth. Concern sat heavy in Lucy's eyes.

Sorren turned away and took the lead. Justice balanced easily in his hands as they moved past the first line of formations. The crystals seemed to shape a path ahead of them. With each step, new clusters came to life in soft colors that lit their way into the strange forest beyond.

The trees were not spared. Trunks and branches were wrapped in veins of crystal that climbed them like ivy. Strangely, the trees themselves looked healthy and full. Leaves whispered overhead, vibrant and green, while the stone at their roots was cracked and worn.

Only when the group approached did the crystals brighten, giving the impression of old things waking as they passed.

Nyla looked back over her shoulder. The little boat sat like a dark seed at the edge of the shore, already half swallowed by mist and distance. She shivered and hurried to fall in step behind Lucy. Akira flew low in the branches, keeping close.

They pushed on until the shoreline vanished from sight. Even though Arlo kept insisting he was fine, they stopped once to let him sit and catch his breath. Deeper in, the plants grew thicker. On one side of their path, the flora was pale and brittle, leaves curled and gray as if bitten by frost. On the other, the growth was wild and lush, swollen with color and strange fruit that seemed to glow faintly in the crystal light.

"Anyone else think it is strange?" Arlo asked. His voice was rough. He rested a hand on a dead branch that crumbled under his touch and looked across to the riot of green on the other side. "Life and rot mixed together. Like someone is playing at picking favorites."

Lucy ran her fingers over a bright leaf. Its veins shimmered with reflected crystal light. "It is connected somehow. The crystals take from one place and give to another. But it is uneven. Like a broken circulation."

She knelt by one of the most withered patches and brushed dirt away from a buried shard. The crystal there was dull and cracked, spiderweb lines etched through its surface.

"Whatever is feeding all this, some of it is empty," she murmured.

415

Nyla hugged her arms around herself and glanced up the path. Bark and branches around them were laced with crystal veins that pulsed like an interconnected web.

"Everything feels wrong," she whispered. "Like something is watching. Waiting."

They pressed on. The forest slowly opened up. The tight press of trees loosened into a wider stretch of tangled roots, broken stone, and crystals growing in thick clusters. Far ahead, always visible through the gaps, was a towering crystalline shape at the heart of the island, a distant spine of light that anchored the horizon.

Branches above twisted and bent, hung with broken shards of gemlike growth that chimed faintly when the wind stirred.

A tall, dark shape moved ahead of them. It slid along a tree trunk, barely visible in the glow. Sorren's hand went to Justice at once.

By the time he blinked, the shape was gone.

"Anyone else see that?" Arlo asked. His eyes scanned the trees, breath shallow. Elduun hung heavy in his grip, more burden than weapon. Half the time it felt like the hammer was helping carry him, not the other way around.

He forced himself onward. The wind shifted. It poured through the crystal forest with a low moan, broken by faint, half formed voices.

"What makes you think you can save anyone?" The words seemed to unravel in the air, incomplete and distant, but one word struck through clean.

Failure.

The sound slid into Arlo's bones. His fist closed around Elduun's handle. Each breath felt heavier. He turned his head, expecting to see Lucy at his side, still braced under his arm.

Instead, for a heartbeat, he faced his own reflection.

Not in a mirror. In the side of a tall crystal to his left. His face stared back at him, the lines sharper, the eyes darker. The reflection smiled. It was not kind.

He stumbled. The image snapped back to normal, just Lucy and Nyla and Sorren around him, Akira flying overhead.

Nyla kept her eyes down, focusing on where to put each step. Her heart pounded. The oddness of the land only made her more homesick. Even Akira, who usually could always coax a smile out of her, was not enough to pull her mind away from home, from her mother.

You do not belong here. You never will.

The thought did not feel like her own, yet it came in her own voice, dry and certain. Her gaze flicked toward the crystals, then the trees. The others moved on ahead, eyes forward, each of them facing whatever weighed on them.

Do you think you can save your mother? You are only a burden. A problem she has to hide. Without your cursed blood, she would be better off.

The words hit harder than any physical blow. Tears stung her eyes. She saw her mother's face, always wary, always tired. Saw the way she pulled Nyla into shadows when others passed, the way she fussed with Nyla's hood, always hiding, always afraid.

She had told herself it was love. Protection. A mother doing everything she could.

The whispers twisted that memory.

You are the reason she is alone. The reason she is sick. The reason she is afraid.

Her throat tightened. She raised her hands and clamped them over her ears, but it did nothing. The voices were inside her, not around her.

She thought back to the night she left. No goodbye. No final embrace. Just the hope that if she found a cure, then it would all be worth it. Now another thought crept in.

Or maybe she was relieved. Maybe when she woke and you were gone, she finally breathed free. No more hiding the Elfar child. No more shame.

Her steps blurred. The path wavered under her feet. The forest bled in and out of focus as the whispers grew louder, overlapping.

You cannot save anyone. Not your mother. Not these people. You are a weak, lost girl who only knows how to run.

They will never see you as an equal. They will abandon you. Half breed. Tainted. Unwanted.

She lifted her eyes to Akira. He flew low along the crystal line, his dark scales catching the light. He glanced back at her, yellow eyes steady and loyal. He had always been there. Always fought for her. She had never deserved him.

Her gaze slipped to Sorren. His shoulders were broad, his walk heavy and sure, the swing of Justice cutting through overgrown brush with ease. He was taller than her, maybe taller than anyone she had met. Strong, confident, guided. She saw something else too, just for a moment. A tightness in his jaw. A shadow at the edge of his stare.

He is fighting something too, she thought. Even if he hides it better.

<hr />

Justice moved easily in Sorren's hands. He hacked through rotten branches and hanging roots, the weight of the sword a familiar comfort. His boots struck hard against the crystal-studded ground.

The island made his skin crawl.

The crystals pulled strength out of the air. Out of Lucy and Arlo, most of all. He had seen both of them grow weaker with every step. He did not like knowing that something unseen could strip away their power. His power. It reminded him of how small they really were here, in a place that did not answer to their gods or their king.

He focused on the path. He did not look at the crystals. He did not want to see his own face staring back at him.

His thoughts drifted anyway.

His loyalty had always belonged to the church and the crown. He had taken the Vow of Zeal without once questioning if it was right. He was proud of it. Proud to serve Heir and the kingdom, proud to be a blade swung in the name of Justice.

Now the buzz of the crystals turned to whispers that sounded too much like doubt.

His mind wandered to the sea. The creak of ropes. The snap of sails. The way salt stung his skin and the air moved freely over open water. Out there, he had been his own man. No council chambers. No sermons. No gilded halls. Only tide, wind, and star.

Out there, no one held his leash.

What good is a god who stands still while men use his name to rule everyone else?

The thought crashed through him like a rogue wave. He faltered for half a heartbeat, then pushed forward.

He saw Davenport in his mind. Saw Dolph standing above the crowd, using Arlo as both shield and banner. Calling him Hero. Pushing him forward as the people's hope while keeping his own hands clean. The king had done little better. Eager to have someone else carry the weight.

For years Sorren believed Heir's will flowed through the church and its leaders. Every order from them, he had treated as if it came straight from the god of war and justice.

Now, away from the marble floors and stained glass, it was harder to ignore the cracks.

Faith should be unshakable.

Brother Jason had said that often. Sorren had believed it. Yet the men who spoke of faith the loudest had the fattest rings, the finest plates, and the softest hands.

If Justice is meant to be my guide, how do I keep following those who twist it for themselves?

The question drove deep. He had always thought his purpose was defending the church. Defending the words of Heir. But the

Gauntlet had peeled that certainty back and left the raw stone beneath. Truth was never what people first showed. Calm seas hid reefs. Gentle waves masked riptides.

Maybe his loyalty had not been faith. Maybe it had been habit. Or fear.

Justice is not blind obedience. It is the courage to see clearly, even when it hurts.

He grit his teeth. Something inside him rose that felt older than his armor and his vows. Heir was a god of war. That did not mean war only belonged on battlefields. Maybe the real wars were fought inside the hearts of men, between what they were told and what they knew was right.

He thought of the sea again.

The sea does not lie. It is wild and ruthless and uncaring, but it never pretends to be something it is not. It tests you, but it does not deceive you.

Faith had become something else. Not a compass, but a chain. A voice that said obey instead of asking why.

If Heir's judgement weighed the Archbishop and the king, would they stand tall, or crack like these crystals?

He shook his head, trying to banish the thoughts. His path ahead was unknown, but it was his. He had sworn an oath. He had meant every word.

"May I be as unyielding as the sea," he whispered under his breath, "as true as the tide. If Justice is to be found, I will find it. Within or beyond Heir's reach."

He slashed through another curtain of dead branches and paused long enough to drink from his canteen. The liquor he had slipped into it burned its way down and loosened the tightness in his chest. This was not the time to drown himself in doubt.

The others filed past him. Lucy lingered. She laid a hand on his shoulder and gave him a small, soft smile. The look said enough. Are you alright. Do you need a moment.

He gave her a short nod and the barest tilt of a smile in return. Just enough to keep her from asking more.

The smile was as much for herself as for him. Her own heart hammered harder with every step, every red pulse of light that seemed to echo her mana. The crystals felt like a thousand eyes. Each beat of their glow tugged at something in her chest, pulling threads loose in the shell she had been building around herself.

Creature of ruin. Darkness. Despair.

The words slid through her mind in her own voice and in a stranger's, repeating and rooting deep. Every ripple of energy in the crystals seemed to speak that same idea. Every hum grew louder.

She caught her reflection in one of the larger shards. For a moment, it was wrong. Her eyes burned with fire. Her skin glowed as if lit from within, cracks of red crawling up her arms. Wings of flame stretched wide from her back, casting everything around her in the promise of ruin.

She blinked, and the image snapped back. Just her. Just a tired woman with messy red hair and soot on her clothes.

This is who you really are. Ruin wrapped in soft words. You pretend you belong beside them. You pretend you are safe. You pretend you will not burn them.

Her fists shook. She dug her nails into her palms. She forced herself to look away from the crystals and down at the ruined path. She opened her hand again.

A faint heat coiled in her palm. Red mana rose just under her skin, eager.

Every smile, every laugh, every good deed is a lie you tell yourself. You were not born to save. Not like Arlo. You were born to destroy.

Fear wrapped tight around her heart. The dream came back more vivid than ever. She stood knee deep in broken wings. Bodies lay everywhere. White and gold feathers stained black and red. Their eyes were empty. Her hands dripped fire and blood.

Her own wings lay tangled beside them, ripped from her back, torn and scorched. Pain had burned through her spine, yet when she looked down at the chaos, she had smiled.

She looked up and saw the hammer falling toward her, the same one Arlo carried now. Bright light swallowed everything.

What if that is all I am. A creature born to burn everything I touch.

A tear slid down her cheek. She tried to picture Arlo's face instead. The way he had looked at her. The softness in his eyes when he thought no one else was watching.

He looked at you with trust.

Liar.

He let you heal him.

You fed on his pain.

He believed in you.

You are using him. A broken man is easy to twist. All you have to do is give him something pretty to believe in.

She saw herself back on the Sea Sentinel. Arlo lying on the bed, still bandaged from Fall Lake. Her body over his, heat rolling off her in waves. She saw her nails bite into his skin as flames bled from her hands, saw him cry out as the fire spread. The room burned. The ship burned. His eyes went from sapphire to molten as he realized the truth.

Monster.

She jerked in the present, breath coming fast. The path blurred. Crystals burned red at the edges of her sight. In the flames around her mind, creatures rose. Winged things with leathery skin and black eyes. They moved aside, making a path.

A throne waited for her. Built of charred bone and ash.

Come sit, it whispered. Be what you are.

The voice grew steady and cruel.

Darkness will always be stronger in you. You cannot cut it out. You cannot change what you were born for. Hope is not for creatures like us. Hope is a lie you tell other people while you burn behind your teeth.

If ruin is all you are, why keep fighting it.

She glanced back at Arlo.

He had fallen behind, his steps heavy, shoulders bowed. He leaned on Elduun as if it was the only thing keeping him upright. Pain tugged at his face with every movement, but his jaw stayed set.

Hope.

He clung to the word like armor. Like a name he was trying to grow into. He repeated it in his mind every time his ribs ached or his head swam. Hope. Hope. Hope.

Here, though, the word felt thin.

Hope is just the story you tell yourself. That you are doing this for others. That you were given that hammer to help them stand. That is not the whole truth.

Images rose unbidden. The orphanage. Sabil. Long nights where he held back his own tears while others cried.

He saw the letter again. His mother's handwriting. Words he had almost memorized. Always have hope. I am watching over you.

He had clung to that line his whole life. Clung to the word like a rope. Told himself that was reason enough.

You have always done this. Played the hero. First for the children at the orphanage. Then for anyone who would let you. You took the beatings so they would not. You did the work no one else wanted. You broke yourself over and over and called it hope.

He remembered standing between the matrons and the other children. Taking punishments he did not earn. Letting Sabil hide behind him. Watching families come and go. Watching them pick smaller, quieter children. Watching their eyes pass right over him and her.

Never chosen.

All your sacrifices, every fight you rush into, are not just for them. They are to fill that empty place. You are afraid of what is left if you stop. If you are not needed. If you are not the hero, then what are you.

His mouth went dry. The wind cut through his clothes, cold enough to sting.

You are not driven by purpose. You are driven by fear. The fear of being left behind. The fear that if no one is leaning on you, you disappear.

He saw himself as a boy, sitting alone on his bed while the other children slept. Listening to the night sounds and the soft creak of the building. Wondering why no one wanted him. Wondering what was wrong with him.

You loved being called the Hero of Fall Lake.

He flinched. He had told himself he hated the title. That it weighed too much. That it did not belong to him. Yet he could still hear the cheers. See the way people had looked at him that day. Like he was something bright and solid.

It had felt good.

Admit it. You needed that. You needed to feel like more than a broken boy from an orphanage.

His knees buckled. He dropped down, one hand catching himself on the cold earth. His head bowed, breath ragged. The crystals around him glowed brighter, trapping his reflection in a hundred overlapping shards.

If you stripped it all away, the hammer, the title, the expectations, what is left. If you were not carrying everyone else, who would you be.

His fingers dug into the dirt. He wanted something steady. Something real to hold onto.

Hope is a mask. You chase other people's pain so you never have to sit with your own. If you ever stopped, even for a moment, you would have to look at what is under it. You are afraid there is nothing there.

His hands shook. His chest felt tight, like something was trying to claw its way out through his ribs. He saw himself alone, standing in a vast, empty space. No people. No hammer. No title. Just him.

"Maybe…" His voice was barely a breath. "Maybe I am nothing. Just a man clinging to hope because I do not know who I am without it."

The words hung in the air. The darkness inside him smiled.

Then, somewhere deep under all the fear, something small pushed back. A single word. Quiet and stubborn.

Hope.

"Even if that is true," Arlo whispered. He pressed his forehead toward the ground, then forced himself to lift it. "Even if hope is the only thing I have left, I will hold onto it. Because it is the only thing that ever kept me from falling apart."

He wrapped both hands around Elduun's handle. His grip steadied. His eyes cleared. He pushed himself to his feet. Every movement hurt, but he rose anyway.

Ahead of them, the crystals had grown closer together, forming a kind of basin. A wall of clear crystal stood in the center of it, tall and smooth like frozen water. As Arlo straightened, the surface rippled.

Shimmering reflections appeared across it.

Four figures stared back. Twisted versions of Arlo, Lucy, Sorren, and Nyla. Eyes dark. Faces warped by their fears. The images shifted through the scenes each of them had just seen in their minds. Nyla's burning village. Sorren in gilded armor with chains in his fists. Lucy wreathed in flame atop broken wings. Arlo standing alone while the people of Fall Lake turned their backs.

The whispers rose to a howl.

Arlo let out a roar of his own and ran forward. Every fear. Every hidden truth. Every doubt that had been placed in him. He took all of it and drove his legs harder.

He raised Elduun high and swung with everything he had.

The hammer met the crystal with a blinding flash of blue light. The impact shook the basin. A crack split across the mirror. Then another. Fractures spidered outward.

"So maybe I am afraid," Arlo shouted as the crystal screamed and splintered. His voice echoed off the stone around them. "Maybe I will never be enough. But if this is what it takes to hold onto hope, then I will break myself a thousand times over. Because that is who I am."

Thunder rolled through the Gauntlet. Lightning flared along the cracks. With a shattering scream, the crystalline mirror exploded into thousands of shards. They rained down at his feet, chiming as they hit the ground.

The air went still.

The whispers cut off.

"Lucy! Sorren! Nyla!" Arlo yelled, chest heaving. His voice carried through the valley of crystals that remained. They no longer looked like trees wrapped in stone. Now he could see the truth of the place. It had once been some kind of structure, now collapsed and hollowed out, its bones left behind as jutting spires and broken walls.

"It is an illusion," he called, turning to them. "Whatever it is showing you, whatever it is telling you, it is not real."

CHAPTER 42

Each of them stood in silence, each of them wrestling with an inner demon of their own. Arlo took several wavering steps forward. Lucy moved to his side, slipping under his arm to help hold him up. Sorren stepped in on Arlo's other side, giving him a second steady anchor.

Nyla stayed just behind them, one hand tangled in Akira's scales as the small Draconis perched on her shoulder. Even he seemed uneasy, his body coiled tight, eyes scanning every shadow.

No matter how much any of them might have wished to turn back, there was no going back now. Among the shattered crystal at their feet rose an archway.

The archway was massive. If it had ever been sized for something to walk through, none of them wanted to meet the sort of being that would fit it. Beyond it, a crystalline path wound upward into the heart of the stone structure they had seen from the shore, built of interlocked rock and crystal. It was all lit from within by twisting strands of blue and red light, the same hues that had been pulled from Arlo and Lucy.

None of them spoke. An unspoken understanding passed between them as they stepped forward together.

A soft, rhythmic hum rose from one of the larger crystal clusters near the arch. It vibrated low in their bones. From the shadowed platform just past the archway, crystals began to rise out of the floor, forming beneath something that stood above them.

One crystal. Then another. Then another.

They stacked and rotated into a staircase as a tall figure descended, each step manifesting under its feet, sliding into place as if the whole structure responded to its presence.

The creature moved with purpose. At first it seemed humanoid. Then the details caught the light. Its skin was dry and gray, almost like worn stone. Crystalline growths protruded from its limbs and shoulders, from its back and head, like living branches of the same mineral that filled the island. Veins of light pulsed along those facets and sank into the cracks of its skin.

Its presence was both beautiful and unsettling. Something that felt like it belonged to another world. Something out of a story a mother might whisper at night, the kind where you never quite knew if the monster was friend or foe.

When it spoke, its voice was soft and precise, but there was power in it that held their attention.

"Who are you, and what brings you here?" the being asked. The tone was measured and firm, with a faint feminine edge.

Arlo drew a breath that burned all the way down. His mana felt completely drained. He knew that if this turned to a fight, he had very little left, but he stepped forward anyway.

"We are here to bring someone back from beyond this land," he said. "Someone who traveled through here years ago. Eckerd Lionhart."

428

The crystals along the being's head flickered, brightening and dimming in quick succession, as if they were sorting through his words.

"This is your reason," it said slowly. "Yes. But why are you here."

Its gaze moved from Arlo to Lucy, then to Sorren, then to Nyla. It felt like it was peeling away skin and looking underneath.

Sorren shifted. His shoulders squared. He placed a fist against the holy symbol at his chest and gave it a sharp pound. "We are here because we must be," he said. "We have come for answers. For allies. And for justice."

"Justice." The being tasted the word. It stepped past Arlo with a slow, gliding stride. There was the slightest hint of amusement in its voice, like it would have laughed if it had remembered how. "Is that why you are here, Sorren? Following the winds of change, or the command of faith?"

His jaw clenched. He could not look away from the Shardkin's gaze.

The creature turned to Nyla next. The light within its crystals softened, its expression becoming strangely gentle.

"And you, child. Why are you here."

Nyla's voice trembled. Her eyes dropped to the ground as she scuffed her boot against the stone. "I... I came to prove myself."

The being tilted its head. The crystals along its neck and shoulders shifted as if considering.

"You wish to prove yourself," it said, "yet you question if you are even worthy to stand here. One cannot prove themselves fully while their heart still doubts the step. You wonder if your mother would be better off without your stained heritage."

Its mouth curved into something that resembled a smile, though there was no warmth in it.

Nyla's cheeks burned. Her fingers tightened on the dagger at her belt. Akira moved in front of her, lowering his head and releasing a low, fierce growl. Nyla wanted nothing more than to sink into the ground and vanish.

The Shardkin shifted to face Lucy.

Lucy lifted her chin, forcing herself to meet its eyes. "I am here to help," she said. "To protect."

Her voice sounded steadier than she felt.

Once more, a faint smile crossed the creature's rough features. "And yet you believe yourself to be the very thing from which others must be protected," it said quietly. "A creature of ruin, marked by fire and shadow."

Lucy flinched. Her breath caught in her throat. She looked away, the words cutting deep.

Finally, its gaze settled on Arlo again. The crystals along its chest flared in a familiar blue, a color that mirrored Elduun's core.

"And you, Arlo." Its voice lowered. "You speak of hope as if it were a weapon, one you wield to break yourself for others. But tell me. When you strip away the burdens. When you set down the need to carry everyone else. Why are you here."

Arlo's chest tightened. The words he had just fought through in the Gauntlet were still raw. He felt the urge to answer, to explain, to confess that half the time hope felt like a mask he wore to cover fear. Fear of being unwanted. Fear of being nothing.

He swallowed and stayed quiet.

The Shardkin took a step backward and lifted its crystalline hand toward the structure ahead. The fingers were fractured and jagged, light pulsing through the cracks.

"Your burdens have brought you here," it said. "Each of you carries a question. An ache that no simple answer can quiet. Yet you seek something beyond yourselves. For that reason, I will allow your passage to the Veil, but…"

"What is the Veil?" Sorren cut in.

The being let its arm lower. A faint, sorrowful curve tugged at what passed for its mouth. It ignored the interruption and continued.

"Know this," it said. "The Prismalith and the Veil have become linked. Outside the Veil, you found the Gauntlet. A mirror of truth, reflecting the deepest parts of who you are. The Veil has fed on the Prismalith, and in doing so, its tests have twisted. Yet that is not all. The Veil is also home to the souls deemed unworthy to return to the realm of the gods. Zenith."

Lucy let out a small gasp. Her hand flew to her chest. Something in those words stirred a cold recognition in her. Souls considered unworthy.

Arlo studied the Shardkin more closely. He tried to figure out if it was a construct given life by mana, or a living being made of stone and crystal.

"What about you?" he asked. "Why are you here?"

Its gaze drifted past them, toward the walls. The light in its crystals dimmed.

Slowly, other shapes began to glow along the walls and pillars. Faint outlines of faces emerged in the stone. Broken forms that had once resembled this same kind of being. Worn down. Weathered by time. Fragments of a people spread through the island.

"I remain because my purpose is not yet fulfilled," it said. "I am the last of my kind. The final guardian of the Prismalith. When it fades, so shall I. Until then, I hold my place. For those who came before me. For those yet to come."

The light along its chest brightened again.

"We had no name for ourselves," it went on. "In ages past, others called us Shardkin. I am known as Korithas. We were shaped by the titan Vyrthalas, wrought from earth, mineral, and residual mana. Vyrthalas took it upon itself to protect this world from the scars of the one that came before."

Sorren frowned. "World that came before. Grace created Lyorion with the other gods. That is what we were taught. What do you mean a world before."

"You are not wrong," Korithas said. "Grace did create Lyorion. Long ago, before this world existed, Grace reached into the chaotic energy of the Drachaos. An endless well of power with no form and no limit. From that chaos she shaped a prototype. A world without walls. It lay open to the Drachaos and the monstrosities born from it. That world was never completed."

The Shardkin turned and began to walk deeper into the structure.

"Upon its remains," it said, "Lyorion was crafted. Layer upon layer, stone upon stone, built over the bones of what came before. If you wish to find the one you seek within the Veil, follow me. I will show you the heart of the Prismalith, where you will find the Veilgate."

The four of them traded uneasy glances. Was this another test. A trap. Had they already failed without knowing.

One by one, they nodded and fell into step behind Korithas, following it along a corridor lined with towering crystals and echoes of forgotten stories.

"So… what exactly is the Prismalith?" Nyla asked, her voice small as she hurried to keep up.

Korithas' light dimmed to a deep, muted glow. The whole hall seemed to hush with it.

"The Prismalith was once more than a source of power," it said. "It is a prison. A guardian. And a lifeline for what remains of this land."

Lucy's eyes tracked upward along the spires overhead. A heavy feeling settled in her chest at the word prison. "A prison," she repeated.

"Yes," Korithas replied. "The Prismalith draws in mana and sends it outward to nourish the land. It is what gave life to my people. It is what kept this island alive."

"What makes it a prison?" Arlo asked.

"It was designed to confine powerful and dark entities," Korithas said. "Those that roamed freely. Those that escaped the judgement

432

of the Veil. Energies too dangerous for Lyorion. The Prismalith fed on them. A silent shield between this world and the horrors beyond."

Lucy's eyes widened. Something in those words rang painfully familiar. "But something went wrong," she said quietly. "Didn't it."

The crystalline walls brightened. Light poured through them, revealing the fractured structure beneath. Along one side, dark veins snaked through the crystal, spreading like rot. Wherever they passed, the light faded.

"Indeed," Korithas said. "The dark energy contained within began to erode its strength. Slowly, it corrupted the Prismalith from the inside. Now it is only a shell of what it was. It can barely sustain the land around it. As it decays, the land decays with it."

A low vibration shook the stone under their feet.

"The storm that surrounds this island is its last defense," Korithas continued. "A deterrent. Its final effort to keep the mana here, to feed itself as long as it can, and to trap any dark entities it draws in. The Prismalith is desperate. It has been for many years. It clings to what little life it has left."

Nyla's shoulders sagged. A tear slipped down her cheek. "So it is dying," she said softly.

"Yes," Korithas answered. "Its light fades. When it goes dark, the last of my kind will pass with it."

It paused and turned to face them.

"I was created to guard the Prismalith," it said. "To protect the Veilgate from intruders. To watch. To wait. And to seek someone capable of taking up the mantle. A new guardian. A new life force to sustain what remains."

Silence settled over them. The weight of its words pressed in from all sides. This was not just an old machine breaking. This was the last remnant of a civilization asking for a replacement heart.

"And if no one is found?" Arlo asked. His voice was low. His mind drifted north, to the war that was brewing. South, to demons already clawing their way into the world. The thought of losing yet another protector made his chest hurt.

"Then the Veil will have no guardian," Korithas replied. "Dark souls will pass through more freely. The Prismalith will continue to drag in mana from anything it can touch. Even now, your own strength is weakened. Your power has been tasted and drawn in. It is searching for one who understands its purpose. Someone who can withstand its burden and defend this world from what lies within Penumbra."

Sorren had grown quiet as they walked. His hand rested on Justice. His eyes never stopped scanning the space around them.

"So it is a test of strength," he said.

Arlo shook his head. His steps slowed as they neared the center of the structure. "Not just strength," he said. "Will. Resolve. It feels like it has claimed a lot of lives looking for the right one."

"Precisely," the Shardkin said. Its arm shot out in a surprisingly quick motion to steady Arlo when he stumbled. "You seek to pass through the Veilgate and enter Penumbra. The Prismalith requires more than travelers. It seeks those who understand sacrifice. Those willing to face the darkness within and beyond the Veil."

"Was Eckerd not chosen when he passed through?" Lucy asked.

"Eckerd is powerful," Korithas answered. "He has many allies. Yet he has proven himself only as one who travels, not as the protector the Prismalith needs."

Ahead of them, a massive archway came into view. Old stone, overrun by creeping roots and veined through with crystal. Beside it, a huge crystalline mass rose from the floor, its veins spreading out through the walls, ceiling, and floor in every direction.

The mana inside it pulsed in shifting bands of color, flowing and circling like blood in a heart.

"It is like a heart," Sorren breathed. For a moment, his usual hard edge slipped, replaced by awe.

"Indeed," Korithas said. "But look closer. Mana should cycle through in a steady rhythm. Instead, when the dark current rises, the rest of it surges in pain."

As if answering the words, a surge of deep red mana tore through the Prismalith. The crystals shuddered. A low, mournful sound vibrated through the structure, like a distant cry for help. New cracks spread along the darker veins.

Without another word, Korithas led them closer. The ceiling loomed high above them, lost in shadow. Spiral staircases wound along the sides, each leading to small, hollow chambers cut into the walls. Arlo guessed those were the prisons. Cells where things once had been held that no one wanted to see again.

Still, it was the archway that held them.

Old. Powerful. Once separate from the Prismalith. Now fused with it. An extension of its body.

"Beyond this passage lies Penumbra," Korithas said. "For your own sake, remember this. The souls that were never privileged enough to ascend to Zenith reside there. Many are restless. Recently, a darkness has stirred among them. The balance has shifted. The souls seek something more."

Its gaze slid to Lucy and lingered there, as if it saw something it chose not to name.

"They now have another place they may go upon their death," it added. "That place is beyond my understanding."

Lucy took a step back. Her mind swirled. Fractured memories surfaced. A familiar chill seeped from the gate, the same cold pressure she had felt in dreams she could never quite recall when she woke.

Arlo tightened his grip on Elduun and stepped closer to her. His free hand found Lucy's, fingers lacing with hers. He could feel the tremor in her hand and squeezed gently.

They had come here together. They would go forward the same way.

435

He looked to Sorren and Nyla. Sorren met his gaze and gave a short, decisive nod.

"Nyla," Arlo said. "We understand if you do not want to go in with us."

She sat bent over, arms wrapped around her knees. All of this, talk of gods and dead worlds and cursed gates, had piled up until it nearly crushed her. She had left home for one reason. Her mother. A cure. That had felt small and simple compared to this.

Her breaths came fast and shallow. Her stomach churned.

"I... I..." She swallowed hard. "I need to..." She wanted to retch, to let the fear out any way she could. But that felt like another sign of weakness. The voices in her head had already given her enough of those.

Lucy led Arlo a step closer and reached her free hand toward Nyla. "If you want to go," she said gently, "we will be with you."

Nyla stared at Lucy's hand for a long moment. Then she reached out and took it.

"I do not think I am meant to be here," she said. "But I have come this far."

Sorren stood at the gate with Justice already drawn. He watched them approach, then turned his eyes to the archway again. None of this matched the stories he had grown up with. None of this fit neatly into sermons.

Arlo, Lucy, and Nyla stepped forward together, hand in hand. The closer they came, the louder the gate hummed. Elduun vibrated in Arlo's grip, as if recognizing an old presence.

He raised the hammer slowly. As he brought it in line with the Veilgate, a blinding light flared to life. A pulse of energy rolled outward, through the arch, into the Prismalith, and then out into the island itself. The ground thrummed under their feet. The crystals answered in waves, each one echoing the call.

The energy pressed against their skin. It felt like a hungry breath, inviting them in.

"So what?" Sorren said. His tone was dry, but there was a thread of nerves under it. "We just walk through and come out on the other side."

"Precisely," Korithas said. It gestured toward the arch.

They moved as one, drawing closer. Determination, fear, and reflection all sat together on their faces.

Just before they crossed the threshold, Korithas lifted one hand. A small crystal slid free from its forearm and dropped into its palm. It glowed with the same faint hum as the island around them.

"Take this," it said. "Carry it with you as you descend and seek the one you are searching for. The gate will not remain open. Our defenses against what lies within are not what they once were. This device will allow us to communicate while you travel. When you are ready to return, I will know, and I will open the gate long enough for you to come back."

Sorren stepped forward and accepted the crystal. He slipped it into a pouch at his side and tightened the flap.

He looked back at Korithas and gave the Shardkin a final nod.

Then, together, they turned to the gate, braced themselves for whatever waited beyond, and stepped into the Veil.

CHAPTER 43

The world around them crumbled.

Each step forward was a hesitation, as if the world they were leaving behind refused to let go. Korithas remained in view for a few lingering heartbeats, its form no longer humming and pulsing in tandem with the Prismalith and the heart of the island. With every step, that image dulled and faded, breaking apart into fragments of light that disappeared into cold darkness. The last traces of color were swallowed, like candlelight snuffed out by a chilling void.

For an instant, the world fell away. No ground, no sky, no sense of up or down. The universe itself seemed to cease to exist. There was nothing around them. Nothing beneath them. Nothing above them.

Nothingness. Except each other.

Their breath refused to come. It felt as if the emptiness had pressed into their lungs and stolen the ability to draw air at all. Warmth became a distant memory. Sensation faded to numbness. For a brief, paralyzing moment, Arlo was convinced this void would be the last thing he ever knew.

Then an invisible burst of wind brushed past them.

Air flooded their chests in a sharp rush. It was still cold, biting and thin, but it was air. They could breathe again. Their hearts pounded, reasserting themselves against whatever nothing had tried to claim them.

The pull of the Prismalith was gone.

Arlo felt it first. Not power, not a sudden surge, but the absence of that constant draining tug he had grown too familiar with. His body remained exhausted, but a thread of strength returned to him, enough to stand without Lucy's full support. Enough to lift Elduun and feel something stir in its core.

As the numbness retreated, reality twisted and bled back into shape.

The air was heavy and thick with an eerie tangibility. It felt wrong. Like the air itself was aware of them and resented their existence. There was a subtle pressure in it, a soft tug at their skin, a faint echo of the Prismalith's hunger, yet different. Less of a drain. More of a presence. Watching.

Shadows writhed at the edges of their vision, weaving in and out of jagged, twisted structures. The land resembled the Gauntlet in the vaguest of ways, a blend of crystal and natural stone, but warped into darker shapes. Where the Gauntlet had been strange, this was sick. Where it had been old, this felt wrong.

The ground beneath them was fractured and uneven. Blackened stone was cut through by faintly glowing veins of mana. The veins pulsed in irregular patterns, every flash a different color. Red. Blue. Gold. Sickly green. They did not follow any natural rhythm. They beat like the heart of something immense and unseen, yet not quite alive in any comforting way.

Above them was not a true sky. A swirling maelstrom of deep purples and blacks rolled overhead with endless motion. Violent streaks of gold, white, blue, and red ripped through it like lightning that never fully faded. A storm frozen in place, yet always shifting. No sun. No moon. No stars. Only chaos.

As they stood there, the amber amulet around Arlo's neck began to glow.

The light was faint at first, a small ember against the oppressive dark. Then it brightened, pulsing in a steady rhythm that did not match the erratic veins around them. The gem tugged gently against its chain, pulling toward some unseen distance.

Arlo raised his hand, fingers tightening around it. His gaze followed the direction it pulled.

"The amulet is glowing," he said. "And pulling. I wonder if it is leading us to Eckerd."

"Convenient," Sorren muttered.

"If not ominous," Nyla added quietly.

"It is like the Gauntlet, but…" Lucy's voice trembled. She stopped to swallow and steady herself. The feeling of unseen eyes on her skin made it hard to breathe. She could not see anyone, yet every instinct screamed that someone was there. Watching. Waiting. And beneath that dread, something else. Something that felt uncomfortably familiar.

"Twisted," Sorren finished for her, his grip tightening on Justice. "This place feels hungry."

Arlo staggered a step, bracing his weight on Elduun. His body still felt drained, but there was no longer that constant pull tugging his strength away, only the hollow echo left behind. Elduun pulsed faintly in his hands, a dim blue ember straining against the oppressive atmosphere.

"It is Penumbra," he said. "A reflection. But broken. A world no longer meant to be."

Akira hovered over Nyla, then descended onto her shoulder, curling his tail around the back of her neck. The small Draconis pressed its weight into her comfortingly. The swirling chaos above cast enough light for them to see a decent distance, but the twisted structures broke the light in strange ways, throwing long, jagged shadows.

Nyla took a few steps away to look around, fear keeping her quiet, although her mind roared with questions. Every surface, every stretch of jagged ground, felt like it held a story she did not want to hear.

Korithas' voice echoed faintly in their minds, a presence without form. The Shardkin was not with them, yet its words were clear, as if carried on the strange air itself.

"You are in the shadow of Lyorion. A prototype abandoned by its creators. Penumbra is a world of imperfection, twisted by chaos and by remnants of souls left to wander for eternity in the void. What you see is a fragment of a greater truth. A land that mirrors your own, but stripped of order. Decayed into its raw, primal form, where only the strongest survive."

Lucy took a step forward, and searing pain flared through her back.

It felt as if hot metal had been pressed into her skin, like something inside her was trying to claw its way out through her shoulder blades. The pain raced up her spine and stabbed into her temples. Along the edges of her forehead, a pressure built until it felt like bone itself strained to push outward.

She cried out, stumbling, catching herself against Arlo.

"Lucy? What is wrong?" he asked.

"It is nothing," she lied through uneven breaths. "This place is getting to me. Let us just go."

Her voice was thin, but she forced herself to stand upright. She would not collapse here. Not in front of them.

The group moved cautiously. The silence was never truly silent. Faint, guttural whispers drifted on the air, never clear enough to understand, but always close enough to unsettle them. The path rose and twisted, leading to a warped set of crystalline platforms that loomed like broken teeth.

"Do you hear that?" Nyla asked softly, her gaze never resting on one place for long.

They stopped and listened. The rustling sound had returned, weaving through the distant dark. A faint glint caught Sorren's eye. A single golden feather lay on the jagged ground ahead, shimmering faintly in the corrupted light.

Sorren knelt slowly and reached out. The moment his fingers brushed the feather, a sharp pulse of energy jolted through him. It was like grabbing a live wire of divine power that had been dragged through a swamp. Familiar yet tainted.

He dropped the feather immediately, grimacing.

"This is not right," he said.

Before anyone could answer, something moved in the distance.

A figure, vaguely humanoid, stood amid the swirling shadows. Its form glowed faintly with a golden hue, but it moved strangely, jerky and unnerving, like it was being yanked through its own body rather than walking of its own will.

"What is that?" Nyla whispered.

They raised their weapons. Arlo and Sorren stepped in front, forming a defensive line. The figure drifted closer, until it emerged enough to see more clearly.

It was tall and hunched. A skeletal frame wrapped in tattered shadows. Its face was obscured, the features hard to discern, but its eyes burned with an unnatural light that pierced the gloom. There was something predatory in the way it leaned forward, inhaling as if testing their scent.

Sorren glanced at the feather, his boot resting near it.

"The feather," he said. "It is Malik's. But this thing... it is not him. I do not think so."

The creature let out a rasp that sounded like stones grinding together.

"Food."

Before they could react, it lunged.

Its limbs stretched forward with unnatural speed, claws reaching. The group scattered, instinct taking over as weapons came up.

Sorren moved with practiced precision. Justice sang through the air, cleaving one of the creature's shadowy limbs as it lashed at him. The limb shredded into tatters of darkness that writhed and then dissipated.

Another similar creature burst from the left, lunging toward Arlo. Its body was a mangled blend of leathery hide and shadow. Arlo raised Elduun and met the strike, deflecting it just enough to knock the creature away. It shrieked, black wings unfurling, jagged and torn at the edges. It dove again. Arlo swung Elduun with all of his might. The hammer erupted in a flare of brilliant blue light, slamming into the creature's chest with a thunderclap. The impact cracked the ground and sent a ripple of force outward.

The creature tore free at the last second, its body bending in unnatural angles as it escaped into the shadows, leaving a smear of dark residue behind.

"Demons!" Sorren shouted. His voice was a mix of fury and disbelief. "I thought they were myths. Stories to frighten children."

"Not myths," Arlo hissed, blocking another strike. The creature's claws wrapped around the head of the hammer, tendrils of shadow writhing along Elduun's surface. "They feel real enough."

Nyla steadied herself, dagger ready, watching for any more that might crawl out of the dark. Her heart hammered. Akira screeched and launched into the air, icy shards forming in his mouth.

"Akira, wait!" she shouted.

He did not. A volley of ice shards tore toward a third demon that had crept closer. The shards pierced its shadowy flesh, forcing a snarl out of it. Another darted past Akira, streaking toward Nyla with its teeth bared.

Nyla barely had time to raise her dagger. The steel met the row of jagged fangs with a screech, sparks flying as black blood dripped over her knuckles. The creature thrashed, and her grip slipped. Its teeth snapped down, grazing her wrist, and she fell back with a cry.

Akira dived, claws sinking into the demon's back. Another blast of ice erupted point blank through its body. The demon convulsed and went limp beside her.

The last of the immediate creatures swarmed Lucy.

They came at her in a flurry of claws and teeth. Instinct took control. Flames roared to life in her hands, hotter and faster than she had ever called them before. The pain in her back surged as her magic flared, but she pushed through. Fire washed over the demon and forced it back with a shriek.

"Correct," Korithas' voice answered in the midst of battle, calm and oddly steady. "These are demons. Souls twisted and made whole by darkness and chaotic energies."

"Not helpful right now," Sorren shouted, parrying a demon's kick. Its claws scraped along his armor with a teeth-grinding screech.

"My apologies," Korithas said. "Carry on with your engagement."

Sorren grunted in annoyance, then seized an opening. He hooked his arm around the demon's leg, dragging it off balance and slamming it into the ground. Justice fell in a clean stroke. Blackened blood sprayed as the demon shuddered and fell still.

The whispering around them grew louder.

Arlo hammered another demon in the chest. Its form exploded outward into a spreading cloud of shadow, hissing as it dissolved. His lungs burned. Every breath felt heavier, the strange air weighing him down.

Nyla and Akira moved in clumsy tandem. She swung her dagger at the last remaining demon harrying her. It was not a clean strike, but it was enough to distract it, enough for Akira to slam into its side and shred it with claws and ice.

Lucy faced her foe with a heat that outmatched its malice. Her flames surged higher, wrapping around the demon in spirals of crimson fire. It screeched, body breaking apart as the flames devoured it until all that remained were drifting scraps of smoke.

Silence crept back in, broken only by the occasional distant skittering and whisper that threaded through the dark.

They straightened slowly. Sorren scanned their surroundings for any further movement. Arlo and Nyla tried to catch their breath. The air burned in their lungs, not from running, but from something in the very nature of Penumbra.

They pushed on.

The crystalline fractures on the ground began to shimmer as they walked. Light skittered along them in thin threads, reacting to their presence. Visions flickered across the surface, refracting like light through broken glass.

Sorren stopped abruptly.

A pale, spectral reflection of himself stood within the fractured surface of one of the crystals. The image grew clearer, spreading out of the shard and into the air around them, painting the space with a scene that did not belong here.

He stood on the deck of a ship beneath a starlit sky.

His breath caught. The vision sharpened. It was not any ship. It was his ship. The Sea Sentinel cut through the waves, worn in all the right ways, every scar on her hull a story. The salt spray hit his face, and for a moment he forgot Penumbra, forgot the demons, forgot the Gauntlet. His chest ached with a sudden, painful longing.

There he was, at the helm, smiling. Free. No king. No bishop. No divine expectations. Just tide and stars.

The vision shifted.

The sea became a fiery battlefield. The Sentinel lay grounded along a ruined shore, flames chewing through her hull. Steel clashed in the background. Men and women screamed. Sorren was no longer at the helm. He stood in a council chamber instead, sword raised in salute. The Archbishop praised his "zeal and dedication to Heir's Justice."

The faces of the council twisted. Their features blurred and warped into masks of greed and hunger.

"Justice," one of the twisted figures hissed. The voice slithered into his ears. "Is that what you think you serve? Or do you serve us, Sorren?"

His grip tightened on Justice.

"This is not real," he whispered under his breath. "It is a trick. A lie."

The scene twisted again. The Archbishop grew larger, looming over everyone else. In one hand he held a scepter of lightning. In the other, a crown. Behind him, peasants knelt in the dirt, hollow and hungry. Soldiers shoved them away when they reached for help.

At the Archbishop's side stood a paladin clad in immaculate white plate, the same armor Sorren had once admired. But when the figure turned, the face beneath the helm was not a stranger's.

It was his.

His own grey eyes stared back at him, laced with sparks of gold and lightning. One hand rested on Justice, the other gripped a chain that snaked out to a line of followers, each with a collar bearing Heir's symbol. Each kneeling. Each bound.

"The strong must guide the weak," Dolph's voice echoed, oily and smooth. "For they cannot guide themselves."

"Guide them?" Sorren rasped. "You do not guide them. You use them."

The Archbishop's image swelled, laughter spilling from his mouth in a cruel wave.

"You are nothing without us," the echo of his voice said. "A pawn. A zealot who mistakes blind faith for purpose. You think the sea is freedom. It is just another lie fishermen tell themselves once they realize they still serve me. When they could serve you."

The vision shifted again.

The council vanished. The waves returned. Sorren stood on the deck of the Sea Sentinel once more. For a heartbeat, he felt true peace.

446

The tide beneath his boots. The open horizon. No sermons. No symbols.

Then the sky went black.

The sea turned into a pit. Chains formed out of water, wrapping around his wrists, his ankles, his throat, dragging him down into the endless dark.

"Sorren!"

Arlo's voice cut through the illusion like a thrown rope. "Stay focused. It is a trick. A vision meant to break you."

Sorren sucked in a harsh breath. The crystalline ground was under his boots again. The images melted away.

Ahead, Nyla let out a startled cry.

Her own reflection shimmered in the crystal, then grew outward, forming another scene that pulled tight around them.

A younger Nyla clung to the shadow of her mother. Her Elfar ears peeked out from beneath strands of blue-tinted hair her mother had carefully pulled over them. The older woman watched the window, worried, always listening, always guarding. Nyla had always thought she knew why. Now the vision showed her more than she ever wanted.

The colors in the vision turned red.

Nyla, now a little older, cried in a corner of their small home. Outside, torchlight flickered. Figures with pitchforks and clubs pounded on the door. Her mother braced her body against it, but the wood cracked and splintered.

"Abomination," a man shouted as he forced his way in. Another followed, torch raised high. "Tainted blood."

Flames leapt to the curtains. Nyla watched as fire spread throughout the vision. Her hands shook. Her knees hit the ground in the present, dagger clattering beside her. The sound echoed louder than it should have.

"It is not real," she whispered to herself. "It is not real."

Her mother's figure stepped forward in the vision, face twisted by grief and illness. The woman looked down at vision-Nyla, eyes brimming with tears.

"It is your fault I am like this," her mother said. Her voice carried across the illusion, merging with the whispers of the realm. "If I was not forced to birth a bloody Elfar, I would not be sick. I would not be at risk. Always hiding. Always lying. Always carrying you."

Nyla's heart splintered.

The others saw the vision as well, but Sorren's focus locked on one detail.

The ears.

Elfar ears. Not hidden, but plain, in a girl that looked exactly like the young woman who had boarded his ship. The realization crashed into him, carrying the weight of every lesson he had grown up with. Every sermon. Every story.

He had let an Elfar onto his ship. Carried her into the Gauntlet. Into Penumbra. Into a realm tied to the gods themselves. And he had done it on the word of Arlo and Lucy.

His jaw clenched. The vows he had sworn rose up in his mind, whispering hard commands into his bones. They clashed with the memory of Nyla's fear, of her shaky laughter, of her quiet courage.

The vision shifted again.

Nyla knelt over her mother's lifeless body on the floor of their home. Flames licked at the walls. Outside, villagers screamed for her death. Akira, younger and smaller, tore at them with furious claws and teeth, protecting her as long as he could.

"No," Nyla whispered, clutching her chest. "I left to save her. Not to..."

Her voice broke.

Sorren's knuckles turned white. Justice trembled in his grip. The weight of command and the reality before him crashed together.

"Nyla," he growled. His voice held a dangerous edge she had never heard before. "You are an Elfar."

448

The words hung in the air like a blade waiting to drop.

Nyla turned, eyes wide and wet. Purple irises, ringed with red from crying, locked with his. She saw it there. The disgust. The fear. The sense of betrayal. Exactly what she had been warned of. Exactly what she had spent her life hiding from.

Her fingers closed around the dagger on the ground.

"Behind you," she choked out.

Sorren turned on instinct.

A massive demon had swooped in behind him, claws reaching. Justice moved in a smooth, practiced arc. The blade tore through leathery flesh. Ichor sprayed, hot and foul, the smell like burnt oil and rot.

The creature stumbled, then shifted its path toward Nyla. Its obsidian claws gleamed. Its crimson eyes locked onto her.

Akira threw himself between them again, colliding mid-air with the demon, the two spiraling through the air in a blur of scales and shadow.

Sorren hesitated.

Nyla was on the ground, bleeding from her side, hood fallen back, ears fully exposed. The demon was a threat, monstrous and obvious, but the indoctrinated part of his mind whispered that the true danger was at his feet.

The crystalline visions bled further across the walls around him. The snow-capped mountains. The massive white and blue serpentlike Draconis coiled around someone that looked like Nyla, sharing a knowing smirk. Another Draconis landed beside the first, dark scaled with blue-tipped edges, treasure piled around them like offerings.

"Sorren, help her!" Arlo's shout tore through the fog.

Another demon swooped in and caught Nyla across the ribs. She cried out, tumbling through the dirt, her hood flying away completely. There was no hiding now. Her Elfar heritage blazed beneath the strange light.

"She is an Elfar," Sorren whispered. Not to them. To himself. To the part of him that clung to old vows.

Visions began to crawl across his sight again. Dolph and Brother Jason appeared within the fractured crystal around him, both shouting the old words of his oath. Demons and Elfar blurred together in his mind. Orders mingled with instinct.

He raised his blade. Justice pointed at Nyla.

"Sorren, slay her," the Archbishop's voice commanded from the illusion. The words echoed everywhere and nowhere. They felt both far away and right at his ear.

"Sorren, help her!" Arlo's real voice shouted.

The illusion faltered. Dolph's face twisted and peeled away, revealing the snarling maw of another demon lunging for Sorren.

Justice flashed, cleaving the creature in two. Black blood sprayed, and a snarl tore out of Sorren's throat as the haze lifted for a brief, painful moment.

Behind him, Nyla struggled to her feet. She pressed a hand against her bleeding side. Tears streaked down her face. She looked at Sorren, seeing every doubt, every instinct to turn on her, laid bare.

"I..." she began, but another demon emerged.

Lucy stepped forward.

Fire already flickered in her hands. It did not feel entirely like her own. It felt like it belonged to something older and more dangerous, something that was only wearing her body.

The demons before her shifted. One moment they were twisted beasts. The next, they were winged beings of white and gold, radiant and sharp. Angels. Warriors of light. Yet every part of her recoiled when she saw them.

Deep inside, Lucy knew the truth.

They were not angels. They were demons dressed in the shape of holiness. Penumbra and the Prismalith had twisted them into things that looked like they belonged in Zenith, yet their eyes were hollow, predatory, and wrong. They were everything from her nightmares made real. Not because they existed, but because they reflected what she feared she was.

The world around her blurred. The battlefield beneath her feet stretched and changed, merging with the scenes she had dreamed of for years. She saw herself again, standing over a field of broken-winged beings. Their eyes bled. Their bodies smoldered. Flames dripped from her hands. Their wings lay in shreds at her feet.

This time, she did not simply witness the nightmare. She felt it.

Heat surged through her back.

Pain ripped across her shoulder blades as if something inside her tore free. She screamed as flames burst out of her spine in violent arcs, taking shape. Fire twisted into the outline of wings, skeletal frames of bone made of flame, every feather a blade of heat that dripped molten embers.

Her head throbbed. A brutal pressure spiked at her temples. A sharp crack sounded in the air as something pushed through. Two fiery horns curled from her temples, jagged and smoldering, as if they had always been there, waiting for permission to exist.

Her skin rippled with patches of deep vermilion that crept across her neck and arms.

"Lucy!" Arlo shouted.

She heard him. Somewhere far away. But she could not reach that sound. The chant of the false angels drowned him out.

"Creature of ruin," they called in unison. "Destroyer of all that is good."

Every word stoked the fire.

"You will never be anything more."

She roared and let the flames go.

Hellfire exploded from her hands, from her wings, from every place her magic could escape. The demons, or angels, or whatever they were, were consumed. Their silhouettes writhed within the fire, laughing even as they burned.

The ground shook. The others watched as those angelic shapes dropped to their knees, bodies contorting between the illusion of holy figures and the reality of demonic forms. Through it all, they knelt in front of Lucy, their golden eyes locked on her in twisted reverence.

"No," she whispered.

Then louder.

"No!"

She drowned them in fire.

The hellfire was beyond what any normal enemy should withstand, but these creatures fed on it. They were drawn to her, to the ruin she represented, to the power that refused to be clean or simple. Tears spilled down her cheeks and burned into trails of blood as the heat from her own wings licked along her skin.

She clutched the flaming bones at her back, as if trying to tear them free.

Sorren stared at her, horror creeping into every line of his face.

"Demon," he whispered. The word escaped before he could swallow it. Then it rose again, louder this time. "You are a demon."

Lucy turned to him.

Her eyes were no longer her soft green. They glowed a deep, burning crimson that matched the demons they had fought. Yet there was pain there. Fear. Desperation.

"Sorren, please," she said. Her voice was small. Raw. She hugged her own arms, wings flaring and dimming with her breath. "I am still me."

Sorren took a step back.

"You have been hiding this from us," he said. "You claimed you did not know anything. All this time, you have been…"

"Enough."

Arlo's voice cut across both of them. Hoarse, but firm. His body ached. Blood marked his armor and skin from multiple wounds. Several demonic corpses lay at his feet, each one proof that he had not stopped fighting even as everything else fell apart.

He stepped between Sorren and Lucy, Elduun still in hand.

"It does not matter what she looks like," Arlo said. "She is still one of us. Same as Nyla. They are still the same people they were before."

"She is a demon," Sorren snapped. His voice rose, full of frustration and disbelief. "They are all demonic beasts. They should be put to the blade of Justice."

"I am still me," Lucy repeated, her voice breaking. The flames around her dipped and surged as if caught between fight and retreat.

She could not hold it anymore.

The weight of Sorren's accusation. The kneeling demons. The visions she just relieved. The fear of Arlo finally seeing her as she feared he would. It all bore down at once.

With a choked cry, Lucy spread her burning wings wide and pushed off the ground.

The fire carried her, hurling her into the sky. Blood streaked from the points where the wings met flesh. She shot forward in a streak of flame, cutting through the heavy air of Penumbra like a comet that refused to fall. A trail of smoldering embers marked her path.

"Lucy!" Arlo shouted after her.

She did not look back.

The air fell still around them for a heartbeat. Just long enough for the absence of her presence to be felt. Then the land answered with its own fury.

The ground trembled.

A guttural roar rolled across Penumbra, deeper and more menacing than any they had heard so far. Shadows in the distance began to shift, thickening and rising. Cracks split the crystalline ground, and something massive pushed through.

A draconic figure emerged.

It was a monstrous amalgamation of scales and shadow. Wingless, yet towering. Its body radiated rage like heat. Molten eyes burned from within its skull, focused and unblinking. Each step shook the broken landscape. Claws gouged deep scars in the stone, carving through whatever remained of the illusory city around them.

Another roar tore through the air.

The vision twisted again. Buildings flickered into place around them. The familiar layout of Fall Lake appeared, broken and distorted, as if someone had tried to recreate it from memory and failed. Houses bent at wrong angles. Streets twisted. The smell of smoke and blood rushed into Arlo's nose.

"No," he whispered.

The draconic beast ripped through the warped buildings. People screamed in the illusion. Half-chewed bodies scattered the streets. Blood rained through the air. It was Fall Lake. It was not. It was worse.

Arlo charged.

Elduun swung in an arc that met the beast's claw. The impact shook everything, sending a shockwave through the city and cracking the false stone beneath them. The illusions fluttered at the edges, like a painting being torn.

Sorren stood frozen. Demons, Elfar, Lucy's wings, the beast of Fall Lake. The teachings of the church. His own doubts. All of it spun together until he did not know where to stand.

"What do we do now?" Nyla asked. Her voice trembled. She pressed one hand to her wounded side, the other clutched at the ground to keep her balance. The beast circled Arlo, each step a reminder of how small they were.

Arlo leapt, meeting another strike. The beast's claws screeched against Elduun. Pain screamed through his arms, but he forced his voice louder than it.

"We fight," he said.

The answer came, not in words, but in intent.

And you will lose.

The battle went on in a blur of chaos. The draconic beast moved with terrible force, carving through the illusionary buildings as if they

454

were paper. Every attack from Arlo chipped away at its shadowed form, yet the beast only seemed to grow more focused, more enraged.

"Nyla, behind you!" Arlo shouted.

She turned just in time to duck beneath a lash of dark energy that whipped out from the beast. The tendril carved through the ground where her head had been. Akira leapt, claws digging into the beast's side, tearing at scaled shadow.

They were thrown back by one sweep of its massive claw.

Sorren still stood, Justice loose in his hands. His eyes bounced between Nyla, bleeding and panting, and the creature in front of them. Between the Elfar he had been told to hate and the obvious monster trying to tear them apart.

"What is the point of this?" he whispered. "Justice. Faith. It is all twisted. What am I even fighting for anymore."

"Sorren!"

Arlo's voice cut through the rising fog in his mind once again.

"I do not care what is going through your head. We need you. Fight now. Questions later."

The words hit like a slap. Sorren drew a breath, then another. He raised Justice, stepping forward. His movements were not as sure as they once had been, but he moved all the same.

Unmotivating.

The whisper dug into Arlo's thoughts, but he pushed it aside. He cast a quick look at Nyla.

"Nyla, stay with me," he said, shifting his stance to shield her.

"I am trying," she gasped. Blood seeped between her fingers as she pressed on the wound under her ribs. Akira stood in front of her, lips peeled in a snarl, every muscle tense.

Never will you be worthy.

The amber amulet at Arlo's neck pulsed again. The glow brightened, as if reacting to the approaching danger. It tugged toward another direction deeper into Penumbra, but the beast was in front of him now, not wherever the amulet pulled.

455

The creature opened its maw.

A torrent of dark energy erupted, searing the air, rushing toward them. Arlo did not think. He slammed Elduun into the ground. Light flared out, forming a barrier. The shield of shimmering energy absorbed the brunt of the blast, but every second it held sent pain up his arms and through his chest. His knees buckled.

Failure.

The shield cracked and dissipated. The beast roared and lunged, punching through the remnants of the illusion around them. Buildings fell apart like shards of glass, revealing more broken space beneath.

Arlo swung again. Elduun blazed. Every blow tore chunks of shadow out of the beast. Yet it remained. Stubborn. Relentless. The more he fought, the heavier the hammer felt. His strength was bleeding away with every breath.

"Stay focused," he called. "We can…"

A thunderous impact cut him off.

The beast recoiled as a new light pierced the sky above them.

Golden light tore through the swirling dark, clean and sharp. A form descended from it, wings spread wide. Radiance poured off him like a waterfall. The realm itself seemed to shrink in his presence.

Malik.

The Deva of Heir descended with a slow, terrifying grace. His wings arched like blades of sunlight, each feather shimmering. Golden armor hugged his form, polished and unmarred by any blade. His gaze swept the battlefield with a divine intensity that made everything else feel cheap and small.

In his hand, he held a blade of pure light. It hummed with power, a sound that settled in their bones.

Arlo's heart sank.

This was no illusion. The realm shifted around Malik, not the other way around. His presence was suffocating.

"You wield Elduun," Malik said.

456

His voice echoed as if it came from everywhere at once, not just his mouth. Each word carried the weight of judgement. "And yet you stumble. Unworthy and frail. Do you think Heir does not see? Do you think you can hold what is not yours and avoid judgement?"

The beast that had seemed so ferocious before cowered.

Its molten eyes dimmed. Its body faded, dissolving into streams of shadow that fled from Malik's presence. The draconic shape tore apart into a storm of darkness and scattered into the distance.

Around them, visions of Fall Lake surged in return. The city lay broken again. Bodies. Fire. Screams. The worst moments of that day replayed in sharper detail than ever before, as if Malik's presence dragged every hidden memory into the open.

Arlo steadied his grip on Elduun. Every wound on his body burned. His muscles shook.

"I do not fight for Heir," he said. He did not raise his voice, but it carried all the same. "I fight for them. For the people who need someone to stand for them."

And how many have fallen because of it?

The world flickered again.

For an instant, he saw a small cottage. A blonde woman lay on a bed, drenched in sweat. A man in a worn uniform stood nearby, helpless. Several women gathered around, helping as she cried out in pain.

A baby's cry pierced the air.

The woman's breaths slowed. Her eyes softened. She held the child, even as her life faded.

Arlo did not know how he knew, but he knew.

She was his mother. He had never seen her. Not really. Not like this. Yet he knew.

"Hope guides you," she whispered.

The words never truly formed in the air, yet he heard them. Or remembered them. Or imagined them. It did not matter. They reached him.

Malik's eyes narrowed with a faint, cruel smirk.

"You claim to fight for hope," the Deva said. "Yet you are consumed by fear. Doubt. Despair. You break yourself for others because you cannot bear to face the emptiness within. Do not think you deceive me, human. The gods see all."

He raised his blade and pointed it at Arlo.

"Prove yourself. Or fall."

The battlefield went still.

Sorren and Nyla stood frozen, each wrestling with their own demons, their own doubts, but neither able to ignore Malik's presence.

Arlo felt his wounds. Felt his fears. Felt his failures.

He also felt the hammer in his hands.

He squared his shoulders and lifted Elduun, even though his body screamed for rest.

"If I fall," he said, voice rough, "then I will fall standing for what I believe in."

Malik's lips curled into a colder smile.

"Then let us see," he replied, "if your faith in yourself can stand against the will of the divine."

He moved.

The Deva descended in an instant, golden blade cutting through the air as he launched himself toward Arlo.

CHAPTER 44

The same blonde boy was brought to a larger building, a place that smelled of old wood and boiled stew, home to other children who no longer had parents. He had no mother, and his father had died while away. The boy felt hollow as he walked in, like someone had scooped everything out of him and left only skin and bone.

Several scenes from the orphanage flickered through the air around Arlo, layered over Penumbra like sheets of glass. The boy lashed out against the matrons, stepping between them and the smaller children. He took the beatings. The lashings. The days of no food. The cramped dark room. Again and again the visions repeated, yet all at once, as if Penumbra and the Prismalith were working together to orchestrate his torment.

You break yourself for others because you cannot bear to face the emptiness within you.

The voice slithered through his mind, curling into the dark corners of his heart. It was not just memory. It felt alive, taunting him, feeding on him.

Arlo gritted his teeth, but the words burrowed deeper, tangling with other whispers that had always been there. They had lived in him for years, quiet and patient, growing louder whenever he faltered. Now they were no longer whispers.

They were a roar.

You are not enough. You will always fail them, like you have failed everyone before.

The view shifted again, faster now, sharper and more vivid. The boy stood in the main hall as families walked in. Each time, other children were chosen, plucked from the dim life of the orphanage and placed into homes that smelled of bread and safety.

But not him. Never him.

No matter how often he protected the others, no matter how hard he fought, he and his closest friend were left behind, year after year, season after season.

Who would want a child so burdened, reckless, and unruly.

Another shift.

His friend sobbed as the matrons dragged her down the hall, her thin legs scraping across the floor. The sound of the lash striking her skin cracked through the scene like a hammer on stone, each hit cutting deeper than the last. The boy tried to intervene, but the matrons shoved him back like he weighed nothing.

"You are the reason she is here," the matrons said together, voices blending into one echo. "If only you would behave. Maybe then someone would take her."

Arlo's fists clenched so tightly his knuckles turned white. The scenes bled into one another, the girl's screams never stopping, only overlapping. The matrons' cruel laughter mingled with the murmurs of families turning away. The walls of the dark isolation room loomed closer, suffocating him as his mind sank back to that time.

You are hiding behind your anger. Behind your defiance. You think it makes you strong, but it only masks your weakness.

His vision blurred with tears. The walls of the orphanage dissolved, giving way to a sky that was too dark and too close. Shadows of Penumbra twisted and threaded themselves through the next scene.

The boy was older now.

He stood over a massive Draconis beast. The city around him lay in ruin. Bodies were strewn across the ground, some partially buried in rubble, some broken beyond recognition. Their hollow eyes stared up at him, accusing and empty. Every face a reminder of what he had not been fast enough to prevent.

Arlo fell to his knees.

The weight of the visions pressed down on him like stone. The core of Elduun flickered in his hand, blue light sparking weakly, then vanishing as it touched his skin. It struggled to reach him, but he was slipping away. His breath came in ragged pulls. The voices did not relent.

His body grew heavier, every injury flaring. For the first time, he truly felt Elduun's weight. It was not just a symbol. It was a burden. He struggled even to lift it in time.

You are nothing. You will always be a lost hope in the void. You cannot save yourself. You cannot save your friends. You cannot save anyone.

He felt the darkness close in around him, thick and cold. For a moment, he believed every word. He felt the emptiness. He felt alone. The crushing weight of failure pressed on his chest, of always being a little too late, a little too small to make a difference.

Gold rushed toward him.

For a heartbeat, he was ready to let it happen. To let it end here. To let this false hero die so that maybe, somewhere, a true one could rise.

Then, somewhere deep within, something sparked.

461

It was not loud. It was not strong. But it was there.

A whisper of the defiance that had carried him this far. The same whisper that had led him up the tower where Elduun came to his hands. The same whisper that made him stand up when older boys pushed him down, made him take blows meant for others, made him refuse to stay in the dark room.

He would not let that spark of hope die.

A blinding light seared through the shadows as Malik's voice boomed, dragging Arlo violently back to the present.

"Is this your strength? Cowering before illusions? How utterly disappointing."

The Deva's radiant form cut through the lingering visions like a blade. Golden light and white lightning tore away the last edges of the nightmare. Malik advanced, golden blade in hand, movements precise and measured. His voice rang sharp, dripping with disdain.

"Pathetic," he said. "To think the likes of you would dare wield such a weapon."

Arlo staggered to his feet. The weight of Elduun anchored him in place when the rest of his body wanted to give in. He raised the hammer out of instinct more than strength, hiding the sluggishness of limbs torn by wounds and strain.

"Do you even comprehend what you hold?" Malik continued, tilting his head back slightly, eyes narrowed in cold superiority. "That hammer is not a shield for the weak. It is a beacon for those worthy to wield its power. And you are not."

Malik closed the distance in a heartbeat.

His strikes came swift and unrelenting. Arlo barely deflected the first blow. The force of it sent him skidding backward through dust and cracked crystal. The clang of light-blade against metal rang through Penumbra, bright and painful.

"You think flailing that thing around makes you some sort of hero?" Malik sneered. "No. You are nothing but a pawn. A hollow vessel pulling a veil over his own eyes."

462

Arlo groaned as he sidestepped the next attack. Elduun flared faintly, but the power within it felt muted, as though it refused to answer fully. He swung the hammer in return, slower than he would have liked. Malik twisted away as if he had known exactly how and when the attack would come. His boot slammed into Arlo's chest, sending him crashing back to one knee.

Pain scoured through him, old wounds and new screaming together. His body begged him to stop. His grip nearly slipped from Elduun's haft. Malik towered above him, cold and unshaken.

"You reek of failure," Malik said. The blade lowered until the tip rested at Arlo's throat. "Shall I carve it into your chest so you never forget?"

Arlo tightened his hold on the hammer. A glimmer of sapphire mana flickered along its surface, answering the faint spark in his own eyes.

"I am not done yet," he managed.

He pushed himself to his feet, the blade never leaving his throat, but he did not look away and he did not back down.

Malik laughed.

The sound was like a bell tolling at an execution. Clear. Cruel. Final.

"Then allow me to educate you on the depth of your insignificance."

He raised his free hand.

The air warped around him, folding in on itself as a storm began to coil into existence. The remnants of Arlo's visions were sucked into it, twisted and shredded until they broke apart into light and shadow. The storm churned into something that was not like the storms Arlo knew. This one burned with holy lightning and divine radiance, uncaring and absolute.

Far above, beyond Malik's storm, the sky of Penumbra groaned. Another storm, distant but coming fast, crawled across the swirling dark. Its presence did not belong to Malik, but it was drawn toward them all the same.

"Behold," Malik's voice thundered. "The will of Heir made manifest. You stand before a servant of the highest order, of the God of Gods, and you dare defy him."

Lightning lashed out from the storm, tendrils of golden energy snaking down toward Arlo. He raised Elduun and met the first few strikes. They crashed into the hammer and were pulled into its surface, absorbed in bright flashes that rattled his bones.

More followed.

They came faster, stronger, more precise. Once Arlo began to regain his footing, the lightning turned vicious. Tendrils struck at his legs, his sides, his shoulders. They wrapped around him like whips, yanking him off balance and dragging him closer. Each time Malik's blade met him at the end of those pulls, crashing into his body with ruthless efficiency.

These bolts were not some distant divine command. They were Malik himself. His will. His power. He had no doubt, no hesitation, no fear.

"You cannot fight what you cannot comprehend," Malik said, contempt lacing every word. "Each strike reminds you of your place in this world. A speck beneath the heel of the divine."

Arlo snarled and swung the hammer in a wide arc, severing one of the tendrils. It snapped apart and dissolved into glittering dust.

For every one he destroyed, two more appeared.

They ripped at his skin, sank into his muscles, tore at everything inside him that dared to stand. He felt like he was being peeled apart, piece by piece.

"Prepare to be extinguished."

Justice flew through the battlefield in Sorren's hands, carving down one demon after another. The air was thick with the stench of sulfur and the metallic taste of blood. Claw and steel collided in bursts of sparks. Each impact traveled up his arm, pushing him on to the next strike.

The noise and chaos did nothing to quiet his thoughts.

Even seeing Arlo's visions, even watching the Deva's storm tear through Penumbra, only added more weight to the questions crushing him.

"Sorren! Behind you!" Nyla shouted.

He moved before he thought, pivoting and raising Justice to meet the leaping demon. Its claws slammed against the blade, forcing him back a step. He grunted and pushed through, slicing through its torso in a clean follow-up. Black ichor sprayed across his armor before the creature hit the ground with a guttural snarl.

Sorren did not turn to acknowledge Nyla.

"I had it," he said, voice flat, almost empty.

"You are welcome," Nyla replied, breath strained. Her dagger trembled in her hand. Her stance faltered as pain from her wound flared up her side. If not for Akira circling her like a shield, she was certain she would already be dead.

Every demon that lunged out of the shadows carried the same face to her. Torches. Pitchforks. Wide, hateful eyes. A crowd surging toward a door her mother could not hold forever.

Sorren's mind was just as tangled.

Lucy's twisted visage burned in his thoughts. The wings of fire. The horns. The demons kneeling before her as if she were their queen. The woman who had healed Arlo. The woman who had laughed with them on the ship. The woman who had stood on his deck, small and human.

Had she ever been just human.

Did Arlo know all along. Should the church have sensed something. Should he.

Then Nyla's ears. Pale, pointed, unmistakable. Why was she on his ship. Why had he agreed. What was Heir doing. Why would the Deva descend only to try to break the man who wielded Elduun, if the hammer had truly been bestowed by divine will.

None of it made sense.

He let out a roar and split another demon in two. Justice's edge clipped close enough to Nyla's hair that a few strands of pale blue fluttered to the ground. She cried out in surprise.

"Sorren, I…"

"Focus on staying alive," he snapped, cutting her off.

His tone was colder than the blade he held. He turned away before she could answer, searching for the next threat. Glancing toward where Arlo and Malik fought, he caught sight of something, a different kind of light threading through the storm.

The amulet at Arlo's neck shone with a brilliant amber pulse. It tugged, insistent, toward some distant point in Penumbra.

Sorren had no time for it.

They could not chase Eckerd while they were barely surviving. They would not find anyone if they all died here.

Akira barked sharply, snapping Sorren's attention back. Several demons hurled themselves forward in a coordinated rush, sliding past the Draconis and rushing Nyla. She lifted her dagger in a clumsy, shaky guard, striking too early and too wide. Her balance faltered.

Sorren gritted his teeth.

He grabbed his cape and swung it around her, pulling her in and turning his body to shield her. With Justice in one hand, he let out a roar and tore through the rushing demons in a single sweeping arc. Limbs and shadows flew. The ground shook with their impact.

He let her go and barely glanced down, but the look was enough. Judgment. Frustration. Fear. Then he turned away again.

Akira darted to Nyla's side as she slumped down upon a crystal formation, clutching her bleeding side.

Nyla knew she was a liability.

She was not a warrior. She had no training like Sorren, no divine weapon like Arlo. She hated how Sorren looked at her, like she was a fragile mistake, like her blood was something that made her less. It bit into her more deeply than any demon's claw, but she refused to let him see her break.

Malik's blade hovered in the air, ready to fall.

Gold energy radiated from his entire form. Arlo's lungs rasped in broken gasps. Sweat and blood blurred his sight. Every breath felt like glass in his chest.

"Why do you persist?" Malik asked. "Is it pride? Foolishness? Or have you convinced yourself you are their savior?"

"You do not understand," Arlo said, pulling himself upright again.

"It is not about being their savior. It is about standing together. Even when it feels impossible."

Malik smiled.

It was not kind.

"A noble lie you tell yourself. Nobility does not absolve incompetence. You are weak, Arlo. The world suffers for your inability to act."

The words cut deeper than any wound. Arlo's grip wavered. His knees buckled. Malik did not wait.

He stepped forward once, smooth and sure. Arlo did not even see the full motion, only the blur of gold.

The blade punched clean through his shoulder.

White-hot pain exploded through him. He felt the metal wedge into bone and muscle. Malik planted a foot on his chest and drove him to the ground. Elduun flew from his grasp, skidding away.

His body screamed from every direction. His head spun. For a moment, he was not sure where his limbs were, if they were even still attached to him.

Malik leaned down and twisted the sword.

"Weak," he said again. "The word repeated, dripping from his tongue. "Worthless. Heir was wise to cast you aside."

Arlo's eyes snapped open.

He forced himself to focus on Malik's face, even through the haze of agony.

"What do you mean?" he managed.

"Do you think you were chosen? That Heir looks upon you with favor?" Malik said. "No, Arlo. You are an accident. A mistake. Proof that Hope is meaningless."

Arlo's heart dropped.

The visions of his childhood pressed in again. The lash. The dark room. The faces in Fall Lake. The roar of the beast. The people he could not save. The feeling of always arriving at the edge of disaster, never fully ahead of it.

He had stood on the ruins of Fall Lake as the Hero, not because he wanted the title, but because they needed someone to stand. He had walked into Davenport with Hope on his lips, because he could not stand to see them break without trying.

Yet here he was, bleeding on the black ground of a world that should never have existed, in a place he should never have been able to reach.

Malik twisted the blade again.

Sparks crawled along the edge as lightning gathered there. Each shift ripped new lines of pain through Arlo's nerves. It was not enough for Malik to kill him. He was going to take his time.

"Weak."

"Beaten."

"Desperate."

"Forgotten."

"Do you truly think you can defy me?"

Arlo's mind drifted.

Not into the same dark corners as before, but to other places. To moments that had defined him, for better or worse.

He saw the orphanage again. But not just the lash and the dark room. He saw the nights he spent teaching the younger kids how to

468

sneak extra food, how to patch clothes, how to hide when the matrons were in a mood. He saw Sabil, thinner than she should have been, laughing at his terrible jokes, even when they both hurt.

He saw himself barely into his teens, making sure Sabil was in the right room, at the right time, saying the right things when a kind-eyed couple came to visit. Saw her leaving with them, clutching a stuffed toy he had given her the night before, tears on her face and something like hope in her eyes.

He saw himself working too hard for too little. As a smith. As a porter. As a nameless hand in a hundred small jobs. Always staying late. Always doing more than asked. Trying to be useful. Trying to be needed.

He remembered walking into the church with a report about the orphanage, voice shaking as he told them what the matrons really were. He remembered Sorren being sent to investigate. That was the first time his path had crossed the paladin's. That choice had changed everything.

He watched Fall Lake again, but this time not just the destruction. He saw himself hauling people behind barricades, shoving them toward safety even while the beast roared. He saw Sorren at his side. Saw Lucy leaning over him afterward. Saw the faces of the people he had helped up from the rubble.

His mind fell gently onto a final image.

Crimson hair and green eyes. Lucy's soft touch on his skin. The way her presence quieted the noise in his mind, even when she herself was falling apart. He tried to smile. He was not sure if his face obeyed.

He could no longer feel his hands properly. He thought he was clenching his fists hard enough to draw blood, but there was no sensation. His body felt like it was drifting away from him.

He let his mind rest on Lucy's face. On Sorren's stubborn loyalty. On Nyla's quiet courage. On Mama Gretta, on the people of Davenport, on the children in the orphanage.

He saw, again, the blonde woman from the vision. Holding a newborn wrapped in cloth. Her breaths ragged. Her eyes tired but bright as she looked down at the child.

From the day he was born, she had given him Hope.

He had clung to it his whole life. Even if he did not know what it truly meant. Even if he twisted it into armor.

He would still give that same Hope to others.

"I may be weak," he said, voice barely more than a rasp. "But I am not alone."

The ground trembled.

The very foundation of Penumbra seemed to shudder as Arlo began to move again. He was still pinned by the sword through his shoulder, but Malik's foot had lifted from his chest, confident that he was beaten.

He was not.

He felt something shift around him. The faint blue spark inside him flared. Not outward from his body, but toward it. For the first time, he did not feel Hope leaking out of him like blood. He felt it coming in.

He heard voices.

Prayers. Pleas. Half remembered and half imagined. Words spoken in moments of fear and heartbreak. Not to him. Not for him. Prayers meant for gods who did not answer. But they were still there, hanging in the world.

He felt them tug toward him like threads.

The storm Malik had summoned above them began to crack at the edges. Bright blue shards broke off from its golden mass and drifted down, pulled toward Arlo, pulled toward that single stubborn spark inside him.

His hand twitched.

Blue energy flickered along his fingers, not trickling out, but gathering. He could feel the sword buried in his shoulder. He could feel the weight of Malik's gaze as the Deva realized this should not be possible.

He had to move. He had to stand. He had to put Malik in his place, or none of them would leave Penumbra.

Arlo forced his eyes to focus.

He saw Malik's hesitation. It was small, barely there, but he saw it. The Deva's confidence had cracked.

He looked at the blade still lodged in his body. At the hammer lying just beyond his reach. At the faint blue motes of light drifting down around him.

He gathered every bit of that blue he could, reaching not just within himself, but outward. To anyone. To everyone. To all those whose hearts still clung to even the smallest ember of hope.

He pulled it all into a single call.

"Elduun!"

CHAPTER 45

Cracks of lightning, the kind Arlo had only truly heard on the day of Fall Lake, split through the warped sky of Penumbra. Bolts tore across the darkness, wild and uncontrolled. But one bolt was different.

One bolt found him.

It struck Elduun.

The hammer ripped free from where it had fallen, drawn through the air by a force that felt older than the world itself. It slammed into Arlo's outstretched hand with enough force to rattle his bones. The impact sent another line of agony through his wounded shoulder, but he gripped it tighter.

Hope answered.

He braced his feet, teeth clenched, and with a roar he twisted his body and brought Elduun down. The sapphire core flared as metal met metal. The golden blade that pinned his arm shattered in a spray of fractured light.

Arlo rose to his feet once more. Battered, bloodied, and still standing.

A last call of defiance against Malik.

Blue energy swirled around him, wrapping him in an aura that hummed against his skin. He knew it would not last. He was in Penumbra, a place shaped by despair, where the voices of hope did not belong. Behind him, past the gate, the Prismalith had already drained him dry, leaving him a husk of who he felt he should be.

But right now, Elduun was a conduit.

The hammer took what little hope remained and pulled more to him, threading it through his veins. Heating his limbs. Steadying his stance. Even if it cost him everything, he would stand in that hope.

"A futile display," Malik said. "You cannot stand against the will of your gods."

"We will see about that," Arlo replied.

He lifted Elduun and moved.

The sapphire glow blurred his outline, so that he seemed to flicker rather than charge. One heartbeat he stood where he had been. The next his hammer crashed into Malik's golden armor.

Light exploded.

Gold and blue flared across the twisted landscape. Malik staggered from the blow but recovered quickly, bringing up the broken remnant of his sword. The blade was shorter now, jagged where Elduun had snapped it, but familiar in Malik's hands. In a single sweeping motion he drove it forward, catching Arlo and slamming him back into a jagged pillar.

"Do you feel it?" Malik asked. "The futility of your struggle. The weight of the inevitable."

Arlo grunted from the impact, but a faint smirk tugged at his lips. He shifted his weight, letting Malik's momentum carry them forward. Malik overcommitted by a fraction. It was enough. Arlo rolled his shoulder, slipped sideways, and brought the hammer around in a tight arc.

Elduun crashed into Malik's ribs.

The Deva flew backwards and hit the ground hard, sliding across the fractured stone.

Malik rose at once, movements sharp and controlled. The battle surged on. Each clash grew more thunderous than the last. Malik fought with the ease of someone who had practiced for lifetimes. Every strike held precision and discipline. Every step an intentional display.

Arlo fought on raw instinct and stubbornness.

He moved with pain in every joint, but his determination and the strange energy coursing through him kept his body from giving in. Hope burned through him like a fever.

"You cannot protect them," Malik said. "You can barely protect yourself."

"You do not know what I am capable of," Arlo growled.

He swung Elduun in another powerful arc, forcing Malik back a step. He did not give him space. He closed the distance and struck again, deflecting a desperate counter and driving the hammer into Malik's shoulder. The snap of bone cracked through the air.

"Impressive," Malik said. "But not enough."

He surged forward.

His strikes came faster now. Sharper. Every swing of his broken blade forced Arlo to give ground. Arlo's breath came in harsh pulls. Each clash sent ripples of gold and blue racing out from them, shaking the broken crystals under their feet.

Through all of it, Lucy hovered at the edge of Arlo's thoughts.

Her absence. Her scream. The look in her eyes before she fled. He could feel something of her still. Distant but near. Just beyond his reach. That sense of her threaded itself through his resolve, holding him upright when his body begged him to fall.

A sudden change in the air ran down Sorren's spine like ice.

The demons' movements faltered. One by one the twisted shapes stopped their assault. Sorren froze mid-swing, Justice held high, as every demon snapped its head toward the clash between Malik and Arlo.

Then they moved.

They broke away from Sorren and Nyla and hurtled toward the center of the battlefield, drawn like moths to flame.

"What is happening?" Nyla whispered.

She leaned heavily against a broken column, one hand pressed to the wound at her side, the other clutching her dagger.

Before Sorren could answer, a voice sounded behind them. Firm. Commanding. Human.

"You need to leave. Now."

Eckerd stepped into view, older and more worn than Arlo imagined. He wore the remnants of royal robes, torn and singed, yet there was still something regal in the way he stood. His eyes flicked over Nyla and Sorren, then to the chaos where Arlo and Malik fought.

He jerked his thumb over his shoulder. In the distance, a rolling wall of storm like fog crawled across the horizon, swallowing what little light Penumbra had.

"Something dark is coming," Eckerd said. "If we linger, there is no telling if we will survive. We need to move."

Sorren clenched his jaw. "We cannot leave Arlo behind."

"There is no time to argue," Eckerd replied. "We go. He will find a way. Here, lass, lean on me."

He offered his shoulder to Nyla. She hesitated only a moment, then took it, wincing as she pushed away from the column. Akira pressed close, eyes still scanning the shadows.

"Sorren," Eckerd said. "Move."

Sorren turned toward Arlo one last time.

"Arlo! We have Eckerd. It is time to go!" he shouted.

Arlo did not answer. He could not. Every part of him was locked in the clash with Malik.

Sorren cursed under his breath and reached for the crystal Korithas had given them. If they could not fight their way out, they needed the Veilgate open. His hands patted over pouches and belts, searching.

Nothing.

"Shit."

He looked back over the ground where they had fought. Bodies of demons lay scattered, limbs twisted at odd angles. Sorren retraced his steps, scanning for even the faintest glimmer.

There.

The crystal was lodged in the chest of one of the fallen demons. Sorren grimaced, set his boot against the creature, and drove Justice down. Bone and warped flesh cracked. He snapped the crystal free and lifted it.

"It is Sorren," he said, voice hard. "We are done. Open the way."

No answer.

The crystal remained cold and dim in his hand. No hum. No shimmer. No voice.

He spat on the demon beneath his boot and clenched the shard tight. There was no time to stand waiting. With a wordless growl, he turned and sprinted after Eckerd and Nyla.

Under the combined assault of the demons and Arlo's hammer, Malik began to falter. Broken wings of shadow and tatters of golden light whipped around him as he spun, golden blade carving through demon after demon. Each stroke was lethal. Each move efficient.

But even a Deva could not strike everywhere at once.

"You are not leaving here alive," Malik said.

He drove forward with renewed ferocity, carving through a demon and stepping past its dissolving form to reach Arlo again. The broken blade lashed out in brutal flurries, each strike aiming to end it.

Arlo met him.

He fought back with everything he had left, Elduun moving in desperate arcs, catching Malik's strikes, answering with his own. Blue and gold clashed again and again.

It still was not enough.

Malik's power pressed down like the weight of a mountain. Blow by blow, step by step, Arlo was forced back. He risked a glance over his shoulder, just long enough to see Sorren and the others near the distant glow of the gate.

They were almost there.

He let out a slow breath, lungs burning, as another wave of shadowy shapes launched themselves at Malik. The demons tore into the storm of light, forcing Malik to turn and cut them down.

The opening bought Arlo a heartbeat to steady himself.

Wind rushed around him suddenly, cold and sharp. The shadows behind him deepened, then split. A figure stepped out of them, wrapped in smoke and fire.

Lucy.

She landed in a spray of embers. Her wings stretched wide behind her, arcs of living flame that sent heat rolling over the broken ground. Her hair whipped around her face. Her eyes glowed like coals. Bone-like protrusions pushed beneath her skin, and the black curve of her horns caught the strange light.

"You are persistent," Malik said, eyes narrowing. "I thought he killed you. I will tell him to be more certain next time."

Arlo's heart stuttered. He did not have breath left to ask who Malik meant. He looked at Lucy instead, searching her face. There was rage there, yes, and something wild, something otherworldly. But beneath it, there was still a glimmer of the woman who had sat at his bedside and laughed at his terrible jokes.

Before he could speak, she moved.

In one smooth motion, Lucy crossed the space between them. Her arms wrapped around him, wings folding close enough that he could feel the heat rolling off them.

"Lucy, what are you…"

"Hold on," she said.

Her wings beat once, hard.

They shot into the air. The world fell away beneath them. Arlo's stomach lurched, but he locked his arms around her shoulders and held on. Below, the storm Malik had woven still raged. Beyond it, the larger storm on the edge of Penumbra was rolling in like a wall, full of screams and lightning.

The land itself seemed to shudder at its approach.

They angled toward the gate, the only true light in sight. The glow of the Veilgate cut through the gloom, growing brighter with every wingbeat. Arlo could see Sorren, Nyla, Eckerd, and Akira as small shapes near its base.

A golden blur cut across their path.

Malik appeared before them, radiant and unmarked in spite of the wounds he had taken. Demons still clawed at his back, but they clung like smoke to a bonfire. His golden eyes seethed as he raised his jagged blade and barred their way.

"You will not escape," he said.

Power flared from him in a wave. The air thickened. Lucy's wings dragged against the force, and she was forced to drop. She landed hard, rolling with the impact so that she took the worst of it. Arlo hit the ground beside her as she wrapped her wings around them both to break the fall.

For what felt like the thousandth time, Arlo forced himself up.

His body protested, every movement a scream, but habit and stubbornness pushed through it. He tightened his grip on Elduun. Lightning ran along the hammer's head, sapphire bright.

"We have to go," Lucy said. "Now, Arlo."

"Not without stopping him."

Arlo stepped forward, dragging pain along with him. He barely felt it anymore. It was just another weight to carry.

"You think hope does not matter," he said, meeting Malik's gaze. "But it is the only thing that keeps some people standing."

Malik's lips curled into a slow, cruel smile.

"Hope," he said. "That fragile ember you cling to. It is nothing but a lie. A spark that dies when it meets true power."

"Then try to snuff it out," Arlo said. "Now."

He charged.

Every part of him screamed in protest, but he did not slow. Elduun swung in a wide, sparking arc. Malik brought his blade up to block, but the impact drove him back. Dust and shards of crystal exploded around them. Malik's boots skidded, carving lines in the broken stone.

"You think you can stand against me," Malik spat. He lashed out at the first opening, a strike aimed to cut Arlo down at the waist.

Arlo twisted.

The serrated edge missed by inches, ripping through his torn clothes instead of his flesh.

"It is not about what I think," Arlo said. "It is about proving that hope does not break as easily as you think it does."

He drove forward on that same turn, shifting his weight and driving Elduun up and in.

The hammer connected with the same rib he had struck before. Blue and gold flared together, a second sun bursting from the point of impact. The shockwave rippled out, blinding and hot. Malik flew backward and smashed to his knees. Cracks spiderwebbed through the ground around him, racing outward like jagged veins.

Malik's eyes burned as he tried to stand.

Arlo was already there.

He raised Elduun high. Blue mana surged along the haft, then down his arms and across his chest. The hammer was no longer just a weapon. It was a promise.

He brought it down.

The impact landed with a thunder that echoed through Penumbra. The sound seemed to punch a hole in the air itself. Light erupted, devouring Malik's form in a blinding blast. The shock tore through nearby rock and crystal. Spires toppled. Shards rained down.

"Hope does not break," Arlo said. "It shatters mountains."

The echo of his words faded into a heavy silence.

Malik's form lay buried beneath broken stone and torn crystal. The Deva was not gone, not truly. Arlo could feel that in his bones. But he was down. That was all they needed.

The storm on the horizon was no longer on the horizon.

It was here.

The roar deepened as the mass of shadow and lightning rolled over the broken land. It felt less like weather, and more like something alive. Something vast. Something hungry.

Lucy's eyes flicked from Malik to the storm to the glowing gate.

"We do not have time for this," she said.

She stepped forward, spreading her wings to their full height. The flames that formed them burned hotter, fueled by something beyond rage. She lifted her arms and let out a sound that did not belong to human throats. A sound layered with guttural growls and soft, haunting whispers.

The demons that had lingered at the edges of the battle froze.

For a heartbeat, their glowing eyes all fixed on her. It was as if some invisible chain linked them to her.

In unison, they turned.

Every twisted shape. Every clawed hand. Every gnashing maw. All pivoted toward Malik.

"Tear him apart," Lucy said.

Her voice held a strange power, heavy and commanding, like someone speaking a language that Penumbra itself understood.

The demons obeyed.

They hurled themselves at Malik in a renewed frenzy. Claws raked through golden light. Teeth tore at the broken armor. Malik roared, his blade flashing as he carved them down, but their numbers and fury slowed him.

Lucy turned back to Arlo.

Her eyes were fierce and wild, but there was tenderness there too, buried under the fire.

"We are leaving," she said. "Now."

She grabbed him again, gentler this time but no less firm, and her wings beat hard, lifting them into the air.

Arlo twisted in her hold, looking back over her shoulder. Through the storm of demons, he caught one last glimpse of Malik. The Deva's face was twisted with fury, eyes blazing.

This is not over, Malik mouthed.

Arlo did not answer.

He knew.

Lucy drove them forward. The light of the portal cut through the darkness, closer and closer. The storm behind them seemed to chase their heels, a wall of shadow and lightning pressing in from every side.

The ground beneath the gate buckled.

Cracks split outward, the stone giving way as if Penumbra itself tried to pull the gate down. The edges of the Veilgate shimmered and flickered as the storm closed around it.

Lucy did not slow.

She pushed through with one final, powerful stroke of her wings. They hit the threshold of the Veilgate. The light swallowed them whole.

The roar of Penumbra cut off.

There was only silence.

For a heartbeat, it felt like falling through nothing. No weight. No sound. No body. Only the echo of everything they had just seen, everything they had just survived.

Then the world caught them.

CHAPTER 46

The light of the portal shattered like glass into fragments of mana that scattered, then were pulled as one toward the Prismalith. Each glowing shard skated along its fractured surface and sank into the massive crystalline core. The chamber exhaled with it. The air felt clean, thin, almost sharp after the suffocating press of Penumbra.

Sorren and Eckerd were already moving.

Together they lifted Nyla, one under her shoulders, the other taking her legs, and hauled her onto a flat slab of stone nearby.

"Lift her higher. We need to stabilize her before she bleeds out," Eckerd said.

"I know what I am doing, old man."

"Then act like it. She has already lost enough blood."

Nyla writhed on the makeshift table. Her breath came in ragged bursts, fingers digging into the stone as she held the torn flesh at her side. Blood soaked through her tunic and smeared the crystal beneath.

"You must lie still," Korithas said, its voice ringing in crystalline harmony.

The Shardkin moved with careful, deliberate steps around her. The facets of its body shimmered in Prismalith light. Several crystalline protrusions shifted and folded together, forming a complex limb that extended over Nyla's wound. A beam of concentrated mana emerged from its palm, a narrow lance of shifting color that pulsed steadily against torn skin, sealing ragged edges with precise, patient heat.

Nyla screamed, the sound raw and small against the vastness of the chamber. Her body trembled as the foreign sensation bored into her.

"I cannot," she gasped.

"You can. And you will," Eckerd said.

He nodded at Sorren to hold her down. Sorren braced her shoulders while Eckerd worked quickly, wrapping bandages over the already sealed flesh to hold it in place.

"Korithas is stopping the bleeding," Eckerd said. "You are going to make it."

Lucy stirred where she had collapsed, propping herself against a jagged rock. Her vision swam. It took several blinks before the shapes around her stopped blurring. Her back burned with phantom agony, her skin prickling where horns and wings had been. Every shift of muscle reminded her that they had not been a dream. The ache sat there, deep and familiar and wrong.

She turned her head.

Arlo lay a few feet away on his back, chest rising in shallow, uneven breaths. His shoulder and chest were dark with dried blood. The wound where Malik's blade had gone through was an angry hole, the flesh around it raw and swollen.

"Arlo," Lucy said, her voice rough.

She dragged herself across the floor, each movement sending needles of pain through her own bones. She reached out and laid a hand on his good shoulder.

He groaned, tried to sit up, and failed. His body simply refused to obey. His face twisted and he dropped back with a hiss. "Lucy," he breathed, barely more than air.

She pressed her palm over his wound and reached for her magic out of habit. All she found was emptiness. Her mana was a scraped-out well. She forced what remained into the gesture anyway, a single ember of heat that slipped from her to him.

It glowed for the briefest moment.

Then the ember flickered blue, as if answering him instead of her, and peeled away toward the Prismalith. It vanished into the crystal along with all the rest.

Here, their power was not their own.

"You are hurt," she murmured.

"It is nothing," he lied.

Sorren's voice cut across them, tight and strained. "The storm. Is it going to make it through?"

He still stood by Nyla, hands pressed to her shoulders, but his eyes were locked on the Veilgate. The portal was closed now, its surface dull and lifeless, yet the image of that wall of shadow and lightning sat in his mind like a weight.

"Can it follow us?" he pressed.

Korithas did not look up. The beam over Nyla's side shifted, pulse slowing as the wound finished sealing.

"The gate is closed," the Shardkin answered. "The connection between both worlds has been severed. It should be unable to build and sustain a passage on its own."

"You sure?" Sorren snapped. His voice climbed higher. "Because if you are wrong, so help me He—"

"I am certain," Korithas said, tone sharpening. "Your panic serves no purpose. Bring Arlo to me next. The girl will live. Her wound has been cauterized and new skin has begun to form. She will survive."

Nyla eased off the table with Eckerd's help. Her legs shook, and she bit down on a groan as she straightened. The pain was still there, hot and throbbing, but it no longer felt like she was being split open.

Sorren muttered under his breath as he moved to Arlo. He hooked his arms under him and lifted in one rough motion.

Arlo's cry echoed through the chamber. His hand slammed down on Elduun's haft, trying to brace himself, but his injured shoulder flared white and the world tilted.

Eckerd shot Sorren a hard look as he guided Nyla to Lucy's side. Sorren ignored him and set Arlo on the stone, jaw clenched.

Korithas turned, crystalline limb already reconfiguring. The beam that emerged this time was narrower, more focused. It hovered over the hole in Arlo's shoulder, sank slowly into muscle. Warmth seeped deep, not soothing so much as stitching. Flesh knit. Torn pathways closed on both sides.

"You will keep use of the arm," Korithas said. "But your other wounds are beyond what I can mend. Your strength must return on its own. Do not test it."

"Thank you," Arlo said.

It took effort to get the words out. He gripped the edge of the stone and forced his body to cooperate, pushing himself upright. Sweat beaded his brow. The chamber swayed around him, but he refused to lie back down.

Sorren paced in a tight line in front of them all. His boots clanged against stone, each heavy step stirring small puffs of dust. His gaze jumped from the Veilgate, to the Prismalith, to the others, then back again. Everything they had seen sat clawing at his thoughts.

"You good?" he asked Arlo. The words were flat. Not quite a question of concern.

"I will manage," Arlo said.

Every movement was a fight. His ribs ached with every breath. His skin felt too tight for his bones. But he found his feet anyway, Elduun serving more as a crutch than a weapon at his side. He had nothing left, yet he still stood.

"Then we move," Sorren said. "No reason to stand around down here any longer. We have a boat waiting. And you have a message for the king."

Eckerd leaned against a jut of crystal, arms folded. He did not bother to hide the amused tilt of his mouth.

"I hate to disappoint you, Porter," he said, "but I have no intention of riding back on that boat to see my brother. Not yet."

Sorren stopped. His spine straightened. His fingers curled until his knuckles popped.

"What?"

Eckerd finally lifted his head, amber eyes calm and steady. "I have other matters to attend to. There are allies I must meet, potential friends to your king and this kingdom. If all goes well, we will convene in a few weeks. Until then, I will not follow you back to Frederick's court."

Sorren laughed.

It was not the laugh of earlier days. There was no warmth, no humor. The sound rang harsh and hollow through the chamber.

"Let me get this straight," he said. "We drag ourselves through Penumbra, nearly die a dozen times over, to find you. And now you are skipping off on some private errand. Not even a thanks."

He threw an arm wide, gesturing at the Prismalith, the Veilgate, all of it. His voice climbed. "You have any idea what I am supposed to do with this?"

"Sorren," Lucy said.

She tried to stand, but her legs still shook. Her back throbbed. The echo of wings that were no longer there made her skin crawl. The single word was all she managed.

Eckerd's gaze cooled. His stance shifted, shoulders settling in a way that said he was done being spoken to like a child.

486

"This is not personal," he said. "The allies I seek may decide whether your kingdom survives. Do you truly believe Frederick can win this war alone. The threats we face are bigger than your orders and your chain of command."

"Bigger than King Frederick," Sorren scoffed. "Bigger than Heir."

He barked another laugh and shook his head. "So I go back as the errand boy who delivers an Elfar, a demon, and a heretic who may have just attacked my god's Deva."

His eyes cut to Nyla, then to Lucy, then to Arlo. Each look landed like a blow.

"Maybe I just hand the four of you over to Fred and Dolph," he said. "Let them decide what to do with you. Maybe I save them the trouble and do it myself."

Nyla flinched. Her hand went instinctively to her side, fingers pressing over the wounds as if to shield herself. Her throat worked, but no words came. Lucy drew her in, one arm wrapping around her and pulling her close. Nyla's head dropped to Lucy's shoulder, tears soaking into torn fabric.

"You think you decide our fate," Lucy said quietly. "You would not even be here if it were not for all of us."

Sorren rounded on her. His eyes burned, not with simple anger, but with something cracked and frightened beneath it.

"Do not mistake survival for absolution, demon," he said. "Every one of you is an anomaly. A danger that should not exist."

Lucy bit down hard on the inside of her cheek. She held Nyla tighter. She had held fire in her hands and bent demons to her will. She had stood with wings of flame and horns of embered bone. Yet one word from him found the parts of her that were still small and unsure.

"And you," she said, voice shaking now, "are a coward hiding behind a god who would sooner strike you down than lift you up."

Arlo moved.

It hurt. Every step hurt. His shoulder throbbed. His ribs screamed. His lungs felt full of broken glass. But he used Elduun as a staff and crossed the space between them one staggering pace at a time.

"That is enough," he said.

The words scraped his throat, but they were steady. He stopped a breath in front of Sorren.

Sorren arched a brow, lips twisting. "You can barely stand," he said. "What are you going to do. Lecture me?"

Arlo's mouth pulled into a humorless smile of his own. "You are damn right," he said. "Someone has to remember what we are fighting for."

He jabbed a finger into Sorren's chest. It was not a strong hit, but it carried weight.

"You think you are the only one carrying anything. The only one who has lost something. We have all bled for this. We have all paid for it. But you."

His eyes narrowed.

"You think turning on your allies makes you righteous," he said. "It makes you pathetic."

Sorren's laugh came back, louder, rolling through the air before dying sharp.

"You really think you understand," he said. "You have defiled the god who blessed you. You struck down his Deva. What happens when Heir decides to finish what Malik started."

Arlo held his gaze. His voice dropped, but it did not shake.

"Then we will face him," he said. "Like we have faced everything else. Together. I am not going to let your fear decide my path."

"And I will not let your suicidal crusade with demons and Elfar tear my kingdom apart."

Silence pressed in around them. The Prismalith hummed softly in the background, as if listening.

Their fists clenched. Their shoulders squared. The air between them buzzed, bright and sharp like the moment before a storm.

Eckerd stepped between them.

"Enough," he said.

He did not shout. He did not need to. His voice cut clean through the crackling tension.

"Your pride does not matter," he said. "Zenaria needs allies, not two fools tearing at each other in a crystal tomb. If you cannot see that, then you are part of the problem."

Sorren's jaw flexed. His hands shook at his sides.

"Maybe I handle it myself," he said. "End this before it lands on Frederick's table."

Eckerd's eyes went cold.

"If you want to play executioner, Sorren, be my guest," he said. "But remember this. Zenaria does not need another sword swinging blind. They need leaders who can keep their heads when the sky falls."

For a long moment Sorren only stared at him. Then he sucked his teeth, turned on his heel, and walked away. His boots hammered across stone, louder than before, until the sound disappeared down the passage toward the shoreline.

Lucy's hands shook where they held Nyla. She watched him go, rage and hurt and something like pity fighting inside her. She knew what it was to feel the ground pulled out beneath you. She did not know what to do with the fact that his first reaction was to draw blood.

"We need a plan," Arlo said. His voice was tired. "Something more than just surviving the next hour."

"There is a plan," Eckerd said. "If you are willing to listen, instead of chewing each other apart."

Arlo shifted closer to Lucy and Nyla and leaned his back against the rock beside them. His legs trembled in protest. He ignored it.

"Then speak," he said.

"In three weeks," Eckerd said, "I intend to meet certain allies just south of Daco. The Nogmi capital."

His gaze drifted to the Prismalith for a heartbeat, then returned.

"These are not simple nobles," he went on. "Not merchants or minor lords. They are powerful. If they stand with Frederick, the war changes. But if I am to bring them, I must earn their trust."

Lucy stroked Nyla's hair absentmindedly, eyes on Eckerd though she did not fully lift her head.

"And us?" she asked. "Where do we fit?"

"Someone must carry word back to Frederick," Eckerd said. "Tell him where to be and when. Travel is not easy for a king in wartime. He will not be wandering for rumors."

He looked to Nyla then.

"And one of those allies is tied to you," he said. "Very closely."

Nyla pulled away from Lucy's shoulder, blinking through the haze of pain and exhaustion.

"Who?" she asked.

"You know her," Eckerd said. "She holds answers about your mother that were kept from you. Answers you deserve. For now, you need to rest. What lies ahead will demand more of you than you think. I suspect each of you will play a larger part in what comes than your Porter friend sees."

Arlo pushed off the rock, forgetting his own fatigue for a moment.

"Why all the secrets?" he asked. "Just tell us everything now."

"Because not all knowledge is armor," Eckerd said. "Sometimes it is a weight that pins you in place. The less you carry before you must, the more you can move when it matters."

Lucy eyed him warily. "Three weeks," she said. "What are we supposed to do until then? Sit here and wait for the world to burn?"

"Hardly," Eckerd said.

A small smile touched his lips, but it did not reach the shadow in his eyes.

"You rest," he said. "Then you learn what you can do. Truly do. I told you once that we need leaders who can stand. That has not changed. You do not see it yet, but the four of you could become anchors in this war."

"What if these friends of yours are not as friendly as you think?" Arlo asked. "What if they lead Frederick into a trap?"

"Then we adapt," Eckerd said. "I did not come this far to fail. I do not believe you did either. You trusted me enough to follow me into the Veil. Trust that I mean to keep my end of this."

Nyla's brows pinched.

"You already know about my mother," she said softly. "Her illness."

Eckerd exhaled through his nose. "Illness," he repeated. "If that is what they told you, you have been kept in the dark longer than I thought."

His tone softened.

"You need to find Zosah," he said. "Let them tell you the truth."

Nyla went quiet. Her thoughts spiraled away from the room. Lucy felt the change in her shoulders and tightened her hold, but said nothing.

"You make this sound like a game," Lucy said. "Some grand board we are all pieces on. What if we do not want to play."

Eckerd's smile sharpened, eyes bright with something unreadable.

"Then the board moves without you," he said. "The stakes do not change. The enemy does not disappear because you step aside. Whether you act or not, what is coming will still come."

Arlo let out a slow breath. He curled his fingers around Elduun's haft and offered his other hand to Lucy and Nyla, helping them stand.

"Fine," he said. "We will play along. But if this is as important as you claim, we need more than hints. We need something real to work with."

"You will have it," Eckerd said. "Find a place to rest. When we meet again, you will not be bystanders. You will be part of the plan."

Arlo, Nyla, and Lucy shared a tired nod. The Shardkin's healing had pulled them back from the edge, but the Prismalith still hummed in the air, quietly drinking in whatever mana tried to stir in their bones. Every step they took cost them.

They turned to leave.

"And so it begins," Eckerd murmured.

A shadow moved overhead.

The faint sound of wings broke the quiet. Slow at first, then louder. The air thickened with power in a way that felt utterly different from Penumbra's storm. The three of them stopped, instincts dragging their hands toward weapon hilts even as their muscles protested.

Arlo lifted Elduun, though his arms shook with the effort. He did not have another fight in him. He readied himself anyway.

The shadow dropped lower through the canopy above the crystalline ravine. Branches groaned. Loose stone rattled and slid. Eckerd's face brightened with something that looked almost like relief. He lifted both arms in welcome.

The roar that followed shook dust from the ceiling.

A great shape broke through the upper trees and descended. Golden scales caught the Prismalith's light and scattered it across the chamber in shards. The ground trembled when it landed. Wind blasted outward in a hot rush, forcing Arlo, Lucy, and Nyla to shield their faces.

The Draconis folded its enormous wings with slow, deliberate grace. Each hinge and membrane moved with an ease that spoke of ancient strength. Its scales were not the harsh gold of Malik's light. They gleamed like metal caught in dawn, shot through with white so bright it seemed to glow from within.

Its head was regal, ridged with horned crowns that refracted light into faint prismatic colors. Its eyes were a deep molten gold, old and sharp and very aware.

Arlo's grip tightened on Elduun. His body screamed at him to put the hammer down, but the memory of Fall Lake's beast and of Malik's blade kept him set.

Lucy stared.

Fear and awe tangled in her chest. Demons, angels, monsters twisted from shadows. None of them had looked like this. If ruin could be beautiful, this creature was its mirror. She could not look away, even when Arlo edged himself in front of her as if he could shield her from a creature the size of a house.

Nyla's breath caught.

She had grown up with one Draconis. She knew the weight of them, the sound of their breath, the heat of their scales. This was different. Bigger. Older. Familiar in a way that a storm is familiar to rain.

Eckerd walked forward without hesitation.

He rested a hand against one scaled foreleg. His palm looked like a child's next to it.

"Zelroth," he said. "It has been too long, old friend."

The Draconis bent its head. Its rumbling voice rolled through them, deep and clear, speaking in a common tongue that still sounded strange from a maw full of teeth.

"Eckerd," it said. "You have aged."

The molten eyes flicked over the others.

"But you still find your way into trouble."

Eckerd chuckled and patted his leg.

"Trouble finds us Lionhart," he said.

Arlo swallowed and took a step closer, his legs still unsteady. "You know him?" he asked.

Eckerd turned back to the three of them with a small, tired smile.

"Zelroth and I go back a long way," he said. "He has carried me through more than one near ending."

Before Arlo could ask more, Eckerd reached for the Draconis' leg and climbed, practiced and sure. Zelroth lowered a wing and shoulder to make the ascent easier. In moments Eckerd was astride his back, seated in a place that looked well worn.

"The journey ahead will test you," Eckerd called down. "All of you. Do not lose sight of why you started down this path. We will meet again in Daco. Zosah will show you where."

Zelroth spread his wings.

The first powerful beat sent a fresh gust slamming into them. Dust and pebbles flew. The Prismalith hummed louder, reacting to the sudden surge of movement and mana. The sound of wings cutting the air was a deep, steady roar that faded only as the massive form climbed higher, then turned and vanished beyond the tree line.

Silence crept in after.

Only the Prismalith's low song remained, a steady pulse beneath everything.

Arlo, Lucy, and Nyla looked at one another. None of them spoke. There was too much that could be said, and no strength left to hold all of it in words.

Korithas stepped forward, crystals dimmed to a softer glow.

"Arlo," it said. "The Prismalith approves of you."

Arlo frowned. His body hurt too much to find room for confusion, but it settled in anyway.

"Approves," he repeated. "What does that mean?"

Korithas tilted its head, facets catching the light.

"Another time," it said. "When your road has carried you further. If you are still the same man, you will return. Then we will speak of it."

Arlo nodded slowly. The answer did nothing to ease the knot in his chest, but he held the Shardkin's gaze.

"I will hold you to that," he said.

They turned from the Prismalith at last and began the slow walk back toward the shore. Every step was a negotiation. Nyla leaned heavily on Lucy's arm. Lucy's own legs trembled. Arlo used Elduun to keep himself upright. His shoulder throbbed with each crunch of

494

gravel. His ribs ached. His head pounded with the memory of Malik's words and his mother's voice.

The deeper they walked into the jungle, the cooler the air became. The distant, familiar sound of waves slowly rose above the Prismalith's hum.

For a brief moment, hope tasted simple.

The tree line broke.

They stepped out onto the beach where they had first arrived. The sand was marked with their old footprints, already half blurred by wind and tide. The water stretched in every direction, heaving against the shore. The sky over the sea was clear.

There was no boat.

No rower. No Sea Sentinel resting beyond the surf. Only open water.

Lucy's shoulders sagged. Her voice came out small. "They left us," she said.

Nyla's knees gave out. She dropped to the sand, hands sinking into it as if she needed to feel something solid. Her fingers shook.

"What do we do now?" she whispered.

Arlo stared at the empty horizon.

The weight of Sorren's absence settled across his back, heavier than Elduun, heavier than any wound. Sorren had walked away from the Prismalith and, somewhere between there and here, chosen his road.

"Sorren is gone," Arlo said. "Eckerd is gone."

He swallowed.

"It is just us now."

Lucy looked to him, searching his face for something to hold onto. Some promise. Some clear next step. His eyes were bloodshot and ringed in shadow. The boy from the Cyril orphanage and the man who had stood against a Deva shared the same body, and both were exhausted.

He had no easy answer for her.

The silence between them grew. Not empty. Heavy. Full of the knowledge that no one was coming to tell them what to do next.

Arlo let out a slow breath. His shoulder screamed. His grip tightened on Elduun until his hand hurt.

"We will find a way," he said. "We have to."

He looked at Lucy. At Nyla on her knees in the sand. At the endless ocean beyond.

"Together."

It hurt to believe it.

But he still had *hope*.

FAREWELL:
A SPOON'S REFLECTION

I stand here now, spoon in hand, watching the flicker of questions in their eyes, the unspoken reflections of the tale we have shared thus far. The fire crackles low nearby, the soft droplets of rain echoing on the shingles outside.

Above us, the rafters creaked with a tiny patter of movement, quick and light, like nimble feet racing across the beams. A few patrons glanced up out of habit, expecting perhaps a loose tile or a settling board, but nothing waited there when they looked. Only a faint sway of a hanging lantern, as if something small had darted past it a moment before.

"Curious thing, isn't it?" I say, intentionally letting the words linger. A quiet bunch, but they have all stayed infatuated in the tale. "To walk through a time not your own and feel its heartbeat. You may reflect on some of the names mentioned along the way, the paths they have walked being similar paths to those you yourself have tread. We witness their trials and triumphs as though they were our own, and perhaps," I tilt the spoon, just enough to catch an ember of light that bursts into a view of a larger scene, "in some ways, they are."

I gesture outward, drawing the room's attention as I rise to my feet.

"Take Arlo, for instance. Elduun was not just a weapon, it was a spark. Not because it carried the power to smite great beasts, or was previously the weapon to the God of Lightning. It instead embodies the hope of Fall Lake, of Davenport, and soon of every soul who dared to dream of a brighter tomorrow. He did not choose this path for himself, but slowly he has begun to accept this newfound purpose. A symbol of resilience, a beacon for those who refuse to be broken. Even in the face of overwhelming odds, he showed us that strength lies in conviction, and that Hope can blaze through the darkest nights."

I let another lingering pause settle the room as they take in my words and the reflections they provide. "And what of Sorren?" My gaze sweeps across the patrons. I see several who possess a similar brawn to the young hero. I cannot help but wonder about their story, what led them here, and what their futures hold.

"A man whose faith in Heir once burned unwavering now finds it flickering in the face of hard truths. To question one's god is to question oneself. Yet in his struggle, there is growth, a sign that perhaps the strongest faith is the one forged in doubt. His armor gleams with the lightning of Heir, but it is the cracks that reveal his humanity. Through Sorren's journey, we see the enduring struggle of a man searching for justice in a world that is anything but just."

I lean against the bar, taking the final swig of my drink. "And Lucy," a soft recognition among the crowd as they show some liveliness. "Faced with trial after trial, her hands are scarred not just by the battles fought, but by the doubts and questions that haunt her.

Her struggles are as much internal as they are external. A woman searching for clarity, but only to be met with a shroud of darkness that answers only with more questions. What does her transformation mean for her, and how will this impact her companions?"

I step away from the bar now, pacing as I let my final words fill the room. I can see Forkner's expression telling me I must wrap up my speech, for it must be very late into the night... But we should not end the show so prematurely.

"Cloaked in mystery, burdened with something more than she truly knows, Nyla's journey began with desperation, a daughter seeking to save her mother. But has the choice to leave led to the consequence of something greater? Her blood carries more than just the ancestral DNA tabooed by the humans of Zenaria. Nyla shall teach us that courage is not the absence of fear, but the will to act despite it. Curious now, are we not, as we see how her challenges lead her to grow."

I lean forward onto a chair next to a powerful muscular individual sitting, his stoic expression harder to muse than others.

"Through all their journeys, through every storm tossed sail and shadowed council room, one thing is clear. None of them stand alone. Each of them holds a different thread in the tapestry of Lyorion, bound not by blood or birth, but by choice, and an unspoken promise to fight darkness together."

Green strands of hair move through, a tap on my wrist indicating my speech should resolve soon. "As the embers of our story begin to cool, we look to the paths ahead. How will our newfound friends escape their desertion on The Gauntlet? How will the promise of newfound allies shape the battles to come? The story is far from over, and the challenges ahead will demand even greater courage and unity than what we have seen thus far."

I raise my voice slightly, letting it carry to the corners of the tavern, my spoon and hands rest behind me. "As we close this chapter, I ask each of you... Are you willing to carry the spark forward? To take up the mantle of Hope, even when the darkness feels insurmountable? If you believe yourself worthy of such a calling, if you dare to strike where few have dared before, then prepare yourself."

A red haired beauty clinks away the remaining dishes upon the tables around me, her soft voice whispering for me to hurry up and end my monologue... But as they are all aware, talking is just the one thing that I love the most. I tap the spoon on the table, letting purple strands of mana streak away into displays of our heroes and heroines thus far.

"Where the wind shifts in this little valley, and the Legends of Lyorion call again, we will return. In our absence of physicality, as long as you keep the spark of Hope within yourself and follow its light, we too shall be connected, and you will never stand alone."

A faint rustle sounded from the rafters again, soft enough that only the closest patrons turned their heads. Something small skittered across the beam, a flash of fur and mischief before disappearing into the shadows. Forkner stiffened. Candy paused mid-step.

I only smiled, tapping the spoon once more.

"Even the smallest companions," I said with an easy wink, "can change the course of a legend, if you give them the chance."

The rustle faded. The room settled. The spark flickered, catching in every set of eyes before me.

Finally, I turned to see young Butters waiting to close up the shop, his anxious face peeking through the dim lamplight. Satisfied that the spark had been planted well within each of them. A spark they would soon need. I raised my spoon one final time.

"We will meet again. The Legends of Lyorion are far from over."

Hammer Fall
Book One of The Hopebringer Trilogy
Within the collection of the Legends of Lyorion Series
ISBN (Paperback): 9798276675237
First Edition: 2025
Printed in the United States of America

Artwork by @d0za.art on Instagram.

A special thank you to anyone who chooses to carry *Hope* forward.

www.ingramcontent.com/pod-product-compliance
Lightning Source LLC
Chambersburg PA
CBHW010811250626
47169CB00009B/2892